DAUGHTER OF HOUSE HILOAR

WAR WIZARD OF CORMYR

RENEGADE

AMIRA

Let Jalan get away. My life for his.

"You are his *mother.*"

"Not his real mother," Amira said, but even she heard the hollowness in her words.

"Would you die for him?" A bit of the anger was creeping back into the belkagen's voice, and he shook his staff as he spoke. "Kill for him? Would you shed your last drop of life's blood to keep him safe? Breathe your last breath?"

"Yes!" Amira looked away from them to wipe away the tears.

"Then you *are* his mother, Lady Amira," said the belkagen. "In all ways that matter."

BUT WILL HER SACRIFICE
SAVE HER SON?

FORGOTTEN REALMS®

THE WIZARDS

Blackstaff
Steven Schend

Bloodwalk
James P. Davis

Darkvision
Bruce R. Cordell

Frostfell
Mark Sehestedt

FORGOTTEN REALMS®

THE
WIZARDS

FROSTFELL

mark sehestedt

Wizards
OF THE COAST®

The Wizards
FROSTFELL

Cover art by Duane O. Myers
First Printing: December 2006

9 8 7 6 5 4 3 2

ISBN-10: 0-7869-4245-2
ISBN-13: 978-0-7869-4245-9
620-95911740-001-EN

U.S., CANADA,	EUROPEAN HEADQUARTERS
ASIA, PACIFIC, & LATIN AMERICA	Hasbro UK Ltd
Wizards of the Coast, Inc.	Caswell Way
P.O. Box 707	Newport, Gwent NP9 0YH
Renton, WA 98057-0707	GREAT BRITAIN
+1-800-324-6496	Save this address for your records.

Visit our web site at www.wizards.com

Dedication

Hey, my first novel! Who'd'a thunk? This one is for Andi, who thunk and never stopped believing.

Acknowledgments

Thanks to Susan Morris for editorial guidance, patience (ah, especially the patience), encouragement, and all the good story suggestions.

Thanks to Don Bassingthwaite, whose gift of the Tuscarora dictionary helped me to flesh out the culture and language of a band of elves roaming the Endless Wastes.

Thanks to Ed Greenwood. When I asked Susan for any additional information on the War Wizards of Cormyr, she suggested I contact Mr. Greenwood. I did, asking if he had any notes on the War Wizards beyond what have already appeared in published FORGOTTEN REALMS® material. He said he had "a few notes"—and sent me forty-nine pages. I kid you not! And he took time from his busy schedule to answer my many questions.

Thanks must also go to James Wyatt, Christopher Perkins, Darrin Drader, and Skip Williams. Their work on the DUNGEONS & DRAGONS® titles *Book of Exalted Deeds* and *Races of the Wild* was a major source of inspiration for the characters in *Frostfell*. If I got anything wrong, the blame is on me.

Special thanks to the many artists whose albums helped the late nights of writing pass with a lot more inspiration—especially the Dropkick Murphys, Garbage, Maria McKee, the Band, the Police, Willie Nelson, the Alarm, and Johnny Cash.

I would like to thank the Academy—

The gods lie dead where the leaves lie red,
For the flame of the sun is flown,
The gods lie cold where the leaves lie gold,
And a Child comes forth alone.

—G.K. Chesterton
"A Child of the Snows"

CHAPTER ONE

*The Year of Lightning Storms (1374 DR)
The woods north of the Lake of Mists
in the lands of the Khassidi*

Dim dusklight bled from the boughs, and Amira ran through a cloud. The mists grew thicker with each step, dampening her skin and hair. It could mean only one thing: They were nearing the lake.

"Run, Jalan! Don't look back!"

Amira ran behind her son, and she had to strain to keep up with him. Over their pounding feet and her heavy breathing, she could hear the men behind them, and they sounded as if they were getting closer. She didn't know if Walloch had brought the hounds. The slaver sliced the vocal cords of his hounds so that they could never bark above a hoarse whisper. Not that he'd really need the dogs. She had no idea where she was going. She and Jalan were running blind. They didn't know this land, and their enemies did.

Jalan stumbled, almost falling. Amira pulled

him to his feet and urged him forward.

"Need . . . rest," said Jalan.

"Not here. Move. Up!"

Jalan pounded on, heedless of the noise he made, and Amira followed. If Walloch had brought the hounds, hiding would do no good. Their one hope was to reach the lake. If they could only make it there, they could hide themselves in the mists and lose their scent in the water.

The trees and underbrush clustered thick before them. The ground became rocky and uneven, and they found themselves running downhill. Amira and Jalan stumbled over roots, branches, and thick ferns, but they kept going.

"Ut ish vet! Ut!"

The voice came from behind them—much too close. During the years Amira spent fighting the Tuigan Horde, she picked up a bit of the speech—enough to understand the meaning behind the words. *Ut ish vet. Ut.* There she is! There!

Amira didn't slow. She swore she could smell the heady scent of the lake, but the mists were growing thicker with the onset of evening, and she could see nothing but more trees and brush in every direction. She dared a look back. Three figures, no more than blurry forms in the mist, ran on the trail behind them—and they were gaining. She could hear more not far away.

The ground fell away before Jalan's feet, and he slid down the slope. Amira half-ran and half-fell behind him. She hit the brushy ground beside Jalan, the sudden stop rattling her teeth, but she pushed the pain away and got them both to their feet. She grabbed Jalan's shoulders, leaned in close, and said, "Keep going! Make for the water."

Jalan turned to look at her, his eyes wide with fear. He looked far younger than his fourteen years. "Mother, no! I—"

She shoved him and said, "Go!" as she choked back tears. "Lose them in the water. I'll find you."

"You promise?"

The earnestness and fear in her son's gaze almost undid

her resolve, but she clenched her jaw, took a deep breath, and pushed him onward. "Go, Jalan!"

She turned to fight, the words of an incantation already forming on her lips. Behind her, she heard Jalan sobbing, then the sound of the boy blundering off through the forest. Amira raked her sleeve over her eyes to clear the tears, then her hands began the intricate patterns to complete her last spell, the one she'd been saving, hoping she wouldn't have to use it. She was Jalan's last hope. Amira had never been much of a praying person, but as the sounds of Jalan fleeing faded behind her, she sent out a silent plea—*Let Jalan get away. My life for his.*

One of Walloch's Tuigan mercenaries came to the slope and began his sliding descent. He saw Amira about halfway down. He hit the ground running, a wild light of triumph in his eyes, and his body slammed into hers full-force.

Amira hit the ground. The full weight of the Tuigan came down on top of her, forcing the breath from her lungs. Bright orbs of light danced before her eyes, and she fought to stay conscious.

The Tuigan grabbed her right forearm in a grip that she thought might crack stone, then seized her collar and hauled her back to her feet. Two other men—another Tuigan with a naked blade in his hand and one whose short, muscular body and long horsetail of hair made him a Nar—descended the slope, laughing at the sight of Amira subdued. The Nar carried a coiled length of rope in one hand and a dagger in the other.

Her captor shook her hard and held her up, displaying his prize. Amira's vision swam. She swallowed the pain, took a deep breath and uttered the last syllable of the spell, grabbing the man under the chin as she did so. She dug her nails into skin, and emerald flame burst from her hand. The man screamed and thrashed away, but too late—the green fire had taken root and blossomed in his greasy hair. He slapped at it, and the flames caught in his sleeves. In moments, brilliant green fire wreathed his upper body, lighting the surrounding mists in eerie ghostlight.

"Down!" said the Nar. "Get him down!" He made a feeble swipe at the burning man's legs with his rope, but he seemed hesitant to get too close.

His efforts brought him a few paces closer to Amira. She lunged and planted her burning fist in his gut—not hard, just enough to get the flames into his shirt. He shoved Amira away. She hit the ground hard, biting her cheek. Emerald flames licked their way up his shirt, and the man screamed, but he had the good sense to drop and roll in the thick brush.

Amira spat blood and planted her hands to push herself up. Her left came down on the thick shaft of an autumn-dry branch. She squeezed, and the green flames bit into the wood, caught, and flared to life. She grabbed the other end with her free hand, pushed herself to her feet, and turned.

"Enough of this!"

Amira looked up. A man stood at the top of the slope. He was taller than the Tuigan and the Nar, but not nearly so thick. In the last of the day's light, Amira recognized him. Though she couldn't make out the details, his outline against the sky was all too familiar. He wore a knee-length Tuigan shirt called a *kalat,* but his ornate cloak and long hair held back by a scarf round his forehead betrayed an origin far to the west. He held a rapier in his hand. It was Walloch, the slave lord who'd held her captive for days.

He aimed the tip at the burning man and said, *"Silo'at!"*

A funnel of frost hissed out of the blade, enveloping the man caught in the green flames and extinguishing them. The man fell only a few paces from Amira. Down in the hollow it was too dark to make out details, but she could smell the sickly sweet scent of scalded flesh and the sulfuric stench of burned hair. He was breathing in quick, shallow gasps.

"Stay right where you are, *bukhla,*" said Walloch. Amira didn't know what *bukhla* meant—it wasn't a Tuigan word—but the slaver's fondness for it said enough. He made his way down the slope, keeping the tip of his blade pointed at Amira.

The other two men kept their distance, their gaze alternating between Amira and their boss. The Nar's shirt was still smoking, but he didn't seem injured.

Walloch stomped to a halt at the bottom of the slope. "Where is the boy?"

Amira glared at him.

The Nar spoke up. "We saw only the woman. Chiet grabbed her, and she burned him. We never saw the boy."

The green flames in Amira's fist were growing smaller with each breath, though the fire on the end of the branch she held still crackled with life.

"Put the stick down," said Walloch.

Amira raised it over her head, ready to strike.

"You really think a torch is going to help you against me?"

Amira glanced at the two mercenaries. They took a cautious step back and looked to their boss.

"Enough of this," said Walloch.

Amira crouched and prepared to spring, her eye fixed on Walloch's blade.

The slaver took one step forward and brought his other hand around in an almost lazy pitch.

Something sharp struck Amira on the forehead, pain flared in her skull, and every shadow in the wood seemed to flood her vision. A roaring filled her ears, then she felt herself being hauled to her feet. The shadows fled, and she found herself looking into Walloch's furious gaze. Her limp hands were empty, and the last of the green flames were dying in the brush at her feet.

"Stupid *bukhla*. You go up against another wizard, all you think about is magic, and I take you down with a rock." He spat in her face and threw her down.

She fell on her side. Her head bounced against the carpet of sodden autumn leaves and mud, and pain lanced through her skull. Light flared in her eyes. She had to fight the pain to stay conscious. Wet warmth pulsed from the point of the pain on her forehead, and when she tried to rise, a mat of leaves and dirt clung to her face.

Blood, she thought. It's blood. That bastard hit me with a rock, and I'm bleeding like a hung pheasant. She cursed her own foolishness.

She made it halfway to her feet, and Walloch's boot struck her in the side. Her breath left her body, and she heard ribs crack.

"Stay down! You get up when I tell you. Not before."

Amira tried to draw a breath into her lungs, but she felt as if her entire upper body were stiff and brittle as cracked wood. Something struck her in the back, hard. Darkness filled her vision—

She was drowning. Water filled her nose, choking her, and she coughed and coughed until she found herself vomiting a pace away from two worn leather boots.

"Careful, boss. You don't want to kill her."

"Those pale-skinned bastards'll kill us all if we don't get that boy back." It was Walloch, nearby and spitting mad.

"No need to hurt good merchandise. That's all."

"If I want your opinion, I'll give it to you. Now get her up."

Amira felt strong hands hauling her to her feet. She opened her eyes and had to squint against the burning light. More men had come, and several held torches. The thick, oily light struggled to burn a halo through the dense mists, but the blow to her forehead seemed to have cracked more than skin, and even the feeble light stabbed into her like hot needles. It was hard to tell for sure, struggling to see through the pain and uncertain light, but Amira thought she saw at least four more newcomers, and one of them held the leashes to two hounds.

"Hey!" More water splashed into her face.

She turned to face Walloch. He still held his sword in one hand, but the other held a dripping waterskin.

"Look at me, *bukhla*. Look at me and listen, or I'll be the last thing you see."

Amira looked. Blood dripped into her right eye, but the men to each side held her arms fast, and she couldn't wipe it away.

"Where's your boy?" asked Walloch.

"He ran."

"He ran?" Walloch looked to his men and laughed, but it held no mirth. "You hear that? He ran!" He turned back to Amira. "I know he ran, you stupid *bukhla*. Where'd he go?"

Amira kept looking at him, feeling the blood trickle off her forehead and down her cheek. She said nothing.

"That's how it's going to be, eh?" Walloch shrugged and turned to his men, pointing at the one holding the hounds and two others. "You three, after him. Don't let the dogs get to him. I want the boy back unharmed."

The men, taking two of the torches, bounded off with the dogs. Amira watched them go, following Jalan's trail. Maybe if he'd listened, maybe if he'd run and kept running, he'd have made it to the lake and then . . . what? Amira's heart sank.

"My hounds'll find him," said Walloch. He was looking at Amira, but his voice was loud enough for everyone to hear. "Damned whelp's probably not far. All he's done for days is whine for his mother."

Amira tested the hold of the man on her right. Her feeble attempt only made him squeeze harder, and she let out a small hiss through clenched teeth.

"He hurting you?" asked Walloch.

"Yes."

"Good. You hold still, or I'll let him hurt you more."

Amira stared daggers at the slaver, but he merely smiled and turned away. At the slaver's orders, the two men sat Amira down and bound her wrists in front of her with a strap of raw leather. They pulled it tight until Amira couldn't help but cry out at the pain. Seeing her discomfort, Walloch walked back over and drenched the leather with water from his waterskin.

"Feel better?"

"No."

"It'll feel a lot worse when that leather dries and tightens even more. If your boy comes back soon, I might cut the straps."

Walloch turned away and began to pace the area, restless as a hound that scents the fox but is kept at his master's leash. When he walked past the steaming body of the Tuigan that Amira had burned, the man let out a faint whimper.

"You still alive, eh? Eh?" Walloch nudged the man with his boot, and the Tuigan cried out. The slaver shook his head, said, "Nothing for you, then," and shoved the tip of his rapier through the man's temple. The charred form jerked once and lay still.

Two of the other men standing nearby were also Tuigan, and they scowled. Walloch cleaned the tip of his blade in the dry leaves, saw them watching, and said, "Nothing for him. I'm a wizard, not a cleric. You? No? Then turn your eye somewhere else. His gold can go to the rest of you now."

The Nar and the other men smiled at this, but the Tuigan's scowls only deepened.

Amira wiped at the blood that still trickled down her scalp. Leaves and dirt were matted in her hair in a grisly mud. "You know what I am." She looked at Walloch but raised her voice for everyone to hear. "Others will come for me. Better if you let us go now. I might try to forget where I left you when the war wizards come for justice."

Walloch laughed. "Come for justice, eh? That's nice. Is that what those three fops I killed had come for? Didn't look like it to me, and you didn't seem happy to see them." He looked to his men and spread his arms, his silver rapier still in his hand. "Let them come!" He spat on the ground. "That for your war wizards! Me and my men'll make belts from their hides."

"You caught them by surprise," said Amira. "That won't happen again."

Walloch shrugged. "And they won't catch me by surprise. Let them come. When our new friends come for your boy, our reward'll be far more than your pretty-robed war wizards can handle."

The evening wore on, and full dark fell. It was still early autumn, but winter often came early to the Wastes, and when a slight breeze set to rattling the boughs, Amira began shivering. Her hands pulsed from the tightness of her bonds, and she feared that before long she would no longer be able to feel her fingers. Not that it mattered. Her spells were spent.

Walloch kept up his pacing, restless as a caged lion. The Tuigan kept their blades handy and their backs to the torches so as not to ruin their night vision. The Lake of Mists had a reputation among the locals, and even the hardiest Tuigan was never quite comfortable around such a large body of water. They were people of the open steppe, and any water that could not be crossed on horseback was water to be wary of. The Nar and the other few thugs huddled near the torches and whispered among themselves while one kept a tight grip on Amira.

"Where are those damned skulkers?" said Walloch.

"If the boy made it to the water, the hounds might've lost his scent," said the Nar.

The flickering hope in Amira brightened at this. The men and hounds had been gone a long time. Amira whispered another prayer, "Azuth, keep him safe. Please. Mystra, watch over him. And Kelemvor, if you're listening, give me a chance. At the least, let me die well. And if you want me to take any of these bastards with me, I am your humble servant."

"What are you muttering about?" Walloch had come back over, and the tip of his sword hovered not far from her face. "I see even a flicker of green fire and I'll do more than hit you with a rock this time."

The man guarding her took a step back.

"How much longer do we wait?" asked the Nar. "Those three know the way back to camp. Why must we sit out here freezing when we could be back at the fires?"

"We aren't leaving until I have that boy," said Walloch. He looked down at Amira, and the torchlight put an evil gleam in his eye. "But my friend here has a point. I'm tired of waiting. You"—he motioned to another of his men—"help him hold her up again. You others stand close with those torches."

The man seemed hesitant to get too close. "What about the green fire?" he asked.

"You think she'd be sitting quiet if she had any spells left?"

"Maybe she's trying to trick us," said the other.

Walloch turned the point of his sword in the man's direction. "You worry about me. Pick her up, damn you."

The men did so, but the man on Amira's right was trembling.

A sudden rustling shook the branches overhead, and a cry broke through the fog.

"What's that?" said the man on Amira's left, and his grip loosened.

"Just a raven," said Walloch. "The lake is thick with 'em this time of year. Now be quiet and hold her good."

The man's grip tightened. The raven cawed again.

Walloch stepped to within a pace of her and put the tip of his rapier beneath her left breast. "You're lucky he wants the boy unharmed, or I'd lop off a few of his fingers to show you what happens to those who cross me. But you? My buyer says whoever else I snag is mine to keep. I might sell you. Pretty western wench like you ought to sell well. Or I might keep you and teach you some manners. Eh, *bukhla?*"

Walloch chuckled and shook his head. "I'm through being nice," he said, then raised his voice to a booming shout. "Boy! Hey, boy! I got your mother! Come back now, boy! Come back and I promise you no harm will come to your mother! You have the word of Walloch! You keep hiding and . . . well, I may have to start cutting!" The slaver brought his waterskin to his lips, took a long drink, then leered at Amira. "Or maybe something else, eh?"

Amira wanted to spit in his face, but her mouth was dry as dust, and cold and weak as she was, she was half afraid it might come out a whimper. She clenched her jaw and looked away.

"Come back, boy!" Walloch shouted. "Come back and we go to the fires for some food, eh? I give you to twenty, then I start on your mother!" He took a deep breath. "One!"

The raven cawed again, and Amira heard branches rustling overhead.

"Two!"

The raven cried out twice. Walloch looked up. "Damned bird," he muttered, then—"Three!"

The count continued, Walloch pausing for a few breaths between each shout and drinking from the skin a few times. The raven continued its cawing, but Walloch ignored it.

"Eleven! Come on, boy! Hurry! Your time's half gone!"

Still the raven cawed.

"Twelve!" Walloch swallowed the last of his water, then looked to Amira. "Little bastard does know how to count, doesn't he?"

The men holding her laughed, and the raven called again. The bird seemed to be making the Nar and Tuigan nervous.

"Thirteen! Thirteen, damn it all!"

Amira heard a faint rustling. At first she thought it was only the raven moving around again, but the sound grew stronger—and it was coming from the direction in which Jalan and his pursuers had disappeared. The flickering hope in Amira sputtered and died.

"Fourtee-ee-een!" Walloch roared.

The sound of someone running through the thick brush grew louder.

Walloch nudged Amira with the tip of his blade. "Seems he can count after all. Maybe we forget the cutting and get to the other, eh? Teach you a lesson. Maybe I let the others have turns and make your son watch."

The sounds of running feet came very loud now, perhaps amplified by the thick mist. Sick to her stomach, Amira forced her blood-caked eye open and watched. The raven cawed and cawed and cawed.

A figured emerged from the mist.

It wasn't Jalan. It was one of the men Walloch sent out—the one who'd held the hounds. His companion was nowhere to be seen, nor were the hounds.

"Iquai?" said Walloch, seemingly more confused than angry. "Where's my dogs, you worthless—?"

The man fell to his knees, one hand gripping his side and one hand holding on to the Nar for support. Even from several paces away, Amira caught the stench. The man had soiled himself. He twisted to one side, turning toward the torchlight, and Amira saw blood leaking between his fingers at his side. The Nar pushed the man away and he fell. An arrow—wood so pale as to be almost white but with fletching black as a raven's wing—stood out from the man's back. The man tried to speak but could not gather his breath.

"What—?" Walloch's jaw opened, shut, then opened again. He seemed more stunned than angry.

The breeze that had been whispering out of the north suddenly picked up to a full wind, setting the branches to rustling and stretching the mists into thin tendrils that fled like ghosts between the trunks. A pale, horned moon peeked through autumn-bare branches and bathed the little hollow in silver light.

A dozen paces or so behind the dying Iquai, standing just outside the shadow of a large tree, Amira saw two shapes. One was a man, tall and thick with muscle, his black hair corded in a long braid. He held a bow in one hand—not the short bows of the Tuigan, suited for loosing from a saddle, but a long horn bow at least a pace and a half in length. Standing to his left was another figure, his hair white as snow, bits of pale skin peeking out amid sinuous tattoos, but he was dressed like his companion in leathers and animal skins. The pale-haired one held a sword in one hand, single-edged and slightly curved near the end. Overhead, the cawing of the raven ceased.

"Release the woman," said the man. His voice held no anger, no threat. It was simply cold and unyielding.

"And who are you?" asked Walloch.

The newcomers said nothing.

"You feathered my man here, eh?" said Walloch, motioning with his sword at Iquai.

Still the newcomers stood silent.

"You an elf?" asked one of the Tuigan, motioning to the figure behind the large newcomer.

The pale-haired newcomer didn't look at the man who'd spoken. He kept his gaze on Walloch. Amira studied him more closely. His hair flowing in the wind seemed gossamer fine. In the merging light from the moon and torches, Amira could see ears that curved upward into sharp points. An elf. He glanced at her, for an instant only, but in that moment the torchlight caught in his eyes and they shone like embers. After first entering the Wastes so many tendays ago, she and her companions had camped on the open steppe. Wolves had come in close to the camp one night. The Cormyreans and their guides had kept the fires going, and the light from the flames reflected back from the wolves' eyes—exactly as they did from the elf's now.

"That's a *vildonrat*," said the other Tuigan. His eyes were wide, and even in the dim light, Amira could see his knees were trembling.

"Vildonrat?" Walloch smirked. "What's that? That mean 'pale elf' or something?"

"Your Tuigan sellswords have thick tongues," said the tall man. "He is Vil Adanrath."

The Tuigan tensed and exchanged nervous glances. One lowered his blade and took a step back.

"Vil Adanrath?" said Walloch. "What's that mean, eh?"

"It means you'd be wise not to anger him."

"Piss on you and the vildonrat," said Walloch. "Off with you both, or you'll join the wench. I could get a good price for you, big one. You'd make a fine pit fighter, I think."

A crackle of leaves and branches, and Walloch turned to see all but one of his Tuigan men running away. He now stood with only one Tuigan, the Nar, and the two men holding Amira.

"Jodai, what's the meaning of this? Your men just lost their promised gold!"

The remaining Tuigan swallowed hard, his gaze still fixed on the elf. "Keep your gold, Walloch. We'll keep our blood. Only fools anger the vildonrat." The Tuigan sheathed his blade, bowed to the pale elf, then turned and fled after his fellows.

"Damned cowards!" Walloch called after them. "Keep your blood! Ha! Forget your gold, you bastards! You'll lose your blood, too, next time I see you!"

The two men holding Amira looked after the Tuigan, but the Nar kept his eyes on the newcomers.

"Go after them," said the tall man. "Leave the woman and go. We'll take care of your friend holding my arrow."

"Piss on him!" said Walloch. "And you! You know who I am?"

"You're a slaver. The caravan trails are thick with them this time of year."

"I am Walloch! Battlemage and master of the arcane arts of Raumathar!"

The tall man raised his head and sniffed. "You smell like a slaver."

Walloch stiffened, puffed out his chest, and took a step closer to Amira. He raised the point of his rapier toward her. "Maybe I kill her first, then you, eh? This is no ordinary blade, my friend. I pulled this from the corpse of a great wizard that died hundreds of years before your whore of a mother first sold herself to your father."

The tall man glanced at Amira, then said, "Durja! *Aniq, Durja!*"

"Mingan! *Aniq, Mingan!*"

Amira jumped, for it was the pale elf who spoke, his voice both light and cold.

"What's that, eh?" said Walloch, and Amira could hear fear and anger in the slaver's voice. "What's that you're saying?"

Amira saw the tall man's grip tighten on his bow. Walloch must have seen it, too, for his sword arm stiffened, aiming the point of his blade at them.

"Enough of this!" said Walloch. *"Sil—!"*

A black shadow struck the slaver's arm. Amira heard the harsh shriek of a raven mingle with Walloch's own shout of surprise. An instant later the man at her right gasped, squeezed her arm so hard that he tore skin, then released her and fell. An arrow protruded from the juncture of his throat and shoulder. His heels hammered the earth as he jerked at the arrow, and he began to shriek.

"Silo'at!" said Walloch.

Amira heard a crackling hiss. She looked up in time to see a funnel of frost spew from Walloch's blade and envelop the trees and brush—but the tall man and the elf were nowhere to be seen.

"Get him!" Walloch roared. "Kill that son of a whore! Now! Now!"

"In the dark?" said the Nar. "You're mad!"

Snarling, Walloch pointed his sword at a large tree. *"Kelenta!"* he shouted, and a sparkling orb, no larger than a pebble, shot out from the tip of his sword. It tumbled and grew in size as it flew, seeming to feed on the air itself until it grew to a huge ball of fire that struck the tree full force. The autumn-bare branches exploded, and the entire tree became a great torch, lighting up the night. Amira flinched and looked away. The blinding light lanced right through her skull.

"There!" said Walloch. "Now get them!"

Something whipped past Amira's face, so close that she felt the wind of its passage, then the man holding her left arm screamed and released her. Amira sat down hard and found herself looking at the man, who shrieked as he yanked at the pale shaft of an arrow protruding from between his ribs. Amira was looking right at him when the second arrow struck him just below the chin.

Amira's numbness snapped, and she lunged for the dagger at the dead man's belt even as he hit the ground.

"Kill her!" Walloch shouted.

The bonds were so tight that she could barely feel her fingers, but she forced them to grasp the hilt of the dagger and pull it free. She turned to see the dark silhouette of the Nar bearing down upon her. Pale moonlight flickered down the length of his blade. He pulled back to strike—

A gray shadow, swift and silent, hit the man, and both

went down. Amira stared dumbfounded. A wolf had taken the Nar's sword arm in its jaws. The wolf shook its head, rending and tearing flesh, its growling so low that Amira felt it in her gut more than she heard it.

The Nar screamed and dropped his sword. His free hand fumbled for the long knife belted at his waist.

Walloch charged, heading straight for the wolf with his sword held high.

"Mingan!" called a voice. "Mingan, *ikwe! Ikwe!*"

The wolf released the Nar, turned, and fled into the safety of the woods.

The tall man stood at the top of the gully, drawn bow in hand, the burning tree a great bonfire at his back. Amira had to squint against the bright light, but she could just make out the pale elf coming from behind the cover of the brush a few paces behind the bowman.

"Kill that *bukhla!*" Walloch pointed at Amira while facing the two assailants. "I'll finish these two!"

The Nar's sword arm was a mangled wreck, and a steady stream of blood dripped from the tips of his fingers, but his other hand held his knife steady. Three steps forward and he swiped at Amira, aiming high for her throat. Still on her knees and bound as she was, Amira's balance was limited. She fell back, and the tip of the Nar's knife just kissed the tip of her nose. She followed through with her fall, rolling, and brought both feet around. Hard as she could, she brought both heels up into the fork of the Nar's legs. He cried out, his eyes squeezed shut—

An arrow struck him in the side of the neck. It went all the way through, one side all pale wood and black feathers, the other a solid wetness that gleamed black. The man fell on his back, and he began to buck and kick and pound the earth with his fists. Amira could hear him trying to scream, but it came out a bubbling gurgle, then a cough that sprayed a fine mist of blood over his torso.

Amira forced herself to look away. Her head swam, and for a moment all went dark, but she took a deep breath, and the bright glow of the dying tree returned. No more than five paces away, Walloch stood, his sword pointing at the newcomers—the bowman still standing against the light as he reached for another arrow; the elf passing him and descending the slope—while Walloch's other hand clutched at something hanging round his neck. Over the roar of the flames and the thrashings of the dying men, Amira could hear the slaver muttering an incantation.

The bowman drew feather to cheek and loosed—Walloch screamed, *"Thranek thritis!"*—the arrow fell, straight and true, but the slaver didn't move, didn't even flinch. The point struck Walloch in the forehead, she heard a sharp *clack!* like the snapping of bone, and the arrow bounced away.

Walloch laughed. "My turn—*Silo'at!*"

Frost swirled out from the slaver's sword. The pale elf had to dive and roll to avoid being struck. Another arrow bounced harmlessly off Walloch.

Amira gripped the dagger and pushed herself to her feet. Agony exploded in her head; she could feel tendrils of pain running down her spine and into her limbs. Darkness threatened to crush her again, but she breathed deep and pushed it back. She knew the spell the slaver was using. The bowman could loose his entire quiver to no effect, but the magic would do little against her steel if she could get close enough.

"Silo'at!"

Amira looked up to see the elf diving out of harm's way again. Walloch's spells were pushing him away. The tall man had dropped the bow and was holding something long in one hand—with the fire so bright behind him, Amira couldn't tell if it was sword or club.

"Let's try something else, eh?" said Walloch. He wove his free hand in an intricate pattern, then swept his sword at his feet, almost as if he were slicing underbrush. *"Sobirith remma!"*

Flame roared to life before the slaver and spread to each side of him as if fed by oil, forming a wall of fire between him and his foes.

Amira took a step forward, then another. Careful as she was, it felt as if each step hammered a spike into her skull.

She clenched her jaw, struggling to breathe through her nose, but still a hoarse cry escaped her throat.

Walloch turned to her. Backlit as he was by the fire, she could not read his features. Desperate, she lunged, but he caught her bound wrists almost lazily and turned the blade aside. He brought his sword around and planted the point in her stomach.

"Seems I won't have time for you after all, *beluglit,* but know this"—he leaned in close over his sword—"I'm still going to find your son."

He thrust. Amira cried out. Through her pain, through the roar of the flames, she heard the blade puncture the muscles over her stomach.

Then Walloch whispered, *"Silo'at."*

CHAPTER TWO

*North of the Lake of Mists
in the lands of the Khassidi*

Worthless sons of whores, the lot of them! I see them again, I'll take their skins to wipe my arse!"

Walloch raged through the camp, slapping with the flat of his blade at anything that got in his way. Several kettles on tripods fell before his wrath. Dogs scurried to get out of his way. One goat tied to a tent post was not so lucky and received two slaps and a kick for daring to be tied in front of Walloch as he paced the camp.

Dremas the Thayan, Walloch's second-in-command, followed silently at a distance, ready to heed his master's command but otherwise content to let the wizard rage. He'd been with the wizard long enough to know when to keep his mouth shut.

"How many?" Walloch turned to look at Dremas, fury still in his eyes.

"How many, Master?"

"How many of those worthless Tuigan curs are left?"

Walloch looked around the camp, and Dremas followed his gaze. The slaves they'd captured on the raid were still tied in the center of camp, watched over by two Nars and one ugly brute that Dremas suspected had more than a little orc blood in him. Leather yurts and a few canvas tents lay scattered among the grass, scrub brush, and few trees, and the handful of horses the Tuigan had left behind were still picketed and under guard. Not a single Tuigan remained in camp, and three of the other men had left with them.

"Faithless, lying bastards." Walloch spat and sheathed his sword. Much of the heat had gone from his voice. "Did they take anything?"

"Only what they brought with them, Master."

Walloch shook his head, muttered a final, "Bastards!" then raised his voice to carry throughout the camp. "Good riddance! More gold for us, eh, men?"

Several cheers answered him.

"Dremas!"

"Yes, Master?"

"Gather the hounds, torches, and . . ." Walloch looked around again. "How many men do we have left?"

"In camp, fifteen, Master. The Khassidi were out scouting, but I fear that if the other Tuigan got word to them, we won't see them again."

"Bastards," Walloch said through clenched teeth, then shrugged. "Can't be helped, eh? I want three men left to guard the horses and two the prisoners. If they get out of line, kill a few till they're down to a more respectable number—the prisoners, not the horses. Get those damned hounds and torches ready. The rest of us are going hunting."

"Yes, Master."

Dremas turned to obey, his mouth open to begin issuing orders, when every animal in camp went skittish. The horses began to pull at their hobbles, snort, and strain at the ropes round their necks. The goats bleated and kicked. The hunting hounds in the pens tried to howl, but with their cut vocal cords it came out a long rasp. The curs roaming through the camp sniffed at the air, whined, and ran out of camp as fast as they could, heedless even of campfires in their path.

"What—?" said Dremas, then stopped.

The air had gone bitter cold. Not the crisp chill of autumn in the Wastes. A frigid, bone-breaking cold seized the air, as if the very dead of winter had come to the steppe, quick as the stopping of a heart.

"Oh, no," said Walloch, and his breath came out in a cloud that hung in the air a moment before it froze and fell to the ground.

"M-master?"

"Silence!" said Walloch.

Darkness pressed down upon the camp, and even the fires seemed to shrink and cling to their coals. Nothing moved. Everyone sat or stood frozen, as if afraid to move. It was then that Dremas realized he was afraid, though he could not say why. An unreasoning terror had seized him, and he found himself shivering. The riffling of the breeze through the grasses and the crackle of the campfires struck his ears as too loud, and in his mind Dremas urged them to hush. Then he heard it—something moving in the dark. Footfalls, unhurried and deliberate.

He saw them—pale forms walking toward the camp, and something dark behind them, almost like a bit of night blown by the wind.

The pale figures, five of them, walked into the camp with the easy gait of tigers, the subdued light from the fires washing over them. They were men, but their skin was pale as snow, and their hair—every man wore it long and unbound— ranged from frost white to the silver sheen of starlight on ice. Their clothes were an assortment of leather and skins, the edges lined with fur. Every man had a long knife belted at his waist and a quiver full of barbed throwing spears on his back. Four had short swords in leather scabbards, but one carried a double-headed battle axe. Dremas thought he saw runes carved into the haft. The belt the man wore across his chest was made from braided scalps.

"Sossrim!" someone whispered behind Dremas.

"Nai," said Gegin, who was from Damara, where people often traded with the Sossrim. "Those be *Aikulen Jain*. Frost Folk. Damn us all, we should have gone with the Tuigan."

Behind his back, Dremas made the sign to ward off evil. He'd never been farther north than Nathoud, and even he had heard of the Frost Folk. People said they drank the blood of their captives and sacrificed to the ancient devils of Raumathar, who granted them sorcerous powers. Dremas looked to Walloch. What had the wizard gotten them into?

"Greetings, my friends!" said Walloch, throwing his arms open wide. Walloch's voice was warm, cheerful, but Dremas could hear he was forcing it. "I did not expect you so soon. I would have prepared a feast to welcome you."

The Frost Folk said nothing. The leader glanced at Walloch but did not otherwise acknowledge his words. He and his comrades spread out so that they faced Walloch in a wide semicircle. They did not look at Walloch, nor at any one thing in particular. Rather they glanced throughout the camp, taking in their surroundings very much as if they were guests invited to a strange home. Dremas shuddered as their gaze passed over him, and his bladder suddenly felt very full.

At first Dremas thought a wisp of fog had risen and was billowing into camp, but then he saw another figure passing through the yurts. Dremas could make out no distinct features, for the walker was swathed head to toe in robes the color of cold ash. A cloak of the same hue covered his robes, topped by a hood too deep for the light to penetrate. The cloaked one glanced neither right nor left, but came straight for Walloch.

The man stopped a few paces before Walloch, who bowed before the newcomer. "Greetings, my lord."

"I come to fulfill the covenant," said the cloaked man.

Dremas had to force his hands down, to keep them from covering his ears. There was something altogether *wrong* with the newcomer's voice. His speech was careful and precise, but it seemed as if there were two voices speaking at once, and one seemed out of tune. Dissonant. Like fingernails scraping over dry stone.

"I was not expecting you so soon," said Walloch. "Tomorrow after sunset, your man said, eh?" Walloch looked to the pale newcomer with the axe. "Tomorrow you said, eh?"

"Where is the boy?" said the cloaked figure.

Dremas could take no more. He fell to his knees and huddled inside his cloak, shivering. He closed his eyes and prayed the dark thing in the cloak would leave.

"Slippery little rat g-got away," said Walloch. "His mother . . . had one spell saved, I guess. She took out two guards and she, uh, she got away. With the boy."

"You let the woman live? I told you not to underestimate her."

"Y-you said any other captives were mine to keep." Walloch gestured to the group of men and women tied not far away. "I took her staff. H-her spellbook too, eh? Took 'em both. Put guards on her. But she hid one last bit of magic away and hit when I was out of camp. We went after them. I led them personally, Lord. I caught 'em soon enough, but my Tuigan betrayed me and left—never again will I hire spineless Tuigan bastards!—then two interlopers attacked and let the boy get away. I killed the woman, though—killed that *bukhla* good! But don't you worry, Lord! You and your men stay here as our guests, eh? I was just about to lead men out with the hounds to find the boy. He can't have gone far."

"The boy," said the cloaked figure, "you left him in the woods?"

Dremas clenched his eyes shut as tight as he could. Blood roared in his ears.

"Last I saw him he was less than two leagues from here. Whelp was running south. T-toward the lake. You'll have him by morning, my lord. I promise!"

"Yes. I will."

"Wh-what are you—?"

"Uthrekh rakhshan thra!"

Dremas opened his eyes. The world went white.

❂ ❂ ❂ ❂ ❂

Arzhan Island, the Lake of Mists in the lands of the Khassidi

She opened her eyes to a ghost of fire. Her right eye would open no more than a slit, but she could see well enough with the other. A figure, not a ghost after all, but an old man painted orange by the light of the flames, leaned over her. His long hair hung in front of his face, obscuring his features. She could hear him chanting in a strange tongue that seemed all hisses and swallows, and he swayed slightly as if in rhythm with the breath of the nearby flames.

"My . . . son," she said, her voice no more than a hoarse whisper. Even that slight breath felt like sand in her throat.

If the old man heard her, he gave no sign.

"My! Son!" she said, and cried out from the pain.

Another figure leaned over her, but his features were hidden in shadow. Beyond him she could see only a hint of branches obscured in fog.

"Rest now," the new figure said in a deep voice. One she thought she'd heard before. "Lendri and Mingan search for your son. Rest now. Let the belkagen work."

What's a Lendri? she wondered.

She fought to keep her eyes open, but they refused her. As sleep seized her again, drawing her back into darkness, she heard the cawing of a raven.

CHAPTER THREE

*The woods north of the Lake of Mists
in the lands of the Khassidi*

Jalan huddled in the hollow of a rotted-out log and tried to still his breathing. The pounding of his heart was so loud in his ears that he could hear nothing else. Full night had fallen. Jalan had always possessed extraordinary eyesight even in the dark. He'd heard it whispered among Amira's family that he had elf blood . . . or worse. But down this close to the lake, the mists were thick off the water, and he was as blind as a newborn pup. Inside the log, he could smell nothing but the sweet resin scent of wet bark and rot. His ears were his best hope at hearing Amira coming for him or—

He swallowed a sob. He dare not think about that. He'd heard the slaver shouting for him, but he ran and ran and ran till he couldn't hear him anymore. He'd crossed another rise, then fell into a creek and down it, hoping the water would hide his scent from Walloch's hounds. He'd thought he heard a distant shout, a scream of surprise—terror almost—chopped off, then silence.

And so Jalan ran again until he came to the lake. Shrouded by the mists that gave the lake its name, he ran headlong into it, only stopping when he was splashing up to his knees.

As his heart slowed and his breath steadied, his teeth began to chatter. Autumn had not yet left the land, but out here in the Wastes, nights came cold early in the season and winter often fell fast. He doubted that it would get cold enough to kill him, but without a fire. . . .

Jalan held his breath and listened. The breeze set the branches rattling like thousands of cold bones, and the faint rippling of the lake kept time, but there was something else. A quick snuffling that came and went. Jalan clenched his jaw to stop his teeth from rattling. There it was again. At first he thought it was hushed laughter, and his panicked mind conjured images of something cold and hungry creeping down from the trees, madness in its eyes, but then he recognized it for what it was. Sniffing. Something was sniffing through the trees and headed right for him.

Jalan scrunched down into the log, wincing at the noise he made. The sniffing stopped. The near darkness just outside his hollowed hiding place moved. Jalan fought the urge to cover his face. He stared, willing his eyes to drink in the meager light. Something was there. Although Jalan could make out no features, he could feel it—something large that kept low to the ground—watching him. It moved again, startling Jalan, but then it was gone. Jalan heard it padding back into the darkness.

He took a cautious breath, confident that he had escaped certain doom, when a voice said, "Boy?"

Quiet as he could, Jalan fumbled about, searching for some sort of weapon—a rock, a stick, anything—but his fingers found only moss and the wet ashy feel of old rot.

"Boy, I know you are in the log," said the voice.

It was not Walloch, nor any of the other slavers. Jalan had

never heard this voice before. A man's voice, though light of timbre. Jalan could easily imagine the speaker singing. The accent was careful, precise, and Jalan suspected that Common was not his native tongue.

"You need not fear me," the voice said. "My brother and I saved your mother, but she is hurt. My brother has taken her to a friend. Come. I will take you to her."

Jalan saw movement again, only this time the lighter shade of darkness was not low to the ground like the first shape, but standing like a man.

"Will you not come out? Are you hurt?"

"I'm cold," said Jalan.

"Then come out, and we shall find a fire."

"How do I know you aren't lying?"

"If I wanted to harm you, I could have done so by now."

Jalan did not move. "I . . . saw something. Before you came."

"Where?"

"Right where you're standing," said Jalan. "Only lower to the ground."

"You have an elf's sight to see so well in the dark," said the man. Jalan could hear the smile in his voice.

"What did I see?"

"You saw it. Not I. Will you come out, or shall you ask me questions till morning? Either you stand, or I shall sit."

Jalan stood.

Holding Jalan by the hand, the newcomer led them up the slope away from the water. They topped a low bluff. The wind was stronger up here, a biting breeze out of the north that pushed back the mists, and in the moonlight that fell between the trees Jalan got his first look at his rescuer. He was not a man at all but an elf, only slightly taller than Jalan but built of a leaner strength. Sinuous tattoos covered his body, but the skin between them shone almost white in the moonlight, and his hair was the silver of starlight on clear water. Despite the cold, he wore only a wraparound loincloth and shoes made of some animal hide.

"How did you know I was out here?" asked Jalan.

"We ran across some slavers with hounds. And we heard their master shouting for a boy."

"My name is Jalan."

"I am called Lendri."

"I didn't know there were elves in the Wastes."

Lendri said nothing. He led Jalan east, skirting the lake. Their trail occasionally dipped back into banks of fog in the shallow valleys and back out again on higher ridges. In the woods, Jalan heard small animals in the brush, and twice he heard the screech of an owl.

"How much farther?" Jalan asked after they'd walked for a league or more by Jalan's guess.

"We must pass four more coves, though I doubt we'll see them in the fog. Past the fourth, a stream enters the lake. At the mouth of the stream is a great rock jutting out of the lake. An island. Your mother is there."

"She isn't my mother."

Lendri frowned at that but said no more.

They descended an easy slope and re-entered the mists. Halfway through, Lendri stopped.

"What—?" asked Jalan.

"Shh!" Lendri released Jalan's hand and crouched, listening, his ear canted into the breeze.

Jalan was about to ask what the elf had heard when he noticed the change in temperature. It was a cold night, and he had been quite chilled sitting wet inside the log. The brisk walk had warmed him, but the air had suddenly gone frigid. The mists in which they stood hardened and fell to the ground in a shower of crystals, leaving Lendri and Jalan standing in the wooded valley, Jalan's dark form against the pale shape of the elf, surrounded by shafts of moonlight and the stark shadows of the trees. Jalan's breath emerged in small clouds that hung before him an instant before they, too, solidified and fell to his feet.

Under the crescent moon and starlight Jalan could see

quite well, though the trees and underbrush were thick. He could hear little but the sighing of the wind, but as he watched he caught sight of pale forms coming at them from the north. Behind them, weaving through the trees like a living shadow, something darker walked. The hair on the back of Jalan's neck stood stiff. He could taste something foul on the wind.

The elf turned and looked at Jalan. His face was in shadow, but Jalan heard the fear in his voice. "Skirt the lake till you come to the stream, then make for the island. Run, boy! Run!"

❧ ❧ ❧ ❧ ❧

Arzhan Island, the Lake of Mists
in the lands of the Khassidi

When Gyaidun entered the camp, the belkagen was sitting close to the fire and sipping from a wooden bowl, his gaze fixed on the woman who still slept beside him. The belkagen had removed her mud- and blood-soaked clothes and wrapped her in elkhides. He had cleaned and dressed her wounds—the blow to her head had bled profusely, and her right eye was swollen shut.

Durja, Gyaidun's raven, was nowhere to be seen. Most likely he'd found a nice spot in one of the trees to sleep. It had been a busy evening.

The belkagen didn't look up as Gyaidun crouched beside him and placed the rolled hide on the ground. Gyaidun was scratched and covered in dirt up to his elbows, with grime under his fingernails from digging for roots. He untied the leather cord binding the hare hide and spread it before the belkagen, revealing an assortment of herbs, roots, chechek stems, and a thick bundle of moss.

"How is she?"

The belkagen swallowed and placed his cup before the fire. "The wizard's spell froze her wounds. In trying to kill her, he kept her alive long enough for you to get her here. If she survives the night, she will live, I think. The plants you found will help her."

"I found everything you asked for," said Gyaidun.

"Well done. If you would be so good as to boil some water, I will do the rest."

Gyaidun took the iron cauldron from the belkagen's small bundle of supplies and went down to the lake. The north wind that had started during the confrontation with the slaver still had not abated, and it whispered cold at Gyaidun's back as he filled the cauldron. He returned to camp, set the tripod over the fire, hung the cauldron, and stirred the fire.

"Is there anything else I—?"

A howl cut him off. It was part call and part cry of defiance, primal and savage. Twice it wafted from the darkness northward, then once again, mixed with anger and pain.

"Lendri!" said Gyaidun.

"Go to him!" said the belkagen. "I cannot leave the girl."

Gyaidun grabbed his club—a black iron rod with woven leather for a handle, thicker on the far end, and nearly the length of his arm—and bounded off. He splashed through the lake—the island was only a few dozen paces offshore and the water never reached higher than mid-thigh—and was running full-speed by the time he entered the woods. The howling had stopped, but the direction from which it had come was fixed in his mind.

The chill wind had blown the mists southward, and the moon, thin as it was, rode high in the sky. Gyaidun's blood-bond with Lendri had bestowed upon him many talents and skills that other humans did not possess, and his keen eyes caught even the meager moon and starlight. His long strides ate up the distance, and he made no attempt at stealth, breaking through bushes and shattering low tree branches as he ran.

A mile or so from the lake he heard another howl. Different from the first call, this was obviously the call of a wolf. Gyaidun knew it well—Mingan's call for help. He followed the signal, weaving through the trees and leaping small streams, the lake always off to his left. He'd followed the howling for almost a mile before finding the wolf.

The wolf stood on a boulder in a small clearing, the Lake of Mists sparkling in the moonlight only a few hundred paces away.

"Mingan," whispered Gyaidun. *"Alet,* Mingan!"

The wolf ran to Gyaidun, a pale shadow in the moonlight. Gyaidun crouched and let the wolf lick his hands and face in greeting. A dark wetness covered Mingan from his snout almost to his ears, and Gyaidun smelled blood.

"Lendri," said Gyaidun. "Where is Lendri, Mingan?"

At the mention of their friend's name, the wolf's ears twitched and he whined.

"Lendri," said Gyaidun. *"Wutheh* Lendri."

The wolf bounded off and Gyaidun followed, away from the lake and slightly westward. They crested the small rise, descended the next hollow, and Gyaidun smelled it—a crisp scent that nipped at his nostrils. It took him a moment to realize what it was: frost. The leaves on which he and Mingan trod crackled and broke, brittle where they had been sodden and soft only a few paces behind. Gyaidun followed the wolf to a spot where the trees grew close together. Thick brush covered the roots of the trees, and every branch was rimmed in a pale skin of ice. Mingan plunged into the brush, leaving a small cloudburst of snow in his wake. Gyaidun followed, pushing his way through the clinging branches.

The roots of the trees spread out in a large bowl. Lendri lay on a bed of leaves, huddled in a fetal position, his wolf standing over him. Little of his pale skin showed, for he was painted in blood. The stench of it filled Gyaidun's head as he knelt beside his friend.

"Lendri!" Gyaidun felt him. The elf's flesh was cold, but only from exposure to the surrounding frost. He was still alive.

Gyaidun tried to pull his friend's arms back, but Lendri's muscles were locked tight. The elf groaned and stirred. "No," he whispered. "Bleed . . . again."

"I need to get a look at your wounds."

Lendri swallowed and pulled his hands back. He'd been holding a fistful of leaves and mud to his side. It was now a sodden mess of blood.

"They . . . had swords," said Lendri. "One stabbed me. Deep."

"I need to get you back to the belkagen," said Gyaidun. He began scooping up fistfuls of the largest leaves he could find. He'd fill the wound with mud, then overlay it with leaves to help keep the elf from bleeding to death on the way back to the island. It might cause the wound to fester, but if he didn't get Lendri to the belkagen soon, the elf would be dead from blood loss anyway. The belkagen could deal with infection if he could first heal whatever was cut inside him, if Gyaidun could get him there in time, if moving him didn't kill him, if, if, if. . . .

The mud and leaves were cold, numbing Gyaidun's hands. He remembered the slaver's sword and how frost had burst from it at his command.

"They . . . took the boy," said Lendri. "I tried. Too many . . . of them."

"You have to try to stay awake, Lendri," said Gyaidun. "I can carry you, but you'll need to hold this to your wound. I'll deal with the slaver later. Get the boy back and bash that slaver bastard's head in. Damn me for not following him when I had the chance!"

"Not the slaver," said Lendri. He winced and sucked in a sharp breath as Gyaidun scraped the old mud off and applied a fresh coat. *"Siksin Neneweth.* Five of them. And . . . something else. Something foul and . . . cold. Ah, I'm . . . so cold."

CHAPTER FOUR

Arzhan Island, the Lake of Mists
in the lands of the Khassidi

Smoke. Scent intruded her darkness, then a thought: Fire. Someone was burning pinewood. Amira recognized the fragrance. It reminded her of winter hearthfires in the Hiloar estates. Home, childhood, winter feasts, laughter cackling like . . .

Flames—a small fire but very close. She could hear it, but more importantly, she could feel it. She was *warm,* which surprised her.

It was some time before she thought to open her eyes. Both of them. The skin on the right side still felt too large, but she could open her eye all the way. She lay beside a small campfire. She was naked but wrapped feet to chin in some sort of animal hides. On the other side of the fire, wrapped much as she was, lay an elf. Tattoos twisted like vines over his ivory-pale skin.

Recognition hit her. Then remembrance. Running

through the woods. Pursuit.

"Keep going! Make for the water."

"Mother, no! I—"

"Go! Lose them in the water. I'll find you."

"You promise?"

Pain . . . fire . . . cold.

"Silo'at!"

Amira let out a small cry and reached for her stomach. She'd felt Walloch's blade pierce her, felt her muscles resist a moment before the sharp steel broke through, kept moving, slicing, then—*"Silo'at!"*—and cold such as she'd never known, a cold that burned.

"Jalan!"

She tried to sit up, and the world swam around her.

Amira heard light footsteps and when her vision cleared, an old man was crouching next to her. Only he wasn't old at all—or even a man. His face was pale like the elf beside her, and his skin was also broken by tattoos twining over his cheeks and round his eyes, but among the black inks were vines of green and even thin streaks of blue. But unlike the other elf, this one had strange, red symbols on each cheek and over each eye. To Amira, they almost looked like runes, but they were like none she had ever seen. His hair was white as snow; he wore it unbound and wild save for two long braids that dangled before his sharp ears. Not a single wrinkle or crease marred his features. His nose and chin were sharp, and his eyes . . . they seemed lit by both joy and sadness, and also something else. Something . . . wild.

"Who?" said the elf, speaking Common.

"Jalan." Amira tried to swallow. Her throat felt raw. "My son."

The elf looked away, but not before Amira saw the look on his face. Regret? No. Resignation.

"What? Where is my son?" Amira tried to sit up, but shadows flooded her vision and she almost passed out again. She lay back down. "I remember. I woke. The big one said that—Lendri, was it?—had gone for my son. Where is he?"

"Try not to move," said the elf. "My craft has done much

to heal your wounds, but you are still very weak."

Amira thrust a hand out from the blankets and grabbed the elf's cloak. It was thick, heavy, made from some animal hide. Her arm felt hollow, her grip feeble, but the elf did not pull away. "Where—?" her throat caught. So dry. She tried again. "My . . . son?"

"A moment."

The elf stood and walked away. He returned a moment later with a wooden bowl cradled in both hands. "Drink this. I will tell you what I know."

He lifted her head with one hand and brought the bowl to her lips with the other. The water was oddly warm and brackish. She winced but swallowed.

"The waters of the Lake of Mists are warm," said the elf. "Many of the streams that feed it come down from the Firepeaks, and there are hot springs everywhere. I have never known the lake to freeze, even in the harshest winter."

"Where is my son?"

The elf placed the bowl beside her and settled himself down. "I am the belkagen. What your folk might call a priest, a shaman."

Amira lay back down and fixed him with the glare that had sent many pages and servants running from her as a child. "I don't care. Where is my son?"

"Gyaidun and Lendri were the ones who came to your aid last night. After the slaver fled, they brought you here, to my island. You would have surely died had they not. Lendri went back out to find your son."

Amira studied the belkagen. Shaman or no, these three could easily be slavers themselves. What had the big one told Walloch last night? "Slavers . . . the caravan trails are thick with them this time of year." Amira had been embroiled in the courtly intrigue of Cormyr before she could count. She hated it, but she could play with the best of them, and she read no deception or malice in the shaman's face.

"Lendri—" the belkagen motioned to the elf who still lay sleeping behind him. "He found your son, but on the way back something attacked them. Gyaidun went to their aid, but by the time he arrived, your son was gone and Lendri nearly dead."

"Attacked? By who?"

"Gyaidun first thought it was Walloch, come back. The woods where Gyaidun found Lendri were coated in frost. But Lendri said it was . . . he said he thought some of them were Frost Folk, but there was . . . something else. Something foul and cold."

Dread, kept at bay these many days, filled Amira's stomach. Oh, no, she prayed. Not again. We were so close!

The belkagen was watching her, his eyes piercing. Under his gaze, Amira felt like a rabbit under the scrutiny of a hungry wolf.

"Where is this . . . Gyaidun?" she asked. "The big one?"

The corner of the belkagen's mouth lifted in a smile, but his eyes remained sharp. "Yes, Gyaidun the big one. I'm afraid my friend has gone and done something foolish."

"He's gone for Jalan?" Hope flickered in Amira—she'd seen the man fight last night; he could've given a Purple Dragon Knight a challenge and then some—but her sense knew it was a feeble hope. No matter how formidable the big man was, the fool had no idea what he was up against.

"No," said the belkagen. "He and Lendri are *rathla*, what the Tuigan call *anda*. Blood brothers. When he found Lendri near dead, a steel rage filled him. I've only seen him like that a few times. After bringing Lendri to me, he went after Walloch."

"But you said it was Frost Folk and . . . something else."

"So Lendri said. But Gyaidun suspected that the slaver was after you two for a reason, and that reason came looking for you and almost killed Lendri." The belkagen shook his head. "I could almost pity Walloch when Gyaidun finds him."

After leaving Lendri with the belkagen, Gyaidun gave serious consideration to picking up the trail of whoever had attacked Lendri and taken the boy. But he knew he'd be outnumbered at least five to one, and they had nearly killed Lendri. Furious as he was, Gyaidun was no fool. But his blood was up, and he could not just sit by the campfire and wait.

He'd picked up the slaver's trail easily enough. That many men and dogs had torn up the woods chasing the woman and her boy. Gyaidun kept a steady pace but didn't hurry. Lendri's people had a saying: *Besthunit nenle.* "Hurry slowly"—go fast, but not so fast that you miss your prey. The slaver had a loud bark, but he had the bite to back it up, and Gyaidun didn't want to rush into an ambush.

Dawn's first light was burning in the east. Gyaidun had left the forest proper behind and was now walking through the beginnings of open steppe, though there were still frequent copses and islands of brush. He knew he was getting close. He could smell horses, dogs, goats, and all the things that came out of them. The smell of cooked food hit his nostrils, though it was old. Apparently none of the slavers were early risers. The stench of the midden pit struck him so hard that he knew they hadn't taken the time to dig it deep enough or bury what was in it. But something else tickled his senses, more taste than smell. Moisture. That was nothing unusual around the Lake of Mists, where half the lake seemed to escape as a cloud every day. But this had a flavor, sharp and hard. He knew it, but it took him a moment to place it, for it was far too early in the year: snow.

Gyaidun stopped long enough to string his bow and nock an arrow. He crept in nice and slow, going low to the ground from cover to cover.

There was no need.

He crested the small rise above a jagged hollow that a stream had cut through the hills. Gyaidun looked down into the remains of the slaver's camp, every bit covered in a thick blanket of snow. Not even the soft, wet snow that could sometimes fall in the autumn. This was a fine, hard snow. It sent up little clouds as he walked and muffled all sound. Nothing in the camp moved, and he knew that the dozens of snowy mounds scattered throughout the camp were bodies.

❧ ❧ ❧ ❧ ❧

"Where are my clothes?"

After eating some dried venison and drinking a great deal of water, Amira finally managed to sit up without fainting. She hunched near the fire, the blankets wrapped round her shoulders.

The belkagen was tending to Lendri, who was still sleeping. He didn't look up as he answered, "You were covered with blood when you came in. Most of it yours. I had to cut the shirt off, frozen as it was. Everything else I washed." He motioned to the far side of the fire. There, spread out over a branch, were Amira's pants, smallclothes, and what was left of her cloak. "I will find you something to replace your shirt later."

"Find it now." Amira stood. The world wobbled for a moment, but it did not spin, and a deep breath set all to rights. "I'm going after my son."

Amira knew the day was wearing on, though she had yet to see the sun. After the night wind had stopped, the fog off the lake rose thick, and she could not see more than a few dozen paces in any direction.

The belkagen finished replacing the poultice on Lendri's wound, then looked up. "And how do you plan to do that?"

"Leaving here is a good start."

"You won't walk a mile before you fall over."

"Watch me."

"My craft mended the worst of your hurts, but you are not yet healed. Your body must do the rest. You need food and sleep."

Amira started toward her clothes—small, shuffling steps. A slight tremble began in her knees on the second step, and by the fourth she had to stop before her legs gave out beneath her. She stopped to gather her strength before she dared reach down for the clothes. The belkagen's eyebrows raised, and she glared at him.

"You find this amusing?"

"No, Lady."

"What then?"

"It is a cruel thing you are doing," said the belkagen. He walked over and held her breeches out for her.

She gripped the blankets round her with one hand and reached for her clothes with the other. She snatched the breeches and clenched them in a tight fist, hoping it would hide her hand's trembling. "They're still wet."

"The mists." The belkagen shrugged. "Put them back on the branch, and I will stoke the fire."

Amira stood her ground. "What did you mean, a cruel thing?"

"You are so eager to rush off so that your son can watch you die."

If Amira had possessed the strength to slap him, she would have.

"I suppose it is a mercy of sorts that you'll never make it to him. If you did, in your condition, with no supplies, not even your spellbook, you'd accomplish little more than giving your son the chance to watch his captors kill you."

Amira's knees trembled again, and this time she had to sit. "How . . . did you know I'm a . . . ?"

"Wizard?" The belkagen crouched and threw more wood on the fire.

"Yes."

"I am surprised you don't recognize one of your own." The belkagen smiled, but there was no humor in it.

A shudder passed down Amira's spine.

"*I* recognized *you*," he said.

"But you said you were a shaman, a priest."

"I am the belkagen. There is no word in your tongue. I am a shaman, a priest, and perhaps what some of the western peoples might call a druid. But I have also studied the arcane arts."

"So you are a wizard?"

"I am the belkagen."

Amira looked off into the mists. "I hate the Wastes."

"Wastes?" The belkagen chuckled. "There is more life in one league of 'the Wastes' than in one of your stone castles."

Amira smirked, then said, "Could you hand me my small-clothes, please?"

"I thought western women did not like men touching their smallclothes."

"Just hand them to me."

He did. "You're still going, then?"

"Jalan is my son. I'll find him or die trying."

"It will be the dying, I think, unless you heed me."

"You mentioned something about a shirt."

The belkagen frowned. "Are all western women so discourteous?"

Amira took a deep breath. She'd dealt with worse growing up amid the courtly intrigue of Cormyr, but she had no time for this. "I thank you for your help, Belkagen. If I can ever repay your hospitality, I will. On my honor and the honor of House Hiloar. Now, if you could find me a shirt and give me some food to set me on my way, I will be doubly in your debt. But I am going after my son."

"Of course you are. But if you will finish healing, you might have some small chance—"

Through the mist came the sound of splashing. Someone was coming through the lake and moving fast. The belkagen went stone-still, listened, then relaxed.

"I thought you said we were on an island," said Amira.

"Arzhan Island," said the belkagen. "I often winter here, but we're only a few dozen paces from the north shore, and the water is no more than waist deep."

The splashing stopped, Amira heard footsteps approaching, and moments later a large figure materialized out of the mist. It was the man who had come to her rescue last night. Gyaidun, was it? She got her first good look at him. He stood tall, and his leather-and-hide clothes obviously covered thick muscle. Tattoos twined down his bare arms, much like those on the one called Lendri, but strangest of all were the scars on his face. He had three long slashes down each cheek, and one slash bisecting them. No battle wounds, certainly. They were too precise. His unstrung bow rode on his back, but Amira's heart leaped when she saw what he carried in one hand: her staff and spellbook.

The man spared Amira a glance, gave the sleeping elf a longer look, concern creasing his brow, then looked to the belkagen. "Dead," he said. "They were all dead. Every last one of them. Captives, horses, dogs. Even that slaving whoreson Walloch. Frozen solid."

CHAPTER FIVE

The Endless Wastes

Out on the open steppe, the wind never stopped. Tucked as he was in the bottom of a dry gully, Jalan could not feel it, but he could hear it whispering over the grasses, and every now and then dirt and late autumn seeds rained down on him. He sat hugging his knees with his back to the dry earth wall. After the five pale northerners and their leader had taken him from Lendri, they ran north all night, leaving the Lake of Mists and surrounding woods far behind. When Jalan's legs finally gave out, one of the northerners grabbed his bound wrists and dragged him, but that slowed their pace, so the northerners took turns carrying him. So exhausted was he that he actually slept while they ran.

When dawn began to paint the eastern horizon, the northerners split up. The sky was just changing from a weak gray to the first yellow of true dawn when they sought shelter in the gully. Their cloaked leader had found the deepest, most shadowed part of the gully and huddled inside his cloak. The northerners ripped dry bushes, their leaves long since gone, out of the ground and covered their leader with them, placed their own cloaks over the makeshift canopy, then covered it all with a thick layer of dirt.

One of them untied Jalan's wrists, gave him a few meager bites of food and two long swallows of water, then shoved him to the ground and said, "Sleep. Now."

Jalan lay on the ground but kept his eyes open. He'd never been so cold. An aura seemed to emanate from the cloaked figure, an almost elemental presence that drained all warmth from the area. It reached beyond the air to seep into Jalan's mind.

The northerners built no fire, so Jalan huddled in his cloak, shivering. He'd been concentrating all his energy into clamping his jaw shut to stop his teeth from chattering when sleep finally claimed him.

When he awoke, the first thing he saw was the crack of sky overhead. Clouds, high and thin, had blown in while he slept, and they were painted the fiery orange and royal purple of evening. Four of the northerners were sleeping in the gully. The pile of brush and dirt that was the makeshift bed of their leader was the same as it had been since morning. Jalan could not see the fifth northerner but assumed he was standing watch somewhere.

Jalan sat up and listened. Nothing but the sound of the wind. The nights had gone cold enough that all but the hardiest of the flies had laid their eggs and died. There wasn't even any birdsong, just the whispering of the wind over miles and miles of grass.

Jalan stretched his legs out and winced. They were stiff. He listened again. Still nothing, and the four sleepers had not stirred. Jalan looked up. Still no sign of the guard. Jalan scooted over to the waterskin. If the guard appeared and questioned him, he could claim he was only going for a drink.

Still nothing. Jalan took a small sip, tied the skin shut tight, then stood up.

The northerners did not stir, but Jalan felt a sudden awareness from the mound where the leader was sleeping. Although it was only an irregular mound with bits of branch protruding from the dirt, Jalan was sure that something inside it was watching him. He still had not seen the leader's face. The man shunned the light and kept his hood up even in darkest night. Jalan pictured him pale as bone with bloodshot eyes, and he felt like those eyes were watching him now.

Jalan looked. The orange in the clouds was deepening to the color of dying embers. The sun would be setting soon.

He looked around for some food. The northerner who had fed him earlier had taken the strip of dried flesh from a leather satchel, which the man was now using for a pillow. Nothing to be done for it. Jalan's eyes were drawn back to the mound of brush and dirt. No change, but he could still feel something inside watching him, could almost picture a pale face and the bloodsh—

No. The eyes wouldn't be bloodshot, Jalan knew, for blood meant life and warmth. Whatever was inside that mound, wrapped in its ash-colored robes, there was no warmth in it. The eyes watching him were ice.

Before his mind could seize up, before sense outdid his courage, Jalan ran. He headed down the gully until he saw a suitable place to climb out, then bounded up the incline, sending dirt and rocks and grass sliding down behind him. His hands found dry grass, his fingers dug in, he pulled himself up, his feet found the ground, and he was off.

Jalan raced over the steppe, at first not caring which direction, caring only to put distance between himself and his captors. But when his fear cleared enough to allow his mind to notice he was heading north—the direction his captors had been taking him—a small cry of frustration shook him and he turned left. His back itched. He feared that at any moment one of the northmen's barbed spears would impale him, that he'd be harpooned like a fish.

He tripped over another tussock of grass, scrambled to his feet, and was off again. Besides the pounding of his feet and his own breathing he heard nothing. No sounds of pursuit. The last sliver of the sun's crown sank into the earth in front of him, and he dared a look back, not stopping but looking over his shoulder as he ran.

One of the northerners—the guard most likely—was standing at the rim of the gully, not moving, not coming after him, just watching. A shadow scuttled insectlike out of the gully then stopped and stood tall beside the guard. Jalan ran into the dying light, the eastern sky darkening behind him. He knew that the dark thing was no shadow at all, but covered in robes and cloak the color of ash.

An unreasoning fear seized Jalan and he ran all the harder, terror giving his legs strength.

The breeze that had whispered through the grasses all day suddenly grew to a full wind, pushing at Jalan from the right and sending stinging dirt and grit into his eyes. He wiped at the muddy tears but did not slow down. Better to run blind than stop. Jalan closed his mouth and breathed through his nose to keep the dirt from his mouth.

The land began to rise a bit, and his legs started to burn. He'd eaten nothing since morning—and barely anything then. His heart seemed to be beating all the way into the top of his skull, and he could not bring enough air into his body. His face twisted into a rictus of pain, but he forced himself onward.

He topped the rise and began his descent. The pain in his legs eased as he went down the slope, but soon he was going too fast. A bloody dusk still lingered in front of him, but the light only glowed in the sky. It blinded him from seeing the ground at his feet as anything but a featureless shadow. His foot hit a thick tussock. He almost fell but righted himself and kept going. He made it another seven steps before his foot hit the lip of a hole—the front door of some animal's home probably—and he went down. The dry grass cushioned the worst of his fall, but the impact drove what little air he had from his lungs.

A sudden gust hit him, almost as if the wind itself were laughing at him. Jalan pushed himself to his feet, and the beginnings of panic set in as he noticed the trembling in his legs. He knew he couldn't keep this pace up much longer.

Jalan looked up. All he saw was featureless steppe in every direction. There might well be other dry gullies, running like cracks throughout the plain, but he'd never see them until he was on top of them.

He forced himself onward but slackened his pace a bit. He'd been lucky. Another foot into a hole and he might well break an ankle. As a boy, he'd seen it happen to horses, and if a healer wasn't around, there was nothing to be done but a quick jab to the thick vein along the beast's throat. A fountain of blood, an ear-splitting cry that would sometimes go on far too long . . . then it was over.

Jalan risked a quick glance over his shoulder. Nothing crested the rise behind him, but when he turned back around he saw pale things flitting over the plain to the north. Gray, in the dusklight they almost blended in to the steppe. Only their movement gave them away—and they were headed right for him.

A sob shook Jalan. He turned and headed south, following the shallow valley between two hills away from whatever the things were. But he'd seen how fast they were moving. Unless he found somewhere to hide, they'd be on him in no time.

He figured he'd gone almost a quarter mile when he saw a ghostly shape pass him several dozen paces off to his right—and two more off to his left. They were surrounding him. He glanced behind him and saw five others a hundred paces behind him. None were close enough for Jalan to make out distinct features, but he could tell that they were large—pony-sized at least.

The ones to the sides began to close in, and soon Jalan could hear them panting. Like dogs. One of the two to his left put on a sudden burst of speed, ran ahead, and stopped a stone's throw from Jalan. It was the biggest wolf Jalan had ever seen. His first impression had misjudged it. This thing was far larger than the Tuigan ponies. Its shoulders were easily the height of the famed Hiloar stallions that were the source of wealth for his mother's family. The wolf, its head low to the ground, stood still, watching Jalan, a deep growl rumbling from its throat.

Jalan stopped and fell to his knees. Part of him was glad. He'd seen wolves take down prey before. It wasn't pretty, and unless they managed to snap the creature's neck, it looked extremely painful. But it was still better than suffering whatever fate the northerners and their cold leader had meant for him.

The huge wolves circled him, pacing and watching and drawing their circle closer until the nearest was no more than five or six paces away. Their breath formed a nimbus of cloud around them. The stink of them hit Jalan and he coughed. Sweat poured freely from his skin, but now that he'd stopped running, he realized how cold it was. He'd slept many times out on the steppe, and the autumn nights often left a covering of ice on water by morning, but this cold was far worse. An uncontrollable shivering seized Jalan's body, and he realized what it meant.

"Oh, no."

The wolves to his left parted for the figure in the ash-colored cloak as he approached Jalan. The grass crunched and crackled beneath his feet, like the breaking of minuscule icicles. Jalan's tears froze on his cheeks.

The figure stopped in front of Jalan and looked down on him. "Our mounts have arrived," he said.

The man's voice made Jalan cover his ears. It was not unlovely, but there was something altogether *wrong* with it. Not just unusual, but twisted, like a choir of voices where half the voices sang off key.

"Good of you to come and welcome them."

CHAPTER SIX

*Arzhan Island, the Lake of Mists in the
lands of the Khassidi*

He's awake."

Amira started. She was sitting by the lakeshore,
her open spellbook in her lap, so absorbed in her
studies that she hadn't heard the man come up
behind her. Gyaidun, his name was. She should've
heard him coming, but the big brute moved with
a panther's grace. That and this damnable fog. It
seemed to cloud her other senses as much as it hid
everything from sight. It unnerved her. The lake, the
woods around it, and the entire damnable Wastes . . .
she hated them. Her home seemed very far away.

"It's about time." Amira snapped her book shut
and pushed herself to her feet. Evening was coming
on anyway, and she'd soon need the fire to read. *"I
felt fine a long ago."*

Gyaidun scowled. "You were brought in before
he was."

Amira said nothing. She knew the elf called Lendri had been clinging to life when Gyaidun carried him in. It had taken all of the belkagen's skills to heal him, and for a while even he had feared the younger elf might not pull through. He'd been unconscious all day, which meant he was sorely hurt indeed, for unlike other races, elves did not sleep.

The big man was still scowling. "Lendri nearly died saving your son," he said.

"Saving my son? Really? And where is my son?" Amira clenched her jaw and glared. She had to take deep breaths to keep the tears back.

Gyaidun looked away, but he seemed more angry than apologetic. "You wish to speak to him? This way."

"I know the way." She pushed past him and headed back to camp.

Despite her words, she almost did get lost on the way back. It was not a large island, but the mists off the lake were thick as wet wool, and this late in the day she couldn't see more than twenty paces in any direction. The trees and the iron-gray boulders strewn about the island were little more than indistinct shadows. She caught the pale nimbus of the campfire off to her right and realized she was passing the camp. She spared a sidelong glance at Gyaidun. He said nothing, but she saw the amusement in his eyes.

Lendri was sitting next to the fire, swathed in a thick hide blanket. One naked arm stuck out, holding a wooden bowl filled with a steaming liquid. He sipped at it and winced. For the first time, Amira noticed that Lendri had the same odd scars on his face that Gyaidun did—three long slashes down each cheek and a fourth cutting through them. He had even more tattoos than the big man. They twined about his arm, neck, and even around his eyes, and they seemed very dark against his pale skin. A huge gray wolf lay on the ground not far away, its head resting on its paws and its eyes closed. *Mingan,* the belkagen had called it.

The belkagen sat not far away. Dark circles rimmed his eyes, and his shoulders sagged. He'd been busy since Gyaidun brought Amira in the night before, using all his arts and herblore to heal her and Lendri. He looked up as Amira approached the fire.

"You are still feeling well, Lady?" he asked.

"I'm fine." Amira sat down across from him. "You should rest. You look as if you're about to fall over."

A faint smile. "I will seek my dreams soon. But first we must make *amrulugek*. 'Hold council,' as you westerners would say."

Amira cast a quick glance at Gyaidun, then fixed her gaze on Lendri. "You . . . tried to save my son. Thank you. I am in your debt."

Lendri bowed his head but said nothing.

"Gyaidun," said the belkagen. "Sit. We have much to discuss."

The big man gave the belkagen a hard look, and it was the elf who looked away first, his eyes downcast. Amira didn't know if it was the weariness or merely the odd behavior of these easterners, but she could've sworn the belkagen looked . . . guilty. Gyaidun definitely looked angry as he sat, his movements stiff, his jaw clenched, and his nostrils flaring like a stallion about to kick his way out of the stall.

Amira held her tongue, deciding that in the tense atmosphere it was better to let one of the others speak first. She busied herself wrapping the leather cord around her spellbook and stuffing it into one of her shirt's many deep pockets. The belkagen had given Amira one of his old shirts. It was shaped much like the Tuigan *kalats*, but rather than being made of cotton or wool, it had been stitched from elkhide with fur trim. It was far too large for her, but it had deep pockets.

Still no one spoke. Lendri sat sipping whatever was in the bowl, the belkagen stared into the fire, and Gyaidun sat feeding small strips of meat to his raven, which bobbed up and down on his lap.

Damn it all. Amira decided to break the silence. "When you and Jalan, when you were attacked, how many were there?"

Lendri took another sip from the bowl, then fixed Amira with his gaze. She shivered, again feeling as if she were a rabbit being sized up by a hungry predator. "The boy," said Lendri, his voice low and hoarse. "Jalan. He told me . . ." He glanced at Gyaidun and the belkagen.

"Told you what?" Amira asked.

"I told him you were here, that I would bring him to you. 'She is not my mother,' he said."

Now all three men were staring at her, the belkagen looking surprised and the big man's eyes narrowed with suspicion. Even the raven stopped eating and fixed its black eyes on her.

Amira straightened, taking on the regal pose she'd been taught by her mother. "I have no husband," she said. "I am sworn to Cormyr, my life one of service. Jalan is not a child of my body, true enough, but I raised him from a babe. I loved—" A sob threatened to break out. Amira felt tears flooding behind her eyes. She bit her lower lip, took a deep breath, and swiped her sleeve across her eyes. "I *love* him as my own."

There was a long silence, then the belkagen spoke. "Among the Vil Adanrath, one who cares for a child, who loves and feeds a child, who would die and kill for a child . . . this is the parent."

Amira nodded her thanks.

"Then why would the boy say such a thing to Lendri?" asked Gyaidun.

Amira shot him a venomous glance. "As you may have noticed"—she looked to Lendri—"Jalan is not Cormyrean."

Lendri said nothing. Didn't even nod. Just kept those predator's eyes fixed on her.

"I am a war wizard," Amira said. "I serve the crown of Cormyr and have done so for almost twenty years, since I was a girl. When the Horde invaded fifteen years ago, I fought for my people. I was at Phsant and Inkar, but mostly my company roamed, harrying the Horde's flanks, killing scouts, and raiding supply lines. I killed. I watched friends die." She closed her eyes, not to relive the memories, but to concentrate on pushing them away. "During one battle . . . gods, we'd been fighting since dawn with no rest. The sun was setting when my company came upon the remains of a Tuigan camp. The warriors fled, for we had won the day. They . . . they slaughtered captives and their own slaves—men, women, children—rather than have them freed. But in their haste to be gone from us, they missed one. A boy, not even walking yet. My captain found him crying over the body of his dead mother, covered in her blood."

Gyaidun spat a curse in a language she didn't recognize, and when she looked up, she saw fury in the man's eyes.

"I was young," she continued, "little more than a girl myself. My captain gave the child into my keeping. I balked at first." Amira smiled. These were the few memories of the war that did not wake her in a cold sweat at the darkest time of the night. "But I grew fond of him. Fondness grew to love. Months later when a suitable mother was found, my captain relieved me of my duty to the child. I told him that if he took the child he'd experience the wrath of a war wizard firsthand. I named him Jalan, after my older brother who'd died in the war."

"Why does he not claim you as his mother?" Lendri asked. The hardness was gone from his eyes. He seemed genuinely confused.

"Jalan is fourteen." Amira shrugged and tried to put lightness in her voice, but even she heard the bitter tone. "And growing up in House Hiloar is not easy, even for one born into the House. For someone who looks . . . 'eastern,' especially after the bloodiest war in generations with the eastern hordes . . . well, many among my family were less than kind to Jalan."

"The boy does not have Tuigan features," said Lendri. "He's far too lean, and his eyes—"

"Tell that to my mother," said Amira. "After the invasion of the Horde, all easterners are savages to many of my people. I shielded him as much as I could, but my duties as a war wizard often sent me abroad, and I had no choice but to leave him with my family. Their treatment of him ranged from coldly polite to cruel. It was . . . not the best childhood for him."

"You *allowed* this?" asked Lendri.

"What choice did I have?" A cold edge tinged Amira's words.

"Among our people—"

The belkagen cut him off. "She is not of our people, Lendri. The bonds of duty to family and clan are not always easy to bear. This we know."

Lendri looked down. "The belkagen speaks wisely," he said. "I ask your forgiveness, Lady."

Amira acknowledged his apology with a nod. She glanced at Gyaidun. Was he *blushing*?

"To answer your question, Lendri, Jalan is on the verge of manhood. He often chafes at his mother's influence—especially the past few years. I fear he blames me for many of the insults and cruelties he suffered from my family. Perhaps the blame is not altogether undeserved."

There was a long silence, then the belkagen spoke. "You are from Cormyr. A war wizard, you said. How did you come to be out here, a captive of slavers?"

"Last year I was sent to High Horn. You've heard of it?"

The men shook their heads.

"It is a castle in the far west of Cormyr. In the mountains. A hard, cold place. Those sent there are either the most skilled warriors and wizards, sent there to make them the best of the best. Or they're considered trouble and are sent there to be disciplined."

"And which are you?" asked Gyaidun. "The best or trouble?"

"I'm both."

Gyaidun smirked and looked away, but the belkagen chuckled.

"We'd been there a few tendays when I was sent out into the field. Some patrols had gone missing, and the knights looking for them wanted a wizard on hand in case they ran into more trouble than they could handle. We found the patrol in a valley, all dead, but only two died of obvious wounds. Scavengers had been at all of them, but using my arts I was able to determine how they died. It was early summer, still cool in the mountains but not cold, and yet—"

"They were frozen," said Gyaidun, his eyes bright and . . . hungry. "Like those slavers. Weren't they?"

Amira nodded. "We gathered the bodies and returned to High Horn. While we were gone, there was an attack. A dozen or so made it inside the castle. Several died. Good men and women. Friends. And the raiders took my son."

"A dozen or so?" said the belkagen. "How could so few breach a castle filled with your kingdom's best and escape?"

"Most of the raiders were pale-skinned men. Warriors. But one . . . it was . . . uh . . ."

"A thing of darkness and cold malice," said Lendri, his voice low. "Hooded in an ash-gray cloak."

"Yes," said Amira. "How . . . ?"

"I saw him last night—or one very like him."

"Him?" asked the belkagen.

"Him . . . it, I don't know," said Lendri. "His presence made my skin crawl and froze the air around me, but I heard him speak the words to his spell, and it was a man's voice." He took another sip from his bowl and swallowed hard. "But something was . . . wrong with the voice. Something twisted, as if the man were not used to speaking."

"He was alone?" asked Amira.

"No," said Lendri. "Others were with him. The whiteskins you spoke of. They are known here in the Wastes. And feared. *Siksin Neneweth,* my people name them."

Amira's brow creased. "I don't know the word."

The belkagen broke in. "Damarans call them *Aikulen Jain,* and the Tuigan *Shen Ghel.* Ice Walkers, Frost Folk it means."

"In the attack on High Horn, three of the raiders died. Two were Tuigan, but the other was one of these pale-skinned barbarians you speak of, these 'Frost Folk.' The senior war wizard at High Horn examined them, probing their minds. The Tuigan were just mercenaries, hired swords. Saelthos said he could read nothing from the other . . . only a sense of cold and frost. But he said he thought the man was Sossrim, not . . . Frost Folk."

The belkagen threw another log on the fire, sending

sparks spiraling upward, where they were quickly snuffed out in the heavy fog. "Sossrim they once were," he said. "But now they dwell farther north than Sossal, in the endless ice where months do not see the sun. You've heard of the Raumathari Empire in your Cormyr?"

"Of course."

"In the years of war between Raumathar and Narfell, many from Sossal allied themselves with Raumathar against the demon hordes of Narfell. But in their desperation, some even among the Raumathari sought power where they should not. I have heard it told that in those ancient days some of the Sossrim swore loyalty to Raumathari wizards who sought power with demons, devils, and other foul beings from the outer darkness. Their own folk shunned them, and so they have lived in the far north, performing their vile rites. In the darkest winters, sometimes they raid far south, taking plunder and captives. But I have never heard of them striking all the way into Cormyr. So far . . . never have I heard of such a thing. And Jalan was all they took?"

"Yes. They slaughtered any who stood in their way, and the . . . uh, the dark one called down a killing frost, but they took no plunder. Only my son."

"Why?" asked the belkagen. "Why travel more than a thousand miles through foreign lands for one boy?"

"I don't know. I wish I did. I only want my son back."

"Have you ever noticed anything special about the boy?"

"You're asking a mother?"

The belkagen smiled, but it did not reach his eyes. "You study the arcane. You know what I mean."

"Dreams."

Both the belkagen and Lendri seemed to tense at this. "Dreams. . . ?" asked the belkagen.

"Jalan was always a vivid dreamer, even as a small child. I can only remember images and words from dreams, but Jalan . . . he could recall sounds, shapes, even smells and touch in solid detail. And he said he often dreamed of a shining song."

"A shining song?"

Amira shrugged. "Only a dream. I never thought about it much."

The belkagen and Lendri shared a look. "The elves do not sleep like other folk of the world. We rest and"—he seemed to be searching for the word—"walk the dreamroad. Dreams can be very powerful and hold great meaning."

"I sometimes dream I can fly," said Amira. "It doesn't make me a bird."

"What did you do?" Lendri broke in.

"About birds?"

"About your son. When you returned to the High Horn and found him gone."

"In Cormyr," said Amira, "the war with the Horde is still fresh in the minds of many, especially among the knights and wizards. I don't know any who didn't lose someone. When it was discovered that Tuigan and other easterners had penetrated one of our westernmost outposts . . . well, it was treated with *extreme* concern.

"Three expeditions were mounted to pursue the raiders, each led by a war wizard. Since the murderers had my son— and since my family has contacts in Nathoud—I volunteered to lead one team. Two of us caught up with them about fifty miles east of the Sunrise Mountains. We caught them late in the day. By surprise. But still they fought like cornered dogs—except for the cloaked one, who cowered and hid and left the fighting to his men and other hired blades. They fled before us.

"But when the sun went down, the . . . dark thing, he . . . uh, seemed to 'wake up' and fill with terrible strength. He killed over half our force." Amira shivered at the memory and pulled her cloak around her. Full night had fallen, and their campfire did little to penetrate the thick darkness. "It was as if he called down the heart of winter itself. Strong men died in their tracks. All but a few of us were killed, but we took many enemy lives as well. A few of us managed to get away with Jalan and flee. We ran through the night. More died. In the end, it was only the sunrise that saved us. Exhausted as we were, we pushed on."

"You said three teams were sent out," said Lendri. "Your

team met with one. What of the other?"

"What few of us survived met them in Almorel. We'd hoped to find a portal thereabouts and make it as far west as we could. We watched for the pale barbarians and the dark thing, but we were foolish." Amira stared into the fire, and her voice hardened. "We underestimated our foe. Whoever is leading them put the word out to every thug and bandit in the Wastes. That loud-mouthed bastard Walloch and a bunch of his men hit us leaving Almorel. Killed the other war wizard, took my staff and book, and when I'd used my last spell . . . well, you figure out the rest. That's where you three enter the story."

"Will more of your war wizards come to help?" asked the belkagen.

Amira looked around and saw a waterskin lying on the ground. She reached for it and took a long swallow before replying. "I wouldn't hope for it."

"Why? Does your order forsake its own so easily?"

"They may not know what happened yet." She avoided the belkagen's gaze. "May not know for days. Tendays even. And even if they do, they have no idea where I am. Our last known location was Almorel. They'll start searching there, but it could take them days to find me. And if I'm on the move every day, it could take tendays before they catch up."

"On the move?"

Amira held the belkagen's gaze. "I'm going for my son. You said that if I waited, you could help. Give me some hope, some chance of success. But that raises another question I haven't been able to answer: Why did you help me in the first place? Outside Almorel, when Walloch's force hit us, there were others on the road. Lots of others. Travelers, merchants, Tuigan warriors . . . those who didn't flee just watched that slaver and his men slaughter us. What makes you three so different?"

Lendri ignored the question. He simply sat drinking from the wooden bowl and staring off into the distance. The belkagen held her gaze for a long moment, then looked to Gyaidun.

The big man shooed the raven off his lap—the bird gave

an angry caw until it saw the remains of the belkagen's dinner lying not far from the fire and went after it—then shrugged and said, "I was born a slave. Never much cared for slavers since. I've made it a point to make their lives difficult whenever I can."

"That's it?"

"We helped," said Gyaidun. "Why suspect our reasons?"

"I'm a stranger to these lands. Trusting doesn't come easy for me."

"If we wanted you dead, we could've killed you or left you to die. If we have not earned your trust by now . . . why chase the wind?"

"Maybe it isn't me dead you want."

Gyaidun snorted. "Don't flatter yourself, woman."

Amira blushed. "That *wasn't* what I meant. How do I know you aren't slavers yourself? Maybe you just saved me to collect the price instead of Walloch."

"I . . . *we* never asked for your trust," said Gyaidun. "Not asking now. No one's keeping you here."

Amira's eyes widened, and she looked to the belkagen. "You convinced me to stay. *I* wanted to leave long ago. It was you who said I should stay, that you'd help—"

"Lendri and I are going after your son," said Gyaidun. "But no one invited you. Best that you stay here with the belkagen."

"Curse my House if I will, you—"

"I care nothing for you or your House."

Amira stood, her face a mask of fury. "You stupid, arrogant—"

"Peace!" said the belkagen, and he stepped between them. "Lady, please sit."

"I've sat enough. Damn you, you convinced me to lie about all day. Jalan's getting farther each moment!"

"Enough!" said the belkagen. The predator's gaze had returned to his eyes, and his nostrils flared in anger. His jaw clenched, and he stood with all the poised authority of a king, his staff held high. "You will sit and hear me or I will tie you down—for your sake and the sake of your son."

Amira sat, her mouth pressed in a flat line. Gyaidun was staring at her, not smiling but watching her.

"And you—" The belkagen turned to Gyaidun. "You will sit silent and ponder the courtesy due an honored guest. Disrespect the lady again, and I'll thump you into the lake."

The big man returned the belkagen's glare. "The . . . 'lady' speaks much of what I'm thinking, Belkagen. The trail goes cold. I could've put leagues behind me before sunset."

The belkagen's staff thumped to the ground, and he leaned heavily on it a moment before sitting. "You would leave your *rathla* behind?" he asked, but Amira could hear the weakness in the elf's argument.

"Once Lendri was healed, he could have caught me. Easily." Gyaidun spoke carefully, with respect, but Amira could hear that it was silk over a blade. Something was going on here. "But you persuaded me to stay," he continued. "Just as you did the lady. Why?"

The belkagen shot them each another look. "Think. Both of you. Lendri says that this dark one is traveling with the ones who have Amira's son. He seems to weaken during the day. Most likely Jalan's captors rest during the day and travel at night. Even if this dark thing does not need sleep, the *Siksin Neneweth* do. Most likely they have slept all day today. We—and I do mean *we*—will certainly do all we can to save the boy. But we cannot rush after them like a pack on a bloodscent." He looked at Amira. "You said that the first time you caught them, that . . . thing killed most of your force by himself. What can four expect to do?"

"We didn't know what we were facing the first time. I do now."

"Do you? What is this 'dark one,' then?"

Amira locked eyes with the belkagen, but it was she who dropped her gaze first.

"I thought as much," said the belkagen. "Then hear me. My people have walked these lands for many hundreds of years, and I myself walked here long before your grandfather was born. Not all lore is kept in books inside your stone forts, and the tales of these lands reach far back to the days of Raumathar and farther back still. You have heard of *Iket Sotha?* 'Winter's Fort' in your tongue, I think."

"You mean Winterkeep?" said Amira.

"Ah, Winterkeep, then."

"It's a ruin on the Great Ice Sea, said to have once been the capital of the Raumathari Empire."

The belkagen smiled, seeming genuinely pleased. "Very good! I see you were a good student."

"My family has had trading contacts in Nathoud for years. Most in House Hiloar study the lore of the East. Knowing your customers and competitors makes for good business."

"You've heard of the legends surrounding the place, then?"

"What ruin isn't surrounded in legends?"

The smile on the belkagen's face fell to a frown. "You study history but disdain legend?"

"Disdain? No. But history is fact. Legend is . . . not. Scholars—"

"Scholars? Pfah! I have met some of these 'scholars.' Half-mad, most of them. Legends . . . well, they are known by the people, who are . . . what is your word? Sane."

Amira chuckled, but it was an empty laugh with no humor in it. She buried her face in her palms and rubbed her eyes. Her head *hurt*. And getting a straight answer out of the belkagen . . . he was worse than any master or teacher among the war wizards. Gods, I hate the Wastes, she thought.

"What do your legends of Winterkeep have to do with me and my son?"

"And you still haven't answered our question," said Gyaidun. "*Why* have you kept us here? The trail goes colder as we sit by the fire, and this is the best lead we've had in over ten years. *Ten* years, Kwarun! If we lose—"

"Peace," said the belkagen. "I know your need, *Yastehanye*. I share your need. But rushing to our deaths—"

"Rushing?" Gyaidun's shout roused the wolf sleeping by Lendri's side, and it sat up, its ears stiff. "Would that we were, *Belkagen*. Instead we sit by the fire and talk!"

The belkagen opened his mouth to respond, but Lendri

spoke first. "Peace, *rathla*. I feel your hunger. But you did not face this . . . thing. Our oaths, both blood and milk, bind us. But we cannot keep them by rushing to our deaths. If making *amrulugek* will give us a chance to bring this thing down, then it is worth a small delay."

"Look," Amira broke in, "you three obviously have much to discuss, but I don't understand half of what you're talking about. All I want is to get my son back. If you can help, I will be in your debt. If not, then speed me on my way. I beg you."

The belkagen muttered a long string of words in his own tongue. The speech was completely foreign to Amira, but she could sense the frustration in his words. He took a deep breath, then stared into the flames and spoke.

"Lady Amira, Lendri and Gyaidun and I have walked many horizons together, few of them pleasant. Forgive us our heated words."

Amira glanced over at Gyaidun, who didn't look at all apologetic.

"You were speaking of Winterkeep . . ." she said.

"Yes, Winterkeep. *Iket Sotha*. It is a place shunned by the people of these lands. In ancient days it was a place of beauty, but foul things happened there, and this cold earth has a long memory. One of the great weaknesses of your 'histories,' Lady Amira"—the belkagen gave her a weary smile—"is that if the tome and scholar are both lost, your 'history' is lost. The people of these lands have a better way of preserving truth. We remember the tales, sing the songs, and dance the fires. Your history is a book. Ours lives in us and our children."

Amira took a deep breath and forced civility into her tone. "Honored Belkagen, *my* child—my only child—is getting farther away as we sit here. I would be most grateful if you came to your point soon."

The belkagen's smile fell to a frown. "As you say. Even a young, upstart people like the Tuigan know of the evil of *Iket Sotha*. They tell tales of how the angry ice gods rose from Yal Tengri and sealed the Raumathari kings and their sorcerers in ice. The Tuigan, who fear very few things in this land, will not go near *Iket Sotha*. But the Tuigan are a young people, and their tales only touch the leaves of a tree whose roots go deep, to a time when the Tuigan still dwelt in the East.

"In the dying days of the wars between Raumathar and the demon-haunted empire of Narfell, the Nars summoned great ice devils to fight for them. Every army sent against them was beaten or pushed back—until the rise of Arantar and Khasoreth. You have heard of them?"

Amira shook her head. "No."

"Many songs are sung of their adventures in these lands. Arantar was a great sorcerer, the greatest of his age. Some have even said that his father was a god or some great being from beyond. Fire was the soul and song of Arantar, and he was its unquestioned master. Khasoreth was his apprentice, but his great love was for ice and cold. Arantar's mother was Raumathari, and together, he and Khasoreth were able to stand against the armies of Nar and their demons. For the first time in many months, the Nar fled the battlefield, and for a time there was peace in these lands."

"I take it the peace didn't last," said Amira.

"No," said the belkagen. "One particularly bleak winter . . . something happened to *Iket Sotha*."

"Something?"

"Here is where even the tales of my people fade to legend. It is not known what destroyed *Iket Sotha,* but one thing is certain: Great powers fell upon *Iket Sotha*. The Tuigan say they came from Yal Tengri. Raumathari legends say they came from the heart of *Iket Sotha* herself. But the one thing that all tales tell the same is that it was in the death of *Iket Sotha* that the Fist of Winter was born."

"The Fist of Winter?"

"A name given to them among the people of the Endless Wastes."

"I don't understand," said Amira. "What are they?"

The belkagen thought a long time before answering. "None know for sure. But they are . . . terrible. Their corrupted flesh cannot abide warmth, and so they dwell in the farthest reaches of the north. But in winter when Yal Tengri freezes, they often roam *Iket Sotha* and the surrounding lands, preying upon the unwary. Over the years, renegade bands of Sossrim have sworn allegiance to them. These are the *Siksin Neneweth,* the Frost Folk, and they worship the Fist of Winter as gods and offer blood sacrifices to them."

"And you believe one of these . . . things has my son?"

Amira had been staring into the fire during the belkagen's tale, but she looked at him now and was shocked at what she saw. The weariness still pulled on him, his shoulders slumping and his eyes seeming empty. But his face was now breaking into what seemed to her a mixture of sadness and fear. The belkagen cast a glance at Gyaidun, then quickly looked away. Amira looked to the big man. Fury seemed to come off Gyaidun in waves, like heat. His eyes were unblinking and fixed on the belkagen, and Amira could see the muscles of his neck standing up taut.

"Belkagen . . . ?" said Amira.

"There . . ." The belkagen avoided everyone's gaze and looked up where the smoke from the fire was curling into the mists. "There is more to the tale. The Fist of Winter and their servants prey upon any who come too close, and I've heard of many fortune-seekers going into the ruins of *Iket Sotha* and never coming out again. But in some years, during the winter months when days are cold and nights dark, the Fist of Winter roams throughout the east, hunting."

"Hunting for what?"

"Boys," said the belkagen. "Some very young and some just shy of manhood, like your Jalan. I've heard of boys being taken from tents, from the heart of cities, boys who are sent to watch the herds and are never—"

Gyaidun lunged over the fire, screaming and reaching for the belkagen. Amira saw murder in his eyes. She grabbed her staff and scrambled away as the belkagen jumped to his feet and ducked. Gyaidun and the belkagen were screaming at each other in their own tongue, and Lendri, weak as he was, had dropped his drink and was trying to pry the two of them apart. Wide-eyed, Amira held her staff ready to strike should the argument come her way.

Lendri managed to push himself between the two combatants. Gyaidun tried to shove him away, but the elf latched onto the man's shoulders and held on. Lendri shouted something, just one quick word in his language, and Gyaidun stopped as if slapped. But he still held his fists before him, and his gaze was burning, looking over Lendri's shoulder to the belkagen, who stood a few paces away, guilt in his eyes.

Gyaidun said something, his voice harsh and angry. The belkagen replied. Amira couldn't tell if his voice was trembling from indignation or fear. Both, she decided. Had Lendri not intervened, she was quite sure the big man would have hurt the belkagen. Gyaidun's whole body was trembling, his face was twisted in a rictus of fury, and tears were running down his cheeks.

"What's going on here?" she asked, her staff still held ready, her mind searching for an appropriate spell should any one of them come at her. "Have you all gone mad?"

No one said anything. Gyaidun was still staring daggers at the belkagen, who was returning the gaze, though he seemed pained and saddened. Lendri watched Gyaidun long enough to be sure the big man was under control, then turned to the belkagen. Amira saw mistrust and anger in his eyes as well.

"*What* is going on here?" she asked.

Gyaidun glanced at her and the tension left his body. He stood straight, looked back to the belkagen, and said, "I will not share a fire with a traitor. *Sumezh.*" He spat in the belkagen's direction, then turned and stormed off. For a moment, he was a shadow in the mists, then they swallowed him.

Lendri watched him go, then turned to the belkagen. "I apologize for my *rathla's* rude words, Belkagen. But you do owe us an explanation. Now."

Defiance and anger flickered in the belkagen's countenance, but neither caught. His shoulders slumped. "My apologies, Lady. You found yourself in the middle of a family quarrel."

"It's more than that," said Lendri. "And you know it. Talk or I may not try to restrain him next time. You've known this—who was responsible for Erun—all these years, after all we've lost, but you said nothing. Why?"

The belkagen looked off into the mists where Gyaidun had disappeared. "Because there is nothing you could have done. Either of you. Or all the Vil Adanrath. You would have only been rushing to your deaths."

"Listen," Amira broke in. "I don't understand any of this. Who is this Erun? I just—"

"Be silent, woman," said Lendri.

Amira opened her mouth to give the insolent elf the tongue-lashing of his life, but she shut it again when he looked at her. The fire caught in his eyes, and again she was reminded of the wolves in the darkness, circling her fire. The tongue-lashing could wait.

"Please, Lendri," said the belkagen. "Sit down before you fall. And there is no need to be rude to our guest. None of this is her fault."

"No," said Lendri. He didn't sit, though Amira could see his arms and legs trembling from the effort of standing. "It is yours. Do not hide behind her. Explain yourself."

The belkagen sighed, then sat by the fire. He placed his staff across his lap, closed his eyes, and said, "I spoke truly. By the time I'd heard of Erun, many days had passed. Although I suspected the Fist of Winter was involved, it was only suspicions. I have become certain in my own mind only in the years since. I know you and your *rathla*. Had I told you, both of you would have rushed off to *Iket Sotha* like a pack on bloodscent. And both of you would have died. What happens to the children taken, I do not know. But whether they are alive or dead, you and Gyaidun could do nothing for Erun if you were dead."

"So you did nothing? All these years, you simply sat?"

"No!" The belkagen looked up at Lendri, and a bit of the heat had returned to his eyes. "I have sought knowledge and chased every rumor, hoping and praying for any sign of Erun and the others. I only became more certain of the boy's fate, but I learned nothing of how to save him."

"I'm going after my son," said Amira. "And don't you

silence me again, elf. Not ever. I have half a mind to broil the lot of you for keeping me here all day. You promised me help, Belkagen. You said if I waited, you might give me hope. Where is it?"

"I believe they are taking your son to *Iket Sotha,*" said the belkagen. "For what reason? I do not know. But knowing what I have told you, we can go after him prepared. Perhaps we can rescue your son. You said you did so once before. If we can get him away—"

"They'll only take him again," said a voice from the darkness. Gyaidun emerged from the mists. He looked down at the belkagen in disgust. "They did so once already. They traveled across half the world to get him." He looked to Amira. "Do you wish to spend the rest of your life—and your son's—running?"

"I'm going after my son," said Amira, though the cold fear had returned to her heart. She had to force a steady calm into her voice. "I don't think I can kill this dark one who leads them. His powers are beyond me. But I'll get my son back or die trying. If I have to spend the rest of my life keeping him safe, so be it. I'm his mother."

Gyaidun smiled, but it was one of the most frightening smiles Amira had ever seen. "Well said. Lendri and I will be going with you."

"And me?" said the belkagen.

"You can sleep in the Nine Hells for all I care," said Gyaidun.

"Rathla!" said Lendri. *"Chu set!"*

The belkagen said nothing, would not even look at Gyaidun.

A spasm seized Lendri and he would have fallen had Gyaidun not rushed over and caught him. The big man helped the elf to sit.

"Your anger is just," said Lendri. "Your disrespect shames us both, *rathla.* The belkagen's silence these years borders on deceit, but his words are not without some wisdom. If our foes are as dangerous as Lady Amira and the belkagen say, we will need help."

"Who would—?" said Gyaidun the same time that Amira said, "There is no time—!" They both stopped and looked at each other.

"Tonight I walk the dreamroad," said Lendri. "Tomorrow you two should follow the trail. I will seek out the Vil Adanrath."

The belkagen hissed. "Foolish. They are more likely to kill you than help you. You know that."

"This concerns Erun," said Lendri. "Haerul may well kill me, but he'd hunt the Beastlord himself if there were a chance of finding Erun. *If* I can find them. If not, I will meet you at *Akhrasut Neth* in three days."

"Wait," said Amira. "Who is this Haerul? And who is *Erun?*"

"Erun is my son," said Gyaidun. "He was taken eleven years ago. Just like Jalan."

CHAPTER SEVEN

Near the ruins of Winterkeep

The old, old woman raised her head and sniffed into the wind. A northern wind, it bit with the promise of ice. Not hard. Not yet. The season was passing, but she still had a few nights before the first snow, a few more days of scrabbling through the ruins. Every evening darkness caught the land earlier and held it longer. She would have to leave soon. Very soon. Old and powerful as she was, even she was not foolish enough to be caught at Winterkeep when the snows came.

As the first rim of the sun touched the western horizon, the old woman stood in a shadow cast by a massive stone. It had once stood tall and proud, and even now after all these years she could make out the remains of designs carved into the stone. They were rounded, smooth, some no more than faint indentations, but for those wise enough to know how to see, the designs had obviously been wrought by human hands. The men and mages who cut the stone and raised the temple had been bones and ashes for thousands of years. Their holy place high on the island had stood longer, but it too eventually succumbed to the never-ending winds off Yal Tengri, and fallen.

The old woman looked to the far shore a few hundred paces south of the island. Only a few broken stones littered the foundations there. Most of once-proud *Iket Sotha* lay underground where the brightest day was dark as sleep and it never grew warm, even in high summer. She'd spent several days scrabbling through the ruins, as she did every autumn, searching for relics and any old thing that might hold power. This season's hunting had been particularly poor. Maybe she'd try the southern stair again tonight.

The wind off the water gusted, and she sniffed again. Yes. Snow soon. In her bones she could feel the clouds gathering far away over the northern ice. This would be her last day on the island.

The breeze died off, almost as if hushed, and inhaling as she was she caught a strange scent. She sneezed and muttered a curse. What was that foul stench? Almost like . . . flowers.

Crouching low and leaning upon her staff, she looked through the jumbles of rubble at her feet. Nothing but moss lined the wet stones. A few stunted shoots had pushed their way through a crack in the stone at the base of the large rock. She considered trampling them but decided against it. With the promise of snow, they would die soon enough anyway. She smiled.

Then the scent hit her again. Very faint but enough to make her scowl. She scrambled through the stones, poking at the rubble with her staff. Some old fish bones there, probably left behind by a tern. The eyes were empty and dead, but a bit of skin still clung round the sockets. The old woman picked it up, plopped it in her mouth, and began sucking on it, trying to soften the bits of skin and tissue.

The breeze brought the scent to her again. *What was that?*
The old woman lifted her gaze and stepped out of the

shadow cast by the stone. It lay at the base of the island's crest, a great pinnacle of rock that thrust out of Yal Tengri. Atop the crag stood a tree, long-dead and blackened by generations of winter. It had been a great thing once, not tall but thick and strong, its boughs twisted. Even the winter gales had never been able to topple it.

Something caught her attention. There it was! Something flickered on the tree, painted orange as an ember by the dying sunlight. Could it be a bird, caught in the ancient tree's tangled branches? Perhaps if she were quiet she could sneak up on the poor thing, snatch it, and have more for her supper than old fish bones.

The old woman had to lean on her staff and took her time climbing the slick rocks. The scent grew stronger as she climbed, and her scowl deepened. That was no bird.

Standing under the great tree, the old woman felt dwarfed. She and the tree were the only upright things on the island, and she seemed small and insignificant next to it. She'd never liked the cursed thing.

She held her staff in a firm hand and raised it, ready to strike. Perhaps she was wrong. Maybe there was a bird up there, and that smell was coming from something else. Should it be a bird, she wanted to be ready. One little rap with her staff. Not hard. Not enough to stop its little heart. Just enough to stun it so she could grab it.

Slow, nice and slow, she crept around the tree, her gaze casting upward. The last sliver of sun sank in the west, and its last flicker of flame caught on the thing waving from a low branch.

The old woman gasped.

It wasn't a bird at all.

It had glowed red as an ember in the dying light when her eye first caught it, then as the first bit of true night fell on the island, all warmth and light left the little thing. It was no larger than the old woman's thumbnail, but there was no mistaking it.

The ancient tree of the Raumathari kings had produced a bud.

CHAPTER EIGHT

The Endless Wastes

Not in all her years serving the crown of Cormyr, all her demanding apprenticeship and training as a war wizard, not even during the longest days of the war, had Amira ever been so tired.

They left Arzhan Island that morning as soon as it was light enough to see. It took all morning and a good deal of the afternoon to get through the woods north of the Lake of Mists. That had been exhausting enough, but once Gyaidun had led them onto the open steppe, he started running, not waiting for Amira but obviously expecting her to keep up. She had, which seemed to annoy Gyaidun, though it didn't entirely please Amira. She knew she'd never have managed it without the belkagen's help.

Before they'd left camp that morning, Gyaidun still avoiding the belkagen and refusing to speak to him, the belkagen had pressed several special roots—he'd called them *kanishta* roots—into her hand and told her to keep quiet about them, but he knew she'd need them after midday when they came to open grassland. She hadn't understood till her legs began to cramp and her lungs refused to fill with enough air. She'd stuck one of the roots in her mouth, chewed, and new vigor and strength had filled her almost at once.

Whether the *kanishta* roots had some herbal property or had been fused with the belkagen's magic—probably both, Amira guessed—they certainly worked. They tasted just shy of foul, but with one tucked between her teeth and cheek, she'd been able to keep up with Gyaidun the whole way, and when they stopped for brief periods to drink, he seemed even more winded than she. His scowl told her he suspected she'd had help doing so, but he didn't say a word.

After midday, after running across the open steppe with only brief periods of jogging for rest, Amira began to hate Gyaidun. Her legs burned and the inside of her chest ached, even with the help of the *kanishta* roots. They kept her going, but she couldn't help feeling as if her endurance were like a bow being pulled farther and farther back, gaining strength but in so doing coming ever closer to snapping. As the sun slid toward the horizon and the ache deepened to pain, then agony, she even considered murdering the man for the unflagging pace he set. Probably the only thing that kept him alive was her knowledge that he was her best hope in finding Jalan. He knew these lands and was able to follow their quarry's trail even through the short grass.

When the western sky began to burn orange with the coming of evening and a violet curtain spread across the east, even her hate for the big man and his long, miles-eating legs faded. Now that they had finally stopped, with the barest sliver of sun peeking over some low hills to her left, Amira just wanted to fall down and die.

"Tired?" asked Gyaidun. A thin sheen of sweat covered his brow, but even carrying most of their supplies he was not breathing heavy. The hate in Amira flared again.

"No." Amira blushed when the word came out a gasp. She

swallowed and her trembling fingers fumbled to untie the waterskin dangling from her pack.

"Let me help you," said Gyaidun, crouching next to her.

"I can do it!" She slapped his hand away.

Gyaidun stood. "What do you think?"

"About what?"

"Light will be gone soon. We should find a place to camp."

"Fine."

"No caves for miles. No copses. Maybe I can find a gully. It'll keep the worst of the wind off us and hide the fire."

"Talking isn't going to find it."

He gave her a hard look then said, "Sure you don't want help with that?"

She let go of the waterskin and let it dangle from her pack. She'd only managed to tighten the knot even worse. "I'm not that thirsty after all."

Gyaidun took his own waterskin, took a long drink, then tied it shut and looked at her. "You sure?"

"You—"

A harsh caw and a rustle of black feathers cut her off. Gyaidun held up his arm and Durja the raven settled on it. The bird flapped his wings and called again.

"Hush," said Gyaidun. *"Dilit, Durja!"*

The raven cawed once more, then settled down.

"What's the matter with him?" asked Amira.

"He's found something."

Under a cloudless sky quickly fading to black, Durja led them less than a quarter of a mile to a dry creek bed no more than five or six paces across and two deep. Amira dropped her pack to the ground next to Gyaidun's and sat on the edge of the gully while the big man climbed down.

"What is it?" she asked.

"They camped here last night," said Gyaidun. He was bent low, his gaze fixed on the ground, and he took the utmost care with each step. Durja perched on a nearby rock and looked to his master. "They lit no fire, but they bedded down here."

"They?"

"Your boy and his captors."

"Jalan?" Even through her bone weariness, proof that they were going the right way gave her a brief surge of excitement.

"Yes. Jalan. And at least four others. Maybe more. They rested here. I'd say they left at sunset yesterday."

"You're certain?"

"Yes."

"How?"

Gyaidun stood straight. "I need to look around. You can start a fire?"

"Yes, but—"

"Then do it." He climbed out of the gully and stood over her. "Down there. And keep it low. We don't want to signal everyone for miles around."

"Where are you going?"

"I won't be long."

"Curse you, where—"

But he was already moving off. In moments, he had disappeared over the small rise.

"I hate the Wastes," Amira said. She stood, dragged their packs down into the gully, then set about looking for something to burn.

There was precious little, and all of it hard to find in the gloom. The gully obviously served as a stream in the wetter, warmer seasons, for the bank was lined with small bushes of hard, twisted wood with tiny leaves. Amira pulled at one and a small pain shot through her finger. The cursed things had thorns. Not large, but they were sharp. She considered lying down by her pack and letting the big oaf build his own fire. But now that the sun was gone and she'd stopped running, the chill in the wind had bite. She'd only spent a few days around the Lake of Mists, and she'd grown used to the heat it gave off. Out here on the open steppe, autumn was cold.

Taking more care, she grabbed the thing at the base and pulled it up by the roots. The soil was dry and the plant came up easily. She gathered five, threw four into a pile and one near the base of the gully wall. Her fingers twirled, she spoke an incantation, and flame funneled out of her fingers into the little bush. The dry leaves caught at once, flared a brilliant orange, and the flames caught in the wood.

It gave her enough light to gather stones to make a little firepit, and she used a larger rock to break up the other bushes without having to risk touching the thorns. She'd just thrown more wood on the fire when Gyaidun returned.

"Here, use these." He tossed several gray chips, each the size of a dinner plate, near the fire.

"What are they?"

"Dung."

Amira put a hand over her nose and scooted to the other side of the fire.

"It's dry," said Gyaidun. "It will burn slow and hot with little light."

"I don't suppose you found any water?"

"No water." Gyaidun crouched next to the fire. He looked grim. "I found something else. Not good."

"What?"

"More tracks besides Jalan's and his captors."

"More Frost Folk?"

"You know *viliniketu?* The Tuigan call them *tirikul.*"

Amira shook her head. "I don't know the word, but *tiri* means 'ice,' does it not?"

"The *viliniketu* are like wolves, but larger and much more cunning. They live—"

Amira's heart skipped a bit. "You mean winter wolves?"

"As you say. A whole pack of them came here yesterday around sunset. No human tracks left."

"What does that mean?" asked Amira. She could not hide the tremor in her voice. "The winter wolves attacked them?" She'd encountered them once before, back during the war. They were dangerous, but she knew they'd be no match for that dark thing that had her son.

"It means that your son's captors are riding the *viliniketu*, and there's damned little chance of our catching them now, even if we ran all night and all day tomorrow."

"This morning when we left the lake, you said we might find Tuigan and obtain horses."

"Might. But even if we found horses tomorrow and ran them till they died, there's no horse that could catch the *viliniketu*."

"You're giving up?" Amira said. Rage and despair filled her.

"No!" said Gyaidun, anger rising in his voice. "We'll run or ride as long as there's a trail to follow. But unless you can grow wings to fly us there, they'll be wherever they're going long before us."

"What if—?" Amira stopped herself.

Gyaidun speared her with his gaze, and she looked away.

"What if what?" he asked.

Amira said nothing but cursed inwardly. She knew Gyaidun's only interest in helping Jalan was in hopes of finding his own son or, barring that, wreaking vengeance on those who took him. She dared not trust him with too much.

"What if what?" Gyaidun grabbed her wrist. "What aren't you telling me?"

Amira slapped his hand away. "Unhand me!"

Gyaidun lowered his hands but leaned in close until he towered over and looked straight down into her eyes. She straightened her back and returned his gaze. One spell, just one, and she could have this brute howling for mercy.

"You think this is a game?" said Gyaidun. His eyes narrowed, and he spoke scarcely above a whisper. "Your son is out there. My *rathla,* my sworn brother, almost died protecting him. I'm risking my life trying to get him back."

"Why?"

Gyaidun flinched, obviously shocked at the straight-forward question, but said nothing.

"I watched you, you know."

"What?" Gyaidun's brow wrinkled in confusion.

Amira had to fight to keep the smile off her lips. She'd never liked the machinations and manipulations of courtly life, hated it in fact, but that didn't mean she didn't know how to play the game when it suited her. Hit your opponent where he least expected. That held true in both court and war—and ten times more so with men.

"When I woke in the belkagen's camp. You treated him with respect. Almost awe at times. Until he told us what he knew of Winterkeep and the . . . Frost Folk, he named them. You tensed up like a drawn bow. I thought you were going to crack a tooth grinding your jaw. Then, when he mentioned other children being taken—"

"Enough!"

Gyaidun stood, and for a moment Amira feared she'd gone too far. The same fury that had clouded his features when he'd attacked the belkagen was back. Amira's hand tightened around her staff, and she started going through the proper spell that could stop Gyaidun without seriously hurting him. But he stopped, and obviously with great effort composed himself.

Finally, his shoulders slumped and he spoke in barely more than a whisper. "My son was taken. Just like Jalan. My wife died, just like your knights. I never saw my son again." A bit of the cold hardness returned to his eyes. "That what you want?"

Amira slapped him, then stepped back, shocked at herself.

Gyaidun glared at her, but he didn't back down. "Hit me all you want," he said. "But if you're keeping secrets from me, you're only damning Jalan. Right now, I'm the only friend you have."

She held his gaze a moment longer, wrestling with her own doubt, then her shoulders sagged. She lowered her staff and sat down beside the fire.

"Sit down."

Gyaidun hesitated, then turned and went to their packs. For a moment she thought he was offended, but he returned with their blankets. He tossed one to her, then sat across the fire from her. He held his blanket in his lap.

Amira wrapped hers around her shoulders, then began her tale.

"I . . . I lied."

She watched him for a reaction. He blinked.

"I was not part of any official expedition from Cormyr. Search parties were sent. That much was true, but I was forbidden from going. It was no simple assignment that I was at High Horn. Over the past few years I have been somewhat . . . insubordinate. They sent me to High Horn in hopes of reining me in. The attack there occurred just as I told you and the others, but when search parties were organized, I was forbidden from going. My *superiors*"—she made no attempt to keep the sneer from her voice—"believed I was too close to the situation, too emotionally attached to serve the crown with proper objectivity. Besides, I am a Hiloar, and my House's relationship with the crown and the war wizards is . . . strained. They assured me they would do all they could for Jalan, but told me in no uncertain terms that I was to remain at High Horn."

Her voice was breaking. She was about to get up and go for her waterskin when Gyaidun handed his to her. She nodded her thanks and took a long drink.

"You're a renegade then," said Gyaidun. "You disobeyed and went anyway."

She held herself erect, proud, ready to defend herself, but much to her surprise she saw approval in Gyaidun's frank gaze.

"I'm here, aren't I?" she said.

He smiled. "Go on."

"I am not without resources, and I organized my own party. Swords for hire, a few good scouts I knew, and even two thieves I thought might prove useful. We ran into one of the 'official' expeditions in Nathoud. Had I run into Strirris or Jamilan's party, they might have arrested me on the spot, but it was Mursen. He and I have a . . . history together, you might say."

Amira watched Gyaidun for a reaction. There wasn't one.

"His knights wanted him to arrest the lot of us, but I talked him out of it. I agreed to submit myself to his authority and face formal charges when we returned to Cormyr, but until then it made more sense to join forces. The knights balked and complained, but Mursen agreed. My family has contacts in Nathoud, and we obtained the finest horses in the area and set off into the Wastes."

Her breath caught. She took another long drink and stared into the fire.

"How many?" asked Gyaidun.

"What?"

"Your parties joined together. How many were you?"

"A score and three. We set an unflagging pace. Lesser mounts would have died, but these were the finest Nathoud horses. We caught them. We caught the whoreson bastards who had Jalan. We saw them around midday and chased them until nearly sunset."

She needed a moment to compose herself. She tied the waterskin shut, tossed it back to Gyaidun, then put a bit more kindling on the fire. The flames burned low, down to little more than embers in ashes, and the fire would go out if no one tended it.

Gyaidun threw some of the dried dung on the fire and said, "What happened?"

"We fought. Those white-skinned barbarians fought like devils, but still we were beating them. Until the sun went down."

"The sun?"

"That . . . thing. The one in the dark robes. He fled before us and hung back. At first we thought him no more than a decrepit old man. But when the sun went down, he . . . he . . ."

"What?"

"It was like . . . like watching a petal unfold. No, it was faster than that. Like throwing oil on a fire. Once darkness was upon us, he became terrible. Knights fell before him like wheat under a scythe. Mursen tried to stop him, and that . . . that monster blocked the spell and snapped Mursen's neck."

Amira closed her eyes, hoping to push back the tears, but it only brought the image back, stark and clear—seeing the slate-gray sky and under it Mursen's head forced all the way around, hearing the final *snap*. She opened her eyes and wiped the tears away on her sleeve.

"Mursen was your . . . I don't know your word. Lover?"

Amira tried to smile, but she could feel it twisting into something else. "Not in a long time, but . . . he . . ."

"I am sorry for your loss. He died well."

"Died well?" The tears were flowing freely now, but she didn't care. "That monster snapped his neck like a twig. Died well or died poorly. Died brave or died a coward. Does it matter?"

Gyaidun's eyes were hard, but there was a gentleness in his voice that Amira had never heard before. "He died fighting. Fighting to save your son. Fighting beside comrades. Better that than a drooling old man whose heart stops in his sleep."

Amira wanted to rail and curse him, pummel him with her fists and maybe sear that damned calm look off his face, but all she said was, "Fool."

Gyaidun sat unfazed. "I did not know Mursen. I do not know your western ways. If I offended, I apologize. I am sorry your . . . friend died."

" 'Died.' " Amira laughed. "You make it sound so simple. He was *killed*. There's a damnably big difference."

"Not in the Wastes."

"You ba—"

"What happened to the others?"

"What?"

"The others. You said there were twenty-three of you when you found Jalan's abdoctors."

Amira snorted.

"What?" asked Gyaidun, his brows wrinkled in confusion.

"Abductors."

"What?"

"You said, 'abdoctors.' The word is abductors."

Gyaidun scowled.

Damn him. Amira found the anger gone. One little word he hadn't even meant to say and the fury at him evaporated. The pain at losing Mursen, the horror of the things she'd seen that night and since, the fear she'd kept barely in check every moment since . . . all of it was still there. But the anger at Gyaidun and his confidence and simple way of looking at the world was gone. Damn him.

"What happened?"

"Mursen's . . . sacrifice"—she almost tripped over the word but forced herself to continue—"allowed me the chance I needed. I killed one of those pale-skinned barbarians, grabbed Jalan, and . . ."

"And what?"

"We come to why I told you all this in the first place."

"I don't understand."

"I grabbed Jalan and cast a spell. One moment we were there out under the darkening sky, death all around us, and the next we were leagues away. What happened to the rest of my comrades, I don't know. Some were still alive and fighting when I made it to Jalan. A few had fled. But at that moment all I could think about was getting Jalan away."

"Wait," said Gyaidun. "You mean to tell me that you know a spell that will take you leagues away in . . . in the blink of an eye?"

"More or less."

"Then *why* did we just spend an entire day running across the steppe, if you could have just . . . just 'blinked' us here or whatever it is you do?"

Amira straightened and propped her staff up beside her. It was a pose and she knew it, but she hoped it would serve to remind Gyaidun with whom he was dealing. She was no fresh-faced maiden in distress.

"Truth be told," she said, "I wasn't entirely sure I could trust you. I'm still not. And part of me . . . a small part, maybe, but a part hoped your belkagen was just a crazy old elf who's spent too many days under the sun. Part of me hoped that Jalan and your friend just ran across bandits and fled with my son. You yourself said the caravan trails are thick with them this time of year."

The big man reached for his waterskin and, watching her, took a long drink. She could see him working all this out in his mind. She let him and didn't rush it.

"And now?" he said.

"As I said, it was a small hope. A foolish one perhaps, but I knew that no common bandits would head due north this time of year. And we've followed them north all day."

"And I don't suppose it hurt to separate these three strangers that you weren't sure you could trust yet?"

Amira said nothing.

"Well played," said Gyaidun. "But I told you already I don't care if you trust me or not. I'm going after your son whether you like it or not. You are here because I let you come."

"Because you *let* me come?" She gripped her staff and balled her other hand into a fist. "What makes you think you could stop me?"

"What makes you think I'd want to?" Gyaidun smiled. "But you need me to track your son's . . . abductors."

"Not if your belkagen was right and they're taking him to Winterkeep."

"You think you can find Winterkeep?"

"I studied maps of the Wastes before leaving Cor—"

"Maps?" Gyaidun laughed. "Did your maps tell you how you will find water when our skins run out? Or food? Did your maps tell you which tribes might help us should we run into them and which will surely try to kill us? Or which plants will keep the sting of the *gaudutu* from rotting away your skin? Did your maps tell you that in midwinter these lands grow so cold that the pines up north sometimes freeze and their sap explodes? Did your precious maps tell you of the whispering of the stars?"

"I told you," said Amira. "I'll find my son. I am in your debt for your help. But I'll find him with or without you."

"As you say." Gyaidun bowed. She couldn't tell if he was mocking her or saluting her.

"But . . ."

"But what?"

"If your belkagen was right, if they are taking Jalan to Winterkeep . . ."

"Yes?"

"If I can take the time to rest and study, I might be able to take us there with a spell. We could get ahead of his captors. Not all the way to Winterkeep. Not with one spell. It's too far. But we could get ahead of them and set a trap."

"The two of us? Alone?" Gyaidun shook his head. "We should wait for Lendri at *Akhrasut Neth* and see if he comes with aid. Then . . . then I like your plan."

Amira smiled. "Gyaidun?"

"Yes?"

"What is 'the whispering of the stars?' "

Gyaidun seemed surprised at her question. "A term among the Vil Adanrath. In deep winter, on the coldest days your breath freezes so quickly that it becomes a fine snow—like little stars—right before your eyes. Listen and you can hear it fall to your feet. Like a whisper. 'The whispering of the stars.' "

Amira shuddered, lowered her staff, and wrapped the blanket back around her. She licked her lips and said, "You . . . do you think my plan will work?"

"Perhaps." Gyaidun shrugged and threw some more dried dung on the fire. "As long as we find them before the first snow."

Darkness on the open steppe. A haze, high but thick, shrouded the sky, and only the waxing moon and the few brightest stars managed to shine through, their milky glow pale and diffuse. Wind came from the north, and it held the scent of winter.

The pack trailed the elk for miles. Normally they did not hunt at night, but with the lean winter months coming, every moment not sleeping or caring for the young was spent on the hunt. The wolves had taken three young bulls from a herd numbering well over a hundred. They'd feasted in the dark and would sleep tomorrow.

The young—only off their mothers' milk for a few months—were just finishing when a howl wafted over the pack from the west. A moment later, another joined it from the south. The scouts.

Every hunter in camp stood still, ears held erect. Several surrounded the young.

The pack did not have long to wait before the scouts ran in, joining them. They spoke in the language of wolves—posture and movement and the flicking of the ears speaking just as much as the yips, whines, and occasional growls. The leader listened, a deep growl building in his throat even before his scouts had finished.

His mate barked, her head held high, looking at the low hills to the south. The short grasses were a black shadow under the iron-gray sky, but something flashed over them— two pale forms moving down the slope at a full run.

Most of the pack circled the young, who had sensed the tension among the group and stopped working at the slick bones of the elk carcasses. The leader led his hunters toward the intruders, his pack forming out behind him, moving silent as ghosts in the grass.

Just shy of the base of the slope, the newcomers stopped. Both were wolves, one a mottled gray and the larger one the color of starlight on new snow. The smaller threw his head back to the sky and let out a long, plaintive howl.

Forsaking silence for swiftness, the pack leader put on a sudden burst of speed. The newcomers did not retreat, though the larger of the two tensed, his muzzle low to the ground and his fangs bared.

The pack leader stopped in front of them, his hunters surrounding the intruders. He did not return the big one's threat. He could smell the southern soils on the newcomers. They had come far. They would be tired. Easy prey.

The largest of the newcomers shimmered in the dim moonlight. Shadows rippled over his fur, stretching and distorting, then disappearing. Where the pale wolf had been, there now stood a pale elf, naked upon the grass, his frost-colored hair falling over his shoulders. Lines and swirls, black in the dimness, covered his body, and three scars bisected by a fourth covered each cheek.

His palms held open, Lendri looked at the pack leader and said, "Greetings, Brother."

CHAPTER NINE

The Endless Wastes

Jalan woke to the feeling of warmth. It came as a shock, for he couldn't remember when he'd last been warm. Not since—

Almorel. Yes, that had been it. At Almorel there had been fire, warm food, a bed . . .

No dreams had come to him since Almorel. Before that, during the days when the first raiders had dragged him through Rashemen and into the Endless Wastes, nightmares had plagued him. Every night he relived the horror of High Horn.

The shouting of the guards . . .

. . . the screaming . . .

. . . his mother's maidservant pulled from the wardrobe and shrieking as the pale man, laughing, slit her throat . . .

. . . blood pooling on the stone floor . . .

. . . the pale men, their eyes wild, blood speckling their skin, beating him down and dragging him outside . . .

The nightmare continued. Jalan had always been a vivid dreamer. His earliest memories were of dreams, and one in particular. For as long as he could remember, he'd dreamed of music, warm and bright, flowing like a breeze that smelled of blossoms. Since that night at High Horn he had not had the dream. Since Almorel he had not dreamed at all. But as conscious thought drifted away and sleep claimed him in that small hollow in the middle of the Endless Wastes, the dream came to him.

Light flooded his mind. Always there had been the almost-voices of the song, a choir that sang beyond words, but now, as Jalan basked in the yellow warmth, he heard a voice, clear and distinct, though seeming to come from far away. What language it spoke Jalan did not know, but he understood the meaning within the words.

Be not afraid.

A tremor of fear passed through Jalan. Not the unreasoning terror the pale barbarians gave him. Not the cold dread of their leader. This was the fear of the unknown, the new, the fear and exhilaration a baby feels taking his first steps, or a bird feels when it first realizes that its fall has caught the wind and the wind is lifting it. It was a fear mixed with joy. It was a feeling Jalan had never known.

His thoughts reached out to the presence, seeking the music, and as he did he heard again the voice within the music. The words were strange, melodic and deep, but their meaning was clear.

Be not afraid.

Gathering his courage, the little bird teetering on the edge of the nest, Jalan called out. *Who are you?* His voice seemed small, a tiny tinkling bell lost amid thunder.

The song swelled, and the voice answered, *I am Vyaidelon.*

The name meant nothing to Jalan, though he felt strangely comforted by it. *Vyaidelon,* Jalan said, savoring the name. It felt right. Maybe even familiar.

Listen, Jalan, the voice sang.

I don't want to go back! Even through the music and light and warmth, Jalan remembered the pale northerners, their huge wolves, and the dark thing, the dark malice, that led them.

Be not afraid, Jalan, sang the voice. *Listen to me.*

Who are you?

You are a closed bud, Jalan, waiting for the sun to shine. I am the root of the tree, buried far away in the cold earth.

What? It was all gibberish to Jalan. A bud? A root? The joy he'd felt at finding clarity within the song for the first time melted away to confusion. *I don't understand!* he called.

You will. Be not afraid. Come to the Witness Tree. It is our only hope.

CHAPTER TEN

The Endless Wastes

One moment thick sleep bound Amira. Instant awareness slapped her awake. She couldn't breathe, couldn't move. Something pressed hard upon her mouth and nose, just shy of pain. She let out a small cry and struck out, but a hand caught her wrist.

"Shh!" A deep voice whispered.

Gyaidun. He brought his hand away, and she took a deep breath.

"We have company," he said.

"What?" Amira sat up. "Who?"

"Don't know. Durja heard them. They're sneaking in quiet. Your spells ready?"

Before sleep last night she'd spent a good while bent over the reeking fire and poring over her spellbook.

"Some," she said, keeping her voice low. "But I was preparing for a journey, not a fight."

"You're in the Wastes, girl," said Gyaidun. "Always be ready for a fight. Start a fire. Be seen. And be ready."

With that, he turned away. The sky was gathering what little light it could from the oncoming sun, but there were no clouds, and the air was thin. Darkness still held the land, and in the time it took Amira to sit up, Gyaidun had disappeared into the shadows. She heard one rustle—the big man passing through the grass—then nothing. She was alone.

"I am *not* a girl!" she whispered after him, but she had no idea if he heard or not.

Annoyed at being ordered about like a lowly apprentice, her every muscle stiff and sore from running all day yesterday, and more than a little frightened, Amira kicked away her blankets and stood. She didn't move, didn't even breathe, but strained her ears to catch every sound. Thunder muttered far off to the south, and she saw little flickers of light. The Lake of Mists and Firepeaks gathered thunderstorms this time of year like summer caravans gathered flies. The slightest hint of a breeze whispered out of the north. She shuddered and only then realized how cold it was. As she bent to the firebed, hands trembling, her breath came out in a thick white fog.

Last night's fire had fallen to a bed of ash, but she could feel warmth coming off it. She took a stick from their small pile of kindling, stirred the ashes, and blew the coals into embers. She added a bit of dry grass, which smoked at once. She blew again, and tiny flames caught and grew. Adding larger twigs and finally several sticks—she would not touch the dried dung no matter what Gyaidun said—she soon had a healthy blaze going.

Light was finally beginning to gather in the grass and tussocks above the little gully, but Amira knew the first sliver of sun would not pass over the horizon for some time yet.

A caw shattered the silence. Amira looked up. Durja was circling the camp in low, erratic sweeps. Every third pass or so he let out a harsh cry.

Amira was about to bend down to add more fuel to the fire when a lump of shadow she'd taken for a tussock or bush moved. She froze, watching it. Whoever it was must have seen her watching, for after a moment it moved again, standing up. It was a man, much shorter than Gyaidun, but stocky with muscle. Another about an easy stone's throw to the man's left stood up, then another just behind them. They started walking toward her, other shapes rising from the grass and behind bushes.

She turned. Four others approached from the other side of the gully. Nine in all.

Where had Gyaidun gone? Damn the man. She knew she could probably manage all nine if she could keep them at a distance—and if none of them had bows. But their build and swagger told her they were Tuigan—she couldn't make out enough details to discern the tribe—and the Tuigan *always* had bows.

Amira retrieved her staff and climbed out of the gully on the east side, putting the wide gash in the earth between her and the four coming in from the west. They'd have to cross it to get at her, and if the sun peaked over the horizon in time, they'd be staring into the sun.

The men kept coming at an easy pace, not hurrying, obviously sizing her up. Tuigan were a superstitious lot, and even if these were nothing more than bandits outcast from their clans, even if they'd forsaken all vows of honor and hospitality, they'd still be wary of anything unknown. Especially a woman alone on the steppe. If she played this right, she might be able to scare them off.

The nearest was only a few dozen paces away.

Amira raised her staff and shouted, "Stop!" in the Khassidi dialect.

The men stopped. They stood in stark silhouette against the brightening horizon. The two on the outside held bows with arrows on the strings. The three in the middle kept their hands on the swords sheathed at their waists.

"You are not Khassidi," said the one in the middle.

"No." She lowered her staff. "I'm not."

"We are not Khassidi."

Amira sifted his words, his accent. The slight roll in his r's and his broad vowels gave him away as a southerner. Commani, perhaps? Maybe raiding into Khassidi territory, if they were clanless bandits.

"Who you are does not concern me," she said. "What do you want?"

"We saw your fire and hoped you might offer us hospitality."

Amira risked a quick glance over her shoulder. The other four had stopped at the opposite edge of the gully. Three of them had bows. Damn, she thought. She prayed for the sun to hurry. Direct sunlight in their faces might give her an added edge. If Gyaidun didn't return soon, she'd need it. Where had he gone?

Durja landed several paces behind the leader and cawed, but the men ignored him.

"Let me gather my things," Amira said, "and you can have the fire to yourselves. I have a long way to go."

"Where is a fine woman like yourself going all alone in these hard lands?"

"I am not alone."

The leader chuckled and looked to his men. "Ah, yes. The big one. We saw him as we came in."

"Skulked in, more like."

The leader shrugged. "One must take care. You might have been bandits trying to lure us in by your fire."

"As I said, let me leave and the fire is yours. There's enough fuel there to last a while."

"Your friend, the big one, where has he gone?"

Durja cawed several times, loud and harsh. It gave her an idea.

"That was my slave," she said. "He displeased me, so I turned him into a raven. That raven." She pointed at Durja with her staff and gave it a theatrical shake.

The men didn't move, but she saw them go stiff and still. The bowmen's fingers tightened round the nocks of their arrows.

"You are a witch?" said the leader. "A Rashemi witch, then?"

"No. I am a War Wizard of Cormyr. Our apprentices practice on the Rashemi witches."

The men made the Tuigan sign to ward off evil, and two of them exchanged nervous glances.

"My father was a powerful shaman," said the leader. "His cloak shadows me. I do not fear you."

"What about your men? I think that one there would make a fine donkey." She shook her staff in his direction, and he started backward, staring nervously at his leader. "I could ride him out of here. Save my feet the journey."

Durja cawed again and flapped his wings. The two men flanking the leader spared the raven a nervous glance, but the bowmen kept their gaze fixed on Amira.

"We wish you no trouble," said the leader. "Nor trouble on us. Give us some hospitality and we will be on our way."

"Hospitality?"

"A drink. Maybe a bite or two and some gold if you have it."

"You are robbing me?" Amira put every ounce of steel she could muster into her voice, stood straight and tall, and readied her staff. *Rise, rise, rise,* she called to the sun. *Come up now!*

The leader feigned shock. "Rob? Curse the notion, holy one! You are a guest in these lands and so do not know our ways. We offer you the gift of our protection. It is custom that you offer us a gift in return. Some food, drink, and maybe a little gold to trade in the caravans would warm our hearts."

Bright light flickered on the tallest bushes and began to bleed downward. The sun was coming up at last. Durja called out again, this time hopping and flapping his wings.

"I care nothing for you or your customs," said Amira. "Be off before I become angry and turn you all into donkeys. I'll herd you to the nearest settlement and geld the lot of you!"

Durja raised a racket and would not stop. The Tuigan

nearest to him, one of the bowmen, scowled and turned to him.

"Ujren!" he called. "Look here!"

The leader kept his eyes on Amira. "What is it?"

"The raven. He's standing on a bit of cloth buried in the dirt, and there's some silver."

"Silver?"

"Looks like a bit of necklace or something."

The leader gave Amira a hard look. "You buried your belongings, did you? Stay there. We will take our gift ourselves, then be off."

"I don't know what you mean," said Amira. "Ravens are hoarders. Probably just a trinket he found on the steppe."

"You said this raven was your slave."

"He wanders." Amira shrugged. "One of the reasons I turned him into a raven. I can't abide a worthless slave."

Still keeping his gaze fixed on Amira, the leader said, "See it, Geshtai."

The bowman looped one finger round the arrow on his bow to hold it in place while freeing his other hand. He approached the ground where Durja was still keeping up his racket. The raven glared at the Tuigan, his cries becoming enraged. When the man was a few paces away, Durja hopped backward, his wings flapping. Finally, he gave up and flew a short distance before landing again and resuming his racket.

Chuckling, the bowman bent over, his free hand reaching out.

The ground at his feet erupted.

Through the spray of dirt Amira saw the glint of the new sun on a blade, and the bowman screamed as if he were being flayed alive. He went down, his shrieks increasing, and through the cloud of dirt, Gyaidun stood, a bloody knife in one hand and his long black iron club in the other.

Amira had an instant to decide—three swordsmen and a bowman facing Gyaidun in front of her and at least three bowmen and two others at her back. She chose.

Amira spun as she fell, whipping her staff around to face

the four bowmen on the other side of the gully. She took a breath even as they raised their bows and pulled feathers to cheeks.

"Vranis!" she shouted.

Flames roared from the ground at the four Tuigan's feet, a gout of fire that turned grass to ash in a rush of breath, caught in the fur lining the men's trousers and continued its way up into their wool shirts—all in the time it took them to gasp in shock. Each man fell screaming to the ground, and their arrows flew harmlessly away. All but one, which skidded through the grass near Durja, who cried out and took to the air.

Amira returned her attention to the foes in front of her. She saw fear in their eyes, but also determination. They knew death was before them, and their only hope was to face it and fight.

Gyaidun had already made it to the first swordsman. With his comrades standing between him and the large warrior, the remaining Tuigan bowman pivoted and brought his aim to bear on Amira.

"No!" she shouted. She'd had no time to prepare any shields.

Her attention focused, becoming acute so that the scene before her seemed frozen. She saw the fingers of the bowman's right hand open, and the tension held in the bow relaxed. Amira took one step back and leaped, partly hoping she'd make it back into the gully and partly dreading the fall.

The arrow passed so close that she heard the buzz of the wind through its fletching as it passed over her. Her hip hit the lip of the gully, and she went down head first into the dry wash. The fall knocked the breath out of her, and when she opened her mouth to fill her lungs, her mouth filled with dirt. She rolled to her hands and knees, coughing and spitting. She could hear screaming, the clash of weapons, the fire from her spell still burning on the other side of the gully over her, and above it all, Durja raising a holy racket.

Though every breath felt as if she were drawing needles

into her lungs, she forced herself to her feet and risked a look above the rim of the gully. Only three Tuigan were still standing, Gyaidun facing off against the leader and the other swordsman. The third had another arrow ready, and as she watched he pulled it to his cheek and took aim at Gyaidun.

Amira thrust one arm forward, pointed at the bowman, and forced out a single word—*"Dramasthe!"*

It was one of the first spells she'd learned as an apprentice, one of the first spells every apprentice learned for its simplicity and sheer effectiveness. A bright beam only slightly longer than the Tuigan's arrow shot forth from her finger and struck the bowman square in the chest. He flew backward as if struck by a hammer, his arrow streaking into the grass a few paces away and his bow falling to the ground where he'd stood.

Amira shifted her aim to the leader and struggled to draw in another breath.

Tuigan learned to fight from horseback not long after they learned to walk. As cavalry, few in Faerûn could match their ferocity. But fine swordsmen they were not, and these two relied upon superior numbers and brute force, charging Gyaidun together, one stabbing while the other swiped his blade at Gyaidun's midsection.

Rather than try to block both swords, Gyaidun simply stepped backward out of their reach.

Amira tried to speak the incantation, but it came out a harsh rasp that turned into a cough. Some of the dirt she'd been unable to spit out had gone down her throat and she couldn't form the syllables.

Gyaidun swiped at the leader with his club, but the Tuigan merely leaned away. Following through, Gyaidun brought the club back around. Again the Tuigan leaned away, but this time Gyaidun let go of his weapon. The long shaft of heavy iron shot forward and slammed into the leader's face. Even over the crackling of the flames and Durja's racket, Amira heard bone crunch. The bandit leader collapsed like a newborn foal.

The handle of Gyaidun's club had about two paces of leather cord braided through it, the other end of which was bound to the big man's wrist. With a flick of his arm he brought the iron club toward him and slapped it back into his hand.

The remaining Tuigan stood alone against a larger foe and a wizard. Amira half-expected him to turn and run. But the Tuigan apparently decided—and rightly so—that it was kill or be killed, and he attacked with renewed ferocity.

Gyaidun blocked two slashes of the man's blade with his club and swiped at the Tuigan with his knife. He missed and the Tuigan lowered his blade and thrust. Gyaidun brought the full weight of his club down on the sword, and the steel blade snapped a hand's length above the hilt. Thrown off-balance, the Tuigan stumbled, and before he could right himself, Gyaidun's long knife swiped under his chin. Blood fountained outward in a long arc as the man fell back.

The Tuigan hammered the ground with his hands and heels. Amira could hear him trying to draw breath into his lungs, and she winced at the wet gurgle. The man coughed, blood and bile sprayed out of the gash in his throat, and Amira looked away. She'd seen worse. Many times. But never did it do anything but fill her with revulsion. "Good," her old master had told her long ago. "That's good. Don't fight the horror. If you do, one day you won't feel the horror at killing anymore. On that day, put away your battle spells and retire to a life of scholarship. Cormyr needs warriors, not murderers."

The fight done, Amira rummaged through their belongings until she found her waterskin. She untied the knot, sloshed water through her mouth and spat, repeating until she could no longer feel grit in her throat. Then she took a long drink, tied the skin shut, and climbed out of the gully.

The fire on the other side was dying. Dry as the grasses were, the cold night had brought dew, and with her magic no longer fueling them, the flames were having a hard time spreading. Steam was rising off four blackened corpses, and for the first time Amira noticed the sweet smell of roasted flesh. She turned away and walked to Gyaidun, who was cleaning his knife and club on the tunic of the dead bandit leader. The Tuigan's skull was bashed in.

The final bandit to fall had stopped his struggles. He lay on his back in a sickly mud, drenched in his own blood, his empty eyes staring up at the cloudless sky. Several paces away lay the body of the first bowman. Gyaidun's blade had cut him deep on the inside of his thigh from knee to groin. Amira knew from her years on the battlefield that such a wound bled a man to death in moments.

Gyaidun stood and sheathed his knife. He was covered with dirt from lying in wait under his sand-covered cloak. He looked to Amira. "You did well, though the fire wasn't the best idea."

Amira bristled. "And why is that?"

"Fire means smoke. A big fire like that made a lot of smoke. Everyone within thirty miles will know right where we are."

Durja landed on a tussock near Gyaidun, let out a final caw, then fell silent.

"I'm a war wizard," Amira said. "I needed something to take them all down fast. It worked."

Gyaidun grunted and walked over to the bowman whom Amira had taken down. Amira followed him.

The man lay in the grass. He clutched at his chest, his face twisted in pain and tears streaking his face. But he was very much alive, though he seemed to be struggling to breathe.

Gyaidun stood over the man. "You and your friends," he said, "you had horses, yes?"

The man glared up at Gyaidun. "Kill me. Spare me my . . . my shame."

"The horses."

The Tuigan took in a shaking breath, then spat on Gyaidun's boots.

Gyaidun shook his head, then placed one heavy foot on the man's chest and pressed down. The man's eyes went wide and his mouth opened as if to scream, but nothing came out.

"The horses," said Gyaidun.

The Tuigan pounded his head on the ground, struggling to breathe.

Gyaidun stepped off. "I won't ask again."

The man raised one trembling hand and pointed northward. "That . . . way. A mile. No more."

"How many guards?"

"One," the Tuigan said. "Ujren's . . . son. Don't harm . . . him. Just a boy."

Gyaidun scowled. "I'll leave him most of your horses. The rest is up to him. Your thievery made him fatherless today."

The Tuigan said nothing, just lay there struggling to breathe.

So fast that Amira jumped, Gyaidun brought his iron club down on the man's skull. Amira looked away, but she heard the wet crunch. Durja cawed twice, and in the following silence, she could no longer hear the man's harsh breathing.

She looked on Gyaidun in shock. "Why did you do that?"

Gyaidun's brow fell as he looked down on her. "I could have used the knife, but he would have suffered. The club was quicker."

"He might not have died. There was no need!"

"You're in the Wastes now, girl. That—"

"Do *not* call me 'girl!'"

Gyaidun continued undeterred. "That man tried to kill you. If we'd left him to recover and nurse his wounded pride, he might well have come after us. The Commani—even outcasts—do not forgive an affront. We have enough to worry about without setting enemies on our trail."

She held his gaze and considered pressing the point. But it hit her: He was right. She was a long way from home, and her notions of honor and chivalry weren't going to get Jalan back to her. And Gyaidun knew this country, knew it like she knew the Hiloar meadows.

Finally, she dropped her gaze, careful to avoid the corpse at her feet, and said, "You won't . . . you won't harm the boy?"

"Not if he's smart. Let's get our things and be gone before anyone curious decides to have a closer look at your smoke."

CHAPTER ELEVEN

The Endless Wastes

Sitting in the grass, his wrists and elbows bound behind his back with rough strips of elkhide cord, Lendri watched the first edge of the sun peek over the horizon. He sat in the middle of the Vil Adanrath, wolves and their elf brothers seeming to mix in equal measure, on a long rise of land that was not quite steep enough to be called a hill. Nearly a quarter mile of land rose at his back, and twice that fell at his feet so that he seemed to look down upon the sunrise. Mingan lay near his feet, sound asleep.

Tension ran through the camp like mice in the grass—more felt and heard than seen. Every elf or wolf walking about or lounging in the grass shot furtive, suspicious glances at them. Some stared in open malice. Still, once Mingan had realized there would be no immediate violence, he had settled down. It was the first time he'd been among his own kind in many seasons.

The elves, both men and women, had the same pale complexion and hair as Lendri, but they wore even less clothing—barely enough for modesty, and none wore any covering on their feet. They too had skin decorated in many swirls and thorns—the younger members of the pack sporting only a few while the elders seemed more black lines than white skin. This had been a hunt, not a permanent camp, and they were still a ways from the nearest cache, so few of the elves had weapons. A dagger or rough spear here and there, but nothing more. Many of the elves walked the dreamroad next to their sleeping wolf brothers, but a half dozen or so of each patrolled the area, scanning the horizon and sniffing the breeze while the others kept close watch on Lendri and Mingan.

Lendri did not know whether to cling to hope or despair. They had not killed him on sight, which was good, he supposed, but every attempt to speak to them had been met with either cold silence or a command to close his mouth. After his fourth attempt, his brother Leren had threatened to gag him, so Lendri sat and waited. Little brother had grown in the years they'd been apart. His limbs were lean but filled with a hard strength, and he walked with the poise and confidence of a true pack leader. Pride and sadness filled Lendri's heart—pride that little brother had taken his place in the pack and sadness that it had to be so.

The bottom rim of the sun was a finger's width over the horizon when Lendri first noticed the long shadows in the distant grass—several of them headed right for the pack. It wouldn't be long now.

Leren, pacing not far away, saw them as well. He was one of the few in camp with a weapon—a long knife that he held naked in his hand. He watched the shadows a while, then turned and looked down on Lendri. "They are coming," he said.

"Thank you, Brother," said Lendri.

"Don't call me that, *hrayek*," said the warrior, and he spat on the ground beside Lendri.

Mingan raised his head, and a growl, more felt than heard, rumbled deep within the wolf's throat. Leren ignored him.

Hrayek, thought Lendri. Outcast. Oathbreaker. This was not going as well as he'd hoped. It was not altogether unexpected, but still it saddened him. He and Leren had been close once.

With full light bathing the rise, the Vil Adanrath stirred out of dreamwalk and sleep. The news spread quickly. The omah nin was coming. Several of the wolves sent up a song to greet him.

A pack of twenty wolves, led by a massive male with fur the color of new snow, ran among the gathered pack. The hunters greeted their lord and his guard, dancing about him, yipping and barking, the greatest of the pack licking his muzzle and bowing with lowered ears and tail. The huge wolf allowed it for a time, then snarled and barked till the others cleared a path for him. He walked up the slope to Leren, wolves and elves following him. Mingan circled Lendri a few times, then settled on his haunches beside his friend and watched.

Leren knelt, lowering his head and opening his palms. "Well come to the pack, Omah Nin."

The wolf looked at Leren, then glanced at Lendri and Mingan. His fur bristled, then began to ripple as if stirred by a hundred tiny breezes. Fur faded to a misty light, the pale shadow within stretching. When the light cleared, an elf stood in front of Leren. This newcomer was the tallest elf in camp. His snow white hair fell well past his waist, and his entire body was a maze of black tattoos and old wounds. Runes the color of fresh blood lined his arms and chest. Three scars marred his skin from scalp to cheek to chin, leaving empty tracks through his pale eyebrows. His eyes stood out like jewels burning with the light of a winter sky. This was Haerul, Omah Nin of the Vil Adanrath. Chieftain of chieftains. What the Tuigan would have named *khahan*.

Haerul knelt by the wolf next to him, which had a light pack on its back. He reached into the pack, removed a loincloth, and covered his nakedness before looking down on Leren. "Rise, my son," he said.

Leren stood, and together the elves turned to face Lendri.

"Hrayek," Haerul said, no warmth in his eyes. "You know the penalty for returning to the pack. There is no help for you here. You know that."

Lendri looked into the chieftain's eyes. "I know, Father."

For the briefest instant, sorrow clouded Haerul's countenance, then he suppressed it and turned to his younger son with his hand open. Leren slapped the blade into his father's palm.

"Then," said Haerul, "I suggest you speak quickly. I would like to know the reason I must kill flesh of my flesh."

Mingan growled at the sight of the blade, but Lendri shushed him to silence. The wolf quieted, but Lendri could feel his tension. His friend's muscles were taut as oak roots, and his hackles stood tall like summer grass.

Lendri kept his eyes low. To look his father in the eye would be seen as a challenge. If it came to the blade, then perhaps he would challenge his father. Until then . . .

Lendri told his tale, of the rescue of Jalan and the war wizard from the slavers, of others—though he did not say who—coming for the boy afterward.

"What does this have to do with the Vil Adanrath?" asked Leren. "Why lose your life's blood to tell us a tale of this outclanner and her son?"

"The ones who came for the wizard's son," said Lendri, "the ones I fought and who almost killed me. They were *Siksin Neneweth.* A man—or something like a man—led them. A man in an ash-gray cloak who walks with winter before and behind him."

Lendri heard several gasps, and even the wolves went silent and still. Every member of the Vil Adanrath, even the youngest, knew the tale of Gyaidun and Hlessa's son. It was told around winter fires and under summer stars.

Leren stared at Lendri with his mouth hanging open. He shut it, looked at his father, then back to Lendri. "You speak of the one who took Erun—or one like him. You—"

"Be silent," said Haerul.

Lendri risked a glance up at his father. A storm was gathering in his winter-sky eyes.

"But—" said Leren.

"Silence."

Lendri could feel his father's gaze upon him, but he did not dare look up. Long moments passed, the only sound a slight breeze rippling the grasses.

"Leren speaks what everyone here knows," said Lendri. "The raiders I speak of, those who took the woman's son, they are the ones who took Erun. Or ones like them. Your daughter's son. Your grandchild. Gyaidun and I are *hrayeket*, but Erun is not. He is your blood."

"Erun is dead," said Haerul. Lendri could hear the rage and sorrow in his father's voice.

Lendri stood in one swift motion and faced his father, only a half-pace between them, his eyes carefully fixed no higher than his father's chin. The surrounding warriors tensed but did not move forward. Lendri said loud enough for all to hear, "Then there is still vengeance."

Snarling, Haerul backhanded Lendri, knocking him to the ground. "You *dare* speak to me of vengeance?" Haerul shouted. "You? Were it not for you, your sister would still be alive. It was your treachery that lost her to us!"

Mingan growled and bared his fangs.

"*Chu set, Mingan!*" Lendri spat blood and struggled to his feet. "Hlessa gave her heart to Gyaidun, and their love gave them a child. It was my sacred duty to her child—beyond all oaths of clan and family. I held my honor, and I would do it again."

"Curse your honor," said Haerul. "Your honor killed your sister and her son."

"Erun may still live."

Haerul's eyes hardened. "Twelve years, *hrayek*. Twelve years the boy has been gone. Even if he is still alive, what will he be? After all these years? He was never more than—" The chieftain stopped and looked to the surrounding warriors.

"Never more than what?" said Lendri, his voice cold. "A half breed? And you curse *my* honor. He is your grandson, your blood!"

Haerul roared, more than a little of the wolf entering his voice. He punched Lendri to the ground and raised the knife.

"Enough!" said a new voice.

The omah nin froze, and every eye turned to the figure approaching from outside the ring of gathered warriors. At first glance, he seemed an old man, for he walked with a tall staff and his hair was long and wild, as if it had seen no brush but the wind for years. Tattoos in hues of black, green, and blue covered his face and arms, and red runes much like the omah nin's shown above and below each eye. He was dressed in skins and furs, but a great elkhide cloak draped his shoulders so that as the wind caught it he seemed some dark and angry bird of prey descending on the scene. But he was an elf, no doubt. Pointed ears protruded from his hair, no wrinkle creased his skin, and his eyes held the cant of the others.

Seeing him, Haerul stepped back from Lendri, turned to the newcomer, and fell to his knees. "Belkagen Kwarun! I did not know you were among us."

"I have just arrived," said the belkagen. He looked at Lendri, who lay in the grass, arms bound behind his back and blood smeared down his chin. He shook his head and sighed. "No matter how old I get, the foolishness of the young never ceases to give me wonder."

"Holy one, I was about to mete out the *hrayek's* punishment," said Haerul, raising the knife. "You need not trouble yourself."

The belkagen rapped his staff across the chieftain's head, not hard but as if chastising a child. "Fool! I meant *you!* The scars of the omah nin are supposed to mean you've learned to think before you act."

"But he has broken the clan oath."

"To keep his blood oath!" The belkagen raised his staff but seemed to think better of striking and lowered it again. He looked down on Haerul and said, "Do you know the meaning of tragedy?"

Haerul opened his mouth, but the belkagen cut him off.

"Hold your tongue, Omah Nin. I am about to tell you." He walked around Haerul and addressed the gathered warriors. "To punish the guilty is not tragedy. That is justice. Tragedy is when two parties are both right but must choose different, even opposing, paths." He looked down at Haerul and Lendri. "Here we have tragedy. The omah nin and his son are both warriors of honor who bring honor to their clan, but in keeping justice each must betray the other's oath. The omah nin speaks of the oaths and laws of the clan—as well he should, for such is the omah nin's duty. But law is not justice. Law is the guide to justice, but in the face of tragedy, law can be an imperfect guide."

"Are you saying we should forsake our law for one warrior?" said Haerul, and a sharp edge had entered his voice. "Even the firstborn of the omah nin?"

Lendri looked at his father. It was the first time in more than sixteen years that Haerul had called him his firstborn and not *hrayek*.

The belkagen turned his back on the pack and looked at Haerul. "Law is the *path* to justice, not its end, as the path to the water is not the water itself. Once you have arrived at the river, you do not forsake the path. You have fulfilled it."

Haerul glared and said, "Lendri betrayed the covenant of clan."

"To keep his covenant of blood," said the belkagen.

"We all know this," said Haerul. His voice was firm, but much of the heat had gone out of it. "It changes nothing, holy one. To keep his honor, a warrior may have to reach into the fire, but honor or no, still he will burn."

"The omah nin is wise." The belkagen offered a small bow. "But that is not why Lendri has come." He looked down at Lendri and raised an eyebrow. "Is it?"

Lendri struggled to his feet and looked to his father. "I

am not asking the clan to help *me*. I am telling you that *your grandson* may be alive. Hlessa's only child. All we have left of her."

Haerul looked at his son a long time. He still held the naked blade in his hand. He turned to the belkagen. "This is true, holy one?"

The belkagen frowned. "Whether Erun is alive or not . . . I do not know. There is hope, but I will not lie. It is a slim one. A small flame in the rain. But another boy—about the same age as Erun when he was taken—has been captured, and the trail is still fresh."

Haerul turned back to Lendri, stepped forward, and placed the edge of the blade against his son's throat. "So, Hlessa's son may be dead."

Lendri looked into his father's eyes, putting every bit of challenge he could into his gaze. "Yes. If he is dead, I can take you to his killers. But time is running out."

CHAPTER TWELVE

The Endless Wastes

Early morning on the open steppe. The sun still ran low on the horizon, and shadows cast by grass and shrub lay long on the land. A hare, the beginnings of its white winter coat just coming in, nibbled at the leaves of a tiny shrub. The owls had gone back to their nests, and the hawks were not yet awake. Best time for breakfast.

The hare sat up, its ears standing straight up, its eyes wide. For ten beats of its heart it sat that way, unmoving, then leaped away, leaving only a tiny cloud of dust in its wake. The last of the dust was just beginning to settle when the air where the hare had sat parted in a great *whoosh* that sent a ring of dirt billowing outward.

Amira looked around, coughing and waving away dirt.

"Ugh," she said. "I hate the Wastes."

Behind her stood Gyaidun, one hand clasping a rope that bound three ponies. With the other hand he cradled Durja to his chest. The raven's eyes were only slightly less wide and frightened than those of the ponies. Amira smiled. Durja let out a harsh cry and took to the air.

They stood in the midst of a gently rolling sea of grass, now turning shades of yellow and brown with winter's coming. To the north of them, painted half in light and half in shadow by the low morning sun, a great hill rose out of the lowlands. Much of it had the rounded-off look of a bastion of rock and soil that had stood through hundreds of years of wind and rain, but the top of it was smooth and almost flat. Standing up there, Amira imagined, someone could see for miles in every direction. Greenery crowned the hill and spread in jagged lines, following the ravines. From this distance, Amira could not tell if they were trees or simply large brush.

"Is this it?" she asked.

"Close enough," said Gyaidun. He pointed to the hill. "That is *Akhrasut Neth*, the Mother's Bed. Lendri will meet us there."

"Mother's Bed?"

"A sacred site to the Vil Adanrath. The belkagenet say it is the place where the Vil Adanrath first came to this world in the time of their greatest grandfathers."

"Is there water there?"

"A sacred spring, yes. Why?" He hefted the waterskin dangling from his pack, then pointed to the two carried by the lead pony. "We have more than enough."

"We spent all day yesterday running," said Amira. "I could use a bath. And so could you."

Gyaidun nodded, his face neutral, but Amira thought she saw a flicker of mischief in his eyes. "Ah, yes. I didn't want to say anything, but . . ."

Amira scowled. "Lead on."

Pulling the tethered ponies behind him, Gyaidun set off toward the Mother's Bed. Amira followed for a while, then quickened her pace to walk beside Gyaidun. He walked at an easy pace, his eyes scanning the horizon.

"Why do we not ride the ponies?" she said.

"Horses."

"What?"

"They are horses, not ponies."

Amira looked at them. "My family breeds the finest horses in Cormyr," she said. "These look like ponies to me."

"We're not in Cormyr. Tuigan horses are smaller than other horses, but they're hardier, as well. Someone who spent so much time among the Tuigan should know that."

"They spent most of their time trying to kill me, so you'll forgive me if I didn't discuss the finer points of horseflesh with them."

"I forgive you." He said it with a perfectly straight face.

"It's an expression."

"What is?"

"Never mind," she said. "You went to the trouble of taking the—*horses,* scaring that boy near to death. Why aren't we riding them?"

"Would you rather I'd killed him?"

"Of course not. But why take horses and then walk all this way?"

Gyaidun shrugged. "Climb on one if you wish. I'm used to walking."

"I thought everyone in the Wastes were famed horsemen."

"Not the Vil Adanrath. Horses cannot abide their presence."

"Why?" she said. "They're elves like Lendri, are they not?"

Gyaidun, not slowing his pace, looked at her sideways. "You Cormyrean wizards are scholars of a sort, aren't you?"

"It requires years of study, if that's what you mean."

"And you still haven't realized what Lendri is?"

Amira's eyebrows creased. "I've never heard of moon elves this far east. His build and complexion are all wrong for a sun elf. I took him to be some sort of wild elf. An offshoot family, perhaps?"

Gyaidun snorted. "Do the wild elves run with wolves?"

"I *said* an offshoot, perhaps. No? Well, what is he, then, he and these Vil Adanrath? The mention of their name certainly made Walloch's hired blades tuck their tails and run."

"The Vil Adanrath are not native to his world," said Gyaidun. "They came here many thousands of years ago."

"That's true of all elves."

"Can all elves take the form of a wolf?"

Amira gasped. She'd heard of such things, down in the Wealdath in Tethyr, but it had been years since she'd studied that particular tome in her old master's library. She scrambled for the memory, and at last it came to her.

"Lendri and the Vil Adanrath, they are lythari?" she said.

"Lythari?" said Gyaidun, and he shook his head. "I don't know this word. The Vil Adanrath are what they are—elves who can walk as wolves. Or wolves who can walk as elves, depending on their mood, I suppose."

"You are not Vil Adanrath, then?"

Gyaidun did not answer.

"May I ask you something?" Amira asked.

The big man broke off his gazing long enough to glance at her. "Ask all you want. Whether or not I answer depends on your question."

"What is Lendri to you? The belkagen said he was your *rathla*. What is that?"

"Lendri is my friend."

"Where I come from, that would hardly explain his devotion to you," she said.

"We're a long way from where you come from." Gyaidun didn't look at her. He continued along the horizon. "We adhere to the old ways out here."

"Old ways?"

Gyaidun spared her a glance, and Amira could tell he was weighing whether to tell her. Finally he looked off into the distance, his attention obviously elsewhere, and said, "You westerners, you shake hands when you take an oath, do you not?"

"There's more to it than that, and customs vary from realm to realm, but yes."

"Do you know why?"

Amira shrugged. "Custom."

Gyaidun smiled, though his eyes continued to scan the horizon. "See. You have forgotten the old ways. When the Vil Adanrath pledge their lives to one another, there is always the mingling of blood. *Always.*"

Gyaidun took the horses' tether in his left hand and raised his right palm toward her. There, Amira saw a deep scar dividing the big man's palm.

"Blood to blood," he said, "oath for oath, and may all the gods damn us and spirits speed us on our way to the grave should we break the oath. It is . . . beyond sacred. The Tuigan take blood oaths as well. You've heard them speak of *anda*—'blood brothers'—yes? But among the Vil Adanrath, the joining of the blood has true power."

"Magic?" asked Amira.

Gyaidun's brow furrowed. "I would not call it that, but I don't know all the theories of you western spellcasters." He shrugged. "Call it what you like."

"You became one of them, the Vil Adanrath?"

Gyaidun shook his head. "I will never be Vil Adanrath."

"Then . . ." Amira shook her head. "I don't understand. If you aren't Vil Adanrath, yet you and Lendri are blood brothers, what does that make you? The other night, you said you were born a slave."

"I was."

"Then how did you come to . . . 'hunt' with the Vil Adanrath?"

Gyaidun did not answer at first. Amira looked at him. His lips were pressed razor thin, and the muscles of his jaw and neck stood out taught and hard. For a moment, Amira feared she'd offended him. The people of the Wastes had many strange customs and traditions of hospitality that were completely foreign to the people of Cormyr. She knew much of the Tuigan's strange ways, having spent much of her youth fighting them, but these pale elves and this big man who lived among them were a new mystery altogether.

Finally, Gyaidun spoke. "My mother was a slave, the *property*"—he almost spat the word—"of Uchun Koro, a merchant who made his living along the Golden Way, trading in slaves, horses, camels, and whatever else he might turn to profit. I do not know who my father was. Another slave, probably, or perhaps a guest to whom Koro sold a night's pleasure with my mother. I was a child on the caravan trails.

"As I grew, Koro took a liking to me and intended to have me as his catamite. But on the night of my . . . 'coming of age,' my mother sneaked a knife to me. When Uchun Koro came to me, I sliced off his manhood and threw it onto the hot coals of a brazier."

Amira swallowed hard. Cormyr certainly had more than its share of lascivious aristocrats and worse. As a young woman, she'd had to fend off plenty of advances by men old enough to be her grandfather, but to do such a thing to a child . . .

"I was frightened as much as furious," Gyaidun continued. "So much blood. And I was still a child, only ten years old. Rather than finishing off the *newetik,* I ran. I fled, but I grew hungry and trailed the caravan, hoping to steal food. Uchun Koro, the whoreson bastard, survived. His men caught me. I found out that he'd had my mother killed. He was planning a suitable death for me when the caravan was attacked by bandits. They killed old Koro. Staked him in the sun and cut off his eyelids. But they took me captive and headed east.

"Gone from the hands of one master to another, I killed the man guarding me and fled. I grew up among various tribes, clans, and nomads. I was fifteen or so when the bandits I ran with were attacked by the Vil Adanrath. They spared me. Why, I don't know, but they did. I spent many days as their captive. Eventually, Haerul, their omah nin—like a chief or a king—set me free, but I followed them, mile upon mile, day after day." Gyaidun shrugged. "It is a long tale, but I came to live among them. Lendri was Haerul's son. In many hunts, he saved my life, and I saved his. We . . ."

They walked on, the horses plodding behind them. Amira

was beginning to fear that Gyaidun had decided against sharing any more with her when he finally spoke up again.

"They named me *athkaraye*—'elf-friend' in your tongue, maybe—and I gained many blessings, both of spirit and body, with the honor, but I will never truly be Vil Adanrath. They are an ancient folk, not of this world. But . . . Lendri and I, we swore our lives to one another. Life for life. Death to death. Blood brothers. *Rathla*."

"*Blood* brothers? Because you cut hands? Mingle your blood?"

"Brothers of the same womb are called milk brothers," said Gyaidun, "because they share the same mother's milk. It is a sacred bond, but only so far. The gods choose your family. *Rathla* choose each other. The pact is sworn before the gods as we mingle our blood. He who breaks the covenant of milk is cast out from the clan." Gyaidun took his free hand and traced the scars along his cheeks. "The scars of an exile, barred from the pack. But he who breaks the covenant of blood is lower than a dog. His own clan and family will hunt him down and scatter his body to the four winds."

"You broke the . . . the covenant of milk? That's why you and Lendri were exiled?"

"Do all ladies of your land ask so many questions?"

"No."

Amira looked at him. His eyes still scanned their surroundings. There had been no malice in his voice. The ways of these easterners were strange to her, and after so long being among them—years fighting in the war and days that turned into tendays searching for her son in these lands—she had learned much, but she'd never been comfortable with their ways. Until now. Though the big man's face was still a mask of serene seriousness, she saw it for just that: a mask. Something in his tone said that he was at ease with her. One desperate parent with another, willing to kill and die for a child. One warrior to another. For the first time since she'd been taken in by this big man and his *rathla* and thrust in the midst of their strange ways, she felt oddly . . . at ease.

"I've never been quite . . . at home among my people," said

Amira. "Questioning my parents, my family, my 'betters' among the aristocracy, my arcane masters. I . . ." She stopped, searching for the proper words. None came.

"Kweshta," said Gyaidun.

"What?"

"Kweshta. It is a word of the Vil Adanrath. There is no good word in the Common tongue. It means a special one. One who does not quite . . . 'fit in.' But in a good way. A special one. Dear. Unique. You stand out among your people, part of them still, but set apart." Gyaidun shrugged, and Amira thought she saw the hint of a blush in his cheeks. *"Kweshta."*

Amira felt her own cheeks growing hot. "You didn't answer my question."

"Question?"

"Why were you and Lendri . . . ?"

"Exiled?"

"Yes."

"Enough talk for now," said Gyaidun, and his countenance had gone hard and implacable. His eyes continued to search their surroundings.

"I did not mean to pry," said Amira. "I—"

"Enough," said Gyaidun. "All you do is pry. No more. Time to walk." He quickened his pace, dragging the plodding horses behind him and putting distance between him and Amira.

Amira could have easily kept up with him. The stubborn side of her nature—the dominant side of her nature—would have and almost did. But this once she let it go.

They walked through most of the morning. Though the Mother's Bed loomed large on the horizon, dozens of small gullies, dry washes, and little valleys broke the land between them and the hill. It was near midday before they came to the first rise in land that marked the foot of *Akhrasut Neth.*

Gyaidun stopped to rest the horses, and Amira turned and looked off southward. By Gyaidun's estimate they had traveled more than a hundred miles with Amira's spell. If Jalan and his captors were indeed on winter wolves—and Amira had little doubt, given the tracking skills she'd seen Gyaidun display the past two days—their quarry could easily cross that distance in two nights.

Amira turned to Gyaidun and said, "If we linger here waiting for Lendri and the belkagen, Jalan's captors will be miles ahead of us."

Gyaidun nodded. "I've considered that. If they're headed for Winterkeep as you say, their path is some miles north of us. We came almost due east. If they continue in the direction their tracks were headed, they're headed northeast—straight to *Iket Sotha* if"—slight hesitation—"the belkagen was right. If you can work your magic again . . . you can, can't you?"

"With rest and study, yes."

"We can get ahead of them. If Lendri can gather the Vil Adanrath, we'll spread out. The pack will find them."

"*If* Lendri or the belkagen can find them," said Amira. "You said yourself that you two are exiles."

"Haerul will come."

"Haerul?"

"My wife's father."

"The one who cast you and Lendri out?" Amira smirked, but Gyaidun was looking off southward and didn't see it.

"Yes," he said.

Amira snorted. "What makes you so sure?"

"If there is even a whisper of hope of finding his grandson, he'll tear a hole to the Nine Hells—and gods have mercy on any who stand in his way."

"We're after Jalan, Gyaidun. *Jalan.* If we learn something of your son, I swear on my family I'll help you if you help me save Jalan. But right now we *know* Jalan is alive. That is certain. Your son is just a . . . a hope."

Gyaidun gave her a dark look, then turned his back and began leading the horses up the hill.

CHAPTER THIRTEEN

The Endless Wastes

Dark and cold. Cold and dark. They had filled Jalan since waking. Through the dried flesh and stale drink that served as his evening breakfast, through the binding of his wrists, the forced march, the wind in his face, the stench of wolf . . . through it all had been dark and cold. Even the distant stars seemed only points of ice in darkness.

But that cold darkness cracked. A fire in the valley below, a distant promise of warmth, broke through the night. From it Jalan could hear the last of the screams. After running half the night, Jalan's captors had come across a band of nomads. They'd fallen on them like an autumn gale, tooth and claw ripping into their sentries, sword and spear stabbing and cutting even as the nomads had struggled out of their blankets and yurts.

Jalan sat on the rise above the carnage. His

guard had dismounted from the huge white wolf and pulled him down after. Better that the wolf not be encumbered as it slaughtered. Tired and terrified as he was, Jalan had not been able to look away. He guessed it was well past midnight but a while still till dawn, the moon long since set, and he could see little but the occasional shadow passing in front of the distant fire. But he could hear them. Hear the nomads screaming—first in warning, then in defiance, then in despair. They did not cry for mercy. Just as well, Jalan thought. The wolves and their riders had none.

Jalan shivered. Even with their cloaked leader down there amid the carnage, still his unearthly cold lingered. Heat, warmth, light . . . Jalan remembered them only as abstracts. Concepts. He knew they existed but could not remember their feeling. Despite the screams and the blood he knew soaked the grass, the deepest part of him longed for the fire glowing in the valley below.

A scream—a woman's, Jalan thought—rose high, then was cut off, almost instantly, and just behind the sighing of the wind over the grass Jalan thought he half-heard and half-felt the sound of jaws shredding and bone crunching. Then the wolves below set to howling, filling the night with their song.

Jalan's guard grabbed his bound wrists, lifted him to his feet, and dragged him down the slope. Jalan's feet moved of their own accord. His body longed for the warmth of the fire, but his mind fled screaming at being pulled nearer to the one in the ash-gray cloak that he knew walked the shadows below.

They entered the camp, passing groups of wolves crouched over the remains of their prey. The guard pulled Jalan to the fire, took the bonds from his wrists, and dropped him to the ground.

The fire burned low, but the light and warmth pulsing from it like lifeblood pulled Jalan in. One of the huge wolves stood just inside the circle of light cast by the fire. It crouched over what had once been a Tuigan nomad but was now no more than an unmoving mass of cooling blood and gore that steamed in the chill night air. The wolf lifted its snout from its feast and looked at Jalan, its muzzle a contrast of white fur and wet darkness that Jalan knew was blood. Light, hungry and hot, reflected in its eyes, then it lowered its muzzle to its meal.

Jalan looked down, forcing his eyes away from the gruesome sight, and fell to his knees beside the fire. He could still hear the chomping and tearing of the wolf's feast, and he covered his ears to try to block the sound.

Beneath his knees, Jalan could feel the ground trembling with the approach of heavy footsteps. His eyes were clenched shut, but he knew whose footsteps they were.

A hand winter-cold grabbed his wrist and pulled it away from his ear. "This disturbs you?" said a voice. The dark one in the ash-gray cloak, Jalan knew. "Our mounts must eat. The miles fill them with great hunger. Be grateful we found these poor wretches. Our wolves were beginning to look to you with ravenous eyes. Now, they will not. At least for a few days. And you, you have fire. Warmth. For now."

The hand released him, and Jalan felt the thing walk away a few steps. He dared to open his eyes. The leader stood at the edge of the firelight next to one of his pale-skinned minions, speaking to him in a language Jalan could not understand.

The guard disappeared behind one of the nomad tents then returned a moment later, carrying a leather satchel. He reached into it, then handed Jalan a few strips of dried meat.

Jalan's stomach gave a wet tumble. With the carnage and horror surrounding him, he knew his stomach would not hold any food.

"Not hungry?" said the leader. "Good. *Good.* Power there is in fasting, in denying the flesh its cravings, the blood its warmth. To your purest essence it brings you. Good."

The thing in the cloak came back and crouched beside Jalan. He leaned in close. Jalan flinched but could back away no farther without going into the fire. He looked into the deep folds of the hood but could see only a sharp chin, likely very pale but now a bright orange as it caught the light from the flames. The leader leaned in close, so close that Jalan could feel the cold bleeding off his skin like the bite off ice. The leader opened his mouth wide and breathed in deeply.

"Yesss," he said. "Oh, yes. Fear. I can taste it. Smell it. It comes off you like mist off the water. Terror burns your blood and smokes out of your very pores. Soon, very soon, you will know no fear, no terror, no nothing. No fire in your blood."

Quick as an adder, the leader's pale hand shot out and grasped Jalan's wrist.

Jalan screamed and struck at the hand, but it was like striking stone, cold and immovable. The leader pulled Jalan's arm to him, in no hurry, moving with slow and unstoppable strength, and in the midst of his struggles, Jalan saw firelight reflect off a blade. Before he could cry out, the dagger whisked across the back of Jalan's hand, then disappeared into the folds of the ash-gray cloak.

Blood, almost black in the meager glow cast by the fire, welled from a perfectly straight gash across the back of Jalan's hand. The ice-grip pulled Jalan's hand toward the blackness waiting inside the dark one's hood. Jalan screamed and tried to drag himself away, no longer caring if he fled into fire, but it was futile. He closed his eyes and felt the thing's tongue, cold and slick as a fish, slide across the wound, then he was free.

He fell to the ground beside the fire and heard the man say, "Yes, you *are* the one. *Yesss.*"

When Jalan dared to look up later—he didn't know how long it had been, but the fire beside him had burned down to coals—the thing in the ash-gray cloak was gone. The wolves were no more than lurking shadows in the near darkness, and the pale-skinned men were nowhere in sight.

Jalan hugged his throbbing hand to his chest and fell into the only peace he knew—sleep.

Just shy of the hilltop Lendri crouched naked in the grass and waited. Mingan was off with the rest of the pack not too far away. Lendri had been running as a wolf most of the night, but he wanted this opportunity to talk to the belkagen and the language of wolves had no words for this conversation.

After the confrontation that morning, Lendri's father had not only ordered all but a few of the hunters of his pack north, he'd sent scouts out to the other packs. In his wildest expectations, Lendri had hoped his father would send his own pack to help them. Haerul had not only done that, he'd called for every pack of Vil Adanrath within a hundred leagues to gather at the Mother's Bed as well. Lendri had seen his father angry many times, had even seem him truly furious once. But this . . . the omah nin seemed almost fey.

Lendri heard the rustle in the grass of another wolf coming up behind him. He didn't turn, but a few moments later the belkagen came forward and crouched beside him. He followed Lendri's gaze. The Vil Adanrath were spread out in the lands below them, rushing northward like a fire in the grass. They'd run all day and into the night, stopping only for enough rest to keep them from dying. Lendri had promised to meet Gyaidun at the Mother's Bed in three days.

"Why?" Lendri asked.

"I knew you'd need help," said the belkagen. "Your father is one of the greatest omah nin I have ever known, but his honor is surpassed only by his pride. I knew you'd need the weight of my testimony."

"You knew that two days ago when you all but begged Gyaidun and me to forsake this hunt."

"I said from the beginning that I would help rescue the wizard's son. With guile and cunning, we may get away with him. But you and your *rathla,* you do not seek to save the boy. You seek vengeance."

"You've given us no reason to think we can't have both."

"This foe is beyond any of you," said the belkagen, and his voice sounded old and tired. "Together, you and I may have succeeded in rousing all our people to lead them to their deaths. You know that, don't you? If we survive, will you be able to live with that burden?"

"Death is part of life, the end of even the most cunning hunter. Our people know this."

"To accept death is not to seek it."

Lendri turned to face the belkagen and gave him a hard look. "Better to die fighting for one of our own than spend the rest of our lives with our tails between our legs."

The belkagen snorted and looked away. "You sound like your *rathla*."

"I take that as an honor."

Silence built between them before the belkagen spoke again. "Gyaidun is one of the greatest men I have ever known. But he is still a man. He is not Vil Adanrath. Like all his people, his flame burns hot and bright, but it is not long for this world. His courage lacks the wisdom of our years."

"Better to die a flame than live as ashes."

The belkagen flinched, and for the briefest moment Lendri saw genuine fear in his eyes. No, not fear. This was colder. Dread.

"What is it, holy one? You hide something in your heart, something that eats at you."

The belkagen looked away, his eyes gazing northward, but Lendri could see that he was looking elsewhere. A long howl drifted out of the north—Mingan inquiring why his brother had stopped. The pack was moving on. Still, Lendri waited.

"Hro'nyewachu," said the belkagen, his voice scarcely more than a harsh whisper.

"The Heart of the Piercing?" said Lendri.

The belkagen nodded. "To become belkagen, one must brave the Heart. It is the source of my power. But not without a price. For all the blessings *Hro'nyewachu* gave me, some days I would give them all back to have not received the burden she gave me. So many years I have seen it before me, like the smoke of wildfire on the horizon. But with the coming of this war wizard, now I see the glow of flames, red as blood, and I smell the smoke. And now, you and your *rathla* have me rushing toward it."

"What is it? This burden? This thing you fear?"

The belkagen looked at him, and in the pale silver of starlight Lendri saw unshed tears welling in the old elf's eyes. "The one burden no warrior should ever bear."

Lendri scowled. He had no idea what the old belkagen was talking about. He did not doubt the belkagen's sincerity—or the depth of his fear—but he had no idea what the holy one feared. And he knew the belkagen would not tell him. The visions of *Hro'nyewachu* were sacred, its mysteries meant for the belkagenet alone. Warriors did not walk that road.

"Are you saying there is no hope?" asked Lendri. "Truly?"

The belkagen turned away and pointed northward. "Mingan returns looking for us. The pack has left us behind. We must hurry."

Lendri grabbed the belkagen's shoulder. "Answer me, holy one. Is there no hope? Do you know this?"

The belkagen gave him a sad smile, but behind it, lurking in the depths of the old elf's eyes, Lendri thought he saw a bit of the young mischievous warrior Kwarun. "Better to die a flame than live as ashes. Your words. You are wise beyond your years, Lendri, and you have reminded me of the path of wisdom. Thank you."

"Then there is hope still?"

"Hope is for those who seize it. Now, run with me."

CHAPTER FOURTEEN

Akhrasut Neth

Amira and Gyaidun made camp on the western base
of the Mother's Bed in a small copse of trees through
which a tiny stream flowed. Just up the rise, around
a bend of the hill formed by a large arm of bare rock,
the stream widened into a small pool. Yesterday,
after setting up camp, Amira and Gyaidun had
taken turns bathing. The water was cold—after
the first teeth-clenching step into the pool, Amira
had been surprised it didn't have a thin layer of ice
on top—but more important, it was clean. She had
scrubbed herself, washed her clothes, then spent
most of the previous afternoon and evening wrapped
in nothing but a thick elkhide while her clothes
dried over the fire. Parts of them still felt damp, but
she preferred that to the unwashed smell.

Gyaidun and Durja had left at first light, scouting
the area. Amira had spent most of the day near the

fire, alternately poring over her spellbook and watching the sky while she listened to the breeze rattle the branches. The wind had been out of the north all day, pushing high, thin clouds ever southward, and even Amira could smell the snow coming. A line of clouds smudging the northern horizon confirmed her fears.

Morning was turning to midday, the cool turning cold, when Gyaidun trudged back into camp. Durja was not with him, for once.

"Are you hungry?" he asked.

"Very," Amira said. "But supplies are low. We should eat no more than once a day until we can get more."

"Not a problem."

Gyaidun stood next to their packs, which lay a few paces from the fire. Methodically, piece by piece, he began to undress, first his belt and harnesses that held his weapon and pouches, then his shirt. Amira had to suppress a gasp at the sight of his naked skin. His torso was warm brown skin over taut, lean muscles, but his chest and stomach were crossed with long scars, one mottled patch that was obviously an old burn, and several spots of puckered skin that she recognized as old puncture wounds. Arrows most likely. Over all was a twisting, turning maze of black, blue, and yellow-gold inks. Her eyes widened when he began to undo the drawstrings of his breeches.

"What are you doing?" she asked, averting her eyes.

"You said you were hungry," he said. "I'm getting dinner."

"You always cook naked?"

"You're cooking." She did not look up, but she could hear the smile on his face. "I'm getting dinner."

"Naked?"

She heard him chuckle and walk toward the horses. She took a deep breath, gathered her courage, and risked a quick glance up. Gyaidun wasn't naked after all, but close enough. He'd stripped down to a loincloth—had even removed his boots—and carried his knife in one hand. He went to the tree where the horses were tethered and huddled together for warmth. He untied one and led it off through the trees.

Amira scowled. If he was going off to hunt, why take one of the horses? He'd been out scouting all morning. Surely he could have taken down a deer or even a rabbit while walking the miles around the hill. And hadn't he said he eschewed horses anyway? And who in their right mind went hunting naked in this cold armed with nothing but a knife?

"I hate the Wastes," she muttered, and went back to her book.

A scream—a high-pitched shriek of agony that set Amira's teeth on edge—broke through the trees from the direction where Gyaidun had gone. The two remaining horses pulled at their tethers, snorting and stamping, their eyes wide and white.

Amira slammed her spellbook shut, grabbed her staff, and ran in the direction she'd watched Gyaidun lead the horse. The ground was rough, uneven, and littered with the detritus of a thousand autumns, and Amira stumbled several times.

Not far away from the camp, in a small clearing ringed by bushes still clinging to the last of their leaves, she found Gyaidun standing over the dead horse. Blood covered everything—the horse, the grass, even Gyaidun. He was more wet red than skin from the waist up, and his right arm—the one holding the knife—was so soaked that blood dripped from his elbow. Amira's shock and fear turned to dismay. She looked at the scene more closely and found the source of the blood—a deep gash across the horse's throat.

"What are you *doing?*" said Amira.

Gyaidun turned and looked at her. "You said you were hungry."

"We need those horses!"

Gyaidun smirked. "Why? We have our legs and your magic to get us where we need to go. Horses are food. Why d'you think I brought them?"

"I thought we were going to ride them."

"When Lendri arrives, you won't be able to keep them. Horses can't stand the Vil Adanrath. They'll break their hobbles and run." He turned and knelt beside the dead horse between its front and back legs. "Why don't you build up the fire? Nothing too big. A good, slow burn. You know how to make a spit?"

Gyaidun thrust the knife into the gut of the horse and began to saw upward. Blood and entrails spilled out of the widening gap. Amira turned away. She could take the sight of the blood and gore. She'd seen far worse in her time. But the sound of the blade cutting through muscle and hide, the entrails falling to a growing pile in the grass . . . too much.

She walked back to camp, taking more care on the path this time and watching the uneven ground. When she entered the camp and looked up, the belkagen was crouching next to the fire and putting the finishing touches on a rack made from branches. Amira could not have been more shocked if King Azoun himself had been sitting there, asking to have his goblet refilled. She stood dumbfounded, her mouth hanging open.

"What . . . what are *you* doing here?" she asked.

The belkagen looked up from his work and smiled. "I suspect that Gyaidun is going to ask the same thing. Let us wait till he returns so that I don't have to tell the same tale twice." The belkagen closed his eyes, leaned his head back, and inhaled deeply through his nose. "He's bringing horseflesh, yes?"

"Yes," she said. "How . . . how did you get here?"

The belkagen tested the stability of the spit. It wasn't like the spits she'd been taught to make. It was more like a miniature rack positioned over the fire. Satisfied with his handiwork, the belkagen sat on the ground, settled into his fur-lined cloak, and said, "What one wizard can do, another can do."

"Magic?"

The belkagen frowned and picked up a stick to stoke the fire. "Sit down, Amira. Please."

She did, across the fire from him, her back to the Mother's Bed.

"You are far from home, Amira. The ways of these lands are not your ways. The powers that walk the steppes and live in the earth . . . they are no less than the powers of your own western lands. But the people of . . . of 'the Wastes,' as you call them, we are . . . more reserved in some ways. There are those among us, like me, who know many of the arcane and divine arts, but it is considered somewhat . . . impolite to speak of them openly."

"I'm sorry, Belkagen. I meant no offense."

He gave her a reassuring smile. "Nor did I take any. One master to another, among ourselves, it is good to speak of such things, to share our wisdom. But very soon we are to be joined by a great many folk who have powers and abilities far older than anything known by the people of Cormyr, and they can be very . . . 'prickly' about their customs of politeness. I urge you, Lady, please, guard your tongue among the Vil Adanrath. You will find no truer or more honorable people in all this world. They are the fiercest friends one can have, but they make terrible enemies and are easily offended. They are a people of pride and honor, and their chief, Haerul, has pride and honor like none I've ever seen. Scratch it at your peril."

Amira thought on this a while. She'd grown up among the aristocracy, and no one played the game of politics and court like the war wizards, but the belkagen's words gave her pause.

"I will treat this Haerul as I would the nobles of my own land," she said.

"You were sent to the High Horn for the way you treated your nobles, were you not?"

Amira blushed. "Not exactly, no."

"I meant no offense, Lady Amira," he said. "But please. Take my words to heart. You saw a bit of Lendri's ire when his hackles were up—and Lendri has traveled among humans for many years. It has softened him toward your kind. Not so with the Vil Adanrath. With Haerul, tread as a fawn among wolves."

"I'm no fawn, Belkagen. I have bite, too."

"I do not attack your pride. You need not bow and scrape and beg. Just . . . use caution. Please."

Amira looked back over her shoulder, searching for a change in subject. "Are you sure that your being here is wise, Belkagen?"

The belkagen smiled. "Gyaidun has a cave bear's temper, but I can take care of myself."

They sat in silence a while, the belkagen tending the fire.

"May I ask you something?" Amira said.

The belkagen smiled. "Please."

"What . . . what are you, exactly?"

"I do not understand your question."

"You speak of the Vil Adanrath as if you are one of them, but Gyaidun told me that he and Lendri are exiles. Outcasts. And I could tell that there was a great deal of tension in Lendri seeking their aid."

" 'A great deal of tension.' " The belkagen put his hands on his knees, leaned back and laughed—quietly but with much enthusiasm. Finally, he settled down and looked at Amira. "Lendri took his life in his hands. Exiles they are. *Hrayeket,* the Vil Adanrath say. Cut off from the pack. The Vil Adanrath would have been within their rights to cut Lendri's throat and scatter his body to the eight winds. He risked a great deal in returning to them. Your presence has lit quite a fire in the grasslands."

Amira did her best to keep her voice mild. "I thank you for all your help, Belkagen. You and Lendri and Gyaidun. I am grateful. But . . . I cannot help but notice the true object of this hunt. Gyaidun and Lendri will help Jalan if they can, I don't doubt. But they're after blood."

"Yes. This bothers you?"

"I want my son back," she said, and the bitterness crept into her tone. "The rest . . . I'll help if I can. But in the end, Jalan is all I care about."

"So you use us and we use you," said the belkagen. She sensed no recrimination in his voice, nor did she see it in his face when she looked up. "Is this not so?"

Amira shrugged.

"You must not despise Gyaidun too much, Amira," said the

belkagen. "He has suffered much. Lost much. He too seeks his lost child. You and he are more alike than you dare admit. Do not resent him for doing the same thing you are doing."

Amira swallowed. "You haven't answered my question."

"Question?"

"You seem as if you are Vil Adanrath, who have exiled Gyaidun and Lendri. Yet you were camping with them at the Lake of Mists. Despite your quarrel, you seem a friend to them."

The belkagen smiled, and Amira saw more than a little sadness in his eyes. "I was born among the *Hinakaweh* clan of the Vil Adanrath and spent much of my youth as a warrior," he said, "but when I became belkagen, I became part of all clans and none. Having no clan, I am not bound by the laws of exile."

"How does one become . . . belkagen?"

The shadow of a high cloud passed over their camp, and a different darkness seemed to fill the belkagen's face. "That," he said, his voice soft, "we will speak of later, for it is part of the news I bear you."

"News?"

"Not now, Lady. First I must deal with your big man."

"My bi—?"

"You!" came a booming voice from behind her.

Gyaidun. Amira turned. The big warrior stepped through the trees, long strips of bloody flesh hanging from his shoulders and arms. In the cold air, the blood and the strips of flesh on his arms and shoulders steamed. Covered in blood almost black, his eyes shone white and hot with anger, his nostrils flared, and the long knife in his hand trembled with the tension in his fist. He seemed the very visage of some savage god of vengeance descending upon them.

"Why are *you* here?" said Gyaidun.

The belkagen remained sitting by the fire. He seemed placid, but Amira could see the anger in his eyes and stiff posture. "I am here to help. Whether you like it or not, you will need my aid before this fight is done."

"Your aid is about twelve years too late, Kwarun."

They stared at each other across the fire, Amira feeling as though she ought to go for a walk but not daring to move.

"Sit, *Yastehanye*," said the belkagen. "Please. Set your burden down and let us talk. When we are done, if you wish me gone, I shall trouble you no more. But you will hear me out. You owe me that."

Gyaidun stood there, every muscle tense, unmoving. At last he gave one swift, hard nod, then stepped forward to place the long strips of horseflesh on the wooden rack the belkagen had built over the fire. A droplet or two of blood fell into the fire and sizzled. He sat.

"You don't wish to wash first?" asked the belkagen.

"I'll wash when this is done," said Gyaidun. "You can be leaving while I'm washing."

"Very well." The belkagen sighed. "First, my news. Lendri found the Vil Adanrath and roused them. Haerul has called the clans and speeds this way. They should be here no later than dusk unless they run into trouble. And I pity whatever trouble places itself in front of Haerul. His exiled son has roused in him a cold fire."

"Lendri," said Gyaidun, "he is . . . well?"

"His father did not greet him with open arms, and he and his brother still stare spears at one another, but he is alive. I would have brought him with me, but there are things that we three need to discuss before they arrive."

A rustle of black feathers descended into the camp, and Durja settled near Gyaidun. It was the first time Amira could remember the bird not raising a raucous noise upon arriving. Perhaps even the raven sensed the tension around the fire. He looked at the three people gathered round the fire, then hopped on Gyaidun's knee and began to peck at the little bits of flesh and gore that still stuck to the big man's skin.

The belkagen had gone silent. Amira looked to him. The elf seemed troubled, his brow creased in concentration and his mouth fallen into a pensive frown.

"Belkagen?" she asked. "What is it?"

He looked up to Gyaidun, who still sat unmoving, and said, "I told the lady a bit of the Vil Adanrath while we waited for you. She asked how one becomes belkagen, and now my answer enters our present tale. These lands in which we sit are filled with an ancient power. It was at this very high place thousands of years ago that the Vil Adanrath first came into this world. *Akhrasut Neth* is very old, a place of great and fell power. She is very ancient. She was old before the Empire of Raumathar was born. Even the Raumathari, great loremasters that they were, avoided *Akhrasut Neth* if they could. The Tuigan shun it altogether. But"—he looked to Amira—"you remember my tale of Arantar?"

"Yes."

"Alone among the loremasters of his day, Arantar would come to *Akhrasut Neth* and seek her wisdom. Some said he had been born here. Whether that is true or not, I do not know. But I do know he came here often, and I believe *Akhrasut Neth* was the source of much of his power and wisdom."

"*Akhrasut Neth?*" asked Amira. "The Mother's Bed? This hill?"

"Yes."

"Gyaidun told me it is a sacred site to the Vil Adanrath. It is something . . . more, then?"

Gyaidun snorted, but the belkagen ignored him and went on. "Much more. It is sacred to the Vil Adanrath for many reasons. Have you been to the top yet?"

"No."

"At the highest point of *Akhrasut Neth*, the bones of the earth break through the soil, a great outcropping of rock jutting from the ground like a weathered fang. At the base, a crevice splits the rock, forming an entrance to a cave that descends into the heart of *Akhrasut Neth*. The heart is a place of great power. *Hro'nyewachu*. What the clerics of the west might call an oracle."

"This . . . oracle," said Amira, "it answers questions? Tells the future? I don't understand."

"*Hro'nyewachu* grants . . . enlightenment. At a price. It

is the place where initiates of my people go to gain their power. Those who survive are the omah, the chosen leaders of our people. But a precious few have a different calling. The belkagen."

" 'Those who survive.' You mean some do not?"

"Some emerge quite mad. Some few never emerge at all. Their fate is unknown, even to me."

"But you," said Amira, "you have been inside the . . . the Oracle?"

The belkagen sighed and closed his eyes. "I have. Once, upon my becoming belkagen. And one time more." He opened his eyes and fixed his gaze on Gyaidun. "Twelve years ago."

Gyaidun blinked once. Hard. Amira saw a tremor run through him.

"When I learned what had befallen the son of Hlessa and Gyaidun . . ." The belkagen lowered his head and closed his eyes. He took a deep breath but did not continue.

Amira waited, not daring to speak. Gyaidun had not spoken of his son much at all, and he had barely even mentioned the boy's mother. That night, after the first mention of Erun, Amira had asked. The belkagen had answered her with stony silence, Gyaidun with a cold glare, and Lendri had simply looked away.

"We were desperate," the belkagen continued. Again his voice sounded old and tired, truly the voice of an old man despite his youthful visage. "I sought the wisdom of *Hro'nyewachu*."

"What did you find?" asked Amira.

"Answers," said the belkagen. He almost gasped the word, then gathered his composure and went on. "Though not the answers I sought. What I told you two nights ago I learned through years of study and searching."

"So all of this tale is for nothing," said Gyaidun, his voice hard and unforgiving. "A history lesson. Your lore will not help us now."

The belkagen sat there, eyes closed and trembling. Amira stared at him, at first thinking he was trembling with fear, but then she saw the iron set of his jaw and his clenched fists. He was *furious*.

If Gyaidun noticed this, he ignored it. "If your tale is done, it is time for you to le—"

"Fool!" the belkagen threw off his cloak and leaped halfway to his feet toward Gyaidun. A growl that was more savage beast than elf rumbled deep in his chest, and his eyes shone with a feral light all their own. With a squawk, Durja took to the air. Gyaidun's eyes widened, but he did not back down.

The belkagen yelled at Gyaidun in his own tongue. Amira couldn't understand it—though she did catch the word *yastehanye* at least twice—but she heard the anger in the elf's voice. Gyaidun's nostrils flared and he breathed like a bellows, but he could not hold the belkagen's gaze. Though she had no idea what the old elf was saying, she felt very much as if she were watching an old patriarch giving a misbehaving son a severe reprimand.

"Te, Gyaidun? *Te?"* said the belkagen after a long tirade in his own speech. *"Kaweh rut, kyed!"*

Gyaidun sat there glowering, his jaw working as if he were chewing on old bark. Finally, without looking up, he said, "I apologize for my disrespect . . . Belkagen. I beseech your counsel."

The belkagen glared at him a moment more, then gave a stiff nod and settled back down into his cloak. Both men sat gazing at one another but did not speak. Durja settled back into a tree near the horses, gave an inquiring caw, then went silent.

Amira cleared her throat. "Listen—"

"Please, Lady," said the belkagen, a bit of anger still lingering in his voice. "Now we come to the part of this tale that concerns you, why I scratched up all these painful memories." He sighed, then said, "What I saw in *Hro'nyewachu* I will not tell. Its part in our hunt is my own burden to bear. But I think *Hro'nyewachu* might be of help to you, Lady Amira."

"Help me? How?"

"Hro'nyewachu is sacred to the Vil Adanrath, but she does

not belong to us. She was here long before us and, I suspect, will still be here long after we are gone. She is a place of . . . need, both in meeting needs and filling her own."

"But you said most who go in never return," said Amira. "I can't help my son if I'm dead or mad."

"I said 'a few,' not 'most.' The belkagenet are few. Since my own master passed, I have walked alone west of the Glittering Spires." He fell silent a moment, obviously wrestling his thoughts, then continued, "Nothing is certain, Lady. Nothing under this sun. But I believe *Hro'nyewachu* can help you."

"How? I don't need answers. I need to save my son."

"I believe—no, I *know* it after Lendri told us what happened. The Fist of Winter has your son. Why? I do not know. They took Gyaidun's son, and the boy was never found. Why? I do not know. I want to save your son, Lady"—he looked to Gyaidun—"and Erun, if we can, but there is too much we do not know. We are running in blind. I fear we are only running to our deaths—and Jalan's."

"And what?" Amira said "You think this oracle can help us? I am not Vil Adanrath. I'm human and not even from here and . . . and I don't even like these cursed lands! What makes you think your oracle will help me? She might just as well kill me or drive me mad. I'll be no good to my son then, and forgive me, but I don't exactly trust Sir Drenched-in-Blood here or your Vil Adanrath to keep Jalan's best interests in sight."

The belkagen smiled and something like pride lit in his eyes. He looked to Gyaidun. "She has a hunter's heart, does she not, *Yastehanye?*"

Gyaidun scowled and said nothing.

"You, Lady," the belkagen continued, "know the arcane powers that spark the world. *Hro'nyewachu* . . . the source of her power I do not know. Divine? Arcane? A power from another world? I do not know. Perhaps she is all these things and more, perhaps none. But I do believe this: *Hro'nyewachu* has a mother's heart. You have a mother's need. Your hearts will beat the same song, I think. I could brave *Hro'nyewachu* again, and if you refuse, I will go. But Jalan is *your* son, Lady, yours the sacred bond. The bond between parent and child is a strength that might avail you much. I will do all I can to help your son, but I am only an old meddler. You are his *mother*."

"Not his real mother," Amira said, but even she heard the hollowness in her words.

"Would you die for him?" A bit of the anger was creeping back into the belkagen's voice, and he shook his staff as he spoke. "Kill for him? Would you shed your last drop of life's blood to keep him safe? Breathe your last breath?"

"Yes!" Amira looked away from them to wipe away the tears.

"Then you *are* his mother, Lady Amira," said the belkagen. "In all ways that matter."

Amira considered his words. She stared into the fire, thinking. Descend into a cave to seek some . . . eastern goddess or spirit or who even knew what it was? It seemed the very height of foolishness.

But she did not doubt the belkagen's power. He'd saved her life and Lendri's and obviously had powers and knowledge beyond her own. Besides, she knew one thing was true with or without his counsel. She'd seen what that dark thing who had her son could do. It had countered Mursen's spell and snapped the man's neck like a chicken. Even if she could find them before they did whatever they were planning to do to Jalan, she knew she could not beat the dark thing.

Her best hope was in cunning, getting close enough to grab Jalan and using her magic to whisk him away. But what would prevent them from coming after them again? They were hundreds of miles from home, tendays away from the nearest aid, even if other war wizards had come looking for them—and she could not be certain of that. Even if other members of her own order did find her, they would be more likely to arrest her and cart her back to Cormyr for trial than believe her wild tale and help her rescue Jalan.

Right now, like it or not, these mad folk of the Wastes and their odd ways were her best hope. Maybe her only hope. They had their own motives, their own hunt, but they were still the only friends she had. Could they protect her and Jalan if she did manage to rescue him? Would they even try? Did she have the right to ask them to do so?

Mad or not, fool's hope or final hope, this oracle was at least that: hope. If there was any way to deal with Jalan's captors once and for all . . .

"I'll do it," said Amira.

"Good," said the belkagen. He did not sound relieved or happy. On the contrary, his tone was grave. Solemn. "You should go at midnight, when darkness and light stand in balance, but there are things we must do to prepare. I will help you."

"Two things first," she said.

"Yes?"

"Several times now I've heard you call Gyaidun *yaste*-something."

"*Yastehanye.*"

"Yes. What is that?"

The belkagen glanced at Gyaidun, and the flicker of a grin crossed the old elf's face. Gyaidun's scowl deepened.

"*Yastehanye* means 'honored exile.' It is a term that many of the Vil Adanrath call our friend Gyaidun—though never in Haerul's hearing. It is a title of sorts. One of honor and respect. Renown. In his anger, Gyaidun called me Kwarun—the name my mother gave me. Very disrespectful to the belkagen. By calling him *yastehanye,* I was . . . *reminding* him of his place—and mine."

"Honored exile, eh? Why?"

The grin faded and died and the belkagen grew solemn again. "A long tale that is. And not mine to tell, Lady. Suffice to say that Gyaidun's exile was both just and tragic. Although the Vil Adanrath honor the omah nin's judgment of exile, still they respect the deeds that earned it."

Amira looked to Gyaidun, whose scowl had not faded. "Sounds like an intriguing tale. Will you tell me?"

"No," said Gyaidun.

Amira had to suppress a snicker. Odd as these folk were,

still no one could pout like a man. They learned it as boys and never outgrew it—in the East or West.

"You said two things," said the belkagen. "What is the other?"

"*Yastehanye* must take a bath. He smells like dead horse."

Gyaidun glared at her and stood. "Your stomach growls for dead horse . . . *Lady.*"

He gave her a mock bow, and before she could reply he stomped away, headed for the pool. Although Amira couldn't see it under the dried horse blood, she felt sure he was blushing.

CHAPTER FIFTEEN

Akhrasut Neth

After washing in the pool, Gyaidun returned, dressed
without saying a word to either of them, gathered
his weapons, and proceeded to leave again. But he
stopped and turned.

"You are really going to do this?"

He was looking to the belkagen, but the old elf
did not answer, instead looking to Amira.

"Yes," she said.

Gyaidun stood there, tense with anger and . . .
something else. Uncertainty? Amira wondered.

"Why?" he asked. "Why . . . honored Belkagen?"

"Why what, *yastehanye?*" said the elf.

"I called you Belkagen."

"Your words. Not your heart."

The big man and the old elf stared at one another,
neither gaze wavering or blinking. The anger was
still there, Amira knew, but the heat was gone. In

a way, this was worse, this cold tension that Amira sensed was born of hurt and loss from both of them. There was a slight curl to Gyaidun's lip that spoke to Amira of derision. The perfect calm of the belkagen's face, so obviously a tight mask, had an air of deep disappointment.

"Why what?" the belkagen said softly.

"Why help this"—he shot Amira an apologetic glance—"outlander seek *Hro'nyewachu?* For twelve years I have walked every horizon, sniffed every trail, and followed every track to find Erun. Not once did you give me this counsel. Why?"

"You are a hunter, Gyaidun." Was that tenderness in the old elf's tone? If so, it was slight. "A warrior. You are not . . ." The belkagen looked to Amira as he struggled for the word. "You have not studied the discipline of magic, nor sought the communion or made the sacrifices to the divine. Some of those taken by *Hro'nyewachu* spent years doing so. *Hro'nyewachu* might give you the answers you seek, but she would devour you. It is folly."

"The omahet are not priests or wizards. They are warriors. Like me. And they have survived the Mother's Heart."

"They are Vil Adanrath," said the belkagen. "You are not. The Mother's Heart, we call her. But she is not your mother. Her jealousy protects our people."

Our people. Gyaidun stared at the belkagen for a long moment, gave Amira a considering look, then turned and walked off. Durja cawed after him, and when the big man showed no sign of stopping or slowing, the raven took to wing after him. Both disappeared into the trees, and the sound of their passage was soon gone, leaving Amira and the belkagen only with the sound of the wind in the branches and the meat beginning to sizzle over the fire.

"Where is he going?" Amira asked.

"He must hunt."

"Now? We have food. I don't understand."

"There is much you do not understand," said the belkagen, and he sounded both tired and annoyed. "No more questions for now. Please. I will tend the fire. You should rest. You have a long night ahead of you."

Though it rankled her to be ordered about, Amira lay down under the small lean-to of branches and brush that Gyaidun had made. She used her pack as a pillow and wrapped herself in the elkhide. Though her breath steamed in the cold, she was quite warm in the thick hide, and she lay listening to the wind as it came around the Mother's Bed and set the trees to rattling. The belkagen muttered to himself as he tended the fire and food. His muttering fell into a half-whispered, half-sung chant, soothing in its rhythm.

Jalan . . . Amira thought, and the next thing she knew the sky was darker, the shadows among the trees thicker, and Gyaidun was walking into camp with a dead deer—a young buck—draped over his shoulders. She could not even remember closing her eyes—or opening them, for that matter. One moment she'd been listening to the belkagen and thinking of Jalan, and the next moment half the day had seemingly passed. Had the old meddler placed some sort of enchantment on her?

Whether he had or not, Amira realized as she sat up, she did feel rested.

Gyaidun knelt and dropped the deer well away from the fire. Aside from two arrow wounds to its throat, the carcass was uncut.

"Why didn't you butcher it?" Amira asked as she emerged from the shadows under the lean-to and came to the fire. "It would've been easier to carry."

Gyaidun didn't answer.

The belkagen, who still sat next to the fire, spoke up. *"Hro'nyewachu* will be hungry. If you have no gift . . ."

"What?"

"Feed *Hro'nyewachu* or she will feed on you," Gyaidun said, though he did not look at her. Instead he gave the belkagen a hard look and continued, "That much I know."

"What kind of oracle is this?" asked Amira.

"I told you," said the belkagen. "She is a being of need—both in fulfilling and needing to be fulfilled. Nothing comes free. Blood for blood."

A flutter passed through Amira's stomach. The war wizards had their own rituals, many of which were dangerous, but she was beginning to regret agreeing to this. Confronting a danger for which she was prepared was one thing. Trusting the word of these foreigners with their strange ways and walking in unprepared to who knew what was something else.

"You are a foreigner here," said the belkagen, and Amira flinched at hearing some of her own thoughts spoken back to her. "I will help you prepare, but you must trust us."

There were a hundred questions she probably should have asked, but she said, "Your oracle doesn't like horses? We have two that Gyaidun says we can't ride. Why go hunting?"

"Hro'nyewachu is . . . *akai'ye,"* said the belkagen. "There is no good word in your tongue. Ancient. Primal. Tame blood will not sate her. She needs the blood of the wild."

"Ah, Azuth," Amira grumbled. "I hate the Wastes."

As late afternoon deepened to evening, Amira saw the sun for the last time for many days. Still wrapped in the elk-hide blanket against the cold, she stood just inside the edge of the copse. The glowing rim of the sun dropped out of the edge of the farthest clouds and was two fingers' width from touching the horizon when Amira heard howling. First she thought it was the wind, but then she caught the mournful melody, rising and falling off the south. Others answered it. Wolves were coming. Many wolves.

She turned and made the short walk back into camp. The two remaining horses were skittish, their ears flicking, their feet stamping, and the whites of their eyes showing as they tossed their heads.

The belkagen still sat beside the fire. He was gnawing on a bit of horseflesh—a *raw* piece, Amira noticed, and turned away. Gyaidun was sitting on the very edge of camp, his back against a tree, Durja nestled in his lap. He was staring off into nothing and did not so much as glance her way. The open hostility between the two men was gone, but there was still a palpable tension in camp. It had been a large reason for her decision to take a walk.

"I heard wolves," she said.

"The Vil Adanrath," said the belkagen. "Haerul is coming."

"Why do they howl?"

The belkagen glanced at Gyaidun. "They announce their presence. They wish us to know they are here, but they will not share fire with Gyaidun."

"It is the omah nin's way of telling me to get back to my camp and stay there," said Gyaidun.

More howls drifted off the southern steppe, and both horses gave a nervous whicker. Amira remembered Gyaidun telling her that horses could not abide the presence of the Vil Adanrath, and something occurred to her.

"Belkagen," she said. "Why do the horses not fear you? You are Vil Adanrath, are you not?"

"Yes," said the belkagen, "and no. The calling of the belkagen leaves us . . . changed."

"I don't understand."

Gyaidun snorted.

The belkagen gave him a dark look, then stood up. "I should lead the horses away. Lendri will likely be arriving soon."

"What will you do with them?" she asked.

"Gifts for Haerul and his pack," the belkagen said as he untied the horses' hobbles. "They will be hungry after such a long journey, and a little hospitality might soften the mood of the omah nin."

Amira found a place by the fire as the belkagen disappeared off into the trees with the two frightened horses. The strips of horseflesh—now cooked—hung from a small rack near the fire. Her stomach rumbled but she winced.

"Not hungry?" said Gyaidun.

"I'm starving."

"Then eat."

"My family raises horses. Some of the finest in Cormyr—the finest anywhere. Horses are for riding, not eating."

In the distance, Amira heard the sudden scream of the horses followed by the sound of galloping hooves.

"Not in the Wastes," said Gyaidun. At first, she thought he was mocking her "outlander ways" again, but his voice held no scorn as he continued. "Even the Tuigan, who care for their horses more than any people I've ever known, eat horseflesh. There is no shame in it."

"Would you eat Durja?"

The raven looked at her, his head twisting sideways, and cawed at her as if he understood.

"Durja is a friend," said Gyaidun.

"When I was a little girl, horses were my friends."

"You're not a little girl anymore."

The breeze slackened, and as the boughs and dry leaves settled, Amira heard another distant whinny, harsh and terrified, almost like the scream of a woman, and behind it she thought she caught the sound of growling. She shuddered.

Amira took a deep breath and looked to Gyaidun. The gloom of evening was deepening, and seated as he was under the tree, she could not tell if he was looking at her or not. "Gyaidun?" she said.

"Yes?"

"Tonight when I . . . seek the oracle, you know I am trying to help my son?"

"Yes." His voice was flat.

"But if . . . if there is anything I can do to help your son, I will."

He said nothing for a long time. She was about to decide she'd offended him again, trespassed on some fragment of eastern manners that she didn't know, when he spoke again. "It's been twelve years since Erun was stolen."

"Then you've given up hope?"

Gyaidun said nothing. Durja set to cawing again, and at the sound a sudden image, a memory, filled Amira's mind.

The field after battle. The sun gone in the west but an angry light still burning in the sky. The air thick with the buzzing of flies and the call of ravens. The stench was the worst. Blood she could handle. But in dying, stomachs were cut open, skulls split, bowels emptied, and spells burned both grass and flesh. For once Amira did not push the image away.

"Despair is for the dead," Amira said. "You are still alive, *Yastehanye.*"

"As is your son," said Gyaidun, though there was no offer of comfort in his voice. Only bitterness. "What of *my* son?"

"I don't know. But if there is no hope for him, there is always vengeance."

CHAPTER SIXTEEN

The Endless Wastes

No dreams—good or bad—troubled Jalan's sleep the night of the massacre of the Tuigan nomads. He slept beside the fire, but with no one to tend it, the fire was nothing but cold ashes by morning. And still Jalan slept. His mind and body wrung out by fear and exhaustion, he did not even turn in his sleep as the thing in the ash-gray cloak fled the coming dawn and buried itself under blankets and hides inside one of the Tuigan yurts. Most of the pale northerners and their wolf mounts slept, scattered throughout the carnage.

Around midday the high slate-colored canopy of clouds fell lower and thickened, deepening to the color of charcoal. The guard pacing near Jalan stopped and, smelling snow in the air, smiled.

Behind the tapestry of clouds, the first edge of the sun was setting in the west when the first spark of awareness stirred within Jalan. Not wakefulness, for his body still slept, his breath even, and his heart beating slow. But something deep within Jalan, something buried far beneath conscious thought, was waking up.

Shadows deepened in the camp, the last of the day's light gathering to a colorless glow in the west. Both wolves and their riders began to stir, the beasts blinking and yawning, the pale northerners kicking their blankets away and setting to packing.

Disturbed by the activity around him, Jalan moaned and woke, though he did not open his eyes. Why bother? He could feel the damp cold in the air, and even with his eyes closed he knew the day was over and they would soon be leaving. More than anything, he wished to fall back into the oblivion of sleep. Lying there hoping for sleep only strengthened his wakefulness, but with it his awareness sharpened and he noticed something. Still he felt hollow, as if the horror of the past few days and the crushed hope of being rescued only to be taken again had scraped his insides clean, but now . . . now floating in that emptiness was . . . something. He couldn't put a name to it. Not light exactly, nor warmth. But there was something very much alive inside him, both a part of him and separate.

Be not afraid. He remembered the words from the dream, the voice amidst the song.

Jalan focused his thought on that something within him and formed a single thought. *Vyaidelon?*

Nothing. No answer, no music, no voice. Still, it did not go away.

Night fell around him. Though he still lay with his eyes closed, Jalan sensed its coming—not the night, but the one who came with it. He was always there, that dark, cold thing, aware of him. Watching. Studying. But in the daylight, the awareness spread out, still there but stretched thin. With the coming of night it pressed upon him again, sharp as new frost.

Jalan, knowing he was coming, squeezed his eyes shut as tight as he could.

He heard the flap of the nearby yurt torn away, wrenched off its wood-frame hinge. Either by dread curiosity or reflex, Jalan started and his eyes opened. The thing in the ash-gray cloak stepped out and straightened to his full height. The air seemed to thicken and become brittle, and Jalan could sense the thing's anger.

The leader paced round the immediate area, moving from space to space in quick bursts of speed then standing still as the shadows themselves. He sniffed at the air, opened his mouth wide, inhaled, then flinched as if bitten.

He looked down at Jalan. "What are you doing?"

Jalan said nothing. He squeezed his eyes shut and huddled inside his cloak. The something, that odd presence inside of him, trembled, but it was not from fear. It was as if a bell had been struck, and the more the thing in the ash-gray cloak exerted his will, the stronger the chime sang within Jalan.

"Stop that," said the leader.

"I . . . I . . ."

"I said stop!" The leader wrenched Jalan up and pulled him close. "I sense what you are doing. I hear it in your heart's beating. Stop now or I'll bleed it out of you."

Jalan heard the rustle of robes and the soft *whisk* of a blade being drawn. He opened his eyes and tears streamed out. Jalan gasped for air and almost gagged at the stench of the thing holding him.

"Heed me, whelp," said the leader, and he pressed the edge of his knife against Jalan's cheek. The metal was so cold it burned. "I need you alive. Not unscathed. Stop what you are doing *now*."

"I . . . can't," Jalan said. "I—"

The knife shifted, the point coming toward Jalan's left eye. He squeezed his eyes shut and tried to pull away, but the thing holding him was too strong. He could feel the point of the blade resting against his clenched eyelid, but he could pull away no further.

"Stop," said the leader, almost a whisper. "I will not say so again."

Jalan's fear had so filled his thoughts that he'd almost forgotten about the thing inside him, that indefinable livingness stirring within. The terror emptied his mind of all else, and in that instant the thing within him resounded, growing from a rhythmic hum to a battle cry. Almost of their own accord his eyes opened. The blade filled his vision, as if all the world had funneled into the knife hovering just beyond his tears. Jalan took the great thing inside of him and focused it there.

The blade *blazed*. A pure orange light glowed outward, but the blade itself was white as the center of the sun.

The thing in the ash-gray cloak shrieked and hurled Jalan and the knife away. Jalan rolled into the cold ashes of the fire, and the knife, still blazing like the noonday sun, tumbled into the grass.

The howling and frightened whines of wolves filled Jalan's ears as he pushed himself to his hands and knees. He saw a pale blur coming at him—one of the northern barbarians—but he was too stunned to move. The boot caught him in the side, and he went down. Darkness and light and a hundred dancing colors filled his eyes, and his body seemed to squeeze in on itself, craving air but finding only pain.

He took deep, choking breaths, his side clenching. When he could hear and see again, the camp was in turmoil. The huge wolves were running around, many growling and snapping at their fellows. The pale northerners rushed to calm them, and their cloaked leader sat in the grass, huddling away from the light and barking orders in a language that Jalan could not understand. His voice sounded stretched and thin. Desperate.

One of the pale men ripped the outer felt covering off a yurt. He dragged it to where the dagger still blazed like a piece of the sun fallen to earth and threw the thick felt over it. The glow winked out, and darkness fell on the camp again.

The cloaked leader stood, his robes falling around him like tides of night, and bore down on Jalan.

Jalan raised his hands before his face, fearing another

dagger or a blast of cold—or worst of all that sharp awareness boring into his mind. Instead, the leader's fist emerged from the folds of his cloak. Jalan saw it, a pallid blur streaking toward his face, then a cold blackness took him.

Akhrasut Neth

The howling had not subsided. In fact, it seemed to Amira that even more wolves had come, and the sounds of their singing came from every direction. Full night had fallen, bringing with it a thick, clinging fog that dampened Amira's cloak and made her hair cling to her scalp.

The belkagen had not returned to camp, and Gyaidun just sat there in the shadows, staring off into nowhere.

Amira heard something approaching through the trees and caught her breath. She hoped it was the belkagen, but she feared it might be Haerul. She could hold her own against this barbarian chieftain no matter what the old elf said, but like it or not she needed their help, and she knew she needed the belkagen's assistance to navigate all the intricate customs and proprieties of these people.

Besides, she'd had a few encounters with werewolves before. None of them pleasant. If Amira was right and Gyaidun's account of the Vil Adanrath matched with her own recollection of the lythari, she knew she had little to fear. If the accounts she'd read were true, the lythari were not afflicted monsters like other werewolves.

Still, she recalled the belkagen's words to her. *They are a people of pride and honor, and their chief, Haerul, has pride and honor like none I've ever seen. Scratch it at your peril.* She'd already seen Lendri angered, and war wizard that she was, remembering the gaze he'd fixed upon her still sent a shiver up her spine.

Amira huddled in her elkhide blanket next to the fire and kept her eyes fixed on the direction from which she heard the sound. More than one person was coming, but she'd only just noticed the second. Both moved with a furtive grace and quiet she'd seen only among animals.

A wolf emerged from the shadows between the trees, bounding through the brush to approach the fire with no hint of fear. Amira recognized Mingan, and Lendri came into view not far behind him. Despite the chill, he wore only a loincloth, and he carried no weapons.

Gyaidun rose to greet him and they embraced, exchanging words in their own language. Lendri gave Amira a small bow, then said, "The Vil Adanrath have come."

"You convinced the omah nin?" said Gyaidun.

"I did little more than offend my brother and rouse my father's ire anew. It was the belkagen who convinced Haerul to come. They are camping on the other side of the spring." A wry, almost mischievous smile broke the elf's grim countenance. "My father has heard you are here."

"He won't even come to greet his daughter's husband?" said Amira.

Gyaidun said nothing, but the look Lendri gave Amira made her wish she'd held her tongue. "Our ways are not your ways, Lady Amira," he said.

"You need not tell *me* that."

"He does, however, send greetings to the War Wizard of Cormyr and bids you well come to his lands."

"*His* lands?"

"*Akhrasut Neth* is sacred to the Vil Adanrath. As the omah nin, Haerul's word is now law here, and he welcomes you as his guest."

Amira didn't know whether to be offended that he hadn't greeted her himself—at the very least with a summons—or thankful that he hadn't ordered her captured for sharing a fire with a man he'd outlawed. She remembered her mother's words, pounded into her from childhood—When you don't know the proper words, courtesy serves best—and so she simply said, "Thank you. Tell him thank you."

"My father's words to me are the last he will speak," said Lendri. "And even those he gave only at the belkagen's urging. No more will his honor permit. You wish to thank him? Thank him yourself. He has sworn to kill me if I speak to him again."

"How many has he brought?" asked Gyaidun.

"Forty hunters arrived with us tonight," said Lendri. "He has summoned more, but I do not think he'll wait for them. A great hunger and rage fills him. Please do not provoke anything, Brother. The omah nin is thirsting for blood. Give him no excuse to spill yours."

Gyaidun opened his mouth to say something, but Durja cut him off, flapping his wings and cawing. Despite the noise, Amira thought she caught the sound of larger wings alighting in one of the trees just outside of camp, and by the time the raven had quieted, settling in atop Gyaidun's shoulder, the belkagen was walking back into the light of the fire.

The old elf held his staff in a firm hand, and he looked grim, reminding Amira of a lord about to pronounce grave judgment on a vassal. He spared Lendri and Gyaidun a glance, then fixed his gaze on Amira.

"It is time, Lady."

CHAPTER SEVENTEEN

Akhrasut Neth

The belkagen led the way, threading a winding path up *Akhrasut Neth* through ravines filled with thousands of years of shattered stone and sand. Low trees with thick, twisted roots clung to the rocks, and even this late in the year their small, waxy leaves were thick and vibrant.

Amira followed the belkagen, staying close, for neither of them carried a torch, and with the canopy of cloud hiding the moon and stars, the night was dark. She knew Lendri and Gyaidun were following—the big man carrying the deer—but she heard them more than she saw them.

In the almost total darkness, her surroundings were little more than varying shades of murk. She stumbled several times and would have fallen once had she not had her staff to steady her. She cursed herself, knowing what a terrible racket she was making, though the others moved with little more noise than the breeze through the brush. Amira knew elves could see like owls in the dark, and even Gyaidun seemed to be having little trouble.

Now and then she heard others following as well—the turning of a stone, gravel sliding under stealthy feet, a branch sliding over a passing body—but she never saw who was trailing them. The belkagen seemed unconcerned, so she followed his lead.

About halfway up, they walked out of the fog. Amira could still see no better, but the darkness didn't seem as thick, and the air that came to her lungs had a dry bite. By the cold, she knew there'd be a thick coating of frost by morning, and if those clouds chose to release their burden, they'd have snow.

The ground grew steeper, the trees smaller and farther between, and Amira soon found herself climbing more than walking, pulling herself over jagged boulders and up shelves of rock. Though she was quite warm in the clothes the belkagen had given her, climbing the rocks made her fingers stiff and cold. She was about to swallow her pride and call for a rest when their trail entered another ravine, and this time there were jagged steps cut into the rock. Though they were cracked and weathered with age, Amira knew they were far too straight and regular to be natural. Someone had carved these.

The stairway doubled back on itself three times, and then the land flattened out. Before Amira's eyes, the darkness bled away into bright contrasts of shadow, gray, and silver, and she looked up. A jagged tear had opened in the clouds, and the edge of the moon shone down on them. Leaning on her staff and breathing hard, Amira looked back.

Akhrasut Neth sat on a sea of fog, unbroken to the farthest horizon. Gyaidun and Lendri climbed the last of the steps, and Amira saw others behind them, the nearest just rounding the last twist of the stairs. She could not make out details in the moonlight, only pale shadows, but there were many of them, dozens at least. Some walked upright while some padded upward on all fours.

Amira turned to the belkagen, who stood watching the sky not far away. "The Vil Adanrath are coming?" she asked.

"The omah nin's pack and a few others, yes."

"Why?"

"They come to honor *Akhrasut Neth*. It is tradition."

"What about . . . ?" Amira looked to Gyaidun, the deer carcass still draped over his shoulders.

"They will keep an honorable distance," said the belkagen. "Haerul knows what you do here this night. He may watch from afar, but he will not approach the exiles."

Amira looked back down. The nearest of the Vil Adanrath had seen them and stopped on the stairway. Even as she watched, the rent in the clouds passed over the moon, and the world plunged into darkness again.

"We must go," said the belkagen. "Midnight is not far off."

They set off, Amira following the belkagen. Again she had to follow him more by sound than sight.

The trail wound through more trees, some of which stood beside the trail itself so they had to duck through branches to pass. After stumbling over the third root, Amira stopped and said, "Belkagen, is there some taboo against torches?"

"Taboo?" said the belkagen. "I am sorry, Lady. I do not know this word."

"Why am I stumbling around in the dark? My toes are bruised and my shins feel scraped raw. Is it forbidden to carry light on the Mother's Bed?"

There was a short silence, then Amira heard the old elf chuckling. "My apologies, Lady Amira. There is no . . . taboo. I merely forgot the limits of your eyes. Forgive my discourtesy."

The belkagen spoke a short incantation, and green flames began to lick up the top quarter length of his staff. They were not the pale sickly green of fire magic she'd sometimes seen dark wizards use, but a vibrant, living flame, like spring sunshine filtered through a canopy of newly sprouted leaves. Amira thought she even caught the scent of blossoms.

The light they cast was meager, but in the near-total dark to which her eyes had become accustomed it seemed like a beacon.

They set off again, and Amira looked over her shoulder to Gyaidun. "How do you see so well in the dark? You're human."

"I am *athkaraye*. Elf-friend. Even though I am now an exile, the blessings remain."

Amira remembered him speaking of this once before, of the "blessings" he'd gained in becoming Lendri's blood brother and elf-friend to the Vil Adanrath. She knew of similar rites among elves to the west, though she'd never met one of the so-called "elf-friends." But it would go a long way toward explaining how Gyaidun moved with such grace and stealth in the wild, how he ran seemingly tirelessly for scores of miles . . . and how he could see on such a dark night.

The group walked on a bit more, and soon the trees thinned as the ground rose. In the clearing, the belkagen stopped, and by the light cast from his staff, Amira saw a large fang of rock breaking through the ground. A great fissure split the stone from the ground to half its height, forming a door into darkness.

"This is it?" said Amira, her voice hushed to a reverent whisper. Even after hearing the belkagen's history of this place, she hadn't put too much weight in it. Every people from the crudest barbarians to the most cultured societies had their own traditions, histories, and legends. She didn't discount any of them, but neither did she accept them without question. She had sifted through the old shaman's tale, hoping that this might be one of Faerûn's sites of power, that she might find some aid in rescuing Jalan. But standing there in a thick darkness broken only by the shimmering light cast from the belkagen's staff, far from her home with shapeshifters at her back and a fell sorcerer somewhere out there, for that moment she believed. Something in her deepest heart, some buried race memory, perhaps, of a time when all men walked in fear of the ancient powers of the world . . . something inside Amira woke up and hummed with life at the sight of the yawning darkness in the rock.

"This is *Hro'nyewachu*," said the belkagen.

Amira heard a rustling in the grass behind her, and she turned. Gyaidun had placed the deer in the grass before him, and both he and Lendri knelt with their heads bowed. Behind them, among the trees, Amira saw silver shadows keeping a respectful distance. They too knelt, and even those that walked on four legs through the trees stopped and lowered their heads.

"From here," said the belkagen, and Amira turned back to face him, "we go alone, you and I."

Amira tried to swallow but found her throat dry. "Lead on," she rasped.

The belkagen knelt beside the deer carcass. "If you would, *Yastehanye* . . ."

Gyaidun lifted the deer and placed it over the elf's shoulders. He moved with a reverence that only deepened Amira's trepidation. The belkagen stood, holding the deer secure with one hand and his staff in the other. If the carcass was a great burden to him, he didn't show it.

"If we are not back by sunrise," said the belkagen, his voice raised for everyone to hear, "do not tarry. Go to the aid of Jalan, son of Amira of Cormyr, and bring the vengeance of the Vil Adanrath upon those who took him."

The belkagen turned and proceeded into the cave. Amira followed. Behind them, the howling of wolves rode the autumn dark. She hoped their song was a salute, but to her the mournful howls sounded more like a dirge.

Their path descended almost at once, the ground beneath Amira's feet ranging from steps hewn out of the rock to gravel-strewn sand. The trail wound back and forth, deeper and deeper into the heart of *Akhrasut Neth*. At times they walked through tunnels low enough that both were forced to crouch, and the green flames from the belkagen's staff lit the path before and behind them a long way. At other times they emerged into caverns so vast the darkness swallowed the light.

Amira expected to hear the chitter of bats or the scuttle of insects, but there was nothing. Save for the shuffling of their feet and the sound of their breath, all was utter silence, a heaviness beyond even sound that weighed upon Amira the farther they went. The beating of her own heart sounded loud in her ears.

They left the biting cold of autumn night behind them and fell into a uniform coolness that did not change through the seasons. The air tasted dry and clean, and the change in it was Amira's first clue that they were approaching something new. Dampness. That's what it was. Amira could smell water in the air.

She and the belkagen descended a flight of stairs in a tight tunnel, then emerged into a cavern, broad beyond the reach of the staff's light but with a low ceiling littered with stalactites. The inverted cones of stone glistened in the green light of the belkagen's flame, and they *drip-drip-dripped* into a pool that filled all but a sandy strip of dry land before them. If the path continued on the far shore, Amira could not see it, for the far side was beyond the reach of the staff's light.

"From here," said the belkagen, his voice lowered to a reverent whisper, "you must go on alone. I cannot aid you."

"Go on?" said Amira. "Where?"

"Through the water. You can swim?"

"Yes."

"It is not deep, but before you reach the other side, the water will be over your head. On the far shore is an opening to the Heart. You must go alone. What happens there is between you and *Hro'nyewachu*."

"And if"—Amira took a deep breath—"if something happens to me, if I need your help . . . ?"

"There is no help I can give you, Lady. If *Hro'nyewachu* takes you, I will honor your memory. But there is nothing I can do to hinder the will of *Hro'nyewachu*."

Amira considered that. It was not bravery or blind faith that decided her, but simple pragmatism. She knew she was no match for the thing that held Jalan. She knew that without help her best hope would be to get away with her son and spend the rest of her life running, jumping at every shadow, never trusting to a night's rest, and putting everyone who aided her in danger. If there was a way to defeat Jalan's abductors once and for all, if even an inkling of the belkagen's suspicions and counsel were true, she'd be a fool not to try.

"You'll be here when I return?" she said.

"I will."

"How . . . how am I supposed to take the oracle's gift?" She pointed to the deer carcass. "I can swim well enough, but not carrying that."

"Take it as far as you can. *Hro'nyewachu* will see to the rest."

Amira wasn't sure she liked the sound of that. No matter. Do or die. Let it be done. She motioned for the belkagen to hand her the deer.

"There is . . . one thing more," said the belkagen, and Amira could not tell if his tone was solemnity, embarrassment, or both.

"What?"

"You can take nothing with you. Your staff, your spellbook, your dagger, and your, uh . . . your clothes must remain here."

"I go . . . naked?"

"The water is not that cold."

"Naked? Why?"

The belkagen lowered his eyes. "It is the way. So it has always been done. So it must be done. You must take with you only your purest essence, no aid beyond body, soul, and spirit."

Amira scowled. It was a trivial thing at which to balk, perhaps, but still . . .

"I am Vil Adanrath," said the belkagen, "not human, and Lady, I am very old, but if you wish it, I shall turn my back to honor your people's customs of modesty."

Modesty be damned. "Let's get this over with," she said

and began to strip, first her elkhide cloak, then her boots, her outer clothes, and finally her smallclothes, all of which she laid in a neat pile not far from the water's edge. She placed her staff, belt with sheathed blade and pouches, and her spellbook atop the pile, then stood and motioned for the deer. Though it was not the biting cold of the outside world, the air inside the cavern was cool, and her bare skin crinkled into gooseflesh.

The belkagen leaned close, averting his eyes, and placed the deer over her shoulders. It was not unbearably heavy so much as awkward in its utter dead weight. The coarse fur made her skin itch.

She turned to the water. "The other side? An opening, you said?"

"Yes," said the belkagen. "Your gods and ancestors go with you."

Amira closed her eyes. A strange feeling washed over her. Dread, yes, but not one that was entirely unpleasant. Fear, yes, but also an odd exhilaration and eagerness. It was not unlike the first time she had been with a man, the one who'd changed her from maiden to woman, the one she'd loved and later watched die. She prayed—*Azuth, Mystra, Kelemvor . . . keep me alive long enough to save my son. If not, grant the enemies of my enemies bloody vengeance.*

She stepped into the pool.

The water was warmer than the air, and it sparked a sharp awareness in her skin. Amira felt every grain of wet sand between her toes, every tiny pebble beneath her feet, and against her bare shins she could even feel the slight ripples caused by the water dripping off the stalactites.

She walked on, dragging her feet through the soft sand, enjoying the sensation. Ten steps and the water was already above her knees. Another four and her hips and waist disappeared beneath the water. The green light cast by the belkagen's staff on the shore behind her grew fainter, and by her thirtieth step she walked in dim, wet shadow with the water caressing the swell of her breasts.

As the darkness swallowed Amira, her other senses sharpened. She could distinguish every drip striking her scalp, feel the tiny waves caused by their impact and her own movement, and she could almost sense a rhythm in dozens of tiny hammer-strikes of water droplets hitting the pool's surface. Almost like sharp heartbeats. Her own pulse slowed and steadied but beat with such strength that Amira could feel blood coursing through her limbs.

When the water reached her shoulders, Amira knelt, allowing the water to lift some of the burden of the deer. It became lighter, but the pull and tug of the water made it even more awkward, and her pace slowed. The belkagen's light was gone now. She knew that if she turned, she could have seen it like an emerald beacon behind her, but before her all was impenetrable blackness.

The water licked at her chin, and her next step fell into nothingness. The ground dropped out beneath her and Amira went down. She felt the water soak through her hair as she entered the thick, pulsing near-silence beneath the pool. She sank less than half a pace before her foot hit solid rock and she pushed. She rose again, but the weight of the deer hindered her, and she had to shrug it off and arch her neck to get her mouth above the water long enough to draw breath.

The deer carcass drifted off her and she held onto its foreleg with one hand as she sank again, farther this time to get more strength for her push. She knelt there in the calm silence of the pool, for just an instant listening to the distant *plip-plitip-plip* of the water droplets striking the surface. Then she pushed off. She broke the surface, took a deep breath—

—and felt the deer yanked away from her. Her breath rose to a scream, then she was below the surface again. Her grip had not been tight—why should it?—but still she'd felt the immutable strength of something take the deer from her. The young buck's antler had scraped the back of her forearm as the head passed, then it was gone.

There, alone in the darkness beneath the water, her heart hammering in her chest, Amira listened. She felt the wake of the deer's passage, and somewhere just beyond hearing she thought she might have heard harsh laughter, then she was alone again.

Enough of this—back to the belkagen! part of her said, but the hard core of her, the part of Amira that fought and strived and killed in battle, recalled the belkagen's words. "Take it as far as you can. *Hro'nyewachu* will see to the rest."

Surprising? Yes. Damned unsettling, in fact, but this was nothing the belkagen had not told her about.

Just get to the other side, she told herself, nice and easy.

The water round her legs seemed to thicken, solidify, and as she opened her mouth to scream, she was pulled under. Water filled her nose, her mouth, and poured down her throat. She clawed for the surface, then the blackness and the thick silence beneath the pool swallowed her.

CHAPTER EIGHTEEN

Hro'nyewachu

Pain pulled Amira back to awareness. Her lungs felt like she was breathing daggers. All she could see was a warm blood red glow, like staring into the sunset with her eyes closed. Panic froze her mind, then her body took over.

She coughed out a great gout of water, drew in a rattling breath, then coughed up more water. She coughed and gagged and heaved until she feared her eyes were going to burst from her head.

When air began to find its way into her body again, her mind was able to emerge from the panic and take stock of her situation. Still on her hands and knees—on a stone floor with a thin covering of grit, she noticed—she looked up through her drenched hair.

The red light hadn't been brought on by her panic. She was in a cavern. Stalactites large as war-horses hung from a ceiling far above. Some had melded with the stone below, forming columns of stone that glistened in the red glow.

Glow—?

She looked around. If the light had a source, she could not find it, but it filled the cavern. Even the great columns of stone cast no shadow. The chamber had no proper walls, but the ceiling formed a dome that fell to meet the floor.

Amira sat up on her knees, brushed her sodden hair out of her face, and looked around. Where is the entrance? she wondered. How did I get here? Where—?

Her gaze stopped on the floor behind her. Not ten paces away lay the deer. It had been cut in two perfect halves, right down the middle, and each half set parallel so that the twin antlers nearly touched. Even the thick bone of the skull and spine had been split. What could have done such a thing?

The entrails and a great pool of blood—black in the cavern's light—lay between them, and just beyond them was a stone pedestal. It looked as if one of the great stone columns had been severed at table-height. Whether it had been carved or formed that way through some craft of magic or by long eons of stone-growth, Amira could not tell.

Upon the stone table was the deer's heart, still beating, slowly but with a steady, unceasing rhythm. With each beat, a small trickle of blood pulsed from the heart. Already a sizeable pool had formed in the concave surface of the stone table.

Amira's eyes widened, and she held her breath. The deer had been dead. How—?

Stand.

Amira gasped at the voice. It came to her mind, not her ears, and the language was one she'd never heard, though she understood it immediately. It was deep, husky, but obviously feminine. Where had it come from? Where—?

Stand.

There. Amira stood and faced the table.

A figure stepped out from behind one of the stone columns that flanked the table. She was tall—she could've looked down upon Gyaidun—but thin. Not emaciated, for the grace with which she moved hinted at great strength, but something about the way she moved seemed . . . unnatural, as if her muscles and joints were not fitted to her bones like other beings. She was quite naked, but Amira could not discern the color of her skin. A slick wetness covered her from head to toe, and in the red light of the cavern it was almost black. Blood. In her heart of hearts, Amira knew it.

The woman's hair was made up in dozens and dozens of tight braids that hung to her waist. Woven among them were bits of bone, feathers, and flowers, which surprised Amira—spring flowers of many colors, here on the verge of winter, some in full bloom and some still in tight little buds.

As the woman walked to the stone pedestal and stood behind it, her eyes held Amira's. They were set deep beneath hairless brows, and they seemed to deny the blood red light of the cavern and shone back a pale, dusty white—the color of the waxing moon on a cloudless winter night.

You bring the gift to fulfill the covenant. As sworn. Name yourself.

"I—" Amira's voice came out a croak. She swallowed and tried again. "Amira of House Hiloar of Cormyr. You are the . . . the oracle?"

The woman raised her right arm and pointed to the bisected deer carcass. *In life, we walk in death. In death, life. Come.*

"Come?"

To me. Now.

Amira took a deep breath and began to walk around the bloody remains of the deer.

Stop! said the figure, though in her head Amira heard the roar of an animal. A predator.

"What—?"

Through death you will walk, or to death you will go.

The woman lifted her head back and took in a deep breath, her nostrils flaring. Though the stench of blood and death filled the cavern, Amira knew the oracle was smelling her, and she knew her promise of death was true.

Amira closed her eyes, took a deep breath, then opened them again and walked between the halves of the deer. The blood was warm—almost hot—beneath the soles of her feet. She winced but did not look down as she almost slipped on the entrails. The stench was overwhelming, and tears flowed down Amira's cheeks.

Amira stood before the table, and the tall figure looked down upon her.

I smell winter upon you.

"I . . . I have come to seek your aid," said Amira. "Something has my son. Something too powerful for me to defeat. I need your help."

The oracle smiled, and it sent a shiver down Amira's back. There was no warmth in it, no pleasure, no human emotion at all. It was merely muscles drawing the lips back over teeth, and the teeth were sharp. The oracle placed her hands on the edge of the table, then bent over and buried her face in the pool of blood and drank, lapping at the blood like an animal. Amira wanted to look away, but she stood frozen.

The oracle straightened, fresh blood smeared over her face and running down her neck and breasts. With her right hand, she seized the still-beating heart, brought it to her open mouth and tore into it. Amira heard the tough muscle snap between the powerful jaws. The oracle put the heart back on the pedestal. Still it beat with a steady, if weaker rhythm.

The oracle chewed and swallowed.

Now, you.

"What?"

Eat. Drink.

"What? I . . . I can't! The belkagen said noth—"

Again a predator's growl cut her off, and this time Amira heard it in her ears as well as her mind. Her own heart skipped a beat, then set to hammering like a bird's. Looking up into the eyes of the oracle, Amira knew beyond doubt that her life now hung by the barest thread.

Eat the flesh. Drink the blood.

Amira placed her hands on the pedestal as the oracle had done. The stone was warm, and Amira almost thought she felt a pulse beating within it. Before her sense and thirty years of ingrained Cormyrean propriety could talk her out of it, Amira plunged her face into the blood. She felt her hair fall around her, soaking up the blood, and she drank. Not just a sip, for at the first taste a thirst she had never known opened in her innermost being, and the blood down her throat seemed both to slake it and make her even more aware of the need to be slaked. Amira drank until her body cried out for air, then pushed herself up.

The oracle looked down on her, eyes still shining, but now Amira thought she could almost see her own reflection in those pale depths.

Now eat and fulfill the pact.

Amira reached out. Her hand was trembling, but not from fear or weakness. Amira could feel the blood coursing through her, filling her spirit with a strength and warmth she had never known. Her skin burned with sensation, feeling even the tiniest stirring of air. Scents overwhelmed her—raw flesh, warm blood, stone older than Cormyr itself, the tiny buds and petals in the oracle's hair, and beneath it all something to which she could put no name but which awoke something ancient and primal in her, some part of her mind that still dreamed of the time before men built cities of stone and kept the wild at bay with their fires and prayers, when the wild was still part of them.

Amira reached out, some part of her registering that her hand trembled not out of weakness or fear, but eagerness. She grabbed the heart, brought it to her open mouth, and bit down. The flesh was tough, resisting, and so she bit harder and harder until her teeth tore through. She grabbed the heart with both hands and shook her head like an animal, rending the flesh and finding herself enjoying it. Against her will, a low growl began to build deep in her throat. The part of her mind that still remembered Amira of House Hiloar, War Wizard of Cormyr, daughter of the royal courts, battered at her mind, screaming—What's happening to me?

The portion of the heart tore loose in her mouth. She swallowed it whole, looked up into the eyes of the oracle——and fell in.

Darkness took her, but it was warm and wet, and when it began to break away, part of her cried out and tried to cling to it.

It will be your death, said a voice.

Whose? She could put no name to it, but she remembered eyes pale as the dust of the moon and the scent of spring blossoms.

She let go. Light returned. Color. And cold. Not the deep cold of the winter or the nameless horror that stalked her memories, cloaked in ashes, but the crisp, clean coolness of the open air. The high, thin clouds of autumn, tattered and torn like rent tapestries, rode across a morning blue sky that stretched from horizon to horizon in every direction except one. Before her, breaking the perfect dome of the sky, rose a high mound, flat and broken on top and bleeding greenery into the grasslands below. She knew it, had seen it from just this view, but she could put no name to it. The name was in her memory; she knew it as she knew breath and blood, but it was closed to her.

Something was moving near the crest of the hill. As if spurred by the thought, her vision flew toward it, coming closer and closer until she could make out the form of a man. Clothes of leather and cloth and robes of animal hides covered his lean frame. His hair was raven black, the top and sides pulled back into a thick braid that fell well below his waist. He walked with a staff that seemed to have been made from three woods, each of a different shade, twisted together and bound with leather and silver. Tassels made from bits of bone, stone, and sprigs of herbs dangled from the top of the staff.

Arantar, said the voice.

The man made his way through the woods. He stopped

before a great fang of rock that broke through the surface of the hill. Again she felt as if she should know this place. The rock almost looked familiar, though taller and sharper than she knew it to be.

The man stood before an opening in the rock, the autumn wind sending the loose bits of his hair waving before his face like tendrils of seaweed tossed by the tide. For the first time, she saw his face. His weather-worn skin was dark, the color of newly tilled soil, and his face was shaven. But his eyes . . . she didn't see them so much as she felt struck by them. They were golden, and even in the shadow cast by the fang of rock they shone with a light all their own.

She had seen those eyes before—or ones very like them. Not quite so intense perhaps, their majesty weakened by the ages, but still she knew them, and for the first time her memory did not fail her. A name came to her.

Jalan.

Those were Jalan's eyes.

Arantar stepped into the darkness within the rock.

Again the darkness took her.

This darkness was different. Not warm but hot and foul. Choking. She fled this darkness, clawing for clean air and light.

And so she came out of the great column of smoke, and beneath her was a field of battle, men and women dying amid steel, flame, and spell. Though death filled the valley, it was near the center, amid the clashing of steel and the cries of dying men, where the battle would be decided.

In the midst of his elite guard stood a man wreathed in tentacles of flame. The fire did not touch his robes nor catch in his thick, black hair. The top halves of skulls—both humans and beasts—dangled from his necklace, and within their eye sockets flickered a terrible life and vitality. The man did not radiate power. He drank it in. Frost spiraled from his fingertips and enveloped entire lines of the opposing forces, freezing them where they stood, still as statues.

"For Nar!" the sorcerer's forces shouted as they ran forward. They struck the frozen soldiers. Limbs broke off, heads cracked, and some few shattered into hundreds of shards.

Still more warriors rushed forward to replace their fallen comrades. The sorcerer sent shards of ice, some large as daggers, some small as needles, into their midst. They ripped through exposed flesh, sending a fine mist of blood to the ground.

Scores of men died this way. Dozens more fled.

The front lines of the opposing armies met, sword and spear clashing on shield. Protected by their line, wizards from the opposing forces summoned magical shields to block the sorcerer's spells. The ice and frost broke on the invisible energy, and for the drawing of a breath the Nar advance faltered.

The sorcerer chanted an incantation, and his own power absorbed the energy from the wizards. Their shields melted away, and he renewed his attacks.

"Gaugan!" shouted the Nar as they renewed their attack. "Gaugan! For Nar! For Nar!"

The opposing force's wizards died beneath sword and upon spear, and for a moment the Nar stood upon an open field, their foes fleeing back like the receding tide. But the tide parted around one who stood in the midst of the slaughter.

She saw him, standing with staff in hand, the winds from the Nar sorcerer's spells sending his robes whipping around him. He was older, but she knew him. Arantar. Beside him stood another, similar in coloring, though his eyes were dark and his frame smaller. Where Arantar stood with the weight of years in his countenance, the one beside him still had the look of youth about him. Fading, yes, but still there.

The two men raised their staffs. Every spell the Nar sorcerer sent against them, these two broke or sent back into the lines of Nar soldiers.

The warriors who had fled before the Nar now turned, reformed their lines, and charged, shouting, "For Raumathar!"

Concern wrinkled the Nar sorcerer's brow, the briefest flicker of what could only have been fear, and then he smiled and began a new incantation. His back stiffened, his eyes rolled, showing only bloodshot white, and the muscles beneath his skin vibrated with a sick vitality.

Behind him the air cracked and widened. Within the torn reality yawned blackness, and a wind poured forth, cold enough to freeze skin and crack bone.

Five creatures, each twice the height of a man, clawed their way out of the ragged portal. They were like nothing that walked under the gods' sunlight. More insect than humanoid, they nevertheless walked on two legs, their mandibles clacking like the breaking of boulders, their long tails, covered in jagged barbs, whipped about their bodies, some even striking into the Nar ranks and ripping through armor and flesh alike.

The Nar sorcerer pointed at the two Raumathari sorcerers. The five abominations struck the earth, tearing through grass and soil, and charged.

The younger of the sorcerers stepped back, eyes wide and rimmed with fear, but Arantar stood his ground. Even as the first wave of frigid wind hit him, he raised his staff, looked to the sky, and shouted, "Father!"

Darkness and cold seemed to falter, as if their foundation had been struck with a great hammer, and now tiny cracks ran through them.

She looked down on Arantar, and two beings seemed to stand there in his frame, two hearts beating in his chest, and two minds looking out from his golden eyes. They shone with righteous indignation and a joy so pure that she cried out in wonder.

The five creatures roared in defiance and agony, then struck at Arantar with claw and spell. The world melted away, flowing in great spirals, and as she fell, she heard Arantar laughing.

In the silence, she wept at the absence of Arantar's laughter. Within it she had heard a power and majesty from beyond the circles of this world, and in its absence her heart felt heavy, yet strangely empty.

Sound returned before sight, speaking a language she had never heard. Still, the meaning came through in her mind.

"He is dangerous, Khasoreth." In this voice, deep and rich, she heard the faintest echo of that sweet laughter. "You know this."

"I do know it," said another voice, this one younger. "Gaugan is dangerous, master. As are you—the most dangerous man in all the Empire."

"I do not use my power to dominate. To conquer."

"Nor did he, at first. He was as much victim as victor. You saw those devils he summoned. They fought at his command, but the leash by which he held them tore at his soul. You sensed it as well as I. They were using him as much as he used them."

"All the more reason to be wary of him."

"Wary, yes. But to murder him—"

"*Execute,* Khasoreth. Execute. You know his crimes. None would call his death unjust."

"No. But what is it that you have told me since before you taught me my first spell? 'In justice, let us remember mercy.'"

Sight began to return to her, slowly at first but growing with each breath. Arantar and the other, younger man, Khasoreth obviously—where had she heard that name?—stood in an empty hall. As she saw it more clearly, she realized that to call this a hall would be like calling the Trackless Sea a "body of water." Words did it no justice.

Stone so white that it almost hurt the eyes made up the floor, the ceiling, and the great columns that joined them. Veins of gold and silver ran throughout the stone, fine as spider silk. The walls were of a darker, though no less smooth, stone. More the color of summer-sky clouds, heavy with rain, though not yet to the point of bursting.

Artisans had carved scenes of battle into the very walls

with such skill that she thought they might move at any moment. The grasses upon which heroes trod seemed to wave, and the blossom-laden trees through which they walked seemed to flutter in a unseen wind. Set between the great columns, brass braziers lit the room and filled it with warmth, their coals glowing with an almost golden radiance.

Arantar stood a few paces away from one of the great columns, his arms crossed over his chest and his brows low and heavy over his eyes. He was dressed much as she had first seen him—in rough cloth and leathers covered by an animal-skin cloak.

Before him stood Khasoreth, resplendent in clothes of linen and silk. The wine-red cloak draping his shoulders had threads of gold and gems woven into the hem, and his boots and gloves were of the finest lambskin.

Arantar looked away, more intent on his own thoughts, and said, "It might be no mercy to let him live, my friend. His heart is dark as winter's heart."

"Is he beyond redemption, then?"

Arantar shook his head, then smiled down upon the younger man, but there was more sadness in the expression than anything. "The emperor has spoken, Khasoreth. Gaugan must die. You know this."

"Yes," said the younger man. "And I know that the emperor's sister loves you, and you her. Were you to suggest—"

"You would have me meddle? Question the word of the emperor?"

Khasoreth laughed. "It's not as though you've never done it before. Were it not for Isenith whispering in his ear, he would have banished you dozens of times already. That business three years ago almost had him ordering your head brought to him on a spear. I'm not asking you to do anything you don't know to be right. 'In justice remember mercy.' Yes?"

Arantar opened his mouth to answer, but what he said she did not hear. The world melted away again, and she felt herself falling.

Images swirled before her, running together so that she could not often separate one from another. She saw—

—Arantar walking the grasslands in summer and through snow, ever seeking, seeking . . . what—?

—the Emperor of Raumathar granting mercy to one of the greatest foes his realm had ever faced. Gaugan the Nar, Gaugan sorcerer, Gaugan summoner of devils knelt before him, swearing loyalty, submission—

—Arantar standing in a royal bedchamber, the only light from one small candle, and the emperor's sister rushing to his arms—

—Khasoreth, his eyes alight with eagerness, standing upon a grassy hill that fell away to a pebble-strewn beach, then endless water. His hands wove intricate patterns in the air, his fingers dancing, and frost and ice came to his command. Laughing, he turned to the Nar sorcerer, who stood behind him, nodding in approval—

—"Take care, my friend," said Arantar. "I do not trust Gaugan's counsel." Khasoreth frowned—

—Arantar stood upon the height of the wooden tower, the Great Ice Sea extending to the far horizon below. The other towers of Winterkeep stood beneath him. He and Isenith stood upon the tallest, the Tower of Summer Sun. The wind off the sea blew back her cloak, and her hands went instinctively to her belly, which was just beginning to swell. Arantar smiled—

—"I beg of you," said Arantar, "do not do this! You are not ready."

"I am ready!" said Khasoreth, more than a little anger entering his voice. "More than ready. Besides, my apprentices will be there to assist me."

"Apprentices, Khasoreth. Apprentices! They are less ready than you. You are endangering those four as much as you. This is madness!"

Khasoreth's eyes narrowed. "Gaugan believes me ready. He said your jealousy would not allow you to see it."

"Gaugan?" Arantar looked as if he had been struck. "His whispers have poisoned your senses. Listen to me, Kha—"

"I am through listening to you, *Master.*" He spoke the last word in a sneer. "I thank you for all your years of teaching and counsel. But I am the master now."

Again the world fell away—

Khasoreth stood upon the promontory, the Hill of the Witness Tree at his back, the Great Ice Sea at his feet. The wind from the north, bringing the season's first snow, made his cloak seem like wings behind him. The hem of the rich garment, a great cloak the color of ash—the royal winter colors of Raumathar—given to him by the emperor himself, slapped at the torso of his nearest apprentice. They too had cloaks like their master, though the clothes beneath them were not nearly so fine. Three more apprentices stood not far behind their master, the last standing upon the lowest step of the hill itself. Gaugan stood off to the side, two arms' lengths away from Khasoreth's outstretched hand.

Khasoreth looked to Gaugan, his face exultant. "I am ready!" he said.

Gaugan nodded and smiled. "Let it be done."

"Let it begin!" said Khasoreth, then began his incantation.

His four apprentices joined in, their tomes held open before them. Khasoreth had no such need. He had long since committed the rite to memory. As the sun set behind the clouds in the west, he would leave these mortal coils behind and achieve the union he had long desired—to become one with the element of cold and ice rather than simply wielding their power. Arantar was wrong. Gaugan had once served dark powers, but upon swearing loyalty to Raumathar he left such pursuits behind. Without him, Khasoreth would never have achieved such power and knowledge so quickly.

The wind increased, driving the snow into his face and eyes and bringing a harsh, stinging spray off the sea that froze before it hit him. Still he chanted, and the wind blew even stronger.

Cold and ice came at his command, and the beings who

knew them as their very nature came at his summoning, answering his call and joining their voices to his. He spoke in rhythm with the crash of the waves, and his apprentices wove their own spells around his, four melodies creating a harmony around his driving beat.

Khasoreth felt ice forming on his skin, in his hair, freezing the water in his eyes, and he smiled. It was working.

Then came the pain.

Slight at first, building not in his body but deep within his mind. The spark of life, the fire of his humanity, flickered and for a moment faltered.

Khasoreth's smile fell, and he added force to the incantation.

The pain increased. He heard one of his apprentices cry out, heard the pages of his tome being ripped away by the wind. Within the howl of the wind, behind the song of the elements, he heard cold laughter.

The pain hit him again, even harder this time.

Khasoreth looked to Gaugan. "Help me!"

Gaugan rushed forward and fell to his knees. "Release me!" He pointed to the collar round his neck. The runes engraved there, the incantations binding his power, seemed to glow as the frost thickened in their crevices. "I cannot help you while bound!"

Khasoreth hesitated, and Arantar's words from years ago ran through his mind—"*His heart is dark as winter's heart.*"

The pain in Khasoreth's mind flared to true agony. His heart hammered in his chest, but every other beat was weaker. His four apprentices were screaming.

Khasoreth brought his staff around, spoke the word of power, and struck the collar round Gaugan's neck.

A flash of light, and the collar fell away in six shards to clatter on the ground. Gaugan stood and laughed. His hands wove an intricate pattern through his own incantation, his back arched, his eyes rolled back in his head, and the muscles beneath his skin tightened to the point of tearing.

The winter sky behind him split, and the wind that came

through it held the stench of death and decay. Five sets of eyes peered out with cold fire, claws rent the air, and they came into the world, screaming.

Gaugan laughed, his voice breaking in his own exultation. It lasted only a moment.

The creatures fell upon him, rending and tearing. "No!" he cried. "No, I—" then he had no more throat with which to scream, and the gale blew his blood upon the stairs leading up to the Witness Tree.

The gash in reality slammed shut, and the five devils fell upon Khasoreth and his apprentices.

Winter howled off the Great Ice Sea. The Road of the Sun, leading from the Royal Colonnade in Winterkeep to the Isle of Witness, could not withstand the onslaught of wind and wave. The wooden bridges fell, their stone supports crumbling. But in their ruin, five shapes, each swathed in a cloak the color of cold ash, emerged from the storm.

Death came to Winterkeep.

Screams still filled the night when Arantar returned to Winterkeep. Too late to save the royal city, he knew, but not too late to save those lives that remained.

He found Isenith just inside the South Wall. She was leading survivors out of the city—servants mostly, but also a few guards, their eyes no less fearful than the others'. Isenith held the baby in one arm while she used the other to issue orders.

"Where is he?" said Arantar. "Where is Khasoreth?"

"I don't know!" said Isenith. Tears streaked her face and froze upon her cheeks. "My brother said—"

"Where is the emperor?"

"Dead!" she shrieked, the first hint of hysteria entering her voice. "Oh, Arantar, they're all dead."

"I must find Khasoreth. Together, perhaps he and I can put an end to this."

"Don't leave me! Arantar, the baby—!"

"Lead the people west. Get them to safety. Trathenik should be headed this way with his cavalry. Tell him what has happened. Tell him to shun Winterkeep until I send word. Allow no one to come near."

"But, Aran—"

A great crash cut her off as the Tower of the Sun toppled into the city, crushing buildings and people beneath it. So great was the storm that even Arantar could no longer distinguish the howling of the wind from the cries of the damned.

"Go, Isenith! Go! Take our child to safety." He gave her a last embrace, placed a tender hand on the bundle of his son, and pushed them out the gate. The others followed, the guards last. Arantar grabbed the final soldier, stopping him. He turned him and looked down into his eyes. "See them away. Should any harm befall my wife and son . . ."

"My life for theirs, Honored One," said the soldier, and he bowed.

Arantar pushed him after the others and turned into the city.

She watched as if from a great height, seeing and hearing everything, even feeling the cold, though it did her no harm. People fled in every direction, dragging children and carrying what few possessions they could. The Royal Guard and City Watch offered some resistance, but the five creatures in the ash-gray cloaks froze them where they stood, destroyed buildings, and summoned the winds of winter to topple the last of the towers of Winterkeep.

Following the sounds of slaughter, Arantar at last came to face the destroyers of the capital of Raumathar. They stood before him, the wind whipping their cloaks like banners. One stood foremost. Upon seeing Arantar, he stopped and lowered his cowl.

Arantar stopped and stared, his mouth hanging open. "Khasoreth? What . . . I—"

The thing that had been Khasoreth laughed and struck, sending shards of ice at his former master.

Arantar rebuffed the attack, then another and another. After repelling the fourth, he struck back, but the five sorcerers absorbed the force he sent against them and used it to fuel their own strength. Spells flew faster than the snows driven by the gale, and shields of magic shattered and reformed themselves. Again and again the five struck at Arantar and he struck back. Their battle raged throughout the city, neither side gaining the upper hand, but Arantar's stand allowed the last of the survivors to escape onto the steppe.

The five sorcerers called forth beings from the darkest planes to fight for them, but Arantar bound them and sent them back. He in turn sent fire and lightning upon his foes, but they blocked every strike. Their battle took them into the skies themselves as the combatants rode the winds of winter and magic.

She watched as Arantar alighted upon the Isle of Witness, now an island in truth since the bridges joining it to the city lay beneath the waves. There, under the winter-bare boughs of the Witness Tree, Arantar made his last stand. His eyes shone forth bright, but with each strike their light was growing dimmer. His foes surrounded him, and she watched as he leaned in weariness against the trunk of the great tree. His hand shook, and his staff fell from his hands to clatter down the stone steps.

Seeing his foes approaching, Arantar smiled, closed his eyes, raised his face to the heavens, and called out, "Father!"

The fabric of creation seemed to vibrate, as if a great bell had been struck or clarion sounded. The gait of the five sorcerers faltered, and when Arantar opened his eyes, they shone a white purer than the noonday sun. Again she looked, and it was as if two beings stood in Arantar's frame, one a man of Raumathar, wanderer of the steppes, and councilor of kings, and the other . . . beyond all that, one who looked down on the petty bickerings of kings and laughed.

The five sorcerers howled in fury and struck, calling upon every spell they knew as they charged up the hill.

Arantar and the Other struck back, and it was as if she could see beyond reality, see every note and harmony within the song of reality. The five were darkness and shadow infusing the bodies of Khasoreth and his four apprentices, and they drank in all warmth and corrupted all life around them. The attack from Arantar and the Other did not strengthen that disharmony, but rather fed it, pouring holy light and life into the never-ending hunger. The five screamed, and four fell to the ground. The dark infusion, the thousands of tendrils of unlife burrowed into their souls, twisted, frayed, and broke.

The thing that had been Khasoreth fell to his hands and knees upon the ice-slick steps and looked up at Arantar. In the light cast by Arantar's countenance, the shadow lifted from Khasoreth's face, and his eyes cleared. "Master . . . please. Remember. Remember . . . mercy."

The exultant smile upon Arantar's face faltered, and his countenance deepened to what she could only call a profound pity. The light dimmed—

—and Khasoreth struck, sending a thick arm of darkness crashing into his former master. The thing within him shrieked in unholy delight.

Arantar stumbled against the tree, and the thing that had been Khasoreth leaped, falling upon his former master with fist, tooth, and spell.

She watched as the Other within Arantar gathered and concentrated his strength to strike.

No! said Arantar, though his lips did not move. *Mercy.*

The pure light in Arantar's eyes evaporated, and the Other began to lift away—

—but the thing that had been Khasoreth struck, its great arm of darkness seizing the Other, tearing at him.

For an instant—she knew it was no more than that, though it seemed to stretch for an eternity—darkness warred with light, then light surrendered. Arantar breathed his last, a small smile upon his lips, and the Other fell.

The five creatures of darkness seized it, and she watched as they battered and tore at it. Again and again they tried, but to no avail.

The Other sought the last bit of warmth, the last living thing upon the island—the Witness Tree—and fell into it. With a cry of triumph, the five struck, unable to destroy the now-hallowed tree, but sealing it with their darkest spells so that the Other could escape to oppose them no more.

Her vision followed them throughout the years. Winterkeep lay fallen and shunned by all people, but true victory had been taken from the five devils. The last attack by Arantar and the Other had warped their spell. Not only were they trapped within the bodies of the five sorcerers, but much to their dismay the bodies of Khasoreth's apprentices grew old, weak, and approached death as all men do. Filled with the dark powers, their bodies lasted many generations, but die they did.

In their desperation the five devils refined their spells and sought the ancient magics of the people of the world in which they found themselves. Try as they might, they could find no way to free themselves from their imprisonment nor stop the decay of their mortal homes. But they did find a way for their fell spirits to seize other mortal forms.

But only a chosen few.

She watched as the years passed and the ruins of Winterkeep blew away with each passing winter or were buried beneath soil and snow. Powerful as the dark arts of the five were, they could not overcome one flaw. No mere mortal could contain them, but only those in whom the blood of Arantar and Isenith flowed.

She watched as Isenith learned the life of an exile, watching her son grow up, often in hunger and want. But he grew to a man that made his mother proud, though the sadness never left her eyes. Her son married, had many children, and his children had children, the royal blood of Raumathar mixing throughout the years with the peoples of the steppes. The first did not disappear until Arantar's great-grandson was a young man. The second a few years after that—and then two others. Then no more for three generations.

She watched as the five sorcerers fled into the dark north, seeking the coldest lands they could find, forever shunning lands of light and warmth.

Her vision narrowed as she followed the strain of Arantar and Isenith's blood down through the ages. A king, warlords, shepherds, farmers, sorcerers, thieves, and slaves—all these and more were the fates of Arantar's offspring. In most, the blood of Arantar grew weaker with each passing generation, the golden eyes fading, the gifts of his heritage becoming only distant melodies in dreams. But in one line the blood ran strong and true, and her vision followed that line through the ages, seeing it mingle, dilute, and fade, only to gather strength as the bloodlines mingled again.

Then came the Horde, and one man's ambition that would bring nations to war and change the fate of Amira Hiloar forever. The young war wizard fought in many battles, killing and almost being killed so many times that she stopped counting. War became her life. Every day different but torturously the same. Until the day of the battle near the Well of the Broken Antlers, when a Tuigan warlord fled his camp before the Cormyrean troops. The warlord's warriors slaughtered every servant, slave, and captive in camp, leaving nothing for the westerners to take. One of Arantar and Isenith's descendants hid her child amid a collapsed tent before her lord's men cut her down. The Tuigan galloped off eastward. The dust of the horses' passage settled, and the little boy crawled from the tentcloth to find his dead mother. He looked up, and his eyes were golden.

Jalan.

Amira's eyes snapped open and she sat up. She was still in the cavern of *Hro'nyewachu*. The stone pedestal, still drenched in blood, was not far away. The remains of the deer carcass and the heart were gone. How long she had lain on the stone floor, how long she had . . . dreamed, seen, whatever it had been. But her hair was dry, and the blood from her grisly meal felt hard and dry on her skin.

You found what you sought?

Amira turned. The oracle was standing behind her, the pale eyes no longer lit with hunger but with . . . what? Amira wondered. Was that sympathy?

"Was it . . . ?" Amira said. Her throat felt raw. Burned. "Was it real? What I saw? What I heard?"

The oracle canted her head—a thoroughly inhuman gesture that reminded Amira of a bird. *The dreamroad,* she said, her lips still not moving, the voice coming straight to Amira's mind, *the waking world, sleeping, waking . . . who is to say where reality begins and ends? The same mind that sees the world around you, that loves and hates and wars and creates, is the same mind that dreams. Why cling to one and discard the other?*

"So Arantar, Khasoreth . . . Gaugan, all of it. I saw it as it happened? It wasn't some dream inspired by the belkagen's fireside tales."

The words of a belkagen spoken by fire are not to be taken lightly. A smile flickered across the oracle's face, faint and fleeting, but in the instant she saw it, Amira thought it looked a little sad. *It has been many turnings of the world since Arantar last came to me. This world has not seen his like since, nor will it again.*

Amira considered all she had seen, and the urgency hit her all at once. "I must go," she said. "Jalan . . ."

The scion of Arantar is in grave danger, said the oracle. *His life teeters on the precipice.*

Amira stood and brushed the sand and grit off her bare skin. She looked up at the oracle, and she was struck by how tall the oracle really was. She would not have looked down upon Gyaidun. She would have *towered* over him.

You have a cold road ahead of you, said the oracle. *Out of affection for a friend long gone, I grant you one last question.*

It came to Amira at once, the only question worth asking, the only answer she needed. "How do I beat them?"

The oracle smiled, and again it was the hungry gaze of the predator. *The Witness Tree. There, all will be decided. Beyond that, I give you no assurances. Death and life will meet. Only those who surrender will triumph.*

"Surrender?" said Amira. " 'Death and life will meet?' What does that mean?"

The oracle's smiled broadened, her full lips pulling back over teeth that were pointed and sharp, fangs that seemed to glisten in the cavern's blood red light.

"Never mind," said Amira. She looked around. There was no sign of the pool where the belkagen had taken her. "How . . . how do I get out of here?"

I said one question, said the oracle. *Now, you owe me.*

Snarling, the oracle struck.

CHAPTER NINETEEN

Hro'nyewachu

The belkagen's concern had long since deepened to worry, and his worry was becoming true fear. Lady Amira had been gone for too long. It had been near midnight when she'd entered the pool, and in his heart that knew the turning of the seasons and the paths of the stars like a husband knows the curves of his wife's body, the belkagen knew dawn was not far away. Amira had been gone too long.

He stood at the water's edge, leaning upon his staff, its green light reflecting off the water. After Amira had gone, the ripples left in her wake had caught the staff's light and painted the cavern in dancing light and shadow, but it had long since returned to a calm broken only by the minuscule plipping of water droplets falling from the ceiling. Now, save for one spot several paces out where the light of his staff floated like a tiny green moon, the water was black as slate.

The belkagen stood waiting, his eyes open but no longer really watching. Alone in the darkness, the words he had spoken to Lady Amira came back to him—

"*Hro'nyewachu* has a mother's heart. You have a mother's need. Your hearts will beat the same song, I think. I could brave *Hro'nyewachu* again, and if you refuse, I will go."

He had said it, had he not?

I could brave *Hro'nyewachu* again . . . I will go.

. . . I will go . . .

. . . I will go . . .

. . . brave *Hro'nyewachu* again . . .

His words came to him again and again, almost as if they were the echoes of the water *drip-drip-dripping* into the pool before him.

Should he go after her? In his heart, he knew there was nothing he could do for her. He'd told her that, as well, and he knew it to be true. But neither could he just walk away. Not without knowing. Even if he couldn't help her, perhaps there was something he could learn to help them, some new vision that—

He heard a splash. Not of something falling into the water. Nothing that hard. But he heard something breaking the surface of the water out beyond the reach of his light.

"Lady Amira?" he called.

Nothing. Just the steady *plip-plip* of water droplets hitting the pool. But as he watched, the small globe of light reflecting on the surface rippled. Something had disturbed the water farther out.

He listened, his ears straining, but there was nothing more.

The belkagen raised his staff and spoke an incantation. The flames flickering along its tip roared to new life, a green beacon in the darkness.

There!

Something was floating in the water. It wasn't moving.

The belkagen tore at the ties of his cloak and left it piled on the shore. It would soak in the water and weigh him down. His clothes would as well, but he didn't want to take the time to remove them.

Staff held high, he charged into the water. The shape floated several paces away, the waves caused by his passage pushed it farther out. He could make out no distinct features, but even in the dim light he could see long, dark hair and fair skin. He cursed and pushed his legs harder.

The water was splashing up his chest and over his shoulders when he drew close enough to reach out and grab the figure. His fingers closed around wet hair and he pulled. It was Amira, floating facedown in the water. The belkagen got a better grip on her forearm, then dragged her back to shore.

He threw her down and turned her over. Her skin was pale, cold to the touch, and her lips were blue. Long, wet tendrils of her hair spread over her bare breasts, and the belkagen saw that her chest did not move. She wasn't breathing.

"No!" He threw his staff aside and knelt beside her. Closing his eyes, he sent his senses through her body, washing over and through her skin, down into muscle, blood, and bone. There! Life still flickered within her, faint and growing weaker with each passing moment, but it was still there.

She is not dead.

The belkagen started and looked up. A great she-wolf, fur gray as clouds laden with spring rain, stood before the entrance, staring down at him with eyes the color of moonlight.

"Hro'nyewachu!" said the belkagen.

The she-wolf walked toward him, and with each step her form blurred and swirled, and motes of light and darkness danced before the belkagen's eyes. When she stopped a few paces away, a tall, lithe woman stood over him. Whatever color her skin was, it was hidden beneath a dark, slick wetness that by the smell the belkagen knew to be blood, though not from any creature that walked in this world. Her hair was made up in scores of tight braids that hung to her waist, and bits of bone, feathers, and spring flowers peeked out from among them. In her right hand she held a staff almost as long as she was tall. It was made from some golden-red wood flecked with darker grains of brown and black. The belkagen had never seen its like.

You remember me, Kwarun. Though her lips did not move, he heard her husky voice clearly in his mind. *It has been many years.*

"I . . . I could never forget you, Holy One," said the belkagen, and for a moment the years did not weigh so heavily upon him, and he remembered a younger Kwarun, who had come here seeking wisdom and power—and the price he'd paid. It had come with pleasure and pain. He remembered the feel of the oracle's skin under his caresses, the burning heat of her breath—even now, his heart beat faster at the memory—and the agony of the burden she'd placed on him.

Not long now, said the oracle. *The burden shall be yours not much longer.*

"That will be both pain and relief."

As are all things worth having.

"Holy One," said the belkagen, and he looked down upon Amira. "Why . . . ? Is she . . . ?"

She lives.

"You did this to her."

Do you care for her so much? The oracle leaned forward slightly and sniffed. *Have you given your heart to her?*

"You know I haven't."

The oracle's eyes flashed. *I do know it. I could smell a lie on you—and I do not. Your truth pleases me. You know my jealousy.*

"Is that why you did this to her?"

No.

"Then why?"

She was impertinent. Arrogant. Still, she has a hunter's heart. Teach her some humility, and she might be great one day.

"What is wrong with her, Holy One?"

The oracle did not answer, and the belkagen looked up. Her form had shrunk somewhat, her features softened into the young maiden that a young Kwarun had first met so many years ago. A small smile played across her lips, but around her eyes was sadness.

I wanted a moment alone with you, she said, *before your final road. We shall not meet again. You should have come to me more often during your time in this world.*

"Our last coupling nearly killed me, Holy One."

You did not seem to mind at the time.

Kwarun blushed at the memory and found himself chuckling.

I have a gift for the girl, said the oracle, and she held up the staff.

"It will help her save her son?"

No, said the oracle as she knelt and placed the gold-red staff in Amira's limp hand. *But it will sharpen the bite she gives her enemies. Saving her son . . . that task is for another.*

"Another, Holy One?" said the belkagen. "Who?"

Amira's hand closed around the staff, she took a deep breath, and the oracle was gone.

CHAPTER TWENTY

The Endless Wastes

Jalan discovered something he had not known since Walloch's slavers captured him and his mother. Hope. That and just a sliver of pride. They swelled in him, giving warmth to a heart that had known only cold for many days.

He still wasn't sure how he had done it, but he knew one thing for certain: He had *hurt* that bastard. Hurt him bad. That thing in the ash-gray cloak had threatened to gouge out his eye, and he had taken the thing's own dagger and made it blaze like the sun. The shriek the cloaked leader had uttered had been surprise, yes, but also pain and *fear*—and that more than anything . . . felt good. Give that bastard a taste of his own toxin and see how he likes it, Jalan thought.

Trussed like the huntsman's catch on the back of the huge wolf as he was, cramped and sore, his skin raw from the ropes' chafing, still Jalan had to fight to keep his eyes open as the wolves ran over the steppe. He'd awakened as they'd left camp, still dazed from the cloaked leader striking him, his ribs still aching from where the barbarian had kicked him. All that after the long rest should have chased sleep far away, but still Jalan had to fight it.

His mind felt thick and foggy. Had his captors given him something, some foul concoction poured down his throat while he was unconscious? He couldn't remember.

Maybe something worse. Maybe the cloaked leader had done something to his mind. He shivered at the thought, but for once the idea of that monster hurting him didn't make him afraid. It made him angry, and he knew he had something inside him that could hurt that monster.

Jalan realized that miles had passed. The air felt frigid and thick. And when had it started snowing? Already the wolves ran through a thick blanket of snow. And still it kept falling and falling from the sky—huge, wet flakes that steamed as they melted off the wolf's pelt in front of him.

True wakefulness returned before dawn, and Jalan passed the time trying to dredge up whatever power had caused that dagger to shine. He knew beyond doubt that he had done it. He'd felt the power flow through him like blood through an opened vein. But how?

He searched for that thing inside him, that living otherness he'd felt so strongly not long ago. When the power had shot through him, it had felt . . . beyond good. Wonderful. Intoxicating. He could still sense it—see it almost, but no matter how hard he concentrated, it remained elusive and distant. It might as well have been the sun shining above the surface of the water, and he the drowning man, reaching out, the light forever beyond his grasp.

The hope that Jalan had cherished all night began to fade again.

He closed his eyes. Concentrating all his will, he prayed, *Vyaidelon! Vyaidelon, help me!*

Nothing. He hadn't heard a thing from Vyaidelon since the dream three nights ago. Maybe it had been just a dream. His heart knew better, but doubt was beginning to nag at him.

Jalan's heart lurched as the wolf on which he rode leaped into the air, then fell and fell. A scream was building in Jalan's throat—he was sure the stupid beast had gone snow-blind and run them off a cliff—when the wolf's paws struck the ground, causing Jalan to bite the inside of his cheek. The wolf ran on, and Jalan heard others making the jump behind him.

The flatness of the land was ending, the steppe beginning to rise and fall in long hills—some miles wide. Amid the rolling snowfields, fissures broke the earth. Most likely gullies where the spring rains gathered and ran on their way to the Great Ice Sea.

The wolves leaped down or sometimes all the way across the smaller valleys. The huge wolves were surprisingly sure-footed and found their way in and out of even the most treacherous of the snow-covered gashes in the earth.

The light was strong enough that Jalan could see several paces in every direction when they stopped at a wide gully with sides so steep that they were forced to search for a safe way down. Jalan watched as their cloaked leader spoke with his barbarian servants. Even a few of the wolves seemed to be attending to the conversation. Although Jalan could not understand their words, he guessed what they were talking about. If he could see this far in such a fierce storm, it meant the sun had risen. Every day so far they had stopped to camp before sunrise. Despite the cloaked leader's power, he seemed unable to abide the daylight.

Scouts scattered up and down each side of the gully, the great wolves pawing and sniffing. A small chorus of howls announced success, and shortly after the entire band was gathering about a small overhang on the northern side of the gully. The body of two wolves, both torn and mangled, their blood spotting the snow, lay on the ground not far away. Tracks led off eastward where more had fled. Jalan watched as one of the pale barbarians crawled out of a shield-sized hole in the gully wall, pulling the body of another dead wolf behind him.

Several of the wolves from the northerners' band began feasting on the remains of the pack whose den they'd just pillaged. Jalan grimaced and turned away. His gaze fell on the leader, snow dusting the ash-gray of his cloak, who had dismounted and was headed straight for him.

Jalan pulled away, but his mount lowered to its haunches, and the leader cut him loose. The wolf bounded away, and the leader grabbed Jalan by the rope around his chest and held him up with one hand. Jalan found himself staring into the darkness of the hood. He could make out no distinct features, just a pale blur hinting at the face within.

"Good," said the leader. "You're awake. It will make our business easier."

Rope still bound Jalan's wrists and elbows, but his legs were free and he kicked at the leader's torso. One blow connected, but it was like striking a tree.

The hand released him, and Jalan fell. After riding for so long in one position, his legs were stiff. Pain shot through his joints. He was halfway to his knees when he felt the leader's hand grabbing his hair. Jalan just had time to take a quick breath before his face was slammed into the snow. The first time was more surprise than pain, for the snow was thick. But the second truly hurt, and with the third blow his face went all the way through the snow to the rocky ground beneath.

"Enough?"

Jalan found himself looking up into the dark confines of the hood, though he had no memory of being picked up.

"Stop struggling," said the leader, "or I will begin truly hurting you."

Jalan tasted blood, snow, and grit in his mouth, but he swallowed it, afraid that spitting it out would be seen as a sign of defiance. Again his mind scrabbled for the power inside him. He found it, but it was dormant, and nothing he did could rouse it.

"This is the very behavior we are about to correct," said the leader, and he set off through the snow, dragging Jalan behind him.

Jalan could see little more than the hem of the leader's cloak and boots and the snowy ground beneath, but judging from the general direction, he knew where they were headed.

The leader ducked into the entrance of the wolf den and pulled Jalan after. As the darkness closed over him, panic set in, and raw instinct almost took over and set Jalan to kicking and streaming, but the last of his conscious mind and will held on. He closed his eyes and tried to prepare for the worst.

The tunnel was short, turned upward near the end, and ended in a fair-sized burrow. It was dim but not altogether dark. The all-covering snow outside reflected the light quite some way into the tunnel. Scraps of bone and tufts of hair littered the ground. Roots from the grass on the surface hung down from the ceiling. Then the light winked out—someone had covered the entrance—and Jalan found himself in complete darkness with the thing inside the ash-gray cloak. His nose was overwhelmed with the thick, musky scent of animal, and what little warmth had been left in the den fell into the presence of the cloaked leader like water funneling down a drain. Jalan shivered.

"Long, long years it has been," said a voice from the darkness. "Long years since we found one where the blood runs as pure as it does in you. I almost wish it were my time. Gerghul will be pleased with you. You will last a long time."

"D-don't make me hurt you," Jalan said, but even he heard the empty threat. His hoarse whisper, just on the verge of tears. "I can, you know. I w-will. D-don't—"

"Yes, you can. I know you can. And that is why we are here. We'll have no more of that."

Hands cold as tomb frost seized Jalan and pulled him close. He kicked and tried to pull away, but the thing's strength was implacable. He could feel breath, cold and fetid on his face, and he choked. Bile rose to his throat and tears streamed down his cheeks.

In the darkness before him, less than a hand's width away, he saw two rings of cold fire, like a starlight nimbus filtered through frost. Eyes. They were eyes rimmed in ice, vast and empty. Portals to nothingness, and Jalan felt himself falling in, trying to find something to hold onto, but there was nothing. Drowning. He was drowning in emptiness.

Then something was with him. In his mind. Something hungry and very much aware of him. He could feel its full attention bearing down on him, coming closer.

Jalan could no longer feel his body, but in his mind he screamed. Then the thing had him.

Hro'nyewachu

During the night, the mists froze on the steppes below *Akhrasut Neth,* and the sky let loose a great cascade of snow—thick, wet flakes that fell harder with each passing moment. By the time the first hint of dawn—no more than a lightening of the dark curtain in the east—struck the sky, *Akhrasut Neth* and all the surrounding lands lay beneath new snow.

Still Gyaidun, Lendri, and the nearby Vil Adanrath kept their vigil. The wolves found shelter beneath the boughs of the nearby trees—all save Mingan, who stayed with his master near the entrance to the cave. But he was restless, partially from the weather that kept trying to give him a blanket of snow he didn't want, but also from something else, perhaps some scent or sound coming from the cave.

It was Gyaidun, who paced only a few feet from the entrance, who saw them first.

"There!" he said.

"What is it?" said Lendri, and behind him he heard the Vil Adanrath rustling among the trees.

"A light."

Lendri saw it then—a faint greenish glow down in the cave that grew stronger with each passing moment. Before long, it was quite bright, staining even the snow outside the entrance the color of new spring leaves.

Mingan hopped around the entrance, barking and yip-ping, and Durja emerged from the folds of Gyaidun's cloak to alight upon an outcropping of stone beside the entrance.

They saw the belkagen first, his staff held high, the flames at its tip the source of the green glow. Behind him walked Amira, huddled in her cloak, her long hair still damp. Her left hand held her cloak closed against the chill, but her right held a staff almost as tall as Gyaidun.

The pair emerged from the cave. The belkagen stopped just outside the entrance, and Mingan came to lick his fingers. Gyaidun stepped to the entrance to take Amira's hand and help her up the final step. She gave him a smile of thanks. Lendri noted the weariness around her eyes.

"Are you well?" Gyaidun asked her.

"Well enough," she said. "Very tired."

"Hear me, my people!" said the belkagen.

Lendri turned and saw that the Vil Adanrath came as close as their honor would allow, hugging the treeline. His father stood just outside the nearest boughs, the falling snow dusting his head and shoulders.

"*Hro'nyewachu* guides our road," said the belkagen. "Lady Amira has sought her wisdom and lived."

The Vil Adanrath, both elves and wolves, let out a great howl, and even Mingan joined in.

"Gather your strength," said the belkagen. "For tonight we hunt!"

CHAPTER TWENTY-ONE

The Endless Wastes

Screaming. Jalan could hear it, made faint by distance or . . . something else. Some barrier or thickness. The voice was familiar. He knew it. He was sure. Then it hit him. It was his own voice, the screams and yells and shrieks finally fading to pleading—all that and more in the den of the dead wolves.

Another sound intruded. Howling. But not the malicious howling of the cloaked leader's pack that reminded Jalan of cold winter and empty places. This howling came from far away, and in it he heard the call of brothers.

Jalan opened his eyes. Again he was tied to the back of one of the great wolves. The sky was dark, but the fresh snowfall seemed to gather in the tiniest bit of light and reflect it back, giving the world a muted ghostly cast. He could make out the large forms of the other wolves and their riders milling about. They'd stopped. Why?

The howling. It came from the distant horizon in front of them. Jalan had once spoken to one of the rangers who patrolled around High Horn. The man told him that wolves have a language all their own, far more intricate than most people knew. They spoke not with words, but with movement, posture, the cant of ears and tail, a look of the eye, yips, barks, growls, and over great distance they howled. What they were saying now, Jalan did not know, but the wolves of the cloaked leader's band obviously did. They seemed agitated, and Jalan could feel the growling deep within his mount's chest.

The barbarians were shouting back and forth in their own tongue. Their leader allowed it for a few moments, then cut them off with a harsh command. The barbarians stiffened, and Jalan could see that they did not approve of their lord's command but were too frightened to disagree.

The leader shouted something, and the company set off again, heading northward, straight into the chorus of howls.

Amira found Gyaidun just under the northern lip of the ridge. The broad valley, now filled with snow, spread out beneath them. She sat down beside him and huddled into her cloak. Gyaidun glanced at her, then continued watching the land beneath them. There was an agitated stirring inside his cloak that Amira knew was Durja, huddled up and trying to keep warm.

"Where is Lendri?" she asked.

"He walks the dreamroad." Gyaidun motioned up the rise, but Amira could see nothing up there but grass and bushes covered in snow. "You have been speaking with the belkagen?"

"Yes."

"Your . . . journey to *Hro'nyewachu*," said Gyaidun, "it went well?"

Amira shuddered and closed her eyes. After their day's journey—two more trips with her magic, followed by a long run; the Mother's Bed was now far, far behind them—she'd spent most of the evening discussing her vision with the belkagen. Even after seeking his wisdom, she still did not understand parts of it, but what she did disturbed her.

She now knew that she was not merely a parent on a desperate quest to save her son. She stood in the forefront of something much larger than she'd ever imagined, perhaps no more than a page or two in a long history that had been going on for thousands of years. It made her feel very small. She'd come to Gyaidun, the only other human for miles, in hopes of feeling a little less small—and not so terribly alone.

"If you don't wish to speak of it . . ." said Gyaidun.

"You want to know if I discovered anything to help your son."

"Did you?"

"I . . . don't know."

"You don't know?" Gyaidun's voice sounded flat, on the verge of anger.

"It wasn't like I thought it would be—me asking the oracle questions, her answering and demanding payment. It was—" Her body began to shiver and would not stop.

"Are you cold?" asked Gyaidun.

"Yes," she said, though in truth she wasn't. The belkagen had given her more *kanishta* roots, and beyond giving her renewed energy, they filled her body—right down to her toes and fingertips—with a pleasant, buzzing warmth.

Gyaidun moved closer, put his arm around her, and wrapped them both in his huge cloak. Durja squawked in protest but soon nestled between them quite comfortably.

"The oracle," Amira continued, "showed me . . . things. The past mostly, farther back even than the wars between Narfell and Raumathar that destroyed them both."

"What does that have to do with my son? And yours?" He was very close, and Amira could feel his breath against her ear. She was shaking so hard that her teeth were chattering.

"You remember the belkagen speaking of Arantar?"

"Yes," said Gyaidun. "Everyone in these lands knows those tales."

"If . . . if I understood correctly, it seems that Arantar is most likely one of your grandsires."

Gyaidun snorted. "You can't meet anyone between the Lake of Steam and Yal Tengri who doesn't claim Arantar or Khasoreth as their grandsire."

"Arantar had only one son before he . . . before he died. Khasoreth had no children." Speaking Khasoreth's name, the warmth coursing through her body seemed to freeze. "But Arantar's son had many children—and each of them in turn had many children. His blood spread throughout the Wastes."

"What does this have to do with Erun and Jalan?"

She had shared most of what she'd seen with the belkagen, his sharp brows furrowing deeper and deeper the longer she spoke. He'd taken it all in, adding his own bits of wisdom gleaned from years of study and learning the lore of the Wastes. And so they knew why young men were taken and who was taking them.

But the belkagen had warned her most strongly not to tell Gyaidun. She'd balked, claiming he had as much right to know as she did—and more than the belkagen—and the old elf hadn't disagreed, but he'd told her, "Gyaidun loved Hlessa and Erun more than anything. More than his own life and honor. He blames himself for their loss, the damned fool. And no amount of reasoning from you or me will convince him otherwise.

"All these years he has hoped of finding his son again. It is the one bit of tenderness left in his heart. Do not destroy that, Lady Amira. Do not. It would be a wicked thing. A cruel thing."

And so Amira told Gyaidun an abbreviated version of what she'd learned, but she did not tell him what the sorcerers did with those they took. That, she spared Gyaidun.

"These five devil-possessed sorcerers," said Gyaidun, "they are the ones who took Erun, who have Jalan?"

"At least one of them, yes," said Amira.

"And what can we do to stop them? To get Jalan back and save Erun?"

"I don't know."

"You don't know?" His voice had returned to the edge of anger. "I'm no mage or shaman, but even I can recognize runes of power when I see them. That's no walking stick she gave you."

Amira looked down at the staff across her lap. She'd spent what time she could studying it, and although the runes were like none she'd ever seen, she understood them. Whether the oracle had opened her understanding or the staff itself gave some power to its bearer, Amira did not know, but already she had learned several of its uses. She didn't know if it would be enough to kill the thing that had her son, but based on her past encounter with him, she thought it would definitely give them an advantage.

"The oracle said . . . said to get Jalan to the Witness Tree. 'Beyond that, I give you no assurances,' she said. 'Death and life will meet. Only those who surrender will triumph.' "

"And what does that mean?"

"I have no idea, Gyaidun."

She felt his entire body stiffen beside her, but he said nothing. Between them, Durja ruffled his feathers, squawked, and pushed himself from between them to perch on Gyaidun's knee.

"May I tell you something?" she asked. She turned to Gyaidun, though in the dark his face was no more than a dim shadow.

"Will anything I say prevent it?" he replied, but she heard the humor in his voice.

"My old master, my mentor, the man who was more of a father to me than my real father, told me something the night before I set out to war. He said, 'The true warrior does not fight because he hates what is in front of him. The true warrior fights because he loves what is behind him.' "

"Lady," said Gyaidun, "the bastards we are hunting took away the only ones I ever loved—butchered my wife and left her body in the open for the vultures and took my son. All I have left now is hate. Hate and a thirst for vengeance."

"And what then? What happens on the day you take your vengeance? What will you have left then?"

He looked away.

"Gyaidun?"

"Yes?"

"Hold me."

CHAPTER TWENTY-TWO

The Endless Wastes

The vanguard of winter wolves kept to their course, their pace unflagging, but every one was skittish. Winter wolves were one of the fiercest predators in the Endless Wastes, and a pack this size should have gone unchallenged. But the land ahead of them was alive with wolfsong, and in the howling the winter wolves heard a challenge. Even a huge pack of wolves should have fled before them. But these did not. They were standing their ground and urging the winter wolves on. That made the winter wolves and their riders nervous, but still their leader urged them on. And so the vanguard, ten winter wolves in all, ran.

On the crest of the rise before them they saw the smaller wolves—four furtive shadows against the white of the snow. The newcomers growled and barked, giving a show of threat, but as soon as the winter wolves headed for them, they turned tail and ran, disappearing over the hill.

The winter wolves pursued, picking up their quarry's scent as they made their way over the rise. Below them the land fell into a stand of trees where a stream most likely flowed in spring and summer. The smaller wolves were just disappearing into the cover of the trees, and the winter wolves doubled their speed, bounding down the slope in great clouds of snow.

The first entered the deep blue shadows beneath the trees, his fellows hard on his tail. A cold fire lit their eyes. As the last entered the wood, the first arrows hissed out from the high boughs, each one flying true into the sides of the winter wolves.

Yelping, the great white wolves stopped, more shocked than hurt, and looked up into the trees. Many shapes were there, silver in the meager light reflecting off the snow, each of them holding a bow. The trees were not that high, and winter wolves were good jumpers. These silver shadows would make easy prey. Their leader growled, baring his fangs, the largest of them as long as a man's hand.

The second volley tore into them, and a third just after. The winter wolves roared in pain, but only two were truly hurt—one with a shaft deep in her throat, another who had taken an arrow in the eye and was taking his last breath.

The winter wolves tightened their muscles, preparing to leap into the trees and feast on their attackers.

Wolves—the four who had acted as bait joined by ten more—hit them from two directions, tearing with their teeth and swiping with their claws. The archers cast aside their bows, drew blade or spear, and leaped down.

It was over in moments.

A hard, cold wind sliced out of the north, driving the snow almost horizontal at times. Although Yal Tengri was many miles away, Gyaidun could taste the tang of salt in the air. He'd hoped the storm would slow their quarry, that they wouldn't make it here until the sun rose beyond the thick clouds.

He remembered Amira's account of her first encounter with the sorcerer in the ash-gray cloak, how the sun had weakened him and how he had been almost no threat at all until the coming of darkness. No such luck this time. The word passed throughout the line of those waiting in ambush on the slopes above the little valley. The attack forces sent out before midnight had done their job. Their prey was being driven right where they wanted them, and they would be here at any moment.

The packs sent out to harry their quarry's scouts had annihilated every one of them, taking only minor injuries themselves. The Vil Adanrath outnumbered their foes by a great many warriors. Gyaidun had even heard—through Amira, who had heard it from the belkagen—that Leren was afraid the pack's honor might be tainted when they won such an uneven fight.

Gyaidun was not so sure. He knew the Vil Adanrath were the finest, fiercest warriors for five hundred leagues. Other than Haerul, Lendri was perhaps the most dangerous being from Yal Tengri to Almorel—and that cloaked horror had almost killed him with seemingly little effort. Had they been able to hit them after sunrise—even a sun hidden through thick layers of cloud and falling snow—Gyaidun might have felt better. But as it was, crouched alone in the unquiet darkness on the hillside, frost thick on his three-day beard, a sickening apprehension filled him. It was not fear. Gyaidun had stopped fearing death long, long ago. This was something else. An unreasoning dread that left him feeling hollow and unready.

The already frigid air went suddenly bone-cracking cold, and Gyaidun knew. That walking terror in the ash-gray cloak had arrived. Out there in the snowblind dark. Even as the knowledge hit him, he heard a great many padded feet tearing through the snow below him.

Gyaidun drew his long knife from its sheath, gripped his iron club, and charged.

Amira had lost sight of Gyaidun some time ago. He'd taken a position only a few dozen paces downslope from her, but in the darkness and driving snow, she was nearly blind. She'd never seen such weather, not even in the deepest winter at High Horn, and it was still autumn here. The snow was already knee deep in places, and the wind blew the flakes so hard that they struck any exposed flesh like tiny stones.

She pulled her left glove off with her teeth, just long enough to rummage in her pouch for another *kanishta* root and put the root in her mouth. Bitter as they were, she was developing a taste for them, and they worked wonders in keeping her warm.

The temperature dropped so swiftly that Amira saw her breath go from steam to snow before being pulled away by the wind. Her next intake of breath *hurt*. In that moment of pain coursing down her throat, she knew that the cold bit deeper than the physical. Knew beyond doubt. The devil-possessed sorcerer had come, and somewhere in the near darkness, Jalan waited for her.

She stood and gripped her new staff so tightly she felt the tendons in her fingers creak. A sudden gust of wind tried to push her over. She uttered a quick prayer and charged.

Gyaidun saw the *viliniket* before it saw him—but only barely. The horse-sized shadow loomed out of the snow, one of the pale *Siksin Neneweth* perched on his back, and almost ran over Gyaidun before it saw him.

He took advantage of the huge wolf's surprise and swung his iron club at its jaws. The beast pulled back, causing the blow to just graze its nose, then snapped forward, its jaws shutting so close that spittle hit Gyaidun's face and froze there.

A quick swipe of his knife sent the huge wolf back, and the creature reared on its hind legs. Gyaidun saw its rider raising his spear—and an arrow struck the rider in the throat. He jerked back, and the sudden change in weight overbalanced the wolf. It fell back, raising a huge cloud of snow that the wind tore away. Now riderless, it regained its footing, faced Gyaidun—and three arrows struck it in quick succession. What began as a snarl ended in a scream, then the wolves of the Vil Adanrath were on it, clawing and biting and tearing.

Amira heard the clash of steel on steel and followed it. In the darkness, she almost ran into the combatants. Two warriors faced off, their swords clashing, and in the murk of the predawn storm, Amira could not at first tell them apart. Both had skin only slightly darker than the snow in which they stood, and both sported a long mane of silver hair tossed by the wind. Each wore clothes cut and sewn from animal hides, but one was taller and had the larger form of a human, and the other—now that she was close enough, she could hear it, no mistake—was growling like a beast unchained.

She raised her staff, pointed it at the larger of the two combatants—and the sky overhead blazed. A burst of light, like a tiny piece of the sun itself, glowed in the air several dozen feet above the valley, lighting all the land beneath in harsh contrasts of frost white and blue shadow. A spell from the belkagen, Amira felt sure. Still, in the fierceness of the snowstorm she could see little but whirling white beyond the two men trying to kill each other.

The human—in the new light, she saw him clearly as one of the Frost Folk—was startled by the sudden flare. The elf before him was not. The Vil Adanrath warrior brought his single-edged blade across the human's stomach in a horizontal swipe—so hard that Amira felt blood splatter her face four paces away. The pale human's knees collapsed even as his entrails spilled on the snow before him, but the elf was already gone, seeking another foe.

Amira followed him.

Even with the new light blazing overhead, Gyaidun could not see more than a dozen paces in any direction. But he knew where to go. Just as a blindfolded man can come to the fire by following the heat in the air, so Gyaidun knew where to find the thing in the ash-gray cloak. This cold was beyond anything an autumn snowstorm could muster. Gyaidun had the protection from the elements offered to him by the blessings of his covenant as *athkaraye* to the Vil Adanrath, and his body was swathed in thick hides and furs, but even he was beginning to feel the harsh bite of the unnatural cold. Rather than fleeing, he waded into it, following the source of the thing that drank in all warmth and life.

Trudging through snow that reached almost to his knees, Gyaidun passed the corpses of one of the Vil Adanrath and his wolf brother, both mangled and torn. The sounds of battle surrounded him—the growling of wolves, steel striking steel, and the screams of men and elves killing and dying.

In the near distance, through the sounds of fighting, Gyaidun thought he heard the belkagen, his voice raised in chant. Power within the words infused the air. Even a warrior like Gyaidun, unskilled in the arcane, could feel it, a drumbeat rhythm in the earth that resonated in the air around him. The wind slowed, then stilled, and like the drawing aside of a curtain, the snow stopped falling. One moment the air in the valley was thick with snow, and the next the night air was clear as starshine.

Twenty paces away, seated on the back of a winter wolf so huge that it would have dwarfed a Tuigan horse, was a figure of frost and shadow, the ash-gray cloak swathing a deeper darkness within. In the bloodied snow before him were two dead winter wolves, their bodies a garden of arrow shafts, two dead *Siksin Neneweth,* one lying a few feet from his head, the other with his throat torn out, and the bodies of a dozen or more Vil Adanrath, both elves and wolves.

Three *Siksin Neneweth* stood before their dark master, two with blades frosted with blood and one carrying a long, barbed spear hung with tiny red icicles. Another *Siksin Neneweth* stood beside his master's winter wolf. In one hand he held a reddened battle-axe and in the other a boy on the verge of manhood, his arms and wrists bound tight behind his back. The boy seemed unharmed, but his eyes stared blankly at the carnage around him.

"Jalan!"

Gyaidun stopped his advance long enough to glance over his shoulder. Amira, her new staff held high, charged down the slope in the midst of a band of Vil Adanrath. Gyaidun turned back around and resumed his advance, slowing a little to give the others a chance to catch up. The boy had looked up at the sound of his name, but he seemed more confused than elated at the sight of his mother.

Arrows fell toward the dark sorcerer and his men. The sorcerer raised his hand, and the shafts burned in midair, raining to the snow as ashes, the metal points falling as bits of molten metal to steam in the snow.

Gyaidun dropped his club and felt the leather leash linking its handle to his wrist pull taut. He grabbed the leash and set the heavy iron to twirling in a figure eight.

The dark sorcerer and his minions stood, seemingly frozen for an instant, staring at the dozens of elves and men descending upon them, then things began happening too fast for Gyaidun to plot and calculate. He became a creature of instinct, action and reaction happening faster than thought.

The *Siksin Neneweth,* except for the one holding the boy, ran to meet their attackers. Their master turned his mount to face them even as his hands began twisting a spell in the air.

Gyaidun was closest. He could hear the Vil Adanrath hard on his heels but knew he would still be the first to face an enemy. The barbarian with the barbed spear was advancing fast. Gyaidun increased the speed of his twirling club. It moved in a black iron blur, humming as it ripped the air.

The dark sorcerer shouted something in a language that hurt Gyaidun's ears. Five seasons ago he and Lendri had spent the winter in the pine forests that clothed the foothills of the Hagga Shan. In the deepest heart of winter, when the sun was no more than a pale, distant fire lingering behind clouds thick with snow, some nights would grow so cold that the woods echoed with the sound of trees exploding as their sap froze and expanded. In the sorcerer's words, the tone haunting his incantation, Gyaidun heard again that sound—a cold so complete that it froze life's blood and cracked bone.

The sorcerer raised his hand—palm open, fingers writhing like the legs of a dying spider—and at the height of his incantation, the air around his hand froze, turning blue-white, and shot forth, gathering force and fury from the air as it arrowed straight at Gyaidun.

Gyaidun tensed his muscles to leap out of the way, but his warrior's instincts knew he'd never make it.

Green fire, a great wall of it three times his own height, erupted from the snow almost at his very feet and spread outward in a straight line to his left and right. The dark sorcerer's magic hit the fire and exploded in a hissing cloud of steam. Wide-eyed, Gyaidun followed its course and saw the belkagen at the base of the far hill, his staff held high as he chanted.

Over the roar of flame, Gyaidun heard the incantation of the sorcerer rise in pitch, and a frigid blast of air shrieked out of the north, stirring up a great cloud of frost from the snow on the ground. The emerald flames bent under the pressure of the wind, flickered and fought a moment, then went out. Still hovering above the battlefield, the belkagen's flare dimmed, and the shadows on the field thickened.

Gyaidun leaped over the trench that the belkagen's wall of fire had cut through the snow. The *Siksin Neneweth* nearest him lunged with his spear, and Gyaidun leaned into it, bringing his club around in an arc before him. The thick iron struck the shaft of the spear with enough force that it should have shattered the staff. Gyaidun had heard that the *Siksin Neneweth* ensorcelled their weapons so that the intense cold would not cause them to become brittle and break. This must be one of them, Gyaidun thought, for his strike only shattered the frozen blood upon its barbed point and turned the spear aside.

The spear point stabbed the snow as Gyaidun followed through with his swing, bringing the club on its leather leash around full circle. It struck the spearman's forearm with such force that bone tore out from muscle and skin, splattering blood onto the snow. The scream died on the barbarian's lips as Gyaidun stepped in, bringing his club round again to smash the man's skull. He stepped over the corpse, and a tide of wolves overtook him, passing in a thunder as their wide paws tore through the snow.

Lightning cracked the sky and struck the ground amidst the wolves. Thunder hit Gyaidun like a club, knocking the wind from his chest, and he saw steam and great gouts of snow explode into the air, the charred bodies of wolves flying in every direction. Some of the wolves had been far enough away to escape the first strike. They scattered, and when the second bolt hit, only three died. The few survivors leaped away from the carnage, then resumed their charge. Gyaidun followed, and from the corners of his eyes he saw Vil Adanrath joining them. The elves were lighter and more fleet of foot than Gyaidun, and they shot past him.

Over the barking of wolves and the battle cries of men and elves, Gyaidun heard Amira shouting, "Jalan! Jalan!"

Gyaidun was still several paces away, wading through the knee-deep snow, when four Vil Adanrath attacked the *Siksin Neneweth* swordsmen. Beyond them, the dark sorcerer raised his arm, shouted an incantation, and thrust his fist at the elves. As he pointed at each of them, they cried out and stopped in their tracks. Two dropped their swords and collapsed to their knees, and another stumbled in the snow and fell forward. The Frost Folk were on them in an instant, their blades rising and falling, throwing streams of blood into the air.

The air in front of Gyaidun seemed to ripple and thicken. His eyes were drawn up to the dark sorcerer, still seated on the back of his massive wolf. The air between them seemed to vibrate, like the plucked string of a harp, and from the inside out, Gyaidun's head went suddenly cold, as if he'd swallowed mouthfuls of snow. Only this was worse. Everything behind his eyes seemed to freeze and crack, and pain such as Gyaidun had never known hit him. He could not move, could not breathe, could not even close his eyes.

Then he saw the fire, tumbling and flickering like a burning sparrow, strike the dark sorcerer in the chest. Tongues of flame burst to life in the ash-gray robes, and the pain evaporated from Gyaidun like water thrown on a hot rock.

Gyaidun took a deep breath as the normal aches and weariness of his body settled back into place.

The *Siksin Neneweth,* blade held high, was almost on him by the time Gyaidun saw him. Gyaidun had just enough time to stumble out of the way. The cold metal passed his throat so close that he felt the wind of its passage. His backside hit the snow, and he scrambled backward, yanking on the leather leash round his wrist to bring his club within reach. The snow hindered his progress, and the *Siksin Neneweth* was quick. The pale barbarian lunged forward, his sword held back, his arm ready to thrust. Gyaidun knew he couldn't get away. Perhaps he could dodge aside and escape with no more than a deep gash, but the white bastard was too close, too damned clo—

An arrow-long beam the color of warm lantern light struck the *Siksin Neneweth* in the shoulder, turning him and knocking him back. It was all Gyaidun needed. He lunged and brought his club around in a wide arc, sacrificing accuracy for power so that it only struck his foe's arm—the one *not* holding the sword. The heavy iron shattered bone and brought a cry of pain from the *Siksin Neneweth*. The man stumbled away so that Gyaidun's return strike missed entirely.

A snarling wolf hit the man, and both went down. The *Siksin Neneweth*, unable to bring his blade to bear, screamed and pummeled at the wolf, but it was no use. The wolf took the man's throat in his jaws, and with one snap it was over.

More flames shot through the air, but by now the *Siksin Neneweth* were aware of them and dodged out of the way. Gyaidun could see several holes in the snow, emitting steam like inverted chimneys, where other shots had missed. He glanced off the field of battle and saw the belkagen standing there, conjuring fire in his outstretched hands and hurling it at their enemies.

Through her gloves Amira could feel warmth and power coursing through the new staff like blood through a vein, and the closer she ran toward the dark sorcerer, the more intense the power pulsed. Fire rimmed the runes along the staff, as if the hot metal that had burned them there had only just been taken away. Still, she saved its power, not wanting to waste it until she was certain she could hurt that pale whoreson bastard holding her son.

Before her, Gyaidun and a wolf leaped over the body of one of the Frost Folk. Several paces beyond them was Jalan, the Frost Folk axeman holding him, and that cloaked monster sitting on the back of his winter wolf. Amira had seen the belkagen's fire catch in his robes, but the fire had lasted only long enough to distract him. The gale the sorcerer summoned had blown the flames out.

Amira ran, cursing the snow pulling at her shins, slowing her advance and keeping her from Jalan. She ran past the corpses of elves and wolves, ignoring the death stench,

all her awareness focused on Jalan. He was so close now
. . . so close.

But as she watched, the sorcerer reached down, grabbed
Jalan, and pulled him onto the back of the wolf. Jalan did not
struggle, his only expression a wince of pain as the sorcerer
hauled him up by the ropes behind his back.

"No!" Amira shouted. "No! Stop him!"

The sorcerer looked at her, and even though his features
were hidden within the cowl, she felt his regard slide over
her like the cold belly of a snake. He raised his free hand
and swept it before him. At his command the air between
him and the advancing Vil Adanrath condensed and froze
into a wall of ice.

"No!" Amira shrieked. Still running, she thrust the point
of her staff before her and spoke a word of power. Light
shot forth and struck the ice, blasting a wagon-sized hole
in the wall.

Gyaidun and the Vil Adanrath leaped through a cloud of
steam, and Amira followed. She heard the clash of weapons
and the battle cry of the Vil Adanrath, and when she emerged
into clear air, she saw the Frost Folk axeman swinging his
weapon back and forth in front of him, keeping an elf and
two wolves at bay. Gyaidun and another wolf were already
well past them, and beyond Amira could see the hindquarters
of the sorcerer's winter wolf disappearing into the cover of
the trees.

"No!" Amira shrieked. She'd come so close!

She pushed the panic down. Time to think more like a
warrior, like a hunter, and less like a terrified mother. She
stopped in her tracks and ignored the men and wolves trying
to kill each other only a few paces away, ignored the stench
of blood and the biting cold, and studied the ground where
the winter wolf had disappeared.

Beyond the reach of the belkagen's magic light, the woods
were all darkness and shadow, but the woods were only a
small strip of foliage in the base of the valley. The sorcerer
had grabbed her son and ran. He meant to flee, not fight.
That meant he'd most likely head to open ground. He'd break

over the rise and be gone like the wind in moments. If he did that, they'd never catch him. Even the Vil Adanrath could not match the stride of a winter wolf.

Amira closed her eyes, concentrated, held the image in her mind—she'd have to place herself just right—and spoke the words of her spell.

The *crack* whipped through the air and brought the belkagen to a stop before the wall of ice. He recognized the sound and knew what had happened. Amira had used her magic to transport herself after the dark sorcerer. The belkagen hesitated. The sounds of battle still echoed in the valley as the Vil Adanrath fought the remaining winter wolves. Those were his people out there killing and dying. They needed him, needed the protection of his Art and prayers.

Do they? said a voice in his mind. That old, nagging voice that had plagued him all these years. He knew it well: his own deepest heart and conscience that always gave the hardest counsel, the one thing he didn't want to hear, but which had always proved right. Every time he'd ignored that still, small voice, he had brought pain to himself and others. Part of him, that part that had felt fear since his first journey to *Hro'nyewachu,* prayed that the voice would be silent. But it wasn't. Do they? it said. Do your people need your protection? Or do you need theirs? You know your duty.

The belkagen cradled his staff close, huddled inside his cloak, covering even his head, and spoke the words of power.

Eyes clenched tight, Amira knew her spell had worked. One moment she was in the midst of the cries of men, elves, and wolves, and the wind howling through the valley, rattling the bare branches. The next, she stood on the bare hillcrest, knee deep in snow, back in the storm with the wind shrieking and the snow hitting her with a million tiny hammerstrikes.

She opened her eyes, but away from the belkagen's spell all was darkness. She could not even see her hair blowing into her face or the snow striking her skin. Straining her ears, she could just make out the distant cries of battle below her and to the right. Then . . . something else. Something large headed right for her. With the realization of what it was, her heart skipped a beat. She'd placed herself too well.

Amira raised her staff and shouted, *"Amalad saisen!"*

Heat flared in the staff and flowed up her arm and through her body. She felt it build in her, permeating blood and bone, then golden light shone around her as if she had become a fragment of the sun, and the entire hillside was bathed in its heat.

The winter wolf bearing down upon her—now only a half-dozen paces away—yelped as if it had been scalded. It tried to stop, but so great was its momentum that its own weight caused it to slide and tumble in the snow. In her mind Amira cried—*Jalan!*—and then the wolf slid past her so close that the cloud of snow its fall produced fell over her like a wave. Still the power of the staff flowed through her, causing the snow to evaporate even as it touched her skin. She felt the unearthly cold radiated by the dark sorcerer strike the aura of light around her and rebound.

The huge wolf regained its feet and turned to face her. She was awed by the sheer size of the beast. Its hackles, raised and trembling, stood as high as the mane of the finest stallions in her father's herds, and its fangs were longer than her hands. Its growl was like tumbling boulders, and its eyes narrowed to slits so that she could see only an ember of fire reflected in its gaze.

The instinct of years of battle-training took over. Holding her staff high in hopes of distracting the beast's attention, Amira thrust her other palm outward and said, *"Dramasthe!"*

A bolt of energy shot from her hand and struck the wolf's face. There was the briefest sound of sizzling flesh, then even the howl of the wind was drowned out by the wolf's shriek. It half-turned and half-fell, then stumbled up the hillside, dragging its scalded face in the snow.

Amira focused her attention farther down the hill. Something lay there, unmoving, and through the gaps in white where the fall and storm had not yet covered it in snow, Amira saw a tattered cloak, set in a pattern of waves. She could not see them at this distance, but she knew those waves were etched in a gold-colored thread. She'd stitched them herself.

"Jalan!" she shouted, and ran down the hill.

But just beyond Jalan another form rose, and the snow seemed to gather and cling to its ash-colored cloak. It took two steps toward Jalan, then bent down to grab him.

"Dramasthe!" Amira shouted, and again the energy shot from her hand.

The sorcerer spoke an incantation and swiped at the bolt with his hand. It evaporated in a sizzling shower of sparks, then the sorcerer stood to his full height and reached within the folds of his cloak. Amira heard the cold whisk of steel being drawn, and when the blade emerged from the depths of the cloak, she recognized it at once. It was Walloch's rapier— the one that had almost killed her only a few days ago.

"Silo'at!"

Cold and frost funneled outward from the blade, but as it struck the core of the golden aura surrounding Amira, it hissed like cold water thrown on hot coals. The shower of frost and ice that raked her face hurt, but it was a bearable pain.

Amira thrust her staff forward and said, *"Keljan saulé!"*

The runes along the staff flared, and a shard of light shot out. It hit the sorcerer in the chest, throwing him away from Jalan and down the slope. Though no sound came to her ears, in her mind Amira heard a shriek that seemed to seek out all the dark places of her mind and rattle there like shards of glass.

Seeing the smoldering cloak hit the ground, she cried

out in triumph and ran for Jalan. But the darkness within the cloak congealed, and in the part of her mind where instinct ruled, Amira sensed fell power gather and spring. The sorcerer leaped and took to the air like a great bird of prey, his cloak rippling like a tattered banner, and then he was falling toward her.

Amira opened her mouth to form a spell, then an image hit her—

—*Mursen charging into the fray, ducking as the broken body of a knight flew past him. A spell passed his lips, the rod in his hand flared—then darkness in an ash-gray cloak lunged.*

Snap! Like the sound of a green branch breaking, the thing's hand reach out, grabbed Mursen by the head and twisted, breaking his neck—

—and the spell faltered on Amira's lips. The light round her dimmed as darkness incarnate descended.

A silver shadow struck the sorcerer the instant before he would have hit her. Silver shadow and ash-colored cloak went down in a snarling explosion of snow. Amira watched, dumbfounded.

The sorcerer threw the wolf off, but it turned in midair and hit the ground running. Four long strides and it jumped again. The sorcerer crouched and brought his sword around in an arc before him. The wolf's snarl turned into a yelp. The animal hit the ground and slid to a stop at Amira's feet. The blade had opened a gash along the side of the wolf's head and haunches, and the sheer force of the blow had shattered bone.

It broke Amira from her stunned silence.

"Dramasthe!" She sent a bolt outward.

The sorcerer swiped it to sparks with his blade and advanced on her.

Again—*"Dramasthe!"*—and again he knocked it away, almost nonchalantly. But that shot had been meant as a distraction.

Amira took a step back and pointed her staff at her foe. *"Keljan saulé!"*

The runes along the staff flared like hot coals kissed by a soft breeze. She aimed for the bastard's head—

—and that was her mistake.

He didn't bother to try to deflect the shard of light, but crouched. The light flew over his head to disappear in the storm. Amira gathered her breath, hoping there was time for another spell.

A shadow emerged from the swirling snow. The light emanating from Amira did not reflect off the club the man was whirling on the end of a leather leash, for it was of the blackest iron.

"Gyaidun, no!" she shouted.

But where her attack had failed, Gyaidun's struck. Perhaps the dark sorcerer had simply been expecting only magical attacks, for the warrior's club swung down and connected with solid flesh somewhere in the folds of the cloak. The sorcerer did not collapse, but he did stumble down the slope.

Gyaidun turned to her and shouted, "Get Jalan and go! Go!"

Then he turned back to his foe, and it was all he could do to stay alive.

Tears welling in her eyes, Amira turned and ran down the hill.

Every childhood nightmare, every horror feared at the back of the north wind, had taken form before Gyaidun, swathed in an ash-gray cloak, and it was coming for him. No battle cry or taunts of defiance did the sorcerer make. He was cold death, and he was coming for Gyaidun.

The muscles in Gyaidun's shoulder were a mass of pain from swinging the heavy iron club, his legs felt both heavy and empty, and every breath of frigid air was like needles in his lungs.

Still, Gyaidun fought, swinging his club and long knife. For the first few strikes, it was attack, if only in hopes of buying Amira enough time to get away. But then every swipe became an effort to keep the sorcerer at bay or to parry a thrust of his sword. Gyaidun retreated, half-stumbling back up the hill and away from Amira and Jalan.

In the confusion of the fight, Amira had lost her bearings, and it took her a moment to relocate Jalan. When she saw him, her first thought was that he had not moved since she'd seen him, her second that the blanket of snow was so thick on him now that he would soon be covered completely, and the third was to wonder at the dark shape that emerged from nothingness over Jalan.

Amira screamed.

But then the shape unfolded and she saw it for what it was—a huge cloak made up of many animal hides and painted in arcane symbols.

The belkagen emerged from the folds of his cloak and stood over Jalan. "Go help Gyaidun! I will take the boy!"

"No!" Amira said as she slid to a stop over her son. "I'm not leaving him again."

"You must!"

"I won't!"

"Lady," said the belkagen, and though he had to shout to be heard over the wind, there was tenderness in his voice. *"Hro'nyewachu* does not give such weapons of power lightly. The staff was given to you for a reason. Do not let it be in vain."

Amira knelt over her son. She brushed the snow away and pulled at the fabric until she could see his face. His eyes were closed—he looked so thin and worn!—but she could see his chest rising and falling. He was alive. If he had been hurt in the fall, it did not seem serious.

"I will see to him, Lady!" said the belkagen.

She rose and looked the old elf in the eye. "Your blood if you don't."

The belkagen flinched, but something told Amira it

was not at her threat but at something else her words had hit.

"On my blood!" said the belkagen.

Amira took two steps up the hill, then turned again. "Tell him . . ." she said. "Tell Jalan I love him."

She looked down at her son, then spun and sped up the hill.

Flickers of light, like minuscule bolts of cold lightning, flashed along the sorcerer's blade. Gyaidun stepped out of range and swung his own weapon, putting every bit of strength into it. The sorcerer's blade flicked down and then up, and Gyaidun felt the leather connecting his wrist to his club part. The heavy weight of black iron flew into the snow-stitched darkness.

Gyaidun scrambled backward, the sorcerer advancing on him, and on the fourth step his heel struck a rock or tussock buried under the snow and he stumbled. He hit the ground but kept going, struggling like a crab on all fours.

The thing in the ash-gray cloak lunged, his cloak flaring in the gale, and grabbed Gyaidun under the chin. The grip was beyond cold. It seemed to leech every bit of warmth from Gyaidun's skull, and he could feel his bones and the fluids in his ears freezing.

The sorcerer stood, and although the arm that gripped him was thinner than a starved cadaver, he lifted Gyaidun's thick frame off the ground and brought him close. Even with his elf-blessed sight, Gyaidun's vision could not penetrate the depths of the sorcerer's cowl, not even when the sorcerer pulled him close. The wind was at the sorcerer's back, and Gyaidun could smell the stench of tombs and worse from the thing's robes.

The sorcerer inhaled deeply—Gyaidun could just hear it over the wind.

"Yes," said the sorcerer. "I know your blood. You might have been the one. Might have—"

Gyaidun thrust his knife into the robes. He kept the blade sharp enough to shave with, and the point punctured through the layers of cloth. Gyaidun felt the steel hit a rib, turn, and plunge deep. The sorcerer gasped, but his grip did not weaken.

"You have bite," the sorcerer said. "Like your pup. He fought, too."

Blind rage filled Gyaidun. He stabbed, slashed, kicked, and punched.

The sorcerer caught his wrist that held the knife, twisted, squeezed—Gyaidun held on through the bones grinding, but when they broke he let go and the knife fell to the ground.

"Enough," said the sorcerer. "Time to die. Time to—"

An avalanche of snarling, whimpering fur hit them. The icy grip under his jaw slipped, and Gyaidun hit the snow and rolled free. A massive paw smashed his shoulder into the ground, then was gone. His body was a mass of pain, but Gyaidun forced himself to keep rolling down the hill. He stopped several paces down and looked up just in time to see white haunches and tail disappearing into the storm. The sorcerer's winter wolf. It was still blinded by Amira's spell and maddened by pain. It must have slammed into them.

Then the shadow was on him again, the life-draining hand gripping his throat and squeezing as the sorcerer lifted him. Gyaidun could feel the blood in his neck freezing, the veins bursting, his skin blistering and cracking from the cold. The grip tightened, and Gyaidun couldn't breathe. Darkness rimmed the edges of his vision, a pulsing mass of it closing in—

—and then Gyaidun noticed a change in the light. It seemed golden. Soft. Even warm. And he had time to wonder if he was crossing over into the afterlife before—

A shard of light struck the sorcerer's midriff. A shriek louder than boulders cracking struck his ears, and Gyaidun went flying. He hit the ground hard, and his first thought was—Why do I smell blossoms?

Gasping for air, he pushed himself up and wiped the snow from his face. Not ten paces away, the sorcerer and

Amira were engaged in battle, spells flying and Amira's golden staff shining like summer's heart. It struck the sorcerer's blade, and sparks of silver and gold mingled with the blowing snowfall.

"Enough!" the sorcerer said, and he flew backward out of the lady's reach. He landed with the practiced ease of a Shou monk, then raised his hands to the storm and shouted, *"Uthrekh rakhshan thra!"*

The gale became a living thing, and Gyaidun felt the already frigid temperature plummet. The air in his throat thickened, choking him. The moisture in his eyes began to freeze, and his skin seemed to turn to stone.

"Kenhakye unethke!" shouted Amira, her staff held high. Warmth and light flowed out from her, pushing back the sorcerer's spell.

The sorcerer stood, arms still outstretched, and stared at Amira. Although Gyaidun could not see his face, he could sense that sorcerer was stunned at the thwarting of his magic. Enraged, the sorcerer took to the air again in a great leap, his sword raised above his flying robes.

Blade struck staff in another shower of sparks, but this time Amira did not retreat and counter. Green fire erupted in her free hand and she reached in, grasping the sorcerer's robe. Despite the wind, the magic fire caught and ignited in the ash-gray robes, and he fell back screaming. But his cries twisted into an incantation, and the wind gusted, blowing Amira back and extinguishing the flames.

Gyaidun, his broken wrist throbbing with pain, pushed himself to his feet and lurched forward. His toe struck something hard. His knife! He reached down, grabbed it, and charged. He knew he was most likely done in and nothing he could do could stop the sorcerer, but if he could add his effort to the fight, perhaps Amira could conjure something strong enough to strike him down—or at the very least buy her time to escape.

The sorcerer stood, blackened holes in his robes and cowl still smoldering, and as his charge brought him close Gyaidun could hear him snarling.

Amira began her incantation, *"Keljan—"*

"Hey!" Gyaidun roared, raising his knife to swipe at the sorcerer's face.

The sorcerer turned his attention away from Amira to Gyaidun, and as he did so the wind caught in his tattered and burned cowl, ripping it off his head.

Gyaidun saw the sorcerer's face for the first time. Older it was, and gaunt like a man long deprived of food, but there was no mistaking the face and the cant of his eyes. His mother's eyes.

It was Erun. His son.

"—saulé!" Amira finished, and from behind him Gyaidun felt the air ignite.

"No!" Gyaidun threw himself between them.

CHAPTER TWENTY-THREE

The Endless Wastes

The wind died near dawn, but the snow kept falling as if Auril meant to bury the world. From the shelter of their camp—at the bottom of a washed-out gully where straggly bushes and long grass sagged over a lip of earth, offering a sort of half roof—Amira watched it come down. Under different circumstances she might have found it beautiful, but now she knew it would be waist deep by midmorning.

Jalan was still asleep, wrapped in thick blankets beside her. She resisted touching him, fearing she might wake him. The belkagen had done all he could to heal him. Jalan's body would have to do the rest. Looking down at him, Amira's heart slowed but seem to beat with twice its usual strength. She had her son back. His cheeks were sunken, dark circles ringed his eyes, his skin had a gray pallor she didn't like, and his breathing was strained, but he was alive and he was *here*. Right now, that was all that mattered.

Amira heard footsteps wading through the snow, and then the belkagen ducked under the overhanging foliage and stepped around the small fire.

"How is he?" she asked.

"Gyaidun?"

"Yes."

"He'll live." The belkagen sat. His skin looked brittle as parchment and his shoulders sagged under his cloak. "Healing the damage from your staff took most of my strength and wisdom. I'll have to rest before I see to his wrist and other injuries."

Amira opened her mouth then shut it again. She was torn between guilt and anger. Battered as Gyaidun had been in the fight, it had been her strike aimed at the sorcerer that had done the most damage. After it had struck Gyaidun in the back, the sorcerer had fled, fading into the deeper darkness of the storm. Gyaidun had lain unmoving in the snow, his torn shirt smoking and the flesh underneath steaming. She'd run to him, finding him breathing but little else. Part of her had wanted to pursue her foe, to finish this once for all, but there was no sign of him.

Looking down at Gyaidun, Amira had known he would die without help—and might well die with it. So she'd used her spell to take them both back to the belkagen. Even after the old elf's first attempt to heal him, Gyaidun had been almost insensate, tears streaming down his cheeks, raving and screaming. Amira had seen wounded men, some on the verge of death, trying to hold in their life's blood as they watched it pouring between their fingers, and she'd understood Gyaidun's cries were from no physical pain. She'd known others like him in the war. He could've swallowed hot iron with a smile. No, this had been something deeper, the cry of anguish, of a broken heart.

The belkagen had poured a syrupy concoction down Gyaidun's throat. A shudder had run through him, followed by a violent bout of coughing. Gyaidun had looked up at her, and his eyes seemed *haunted*. He told the old elf what he'd seen. Amira had been standing nearby, and she heard it all.

"Erun!" he said. "It was Erun. My son! My son, my son . . ."

"Erun?" said the belkagen. "That thing had Erun?"

"No!" Gyaidun grabbed the belkagen's shoulders. "It *was* Erun. That thing was my son. My son!"

That had shocked Amira as much as anyone—and filled her with a cold dread. So much of the past several tendays— Jalan's abduction, that damned sorcerer's dogged pursuit of him, the vision in *Hro'nyewachu*—was beginning to come together in her mind.

Now, with Gyaidun off somewhere else, she voiced her concerns to the belkagen.

"Gyaidun's son . . ."

"Erun," said the belkagen, his voice thick. "Erun is—*was* his name."

"Erun. He was taken, just like Jalan?"

"Fifteen years ago."

"Out there . . ." said Amira. She stopped, gathering her thoughts. "In the darkness, in the storm, Gyaidun was . . . beyond hurt. I've seen the carnage of battle, and I've seen few men take a beating like that and still remain on their feet. But Gyaidun was still fighting. He must have been running on will alone. Is it possible that . . . that—"

"That he imagined the whole thing?"

"Yes," she said, her hope gathering strength. "His search for his son has consumed him for so long. It's been the one thing that kept him going. Finding Jalan . . . I knew from the beginning, since that night by the lake when we first spoke, that Gyaidun was after Erun, not Jalan. Is it possible he wanted to find his son so much—maybe too much—that his mind saw what it wanted to see?"

The belkagen sat in silence for a long while. When he spoke, his voice was cold and hard. "You think Gyaidun *wanted* to see his son warped and twisted into that . . . thing? That horror?"

"No," said Amira. "But if the heart wants something strong enough . . ."

"You told me what you saw in *Hro'nyewachu*. The road of years you walked. You saw the fate of Khasoreth and his apprentices. Jalan's forefathers. Did your heart . . . *imagine* that?"

"No. Mystra help me, no. If anything, I would want to believe it was all some twisted dream. But I know it wasn't."

The belkagen gave a deep sigh and nodded. "I know it also. I never walked that road, but I have walked many others. Long roads through doubt, darkness, and worse. I believe what you saw in *Hro'nyewachu* was truth. I do not doubt it. But my question is: Why?"

Amira scowled. "Why?"

"You went seeking aid for your son, not . . . what you would call 'a history lesson.' "

"The staff—"

"Was given to aid your fight. But it was not the help you sought. *Hro'nyewachu* told me the staff would 'sharpen the bite' you gave your enemies, but that it was for another to save Jalan."

"Sharpen the bite?" Amira's mouth opened and closed twice before more words would come to her. *"Hro'nyewachu* . . . told you? She *told* you? What else did she tell you?"

The belkagen looked up, and again Amira felt herself caught in a hunter's gaze. "Many things, sacred things for her and me alone. But she told me that for you. The staff is meant to aid your fight, not win it. That task is for another."

"Another?" she said. "Gyaidun? You mean Gyaidun?"

"I mean no one," he said. "They are the words of *Hro'nye-wachu,* not the words of the belkagen. Is the other Gyaidun?" The belkagen shrugged. "Perhaps. Perhaps not. Who can tell?"

"Then what damned good is it?" Amira said. "If we can't understand any of it, what does it mean?"

"It means this fight is not over."

"What?"

Amira could not look away from the belkagen's wolf stare. He'd run last night while she stood and fought, yet here she sat feeling like a snowblind hare caught in the open.

"You are thinking about taking Jalan back to Cormyr," he said. "Back to the safety of your knights, wizards, and castles."

"And if I am?"

"Your knights, wizards, and castles could not protect him before."

"They cau—!"

"And they will not protect him now!" said the belkagen. "Nor you. You did an amazing thing last night, Amira Hiloar. You hurt . . . the sorcerer. You did something that no one has done in many ages, I think—not even your own precious knights and wizards. But now he *knows* it. And he knows you. He will come upon you when you least suspect it, when you are tired or alone. Whatever Erun has become, it is a thing of cold and darkness. He does not care for honor or fairness. He will come upon you when you are at your weakest. You will not survive that, I think. You will die, and he will have Jalan again."

Amira said nothing, but she did not look away. Wolf's gaze or no, her Hiloar pride would not permit it.

"You saw the sorcerer," said the belkagen. "If that's what he is. It was Erun, twisted into something . . . vile. Unholy. *Think*, Amira! It was Erun."

"We've established that."

"Erun. Gyaidun's son. Erun, who was taken *just like Jalan*."

The reality of it hit her. How could she have been so foolish? All she'd seen! All the oracle had shown her. How could she not have seen this herself?

"What happened to Gyaidun's son," she said. "They mean the same thing for Jalan."

"You saw Khasoreth's fate. You saw him and his pack of devilspawn walking through the years, not living but never dying, taking new vessels to contain the darkness within them. You saw this, Lady. You told me so."

"I did."

They sat together in silence for a long while, the belkagen watching the snowfall while Amira watched nothing at all. She sat looking inward, going over every detail of the oracle's visions, looking for some flaw in the elf's reasoning. There was none. Her shoulders slumped and she sighed.

"Have you," she said, "have you . . . told Gyaidun?"

"Told him what has happened to Erun?"

Amira nodded.

"Not yet. You said it yourself. The hope of finding his son has been the one thing giving him life and purpose all these years. If we take that away . . ."

"Hope," said Amira, wishing she could find her own. "You think he has any left at this point?"

"Hope is for those who seize it," said a voice above them.

Lendri leaped off the lip of the gully and landed in the snow. Mingan followed. Elf and wolf looked at Amira and the belkagen, then joined them under the overhanging grass. Lendri sat down beside the belkagen while his wolf-brother sat with his head on his paws and watched Jalan. The wolf's ears twitched, and he let out a long whine.

"How long have you been there, pup?" asked the belkagen.

"Not long," Lendri answered, though his eyes were fixed on Amira. "I heard you discussing my *rathla*. I listened."

The belkagen scowled. "You listened to a private conversation of the belkagen. Very rude. Almost dishonorable."

Lendri shrugged, not seeming the least bit chagrined. "She is not belkagen, and I am *hrayek*. My honor is sullied already." He looked at both of them and steel entered his voice. "If you know something about Erun, something you are not telling Gyaidun . . ."

"How much did you hear?" asked the belkagen.

Lendri looked at Amira a long moment, then turned his gaze back to the belkagen and said, "Have you ever haggled with the merchants along the Golden Way?"

The belkagen scowled. "What does that have to do with—?"

"They are liars," said Lendri. "Unrepentant liars. I learned long ago that the best way to judge the honesty of someone is to ask them a question to which you already know the answer and see what they say. I have yet to meet a merchant who does not make a practice of lying."

The belkagen's eyes narrowed to slits, and his voice became soft as velvet over a knife. "You accuse me of lying, Lendri *hrayek?*"

Lendri shrugged. "I accuse the belkagen of nothing. But I'm not going to answer his question until he answers mine."

"Where is your resp—?"

"Please!" Amira cut them off and looked to Lendri. "Do we know what happened to Gyaidun's son?" She cast a quick look at the belkagen, who was scowling. "Yes," she continued, "gods help us, I think we do. But what you are really asking, I think, is, 'Have we found a way to help him?' And the answer to that, Lendri, is no. Damn it all, we haven't. I swear by my gods and my House that I'm telling you the truth."

"Your House is a house of merchants, is it not?"

"They are," she said. "Liars, the lot of them. I can't stand them either."

Lendri smiled, but his eyes were sad. "That, I understand. Family troubles seem to plague all peoples."

"Then you believe me?"

"I see no reason for you to lie. But why do you hide the truth from Gyaidun?"

"What good would it do him?"

"None," said Lendri. "But *na kwast wahir athu kyene wekht unarihe*—'better a cold truth than a warm lie.' I know my *rathla*. He would rather be hurt than ignorant."

"This hurt might be more than your *rathla* could bear," said the belkagen.

"That should be his decision. Not yours."

The belkagen sighed. "You must choose your own path, even if it means destroying your *rathla,* but I will tell you this: You have no truth to give your *rathla.* We know only that the Fist of Winter took Erun and twisted him into something vile and evil. That much Gyaidun already knows. His greatest hope—that his son is still alive—has met his greatest fear—the one who took him—and they are one. Your *rathla* is . . . confused now, Lendri. Hurting. Despair has gripped him. What we know, what Amira learned in *Hro'nyewachu* will only deepen that. Consider my words. I will argue this with you no more."

They sat in silence for a long while, the belkagen's scowl deepening, Amira watching her sleeping son, and Lendri scratching Mingan behind the ears. "I will think on what you have said," said Lendri, and stood and walked away, Mingan at his heels.

"You think he's going to tell Gyaidun?" asked Amira.

"Most certainly," said the belkagen. "I love those two like sons, but they can be stubborn as dwarves. Gyaidun is more obvious about it because he blusters and roars, but Lendri . . . that one, he is quiet and so hides it, but he's even worse."

"What will Gyaidun do, do you think?"

"Knowing him as I do, I can only be sure that it will be something foolish."

"And you aren't going to stop him?"

"He's a grown man, Lady, and Lendri is five times your age, at least. If those two want to rush off and get themselves killed . . . well, it won't be the first time they've tried, and they're still here. Stubborn and hotheaded as they both are, they never cease to surprise me. I must trust them to follow their own path. But you . . ."

"What about me?"

The belkagen fixed her with that predator's gaze that made her feel so small and said, "Now that you have your son, what will you do, Lady?"

"Winterkeep," said Amira.

"What?"

"Winterkeep. *Iket Sotha* you called it. That's where the sorcerer was headed with Jalan."

"You are certain?"

"Yes," Amira answered. "Mystra help me, I am."

CHAPTER TWENTY-FOUR

The Endless Wastes

The sorcerer, still swathed in his scorched and torn ash-gray cloak, and his three remaining Frost Folk rode upon winter wolves to the shore of the Great Ice Sea. One riderless winter wolf trailed them. It was past midday, but the unrelenting storm was so thick, and the sky so dark, that it gave them enough cover to keep moving throughout the day. This close to the water the air was heavy with moisture, and the snow fell in great clumps, some almost as big as a man's hand.

One of the Frost Folk fell from the back of his wolf and lay in the snow. The man had half a Vil Adanrath arrow in his ribs. He had spent most of the day coughing, and the front of his body was smeared with his own blood. The wolf he'd been riding sidestepped and looked down on him. The man lay in the snow, unmoving except for the swift rising and falling of his chest.

Another of the Frost Folk lifted his leg and slid off his own mount. He knelt beside his fallen companion, examined the wound, then stood and spoke to his master.

The sorcerer still sat atop his wolf, both of them staring into the face of the storm. He turned at his servant's words and looked down on the fallen man.

"He is beyond help," said the sorcerer in the tongue of the far north. "And the wolves are hungry."

The sorcerer dismounted. His wolf turned and joined his fellows in their meager meal. The man never even screamed. One swift snap from a wolf's jaws, and it was over for him. The two remaining Frost Folk turned away from the carnage and watched their master.

Ignoring them, the sorcerer climbed to the very lip of the promontory. Standing in the full force of the wind, the remains of his cloak and robes fluttered and cracked. It didn't seem to bother him, not even when his cowl flew back, exposing his long hair and pallid skin to the biting frost. The Frost Folk watched as their master basked in the frigid wind off the Great Ice Sea. The intense cold and fury of the storm seemed to lend him strength, reinvigorating him, but still he leaned heavily upon his staff. A foe—a *woman!*—had managed to do something no other had in generations. She'd hurt him. Hurt him badly.

The sorcerer stood there a long while, his men watching. When he sat upon the very edge of the rock, the Frost Folk exchanged a furtive glance. Their forefathers had served the Fist of Winter for hundreds of years, their devotion born out of the rewards given to them by the dark sorcerers, but also out of fear. They served their fiendish masters because the Fist of Winter gave them the gifts necessary to survive in the far north, where months passed without the light of the sun. The Fist of Winter gave the Frost Folk power to overcome their enemies and to eke out a living in a world of ice and darkness. But the glance these two exchanged said something that none of their people had dared speak aloud for generations. They had a new fear: that their masters could be beaten, that there were stronger powers in the world.

The sorcerer clutched his staff to his chest and leaned back, breathing deep of the storm's fury. Slowly at first, but gathering strength as he found his rhythm, the sorcerer began an incantation.

What little warmth still gripped the air lost its hold. No longer did the snow fall in great, wet clumps. The flakes shrank and froze, hard as minuscule diamonds. Even the gray daylight dimmed to a thick gloom.

A silver eldritch light flickered around the sorcerer. Beyond the sound of his voice, the hiss of driving snow, and the hard slap of the waves on the rocks below, came the sound of voices riding on the wind.

Amira finished stuffing the last of her supplies into the pack and pulled the straps tight. Jalan lay beside her, still sleeping beside the fire. She'd have to wake him soon. He'd awakened a while ago, but only long enough to have a few bites of food and swallow a mouthful of water. She had held him while he ate, and the fact that he let her filled her with a mixture of relief and dismay.

Jalan had not let her hold him like this for years. He was on the verge of manhood, and though she missed holding her son, she understood why it made him uncomfortable. She'd welcomed holding him this morning, but doing so only emphasized how deeply Jalan had been hurt. Not so much on the outside—he looked underfed and exhausted, but other than the torn and bruised skin from too-tight ropes, his captors had done him no real harm. But his spirit had been hurt. Pensive and sometimes sullen Jalan had been replaced by a scared little boy who jumped at sudden sounds and huddled away from shadows.

Amira heard footsteps behind her—heavy and deliberate, so unlike the furtive tread of the elves—and she knew at once who it was.

She stood and turned to look up at Gyaidun. She almost

didn't recognize him. His countenance had lost all vitality. His features, which she had first seen as hard and chiseled, now seemed merely haggard and tired. Even his eyes seemed fragile and hollow.

"Amira," he said. He stopped, his mouth hanging open as if he meant to continue, but then he shut it and shook his head.

"Gyaidun," she said, and was ashamed to hear the accusation in her voice. Her head knew she should feel pity for the man, but her heart was angry. "Did you come to say your farewells?"

"Farewells?"

"Lendri told me you aren't coming with us." No, she thought, you are staying here while your blood brother goes off to face certain death.

"I can't, Amira," he said. "I can't come and . . . and try to kill my own son."

Amira stood and hefted her pack. She felt no pity for that monster in the ash-gray cloak, not even a little, but still she tried to force some gentleness and warmth into her voice. "Gyaidun, he . . . he isn't your son anymore. You know that, don't you?"

Gyaidun looked away.

"I am sorry," she said. "I really am. What happened to your son, to Erun, it's . . . unforgivable. Monstrous. It's . . . blasphemous. But it happened. That thing you saw may have been wearing Erun's body, but the heart of what made him Erun isn't there anymore, Gyaidun. I know."

"You learned this," he said, his voice raw, "in *Hro'nyewachu?* She . . . she told you this?"

Amira hesitated. The belkagen had warned her of the dangers of sharing the secrets of the oracle. "Told me?" she said. "No. I *saw* it, Gyaidun. I saw it happen again and again through the centuries."

Gyaidun stood there, letting that sink in, then said, "You're going to kill him."

Amira took a deep breath and looked Gyaidun in the eye. He towered over her. Still, as he was now, broken and hurt, she felt stronger, felt as though she should be the one protecting him. But this was one truth from which she could not protect him. That would be no mercy.

"Yes," she said. "I'm going to try. If I don't, he'll do the same to my son. And others."

"You know this?" he said, and the slightest flicker of the old Gyaidun's fire lit his gaze.

"I do know it," she said. She put her gloved hand on his forearm and squeezed.

He stared down at her hand, then looked up at her. "Watch out for Lendri," he said. "The Vil Adanrath will fight to the death, but they won't help him. He'll be on his own out there."

Not if you'd come with us, she wanted to say, but she didn't.

Gyaidun turned and walked away. She watched until he was little more than a pale shadow cloaked in falling snow, then there was only the snow.

"Don't judge him too harshly."

Amira turned, and the belkagen was standing only a few paces away.

"I really thought he would come with us," she said. "Even with hope for Erun gone, I thought he'd want vengeance at least. Not, this, this . . ."

"Despair?"

"Yes."

"Gyaidun is not a coward, Lady."

"I know he isn't."

The belkagen looked down at Jalan and asked, "Do you pray, Lady?"

"Sometimes, yes."

"Pray for Gyaidun. After what happened, he has embraced one of the gravest sins: Despair."

"I have never seen despair as a sin."

He looked her in the eye and smiled. "Then you've never considered it."

"What do you mean?"

"Despair is the forsaking of hope, believing that you

know all paths. Embracing doom. But no mortal can see so far—even those like us who have been shown"—the belkagen stopped and swallowed—"shown such things. We are given the greatest burden of all, I think, to be shown some of what lies ahead that we might still dare to hope."

Amira scowled. She had the feeling that the belkagen wasn't talking about Gyaidun anymore. What had the old elf seen in *Hro'nyewachu?* She'd asked, but he'd refused to answer. In some ways, he seemed little more than a simple, old mystic who'd spent too long out in the sun, but at times like now she found him more inscrutable than the greatest masters of her Art.

"I know Gyaidun is no coward," she said.

"You know it now, but later, when this fight is done . . . the thought might come to you. When it does, know that it is a lie."

Amira looked down at Jalan, who was still sleeping. She didn't look up as she said, "You really think there will be a later?"

"Dare to hope, Lady. We must dare to hope."

CHAPTER TWENTY-FIVE

The Endless Wastes

The land lay on the verge of true darkness when the lone guard saw them. They came from the west—a dozen ghostlike shapes only slightly darker than the surrounding snow. Still crouching in the shadow of the great rock, the guard took a wooden pipe out of his belt pouch and put it to his lips. He blew a long note that rose and fell with the wind. The nearest of the approaching shapes stopped. The guard stood and stepped out of the shadows. He waved his spear in three wide arcs.

The figures resumed their run, and by the time full dark had fallen they had gathered around the rock—twelve winter wolves and eight Frost Folk riding. Their leader brought his mount forward until he towered over the guard. Steam from the great beast's breath enveloped the guard in an icy cloud.

"We have come," said the new arrival. "To where does the master call us?"

The deepest shadow under the great rock moved. It stood, a tall man wearing the tattered remains of an ash-gray cloak and cowl. Snow and frost clung to him, and there was no warmth in his breath to cloud before him. He stepped forward until he stood beside the guard. The winter wolf before them let out a small whine and took several steps backward, its ears low and its tail between its legs.

"To Winterkeep," said the sorcerer. "We go to Winterkeep."

Sitting before the meager fire, Jalan curled up next to her, Amira gripped her new staff as she studied its runes. She'd never seen their like, and she had studied most of the languages of Faerûn, both ancient and modern, living and dead. Still, there was something familiar about them, something she felt she ought to recognize. It nagged at her, just as the staff itself seemed to . . . to sing to her.

It was not unlike the times she'd lulled Jalan to sleep as a baby with a lullaby—oftentimes nonsense words where the sound and melody were more important than the meaning.

Something within the staff spoke to her like that—not in words or even meaning, but in a deeper connection that had more to do with the beating of her heart and the passions of her flesh than the knowledge of her mind. Even now, she could feel it flowing through her, and she felt a strange communion with the golden wood, and through it to all the land around her. So strong was the sensation, that she could *feel* the sun setting in the distance, even though it was hidden behind countless miles of falling snow and cloud.

She heard movement and looked up to see a pale elf sitting down across the fire from her. At first she thought it was Lendri, but it was not. In his exile, Lendri had collected various bits of other cultures upon his person. His clothes and supplies showed he had traveled among half the peoples of the Wastes, but the one before her now was all Vil Adanrath, dressed only in leathers and the fur of various animals. His hair was wild and free, and though it was now sprinkled with snow, still it drank in the firelight and seemed to glow with its own warmth.

"I am Leren," said the elf, speaking each word with careful precision. He held his palms open before him and offered a small bow. "Son of Haerul, Omah Nin of the Vil Adanrath."

"I am Amira," she said, her voice low so as not to wake Jalan.

"Amira Hiloar, War Wizard of Cormyr. Yes, I know."

Amira did not know what to say, so she said nothing.

"I have seen you with the belkagen. He speaks well of you."

"He saved me and my son," she said, and placed a gentle hand on Jalan's shoulder. "He and Gyaidun and Lendri. They saved our lives."

Leren flinched at the mention of his brother and Gyaidun's names. "I did not come to speak to you of the *hrayeket.*"

"Then why did you come?"

"My father sent out summons to all the packs. Many have come, and others may come still, but he and the belkagen agree on this: We cannot wait. The belkagen says our enemies will be here soon, and he says you know this also."

Amira nodded. "The belkagen speaks the truth."

"Then we must prepare. The omah nin will make *amrulugek.* You know what this means?"

"Yes. A council."

"Council, yes. The omah nin asks you to come."

A shiver went up Amira's spine. She'd spoken with a few of the Vil Adanrath over the last day or so, but for the most part they kept to themselves. She thought it was mostly because they avoided Lendri, and when he was in camp, he was most often around Amira's fire. The belkagen had acted as a sort of go-between, and Amira had liked that just fine.

The Vil Adanrath made every hair on her body stand

on end. She'd known elves all her life, but none like these. Shapeshifters who could walk as wolves as easily as elves—and even when they walked on two legs the wolf never quite left their stride or their eyes.

"Will the belkagen be there?" she asked.

"He will."

"And Lendri?"

Leren flinched. "That one is *hrayek*. Exiled. He cannot join our council."

"He may join our fight and risk his blood but not sit at our fire?"

Leren said nothing, simply sat and watched her.

"I will come," she said. "But I do not like Lendri being excluded."

"You do not know his crimes," said Leren, though there was a tone of respect in his voice.

"And you do not know mine, but still you ask me to your council."

"Your crimes were not against the Vil Adanrath."

Amira scowled. "Fine. When is the council?"

"The scouts should return soon. We meet then. Someone will come for you."

Leren stood to go.

"My son," said Amira. "I will not leave him."

The elf looked down on Jalan. "Your son may come."

Amira did not have long to wait. Leren had been gone just long enough for full dark to fall when the belkagen trudged up to her fire, his long cloak trailing in the snow.

"It is time, Lady," he said. "The council of the omah nin gathers."

Amira gave Jalan a gentle shake. "Jalan," she said. "Jal, you must wake up."

He stirred, turning so that the blanket fell away from his face. His eyes went wide and he gasped.

"It's dark," he said.

"I know, dear. We're in camp. We're safe. But you must wake up, just for a little while. You and I have been invited to a council."

Jalan squeezed his eyes shut, and his whole body shuddered. But he forced himself up, and he and Amira followed the belkagen, his staff emitting its cold green fire and lighting their way. The camp was spread out in a shallow valley that probably turned into a river in spring and early summer. Autumn-bare trees, their branches drooping under a heavy load of snow, lined the ground between the valley and steep embankment, and the Vil Adanrath had made fires and erected small lean-tos beneath them. Wolves and elves slept in some of the campsites, others were empty, and a few sat beside fires and watched the trio pass.

The omah nin had built his fire at the very edge of the camp where the eastern embankment fell to a flat area of scrub and boulders, all made into formless humps of snow.

Behind a large fire stood Haerul himself, shirtless but with a long cape of black fur draping his shoulders. His hair was unbound and hung heavy with snow well below his waist. He was almost as tall as Gyaidun, but his frame had the lean strength of the elves. Scars crisscrossed his torso, and one particularly nasty gash, long healed, streaked down his neck and chest. Like the rest of the Vil Adanrath, only bits of pale skin peeked out from a twisting maze of black tattoos.

As she approached the chieftain, Amira caught glints of red among the darker inks and thought at first that they were new scars, still raw from healing. But her breath caught in her throat when she took a closer look. They were runes, and although there were differences, she recognized them. She couldn't read them, but there was no doubt that they were the same language as was carved into her new staff.

"Belkagen," she whispered. "Those marks upon the omah nin. What are they?"

The belkagen slowed his pace and turned to her. "Those are the marks of a chieftain. In the west, your kings wear crowns and wield scepters. Among the Vil Adanrath, those red runes mark him omah nin."

"What do they say?"

"Not now, Lady."

"But they are much like the runes on the staff given to me by the oracle."

The belkagen nodded. "Most likely they were carved by the same hand."

"You mean the omah nin has been to the oracle?"

"All omah seek *Hro'nyewachu,* who chooses the omah nin. Now hush, Lady. Please. This is not the time."

They walked amid the gathered crowd. Amira counted ten other Vil Adanrath gathered—elves anyway. The wolves milled about so that she had trouble counting them, and they came in every color, from a black deep as coal to a white that became one with the snow. Among the elves, Amira was surprised to see three women. They looked no less fierce than the men. One had a disfigured face, half of which was a mottled burn-scar, and one eye stared out milky white.

The belkagen stood across the fire from the omah nin and bowed. "Omah Nin, I have come to your council, and I bring Lady Amira Hiloar, War Wizard of Cormyr, *Inisach tin Nekutha Hro'nyewachwe.* I request that those who speak the common tongue of the west do so, that we might honor her presence."

The omah nin turned his heavy gaze on her, and she was bowing before she realized it. "Well come to my fire, Lady Amira," said the omah nin. "You honor us with your presence." He motioned to each of those seated around the fire, calling each of their names. Leren was the only one she had already met. "Please, sit. We have much to discuss."

The belkagen sat on the ground amid the ring of elves.

Amira and Jalan settled in beside him, and she leaned toward him and whispered, "What was that you called me? *Inisaktin Neku*-something?"

The belkagen turned to her and said, *"Inisach tin Nekutha Hro'nyewachwe.* It means you sought *Hro'nyewachu* and lived."

"Why did you tell them that?"

"So that they will know you are their equal."

"I—"

A great howl from beyond the camp cut her off, and everyone seated round the fire stiffened. The wolves stopped their pacing and stood still, only their ears moving.

"The sentries—" said one of the elves beside the omah nin.

The wind, which had blown out of the north all day, suddenly rose to a tumultuous gale and blew up a great cloud of snow. The fire went out, and as darkness gripped them, Jalan grabbed his mother. She could feel him trembling beside her.

Amira felt the belkagen rise beside her and heard his incantation. A moment later the green fire from his staff lit the camp, reflecting off the snow in the air so that it seemed as if they were suspended in a spring-green cloud. The wind shrieked even harder, and the belkagen shouted, "No one move! Be still!"

A cackle came from somewhere in the blizzard. It was one of the most inhuman sounds Amira had ever heard, like the sound of breaking icicles given life and a gleeful malice.

"Behind me!" shouted the belkagen as he stepped away from the main body of the camp, his staff held high, the flames on its tip blazing like an emerald star. "Everyone back! Stay behind my light!"

The wind blew even stronger, sending the belkagen's great cloak billowing behind him. Amira could hear him shouting but could not understand the words. The gale pummeled them, blowing no longer from the north but switching direction again and again. Amira thought it was beginning to slacken a bit, but then she realized that it was only gathering in the darkness just beyond the reach of the belkagen's light.

Amira watched in horror as the wind gathered into a single cyclone, dozens of feet high. It stayed in one spot, gathering snow, ice, leaves, and other bits of debris as it swayed back and forth.

Gripping her staff, Amira began to form the words of a spell.

"Be still!" said the belkagen. "I beg you, Lady."

Out of the snow, a small form staggered, leaning heavily upon a gnarled staff dangling with thorns and bits of hair and bone. She stepped into the green light, and Amira saw that it was indeed a she—a hideous old crone, her skin blue as a drowned corpse, the flesh round her rheumy eyes black with decay. She seemed about Amira's height, but bent over as she was, Jalan could have looked down on her. Gripped in one hand she was dragging a pale, silver-haired body—one of the Vil Adanrath, either dead or unconscious; Amira could not be sure.

The old crone came forward until she was only a few paces from the belkagen, then she spat. "Ach! Cursed wolf-elf. Blech! Who could eat such a thing?" She dropped the unconscious sentry into the snow, sniffed the air, and fixed her eyes on everyone gathered around the dead fire. "But I do smell a human. Tasty manflesh."

The belkagen lowered his staff, and it seemed to glow even brighter as he spoke. "There is no meal for you here, Tselelka. Leave our sentry there and be off."

The old woman cackled and thrust her staff toward them, and a great deluge of hail and ice fell with a loud roar. Only a few shards hit before the belkagen raised his own staff, spoke a harsh incantation, and a half-globe shield, faintly sparkling, covered them all.

The old woman stamped her foot, and the ice storm died away. "Kwarun. It is you, eh? I feared as much. Damn and damn. I thought you were meddling in the south these days."

The belkagen lowered his staff, and the magic shield flickered away. "How was your hunting this season, Tselelka?"

"Pfah. No more than a few gems and an amulet. Hardly worth my time, though the amulet will give me something to puzzle over this winter. What might you be up to, old meddler?"

"Our business is none of your concern."

"If you're here, your business is Winterkeep. Tselelka is old, but she's no fool. And only fools find themselves at Winterkeep after the first snow falls."

"You're here."

"I am leaving."

The belkagen fixed her with a hard glare. "Then don't let us keep you. But leave our hunter behind. If you've hurt him, I'll make finding you my first order of business come spring."

The old crone cackled. She seemed genuinely pleased. "Kwarun, you always did know how to warm a girl's heart. Don't worry. I took no more than a nibble out of your watchdog. He can tell the rest of his litter it's a love bite from old Tselelka."

Amira pushed her way forward. "You've come from Winterkeep, old woman. What is there?"

Tselelka's eyes lit with a sudden fire at the sight of Amira. Her nostrils flared and she licked her lips as she took an eager step forward.

The belkagen stepped in front of Amira and pushed her back. "Back, hag! I said you'll find no meal here."

The old woman scowled, and the hunger in her eyes only seemed to increase. "Cruel, Kwarun. Poor old Tselelka's had nothing but rats and worse for months. Haven't had a bit of manflesh since last summer, and this one smells *sweet*."

"I said no, Tselelka. Now be gone."

The old woman craned her neck to try to catch a glimpse of Amira. "Give old Tselelka a taste and I'll answer your question, girlie."

The belkagen flicked his staff and said, *"Crithta!"* White fire shot from his staff and struck the ground in front of the old woman.

Tselelka shielded her eyes and stepped back from the steaming hole in the snow before her. "Missed, old meddler!"

"I hit where I aimed," said the belkagen. He lowered his staff, pointing the end right at the old woman. "And the next one will hit as well. Now off with you! You and your orglash!"

The hag looked at the belkagen through narrowed eyes. "I hope we meet again, meddler, when Tselelka is rested and fed. I hope you survive your latest folly so that I can teach you some manners. Flee Winterkeep. Listen to the wind, and perhaps we'll meet again."

The old woman motioned to the cyclone behind her, which suddenly grew and spread, hitting everyone with galeforce winds and blinding them in the snow. Amira had a spell half cast when the wind died away and the snow settled. The old hag was gone, leaving the senseless sentry on the ground.

"Listen to the wind?" Amira asked. "What's that mean?"

"Listen," said Haerul.

Amira did. With the orglash gone, the north wind had returned, but now it seemed colder, and besides the hissing of the snow, Amira could almost swear she heard voices, fell and dark, chanting at the back of the wind.

Far away, on the tattered edges of the storm, a long tear opened in the clouds, and the waxing moon shone through like a baleful eye peeking through a torn curtain. Its pale light reflected off miles of steppe, now covered with a fresh blanket of white.

On the very edge of the moon's light, the blanket of snow rose, shedding snow in places as the ground rose to a great height—a high hill shaped like a broken and weathered fang that had long since given up biting at the sky. The Mother's Bed.

At its summit, amid a thick grove of trees that even now still bore green, a large rock leaned out of the soil, a great crack forming a cave at its base.

Gyaidun, all alone, no sacrifice in hand, watched that yawning darkness a long time. He remembered the words spoken only three days ago.

"*Hro'nyewachu* will be hungry," the belkagen had said. "If you have no gift . . ."

"What?" Amira had asked.

"Feed *Hro'nyewachu* or she will feed on you," Gyaidun had told her.

"What kind of Oracle is this?"

"I told you," the belkagen said. "She is a being of need—both in fulfilling and needing to be fulfilled. Nothing comes free. Blood for blood."

"So be it," said Gyaidun. "Blood for blood." He raised his knife and walked into the hungry darkness.

CHAPTER TWENTY-SIX

The Endless Wastes

Dawn was no more than a dim gloom bleeding through the deep darkness. Huddled near the fire, unable to sleep, Amira clutched her staff tight. In the back of her mind, she knew that far beyond the storm the sun was rising in the east. Part of her welcomed the knowledge that somewhere out there, light still shone through open skies and brought warmth to the land, even if she could not feel it here. But the foremost part of her mind dreaded the coming of dawn. At first light—or what would pass for it today—the last of the scouts would return, and they would set their plan into motion.

Regret and worry tugged at her heart, and she cursed herself for agreeing to the belkagen's plan. Not the taking of the fight to the enemy. In that, she was steadfast. But after the hag's departure, their council had resumed, and after much debate, the old elf had put forth his plan.

"The Vil Adanrath should attack *Iket Sotha* in force. Be seen. Draw our enemies to you." He hesitated—in hindsight Amira knew why—then looked to her. "You should lead them, Lady Amira."

She opened her mouth to respond, but Leren beat her to it.

"Her? The people speak of the prowess she showed in battle, but outlanders do not lead the Vil Adanrath."

"Lady Amira led the forces of her people against the Horde," said the belkagen. "None doubt her courage or prowess. But many days ago she was taken captive by an oathless slaver. A man little more than a common bandit bound her and made her his slave."

Amira considered pointing out that she'd been taken by surprise and that Walloch had been much more than a "common bandit." A slaver he might have been, but he'd studied the lore of Raumathar for years and had turned out to be quite a formidable wizard in his own right. All this was true, and although it stung her pride, she kept her mouth shut. In this, she agreed with Leren. Let the Vil Adanrath fight their own way. Her place was with Jalan.

"But," the belkagen continued, "that was before she sought *Hro'nyewachu*. Lady Amira is chosen."

"She does not bear the . . . the *uwethla*," said one of the Vil Adanrath women. "I am sorry, Lady Amira, I do not know your words for this."

The woman stood, pulled back her cloak, and much to Amira's shock lifted her buckskin shirt to display her torso and breasts. Like Haerul, her skin was a mass of black, blue, and green inks, but over them were red runes that seemed to drink in the light of the fire.

She sat back down. "Lady Amira is not omah. Are you saying she is belkagen?"

Her cheeks burning, Amira glanced down at her son. If the sight of a comely woman lifting her shirt before him disturbed him at all, he didn't show it. He simply stared into the fire, seemingly oblivious to his surroundings.

The belkagen nodded as if considering the woman's words, then said, "I hear you, Turha. No, Lady Amira is not omah, nor is she belkagen. In truth . . ." He paused letting his words hang. "In truth, I do not know what she is. Not in all my years, nor the times of my greatest grandfathers, has an outlander sought *Hro'nyewachu* and lived. Yet here she is. The omah nin himself bore witness to her journey. Would any here doubt the word of the omah nin?"

There were several gathered who had arrived lately and had not been there at the Mother's Bed. They looked to their high chief. He did not return their gaze but fixed his stare on the belkagen.

"The belkagen speaks the truth," said the omah nin. "Lady Amira entered the cave in darkness and emerged at dawn."

"But do we know she saw *Hro'nyewachu?*" asked another omah.

The omah nin gave him a hard look but said nothing.

"You doubt the word of the omah nin?" said Leren. "Of the belkagen?"

The elf looked at Amira and shook his head. "I do not. But as you have said, this is most strange. Never in all our days have we heard such a thing. It is a hard bite to swallow."

Another opened his mouth to speak, but the belkagen cleared his throat. The younger elf shut his mouth, and all eyes turned to the belkagen.

"I hear you," he said. "Turha spoke truly. Lady Amira does not bear the *uwethla*. Such was not the gift of *Hro'nyewachu*. But do not think that Amira left giftless." He turned to Amira. "Lady, stand and present the staff."

All eyes turned to Amira. Her heart hammering in her chest, she reluctantly peeled Jalan off her side and stood. The staff was longer than she was tall, but she had kept most of it huddled inside the cloak with her. She thrust off the side of her cloak, a blast of cold hit her, and she raised the staff before her. The light from the fire caught in the gold-red wood and flickered along its length. The runes etched along the staff's surface blazed, and Amira heard several of the gathered elves gasp.

"What is this, Belkagen?" said the omah nin, and even his proud voice held a tone of awe.

"When *Hro'nyewachu* gave this to Amira," said the belkagen, "these were her words: 'It will sharpen the bite she gives her enemies.' Thus I name the staff *Karakhnir*. It was *Hro'nyewachu* herself who counseled us to take Amira's son to the Witness Tree in *Iket Sotha,* and it was *Hro'nyewachu* who gave Amira this staff to hurt those who would hurt her son. Do we doubt the word of our people's most sacred heart?"

That silenced all argument. Feeling suddenly exposed and on display, Amira lowered the staff and sat back down beside her son.

"We make war upon the Fist of Winter and their minions," the belkagen continued. *"Hro'nyewachu* bids us to do so and gives to Amira the weapon to lead us." He glanced around the gathering, then said, "I have spoken," and sat down.

All eyes turned to the omah nin. He sat in silence a long while, looking at no one. When he looked up, his gaze fixed on Amira. "We will attack *Iket Sotha* as *Hro'nyewachu* commands. We will bring fear to our enemies. And Lady Amira will lead us. The omah nin has spoken."

"Wait!" said Amira. "No one has asked me what *I* think of this."

Turha frowned at her. "The omah nin has spoken."

Amira thought of a half-dozen ways she could point out that omah nin or no, she was not Vil Adanrath and no matter how many oracles this man consulted, he was not her lord. Instead, she said the one thing she meant most.

"I'm not leaving my son. Not again. He's been taken from me twice already. Until we've dealt with this . . . this monster, Jalan isn't leaving me."

The belkagen said, "Lady—"

"No! Don't you 'Lady' me. You said it yourself. This staff, this *Karakhnir* is our best defense against these fiends who want nothing more than to take my son. I'm his best hope of staying safe."

"Lady Amira, I—"

But this time it was the omah nin who cut him off, simply by raising one hand. Haerul waited for silence, then said, "Your son's best hope is to kill those trying to harm him, and your best hope for doing that is to attack them before they attack you. Do you truly wish to take your son into battle?"

"No, of course not, but . . ."

The omah nin raised his eyebrows and nodded. It was the same expression her brother used to make at her when besting her in some argument, and Amira almost threw her staff at the high chief.

"Lady Amira," said the belkagen, his voice mild, "will you hear me?"

Amira looked at him, her mouth a razor-sharp line, and gave one stiff nod.

"Remember the words of *Hro'nyewachu.* Jalan must go to the Witness Tree. Whatever is going to happen there, we must buy Jalan time. We must keep the Fist of Winter distracted at all costs. You and *Karakhnir* will do this like no other. The Vil Adanrath will fight, but it is you and your staff that the Fist of Winter will fear. You know this."

Amira did know it, though she hated every bit of it. Sifting through the oracle's words, she grasped the last tattered string of the unraveling cloth of her argument.

"I will give you the staff, Belkagen. Lead your people to victory. I will take Jalan to this Witness Tree and do . . . whatever must be done."

The belkagen shook his head and sighed. "I cannot. The staff is for you and you alone. I will not desecrate the gift of *Hro'nyewachu.*"

And so it had been decided. And so it would begin any time now—Amira leading the first strikeforce upon Winterkeep while other packs came in from every direction. The plan was simple: Keep the enemy's attention fixed on Winterkeep. The belkagen and Lendri would take Jalan to the Witness Tree.

By sunset tonight, all this would be over, one way or another. Amira swore to her gods that Jalan would be free today, or she would be dead trying to free him.

❦ ❦ ❦ ❦ ❦

The belkagen and Lendri came to her not long after. Amira's heart lurched, and she swallowed. The elves stopped near her fire.

"It is time, Lady," said the belkagen.

Amira looked down at her son. "I don't know if I can do this," she said.

"You must."

"Please, Belkagen," she said, her eyes welling with hot tears. "He's just a boy."

"This is a cruel world, Lady," said the belkagen. "You now face what all mothers face. Your boy can be a boy no longer. You cannot protect him forever. He must stand on his own."

"I don't fear him standing on his own," she said, and the tears fell, freezing on her cheeks. "I fear him falling alone. He's not ready for this. Not yet."

"He will not be alone," said Lendri. "The belkagen and I will watch over Jalan. If anything tries to harm him, it will have to take our life's blood first. If it is the will of your gods and ours that Jalan die today, he will die beside friends. That is the most anyone can ask of the gods."

Amira sniffed, trying to contain her tears. She did the one thing she'd learned to do at a very young age: She turned her grief and heartbreak to anger. "I hate the godsdamned Wastes," she said. "I hate them."

"She is a hard land," said Lendri, "and she breeds hard children. Take heart and give grief to your enemies."

Something that was half-sob and half-chuckle shook Amira. "Ah, Lendri. Someday I'm going to introduce you to my mother. You'll learn hard then." She stepped forward, twisted a brass ring off her finger, and handed it to Lendri. "Here. Take this."

The elf took it and studied it, turning it in his fingers. "What is it?"

"Something a dear friend once gave me. It's magical."

"I am no wizard, Lady."

"You need not be, not with this ring," she said. She explained to him what it did and how to use it. "It will work only once, so don't waste it. It may not be much, but it helped me escape from that lecherous bastard Walloch when all my best spells were spent."

Lendri put the ring on the middle finger of his right hand and bowed. "Thank you, Lady. I will use this gift in service to your son."

The belkagen cleared his throat and said, "Amira."

"Yes?" Only a slight flutter shook her voice.

"It is time. We must wake Jalan and go."

CHAPTER TWENTY-SEVEN

Winterkeep

Late morning. The low, slate-colored sky threatened overhead, and Amira looked down for the first time upon the ruins of Winterkeep. Only the seven pillars—all broken at various lengths—were visible. The piles of broken stone and boulders that the belkagen had told her littered the ground were now only great drifts of snow.

But Amira had seen it all before. In *Hro'nye-wachu* she'd seen *Iket Sotha* die, and in her mind's eye she could still see the seven-pillared colonnade, the wooden mansions and outbuildings, and the wall of finished logs painted in the royal colors of Raumathar.

The air was so cold that the snow seemed more of a frozen mist coming off the sea. From where she crouched on the slight rise of land, Amira could see the ruins, but beyond that was only a constantly shifting canvass of white and gray.

She turned around. Leren and two massive gray wolves crouched behind her. Fanning out behind them were more Vil Adanrath, both elves and wolves. Some of the elves carried weapons, but a few had stripped down to loincloths so that they could change to their wolf forms in battle. Even with the small bit of *kanishta* root wedged in her jaw, flooding her body with warmth, just watching the nearly naked elves crouched in the snow made her shiver.

"Any sign of the enemy?" asked Leren.

Amira found it an odd question, elf eyesight being far superior to her own. But then she realized that she *could* sense something. Through the thick hide of her gloves, she could feel power pulsing through the staff, connecting her to their surroundings, almost as if the staff were a young sapling with thousands upon thousands of roots spreading throughout the ground. To the north, scattered throughout the ruins of Winterkeep, that life seemed to twist and warp, as if shunning something there.

"Something's down there," she said. "I can't see it, but I can sense it."

"*Iket Sotha* is very old," said Leren. "Terrible things happened there long ago, and many foul creatures lurk in its depths. Perhaps that is what you are sensing?"

"Perhaps," said Amira, but she didn't believe it.

Off to their right in the distance came a long howl, plaintive and ending on a low note. It was the signal to begin their advance. One more off to the south would be the signal to the belkagen to get Jalan to the Witness Tree.

They set off at an easy trot, Amira leading them. The wolves fanned out, flanking them but slowing their pace so as not to outdistance the others.

Two-thirds of the way down the slope, they were approaching a series of humps that Amira had taken for snow-covered boulders. But as they drew close, the mounds erupted, and a half-dozen Frost Folk threw off their blanket of snow and the cloaks under them. Axes and swords raised, they charged Amira and the Vil Adanrath.

Amira raised her staff, and a wave of elves and wolves swept past her. She cursed as an elf and his wolf-brother leaped between her and her intended target.

But the Frost Folk turned and ran, heading for the ruins. A Vil Adanrath arrow sent one crashing into the snow, and three wolves fell upon him, rending and tearing. The tall men were surprisingly swift, not outpacing the elves but matching their speed. When they reached a large snowdrift they stopped and turned. A pair of winter wolves came round one side, three round the other, and two climbed the crest of the drift. Upon the topmost wolf—a great white beast larger than a stallion—a figure hunched inside an ash-gray cloak.

Amira screamed and charged.

The Frost Folk and winter wolves held their ground and waited for the Vil Adanrath to come to them. To Amira, the battle was a cacophony of growling and shrieking wolves, shouting men and elves, the clash of steel on steel, and the cries of the dying. Once the forces met, all was chaos, but Amira kept her focus on one thing only: the sorcerer.

He came down at them, his winter wolf charging the smaller wolves, teeth bared and a growl coming from its chest that caused the air itself to tremble. Amira saw one of the black-feathered arrows of the Vil Adanrath pierce its side, but so great was its battle-rage that it didn't seem to notice. Three wolves and an elf stood between it and Amira, but they scattered as the great wolf bore down upon them.

Amira held her ground—she could feel it trembling beneath her feet—and raised her staff. The winter wolf was coming so fast. She knew she'd only have one chance at this.

She thrust her open palm at the wolf's head and shouted, *"Dramasthe!"*

The bolt of yellow energy shot from her hand. It struck the beast full in the face, and in the moment of clarity that often came to her in battle, when moments seemed to stretch out to days, she saw bits of scorched flesh and skin shower outward, and the wolf's left eye exploded.

Its growl rose to a shriek, and the animal tumbled into the snow face first, sending up a great cloud of frost mixed with bits of smoke and blood. The rider in the ash-gray cloak went down as well, and Amira lost sight of him in all the flying snow and debris.

The winter wolf jumped to its feet and ran off northward, shaking its head in agony.

Amira saw the ash-gray cloak rising, perhaps even shaking a bit, and she thrust her staff forward with a cry. *"Keljan saulé!"*

The runes etched into the staff flared, bathing Amira and the surrounding snowfield in a warm glow, and a shard of light shot out. It struck the ash-gray robes, and the figure flew backward as if struck by a giant's club. He hit the ground several paces away and fell into a smoking heap. Amira watched, ignoring the carnage around her and preparing another strike, but the sorcerer did not move.

She ran forward, her staff ready. Out of the corner of her eye. she saw one of the Frost Folk fall, a black wolf's jaws locked around his throat.

The sorcerer still had not moved. The mass of gray fabric smoked from her strike, and the surrounding snow steamed as it melted. She slowed as she approached, and still the figure had not moved.

Keeping the point of her staff aimed directly at the dark mass, the words of the spell ready on her lips, Amira stepped forward. The stench hit her—a foul odor of burned fabric and flesh. One hand, pale as the snow in which it lay, was flung outward, almost like an orator's motion in mid-speech.

Amira put the tip of her staff inside the cowl and pulled. The fabric came away, and a lifeless head fell backward against the outstretched arm. It was not the emaciated face she remembered, the corpselike visage covered in pallid skin. This man's features were white, his hair whiter still, long and healthy.

It was one of the *Siksin Neneweth,* one of the Frost Folk, and he was quite dead.

The knowledge hit Amira, freezing her insides.

They'd been fooled.

Only one thought came to her mind, and it passed her lips unbidden.

"Jalan!"

CHAPTER TWENTY-EIGHT

The Isle of Witness

Nothing moved on the Isle of Witness. The island itself was really just a huge pinnacle of rock breaking the surface of the Great Ice Sea. Nothing but moss and a few shoots grew there. The soil was too rocky and the wind was too harsh. Even the great dead tree at the island's summit stood implacable, as it had for hundreds of years. Only the thickest boughs remained, and they were hard as iron from the countless ages of bitter cold and salt-tinged air.

A stone stairway—once decorated with many signs both sacred and arcane, but now weathered and broken—descended from the base of the Witness Tree to the northern shore of the island. At the base of the stair the air rippled, almost like a heat mirage, then darkened and solidified into the folds of a greatcloak. It was made from the skin of some great animal, and bits of fur lined the hem. The arcane symbols upon it glowed briefly, a warm green light. The great hump of a cloak rose and billowed. Straightening, the belkagen drew back the folds of his greatcloak, and Lendri and Jalan emerged.

The trio straightened. Lendri's eyes were wide with uneasiness, and he flinched at being exposed to the wind off the sea, snow and sleet striking his face. Their breath steamed for an instant before crystallizing and joining the snow, and even Lendri, who was seldom bothered even by intense cold, shivered. Only the boy seemed unaffected, and his eyes had a dullness to them, like resignation or even drunkenness.

The belkagen's brow creased. Cold was to be expected, but this . . . already his hair had frozen to bits of ice, and even blinking hurt. Realization of what this meant hit him.

"No. Oh, no!"

He turned. On the hill above them, emerging from behind the thick trunk of the Witness Tree, stood the Fist of Winter—all five of them, and they looked down at the belkagen and his two charges.

"Back!" shouted the belkagen, throwing the folds of his cloak around Lendri and Jalan. He held them tight and ducked under his hood.

One of the sorcerers stepped forward, laughing. He lowered his tattered hood. Pallid skin and dead, black eyes seemed unconcerned as he smiled into the full force of the storm. It was Erun. He motioned with his hands and mouthed the words of a spell.

The belkagen froze. His cloak wasn't working. Erun—or what had once been Erun—had used his own foul arts to nullify the power in the cloak.

"Give us the boy," said Erun, shouting to be heard over the wind and waves. His voice was harsh and subhuman, as if his will forced his throat to utter sounds strange to it.

The belkagen stood and pushed Lendri and Jalan behind him. He held his staff up, shielding them.

"You cannot have him," said the belkagen. "Not again."

But the belkagen stumbled forward as Jalan pushed

past him and rushed up the stairs.

Lendri lunged after him, but Erun drew a single-edged sword with one fluid motion and shouted, *"Silo'at!"*

Biting frost funneled outward against the gale and struck Lendri full-force, sending him flying back into the rocks, frost and ice coating him from chin to waist. He hit hard then rolled over, groaning, trying to rise only to have his body betray him.

Jalan ascended the last few steps on all fours, then fell and hugged Erun's legs. While the belkagen watched, dumbstruck, Erun placed one emaciated hand on the boy's neck and spoke an incantation. Jalan flinched as if he'd been slapped across the face, then collapsed.

"What—?" the belkagen spoke his thought aloud.

Erun smiled. There was no humor in it, merely the baring of teeth. "My hold on him is no longer necessary."

"All this time . . ."

"I *let* you take him, old fool. You think that wench could have beaten me so easily? I let him go, and through him I watched you. Heard you. And so when I knew you'd be bringing him back to me, I . . . let you." He shrugged, though coming from the sorcerer it seemed an obscene gesture, unnatural. The shoulders moving beneath the tattered cloak and robes reminded the belkagen of a dung beetle flexing its carapace. "It has long been a weakness of mine," Erun continued. "I like to play with my prey."

The enchantment broken, Jalan, trembling from cold and terror, tried to scramble back down the steps, but the sorcerer bent and snatched him, quick as a scorpion. He held the boy by the hair and pulled him back. Jalan screamed.

"Jalan, no!" said the belkagen. "Erun, don't hurt him!"

The sorcerer shook the boy until tears leaked out of Jalan's terror-stricken eyes and froze on his cheeks.

"Erun?" said the sorcerer. "That is not my name. I merely wear that boy's skin. What was Erun has been sleeping for a long time—and having most unpleasant dreams. Oh, how the boy screams."

✧ ✧ ✧ ✧ ✧

Amira stood on the black, ice-slick rocks of the shore, looking across the water to the island. Staring into the storm, snow and sleet stinging her face, she could just make out five figures standing beneath an old, long-dead tree. The wind off the Great Ice Sea tossed their cloaks, but through the waving fabric she was sure she saw Jalan.

She clenched her fist and punched her hip in frustration. The great pinnacle of rock was several hundred paces offshore, but it might as well have been a league. She'd tried again and again to use her magic to transport her out there, but something was blocking her spell. The core of her mind could feel the power hammering against some unseen barrier, and nothing she tried could break through. Even if the water hadn't been broken by tall white-capped waves, the temperature itself would've made swimming impossible. She'd freeze before she got halfway, assuming she didn't drown.

She turned to the elf who had accompanied her to the shore. It was Turha, one of the female omah from last night's council. "Is there any way out there?" Amira asked. "Boats? Anything?"

Turha shook her head. "Nothing. In summer, one must swim. In winter, we walk the ice. Now . . ."

Two other Vil Adanrath, one coated in blood, were coming toward them, three wolves at their heels. The bloody one had a bow.

"You!" Amira shouted. She pointed to the figures on the island. "Can you hit them from here?"

The elf looked at the target. "Not in this wind. Even if I could, my arrows would not stop th—"

"Damn you all!" Amira shouted. "Does no one have anything useful to say?"

Desperate, Amira peeled her gloves off with her teeth, dropped them, and began to work at the knot of her cloak.

"Lady," said Turha, "what are you—?"

Tears were filling Amira's eyes. "If I take off most of these damned clothes and the boots, maybe I can make it."

"The cold will kill you," said Turha. "Even the Vil Adanrath would not attempt this."

"I'm not one of the damned Vil Ad—"

A great commotion behind them cut her off. Elves shouting and wolves growling. Amira turned, fearing that more Frost Folk or winter wolves had found them. Three elves, their wolves milling about, were trying to restrain a huge figure, covered head to heels in thick, dark blood so that his eyes shone bright from his feral visage. The elves were armed, and their shouts and enraged faces showed their fury, but they did not attack the figure. They seemed to be trying to restrain him and were cursing him in their native tongue. But they were unable to slow him.

Amira's hammering heart skipped a beat and she held her breath, for as the figure drew close she recognized him. It was Gyaidun, his shirt hanging off him in tatters, his pants ripped, his hair unbound and sticky with blood, his iron club in one hand and his knife bare in the other, both thick with gore. From the scratches and cuts lining his torso, Amira knew that at least some of the blood was his. He stopped before her, panting, and the stench hit her—the salty tang of blood, the acidic bite of darker heart's blood, and wafting through it all the scent of spring blossoms. The smell caused a memory to hit her like a club: *Hro'nyewachu.* No other odor matched it—the stench of death and the fragrance of new life.

Amira blinked. "Gyaidun? How . . . ? What hap—?"

Turha looked as if she were ready to stab Gyaidun with her spear, and three of the surrounding elves grabbed at his arms and tried to drag him away, one of them shouting, *"Hrayek!* You have no place here!"

"Stop!" Amira shouted. "Let him be! Gyaidun how did you get h—?"

"He is *hrayek!*" said Turha. "He cannot be in our presence!"

Amira glared at the lady omah. "Then leave, damn you."

Turha turned to the Vil Adanrath warriors and said, "Get him out of here. Drag him if you must."

But Gyaidun held them off with his knife and club. "No time!" he said. "That bastard out there has some sort of link with Jalan. He knows everything you've planned."

This renewed Amira's panic, and she finally managed to tear loose the knot of her cloak and throw it to the ground.

"What are you doing?" Gyaidun said.

"I have to get out there!"

"Swimming? You'll never make it. The cold will kill you."

"What choice do I have?"

"Your magic," he said. "It brought you here last night. Use it to get us out there."

"Us? But Erun—"

"I know how to stop this!" he said. "But I have to get out there before it's too late."

The words of the oracle came back to her. She hadn't heard them, had been lost in some dark dream forced on her by the oracle. But the belkagen had asked the oracle, face to face, if the staff she'd given would save Jalan, and she had replied, *No. That task is for another.*

Hope and despair tore at her heart.

"Amira!" Gyaidun said. "Get us out there. Now!"

"I can't!" she shrieked. "Don't you think I've tried? Something is blocking the magic. Some counterspell—"

"Can you get us above it—out of range?" asked Gyaidun.

"In the water? But . . . the cold. You said—"

"Not the water!" He pointed to the sky above the distant island. "The air!"

"The fall will kill us!"

"You're a wizard, aren't you?"

CHAPTER TWENTY-NINE

The Isle of Witness

Lendri was still down. Not dead, but in such agony he could scarcely move.

The belkagen looked up to the pinnacle where the five sorcerers stood beneath the Witness Tree. The old elf's hands trembled, and his knees felt weak. The burden he had carried down the long years, the knowledge no living being should ever have, had come to him at last. Here it was. The fear hit him as it always did when he recalled the vision of *Hro'nyewachu*, but this time he did not let it weaken him. The fulfillment of his vision, the consummation of his mission, was here. The final reward. But as he'd told *Hro'nyewachu*, it could come only through pain.

"As are all things worth having," he said, remembering her words. "So be it."

The belkagen raised his staff, knowing the futility

of what he was about to do. But instead of letting it weaken him, he accepted the knowledge and embraced it. Knowing the ending—or at least part of it—was oddly liberating.

"Jalan!" he shouted. "Hold on to something!"

The five sorcerers looked down upon him, and two of them began to weave their hands in their own summoning, but the belkagen was quicker. He raised his staff and said, *"U werekh kye wu!"*

The galeforce wind at his back switched directions and hit him from the left with a force beyond any hurricane. Waves broke against the side of the island, and the great mist tossed upward froze to ice and shot across the island like millions of tiny arrows. The wind caught in the cloaks and robes of the five sorcerers and they tumbled off the pinnacle. Four splashed into the water while Erun clung to the rocks like a barnacle.

The wind died off, then resumed its normal course. The belkagen spared a glance upward to make sure Jalan was unharmed. The boy clung to the twisted roots of the Witness Tree and looked down on him with wide eyes. Sweeping his staff down toward the water, the belkagen said, *"Kaharenharik ket!"*

Five bolts of lightning cracked the sky and hit the water. For the belkagen, all sound ceased and the world went white. His hair stood on end and flickers of blue electric light danced around his outstretched arms. Sound returned to the world as a great clap of thunder rattled the sky and shook the rocks beneath his feet.

The belkagen blinked, and when his eyes opened he saw Erun scrambling up the rocks like a spider, but upon reaching a small outcropping he jumped into the wind, which caught in his robes, causing them to billow like a great bat. He flew into the air and landed on the stone stairway halfway between the belkagen and Jalan.

A great cracking hit the belkagen's ears, and his first thought was that the rock had been split by the lightning, but then he saw the ice. The very waters of Yal Tengri were freezing in a column at the base of the island, and riding atop it were the other four sorcerers. The robes and cloaks were sodden, and the belkagen could see bits of flesh hanging off the hands of the nearest, but they otherwise seemed unharmed.

The column of ice twisted and turned at the command of one of the sorcerers until it reached the side of the island. The four sorcerers stepped off the ice. One of them, the one whose flesh hung off the bones of his right hand, shambled as if weighed down by sickness or great age. It was to him that Erun pointed.

"Take Gerghul to the boy," he said. "I will deal with this meddler."

"No!" said the tallest of the four, and the belkagen cowered at the sound of his voice. This one had no cloak and cowl like the others, but his robes were of the same ash-gray color, and it was as if the heart of winter had taken form inside those robes. The voice sounded of the darkest, emptiest places the belkagen had ever imagined. "I will deal with this one. You will see to Gerghul before it is too late."

"Jalan!" shouted the belkagen, ashamed at the quiver he heard in his voice. "Run, boy! Run!"

But Erun was too swift—far beyond any natural ability—and he shot up the steps. Jalan made it no more than two steps before he was caught. The other three took their time, two helping their weaker companion ascend the hill.

The tallest came at the belkagen, not hurrying but keeping a slow, deliberate pace, his corpse-pale hands weaving the motions of a spell. The belkagen could feel a sudden brittleness taking the air, and a coldness began to grow in his heart, as if a small hole had opened in him and was swallowing all the warmth and life in his body. He clutched at his chest and fell to his knees. His staff clattered on the ground beside him.

The sorcerer grabbed the belkagen under the jaw and lifted him until the old elf was staring into the impenetrable darkness of the cowl. Somewhere he could hear a boy screaming.

"My children have spoken of you," said the sorcerer. "In the north, they fear you, you and your mongrels. I am unimpressed."

The grip tightened, and the belkagen felt a tooth snap loose. Blood filled his mouth, but it held no warmth. The coldness inside him seemed to have filled his entire chest, and he could no longer move his limbs.

A snarling silver shadow hit the sorcerer, and the belkagen fell. He dropped in a heap and struggled to breathe. Each breath sent lances of pain through his head, but with it came warmth.

The belkagen looked up. The sorcerer was on the ground, his mass of robes tangled round a snarling, biting silver-white form. Lendri!

The sorcerer hit the smaller elf, and Lendri went flying. But he hit the ground running, and the belkagen saw that the elf's eyes had turned gold, his teeth grown long and sharp, prominent in his elongated, beastlike jaw. He shrieked—a sound that was half battle-cry, half beast, and all fury—and charged, his knife in one hand.

Hot courage building in his heart, the belkagen scrambled for his staff.

The sorcerer's grip on his shoulder was so cold that it stung, even through the layers of clothes. Screaming, Jalan kicked and hit at the ash-gray robes, but he might as well have been striking the petrified tree. Desperate, he bent his neck and bit as hard as he could, but the taste was so foul that his throat closed and he gagged.

"Yes!" said the sorcerer as he pulled Jalan close. "Struggle. Scream! Your pain will make this all the sweeter."

Still trying to breathe and spit the foul taste out of his mouth, Jalan looked up. Two other sorcerers, much like the one he'd known for days save that their robes were drenched, stood over him, seemingly tall as towers. Another hunched between them, and even Jalan could see he was trembling and shaking.

"Hurry," said the cowering sorcerer. "I can . . . feel this husk dying."

The sorcerer holding Jalan thrust him toward the trunk of the long-dead tree, and the one who'd spoken half-stepped and half-fell forward. He was between Jalan and the wind, and the smell of tombs hit Jalan full in the face.

Jalan screamed.

"Yesss," said the weakened one. He pawed at Jalan, almost like an old crone stroking her favorite pet. "Oh, I like this one. I can . . . c-can taste him."

Lendri leaped, one hand extended in sharp claws and the other bringing his knife forward in an arc that hissed as it cut the air.

The sorcerer caught his forearm in one hand, his long arm gripping the bestial elf in an iron hold. Choking and spitting, Lendri stabbed and cut at the arm again and again, but the grip did not weaken. The sorcerer's arm did not even tremble.

The dark cowl turned to the belkagen. "I grow tired of your mongrel pets."

He pulled Lendri in close as his grip tightened. The belkagen heard bone snap, and he raised his staff, a spell forming on his lips.

Lendri dropped his knife and screamed, but it was not wholly in pain. *"Lamathris!"* he shouted.

Flames swirled out of the ring on his finger—the ring Amira had given to him—and with his fist wreathed in flame, he punched the sorcerer in the stomach. Wet and stiff with ice though the robes were, the magic fire caught in them and blazed upward.

The sorcerer screamed—

Vyaidelon! Jalan prayed. *Help me! Help me, please!*

But no answer came, and the power that had awakened

in him that night on the steppes was beyond him. He could sense it, feel it growing in him, but it was as if an unbreakable barrier—one made of ice—separated him from the the light.

"Help!" Jalan screamed, his voice breaking. "Somebody help me!"

"There is no help for you now," said the sorcerer—the shambling one who reeked of death and decay. He pulled Jalan close to him. "Tonight you will dream in endless darkness, the utter cold of—"

A scream, so loud and piercing that it was almost beyond sound, broke the air, and the four sorcerers over him staggered. The one holding Jalan lost his grip altogether and fell on his hands.

The shriek died away and one of the sorcerers—the one who had kidnapped Jalan and dragged him across the Wastes—looked down the hill.

"Go . . . to h-him," said the one near Jalan, and he crawled forward and grabbed him once more. "I will deal with this one."

The three other sorcerers swept away, like clouds blown by the wind, and Jalan looked up into the cowl of the one remaining. He could feel the cold emanating off the sorcerer in waves, and behind it all was an insatiable *hunger*.

Jalan kicked at him. Bits of skin and flesh flew off the bones of the sorcerer's arm. Some of it, greasy and sticky with decay, stuck to Jalan, but the grip did not lessen.

The sorcerer struggled to his feet, but only made it halfway, standing hunched over and weaving in the wind like an old man. With his free hand, he reached into the folds of his robes and drew forth an ornate blade. It seemed part steel and part ice. Sharp, jagged runes covered the blade, and they glowed with a cold, blue light. Jalan could feel it pulling all warmth and life from his body.

Jalan cringed, a whimper escaping his throat.

The sorcerer laughed, a rasp like dust sliding down gravestones, and said, "This blade cuts more than flesh, boy. You're right . . . to fear it. To fear me."

He raised the blade.

Jalan continued to kick and punch, but to no avail. He thrashed and turned, hoping against hope to be able to avoid the dagger.

"Don't struggle, boy," said the sorcerer. "Soon all will be . . . over. For you. Darkness. Cold. But for me . . . tonight I'll wear your . . . s-skin when I find your mother. When I . . . eat her heart."

Unable to look away, Jalan watched as the decaying muscles tightened in preparation for the downstroke—

A dark shape fell out of the sky and struck the sorcerer in the back, smashing him into the rocks. Jalan screamed. A demon! The sorcerer had summoned a demon to take his soul!

But the figure that struggled to his feet was no demon. He was a man—tall and thick with hard muscle, dressed in torn bits of leather that might once have been clothes, and every inch of him coated in dried blood. From the near-black blood, the man's eyes seemed to shine forth with both fury and pain. In one hand the man held a single-edge knife, the blade of which was almost as long as his forearm, and in the other he held a black iron club.

The sorcerer stood. His robes and much of his cloak had been torn away, and in the rents Jalan saw bits of ribs broken through the emaciated, gray skin. But even as he watched, the bones sank back into the flesh, mending with a sickening popping and crunching.

The man brought his club down in a fierce strike aimed for the ash-gray cowl, but the sorcerer caught the club in his hand. Bone cracked and tiny bits of flesh flew away, but the sorcerer did not weaken his grip. He twisted the club out of the man's hand and brought the club back around, striking the man with his own weapon. The club caught the man in the gut and he folded in half as he tumbled off the hill.

The sorcerer turned back to Jalan, but the boy was too frozen with shock and fear to move. Where had the man come from? Who *was* he?

Dropping the club, the sorcerer snarled and shambled forward, but he made only two steps when another figure dropped out of the sky, more gently than the man had, and landed between them. The clothes and cloak were strange, but Jalan recognized her at once.

"Mother!"

She kept her back to him and turned to the sorcerer. "Get away from my son, you bastard!" she roared. She thrust forward a strange golden-red staff and shouted, *"Keljan saulé!"*

CHAPTER THIRTY

The Isle of Witness

The sorcerer screamed and flung Lendri away. He thrashed, his shriek rising in pitch until it passed beyond hearing. Still, the belkagen could sense it rattling inside his skull. The flames caught in the sorcerer's sleeves and lower robes, then ran down as if he were dipped in pitch.

Three shadows fell out of the storm sky and landed around the burning sorcerer. The tallest of the newcomers flung his palms out in an arcane gesture and screamed the words of a spell. A channel of wind filled with snow and sleet hit the gathered sorcerers, and so great was its force that the flames sputtered and died.

Most of the sorcerer's robes had gaping holes. His face was that of a cadaver kept alive by dark magics, his skin withered, gray, and stretched over a hairless skull. His nose was long gone, leaving only a desiccated hole. His eyes were deep pits rimmed in cold frostfire, and they bore down on the belkagen, who still lay prostrate on the rocks. The sorcerer raised his hand and pointed even as he spoke the words of his incantation.

The belkagen was halfway to his feet when the air around the sorcerer's hand coalesced and froze into a blue-white light and shot forth. The belkagen spoke his own spell and raised his staff just in time. The light struck the staff—

—a sharp *crack,* followed by a flash of darkness that the belkagen saw behind his eyes—

And the staff shattered, splinters and tiny shards of ice flying into the old elf's hand and face.

The belkagen screamed but kept moving. He turned his cry of pain into words of power and spread his arms wide as he leaped. The wind caught in his cloak, and as the hide billowed it rippled with magic, forming wings even as the elf's form shrank, his legs shortening and his feet stretching into claws, feathers covering his body. In a breath's time he transformed into an eagle and caught the wind current.

Too late.

Fierce channels of wind, twisting like tentacles and filled with ice, roared from above at the sorcerer's behest and struck the great bird from the sky. The belkagen lost his eagle form a dozen feet above the rocks and fell. He struck the rocks, bones shattering, not far from where Lendri was just now stirring. All breath left the belkagen's body, and dark clouds swam before his eyes.

Spells forming on their lips, the four sorcerers stepped toward the fallen elves.

A flash of golden light lit the sky above them, and for an instant everyone froze. All eyes looked up in time to see the fifth sorcerer, flame and a summer-golden light enveloping him, fly like a comet overhead. He shot over the island, trailing a silvery-white smoke, and landed with a splash in Yal Tengri.

The belkagen, struggling to breathe, and the four sorcerers, their spells frozen on their lips, turned to look up the hill. There, under the black boughs of the Witness Tree, stood Amira, her golden staff raised and Jalan clutched protectively under one arm.

Amira's eyes widened as she saw the four sorcerers coming straight at her. They didn't rush but walked at a deliberate pace. Their gaze, the light like a cold halo around their eyes, seemed to freeze her blood.

"Amira!" said a rasping voice behind her.

She turned. Gyaidun, fresh wounds scraping his already-bloody skin, was crawling over the broken remnants of the wall.

"Hold them off!" he said. "Just a few moments. I know how to stop them."

"What?"

"Just hold them off! And don't . . . don't hurt Erun. Please."

She turned to look back down the hill. They were almost to the bottom of the steps. Behind them, beyond the broken bodies of Lendri and the belkagen, just crawling over the rocks at the edge of the island, was the sorcerer she'd sent sailing out into the Great Ice Sea. A snarl of rage twisted his rotting visage, but aside from the scorched robes he seemed unharmed.

"I don't think that's going to be an issue." She looked down at her son and said, "Jalan."

He looked up at her, his golden eyes wide, and in that instant she noticed that color had returned to his cheeks. He looked warm. And something else. His eyes had been golden all his life, but now there was a light behind them, still small and uncertain, but growing.

"I love you, Jalan," she said, then pushed him away and charged down the stairs.

The belkagen watched the sorcerer emerge from Yal Tengri. He was soaked, most of his robes had burned away, and his decayed flesh hung off him, but still he pulled himself up the rocks and followed the others. His anger and malice seemed to fuel his strength.

The old elf tried to take a deep breath, and pain shot through him. That fall had cracked ribs, his right arm was broken, and he couldn't feel his fingers on that hand.

The words *Hro'nyewachu* had given to Amira came to him—

"The Witness Tree. There, all will be decided. Beyond that, I give you no assurances. Death and life will meet. Only those who surrender will triumph."

—and those she'd given to him—

"That task is for another."

The belkagen pushed himself to his feet. A cough that felt like sharp stones in his lungs shook him, and he saw bits of blood spatter from his lips. Lendri was struggling to his feet as well.

God of my ancestors, the belkagen prayed, *and you,* Hro'nyewachu, *if you can hear me . . . whatever is going to happen, please make it happen soon.*

He saw Amira charging, a golden light enveloping her. It lent him courage, for she looked like a goddess of summer incarnate—if summer were fury and fire.

The belkagen spoke the words of power. They tore at his throat, but he forced them out—*"Crith kesh het!"* A globe of searing radiance, like a tiny sun, enveloped him. *"U werekh kye wu!"*

The steady wind at his back gusted, grasping and lifting him, and he flew forward into the midst of the sorcerers.

The nearest turned to him, the wind blowing off the tattered cowl, and the belkagen saw that it was Erun. The boy the belkagen had watched take his first steps under the autumn boughs—

No! the belkagen reminded himself. That is *not* Erun, but the thing that killed him!

—snarled and raised a rapier, its silver steel glistening with fell magic.

The sorcerer flinched as the globe of light enveloping the

old elf hit him, but he held his ground. Too weak to control his flight, the belkagen could not avoid the blade. His eyes went wide the instant before the point shattered his cracked ribs and tore through his heart and lungs.

The belkagen's light went out, but he was smiling as the darkness closed in.

Amira saw the belkagen impaled upon that monster's sword, and she screamed, rage and sorrow cracking her voice. She hurled spells at her foes, magic flying from her staff and hands, but they bounced or shattered off the sorcerers' shields.

Erun flung the body of the belkagen off his blade and turned. He looked up at Amira and began an incantation, his free hand weaving an arcane pattern that cut the air and left a blue light in its wake. Amira could feel the air crackling with gathering power—

Then the wolf struck, a white mass of snarling fur and fangs that hit the sorcerer in the back, throwing him off balance.

More annoyed than hurt, Erun whirled, swinging his blade. The wolf dodged and backed off, favoring one leg, and in that moment Amira knew the wolf was Lendri.

She renewed her attack, loosing spell after spell, but every one broke on the sorcerers' shields.

"Enough of this!" the sorcerer that had been Erun roared. He raised his arms, the golden aura that still flickered round Amira glittering off his blade. *"Uthrekh rakhshan thra!"*

In the time it took Amira to draw a breath, the air round the island froze, going from mist to ice. Amira felt the moisture on her eyes freezing, and her inner ears began to pop and crack. Dizziness and nausea gripped her.

With what she felt sure would be her last breath she raised the staff the belkagen had named *Karakhnir* and shouted, *"Amalad saisen!"*

Heat. She felt it rising from the earth and flowing

through her. It flared from the staff, struggling to push back the unearthly cold. The ice—for it was truly ice, hard and biting, not snow—falling from the sky struck the wave of heat and steamed, but Amira could feel the cold pressing down upon her, almost like the weight of the sky itself, and she fell to her knees.

The cold hit Jalan, stealing all breath from his body. The air bit through his clothes, and he could feel his skin contracting, ice forming over his body, then he heard his mother shout words he didn't recognize, and the cold retreated . . . a little.

Jalan took a shuddering breath, then he saw his mother fall. He screamed.

The blood-covered man grabbed him and pulled him under the lowest bough of the great tree. Jalan struggled—he had no idea who this blood-covered man who fell from the sky could be—but his mother had spoken to him as if she knew him.

"Jalan!"

He looked up at the man.

"Jalan, you must trust me! There's still time to save your mother."

Jalan swallowed and said, "What do you want me to do?"

The big man bent and picked up a knife that had fallen on the ground. It was sharp only on one edge and nearly as long as the man's forearm. The man grabbed Jalan's wrist and brought the knife close.

Panic seized Jalan and he struggled, trying to get away, but the man's grip was too strong. Jalan punched and kicked.

"Jalan!" said the man. "Jalan, stop it! You must trust me!"

All the memories and horrors of the past days hit him—the sorcerer's blade drawing blood in the darkness, then coming at him, invading his mind—and he screamed and kicked all the harder.

But through his panic and the memories came a voice that he recognized at once, saying, *Surrender, Jalan. Trust him. Trust* me.

It was Vyaidelon.

Panting, his eyes still wide with fear, Jalan relented and relaxed his arm.

The big man nodded. "Good," he said. "I'll go first so that you will trust me."

With that, the man grabbed his knife and yanked it down, opening a deep gash across his palm. Fresh blood poured down his forearm, mingling with the older blood and mud dried there.

He reached for Jalan's hand, but Jalan flinched.

"Trust me, Jalan," said the man.

Jalan could feel the cold pressing in again, could hear his mother crying.

"Trust me."

Trust, Jalan. Be not afraid.

Jalan extended his right hand. The big man brought the edge of the blade across his open palm—Jalan winced—then brought their open palms together in a tight grip. Jalan could feel their blood mingling. It seemed hot and cold at the same time, soothing and biting.

A large drop of their blood fell onto the root of the great tree. Jalan watched, his eyes going even wider, as the iron-hard wood of the long-dead tree drank it in, like dry earth soaking up spring rain.

The cold pressing upon them faltered, and in his deepest heart Jalan could feel cracks running through the dark power at work. Beyond it all was the sweet singing he remembered from his childhood dreams—and it was growing stronger.

"No!" came a shout below them, and in the back of his mind Jalan recognized the voice of the sorcerer who had taken him, who had dragged him across the Endless Wastes, tormenting him all the way. A smile crept across Jalan's face, for he heard something new in the voice: despair.

A pale flutter overhead caught Jalan's eye, and he looked up. There, just at the limit of his reach, was a pale bud, fluttering in the gale. Even as he watched, the bud opened into a full blossom, white petals round a gold center.

Grab it! said Vyaidelon's song inside him.

He did.

CHAPTER THIRTY-ONE

The Isle of Witness

Father!"

The cry went out, echoing into realms beyond the paths of mortal men, and Vyaidelon answered.

Arantar, his son, his only son born to him of a mortal woman, stood beneath the Witness Tree. Weariness hung upon him, and the light in his eyes was dim. Five sorcerers, clad in the royal gray of Raumathar, surrounded him. Vyaidelon could look beyond the scope of mortal eyes, and he saw the cold, hungry darknesses writhing within them, giving them great strength even as the darknesses consumed them.

Vyaidelon merged with Arantar, combining their spirits and lending his strength to his son.

The five sorcerers howled in fury and struck, calling upon every spell they knew as they charged.

Arantar and Vyaidelon, two beings sharing one

body, struck back, pouring holy light and life into the never-ending hunger that filled the sorcerers. The five screamed, and four of them fell. The dark infusion, the thousands of tendrils of unlife burrowing into their souls, twisted and frayed.

The leader, the one that had been Khasoreth, fell to his hands and knees upon the ice-slick steps and looked up at Arantar. The shadow lifted from Khasoreth's face, and his eyes cleared. "Master . . . please. Remember. Remember . . . mercy."

The words hit Arantar stronger than any of their spells had. They cut to his very heart, for they were ideals by which he had tried to live his entire life, as a servant to the people of the steppes, as a husband and father, and most of all as a man.

In that moment of hesitation Khasoreth struck, sending a thick arm of darkness crashing into Arantar. The thing within Khasoreth shrieked in unholy delight, and Vyaidelon's song faltered.

Arantar stumbled against the tree, and the thing that had been Khasoreth leaped, falling upon him with fist, tooth, and spell.

Vyaidelon concentrated his strength to strike.

No! said Arantar, calling to his father in the mind they shared. *Mercy.*

He began to lift away, but the thing that had been Khasoreth struck, its great arm of darkness seizing Vyaidelon, grasping and tearing at him. Darkness warred with light, but this time Vyaidelon did not fight it. There would be another way. Another day when justice and mercy could meet as one.

Do not fear, Vyaidelon told his son. *You have planted the seed. It is not for you to see the flower bloom.*

Arantar breathed his last, a small smile upon his lips, and Vyaidelon fell. The five creatures of darkness seized him and battered at him, but their attempts were futile. Light was stronger, and Vyaidelon knew it even as he fell into the darkness.

Vyaidelon sought the last bit of warmth, the last living thing upon the island—the Witness Tree—and fell into the pure essence of the tree. The five sorcerers struck, but try as they might, they could not destroy the now-hallowed tree. Spell after spell and the darkest of magics broke upon it.

Knowing that the murder of the tree was beyond them, the five sorcerers used their darkest spells and imprisoned Vyaidelon in the lifeblood of the tree.

Through the long years, through the coldest winters and darkest nights, the deepest heart of the tree remained alive. Warmth and life still lived there, waiting.

Waiting for the true blood of Arantar to set free his celestial father.

Every bit of Gyaidun's body, both inside and out, pulsed with agony. Cracked bones, bruised muscles, skin cut and scraped—all of it clawed at his mind, trying to drag him down to unconsciousness.

He fought it, willing his eyes to stay open, forcing his lungs to breathe, as he watched his life's blood pouring out of the gash in his hand. *Damn my haste,* he thought. *Cut too quick. Too deep.*

Gyaidun heard Amira cry out, saw the blood from his and Jalan's hands soak into the roots of the tree—that thing at the bottom of the stairs cried out, *"No!"*—then the boy stood, stretched out his hand, and grabbed a pale blossom fluttering in the wind.

A blossom? Gyaidun thought. *Hro'nyewachu* said nothing about—

Jalan's hand *blazed*.

It was as if a thousand suns had condensed into the boy's fist and exploded with all the light they'd ever held or would hold.

And then, in the deepest recesses of Gyaidun's mind where he walked in dreams, Gyaidun heard music. It came as if from a great distance, but in the melody he felt warmth and light filling his soul, and in the corners of his mind that had known only darkness for years, something old and buried awoke: hope.

Jalan looked down at Gyaidun, and the scared boy was gone. In his place stood a lord, a hero, and in that moment Gyaidun believed Amira's words, that the boy was of the line of Arantar himself. Jalan was smiling, and his eyes sparkled like sunlight through amber.

A shard of blue light struck Jalan, and the boy stumbled.

Gyaidun turned. Three of the dark sorcerers had come; the tallest led them, the magic of his spent spell still sparking minuscule lightning around his fist.

Two of the other sorcerers struck, one sending a funnel of frost spiraling at the boy, the other loosing a barrage of blue-white light that seemed to devour all warmth from the air.

With a wave of Jalan's hand, the air before him solidified into a concave golden shield, and the sorcerers' spells shattered against it.

"Kneel, worm!" said the sorcerers' leader. "Submit, and I will make your death swift."

Jalan laughed, and Gyaidun heard two voices—one young and full of life, the other old beyond the reckoning of human minds.

"Your time has come," said Jalan. "Time to release them."

The leader snarled and turned, motioning behind him. Up the stairs behind him came the two remaining sorcerers—one who shambled, almost on his hands and knees, and the other was Erun. He held Amira under her arm, the point of his sword resting against her neck. She struggled to walk, arching her back to keep the blade from piercing her skin.

The leader turned back to Jalan. "Surrender and die quickly," he said, "or he will kill her slowly."

Jalan glanced down at his mother. His smile faltered, for a moment seeming almost sad, then he said, "No, he will not." A look of triumph and utter joy filled Jalan's countenance. It looked as if the boy's skin were glowing, as if a power so great filled him that it was leaking out through his pores.

Jalan extended both hands, palms open, to Erun and began to sing a music that was beyond words. Gyaidun gasped as he saw Erun's muscles tighten to thrust the sword, but then he sensed something ripple between Jalan and the sorcerer, and Erun trembled. He blinked and shook his head as if confused, then his muscles spasmed, his back arched, and a scream beyond sound was torn from him. Amira ripped herself away and stumbled down the stairs. The sorcerer's blade clattered to the stone.

Jalan's song filled Gyaidun, awakening his senses beyond anything he'd ever experienced. He'd sometimes heard the belkagen speak of the heart's eye, the vision that the enlightened were granted on the dreamroad, and for the first time he understood it. He saw beyond fleshy reality to the deeper life within it, saw Erun's tortured and tormented body, his imprisoned soul; latched onto it like a parasite was a cold darkness, a thing of never-ending hunger and malice. But even as Gyaidun watched, the dark thing's grip weakened.

Three of the other sorcerers shrieked in confusion and fear, and their leader screamed, "No! You dare not! You dare not!"

And then the dark thing was gone, and Erun fell upon the stone steps. He did not move, but with his new sight, Gyaidun could see life there—weak, faint, and hurt, but there.

The remaining sorcerers turned all their strength and spells upon Jalan. Even the weak one loosed spell after spell as he clawed his way up the final steps.

Jalan blocked or turned most of their spells, but some few managed to break through, and Jalan fell back, frost and ice forming where the blue shards of light struck him. Walking backward to Gyaidun and continuing to try to block their barrage, his song changed. It did not lessen in power but broadened in scope, and even Gyaidun, who had never studied the ways of priests or sorcerers, recognized it for what it was: A call. A summons.

The sorcerers doubled their efforts, fanning out to hit Jalan both in front and to the sides.

Still smiling, Jalan shouted, *"Wed chai'el!"* and a great wall of flame roared from the stones of the island between him and his foes. So great was the heat that Gyaidun backed away.

In that moment of respite, his enemies cut off, Jalan turned to Gyaidun and extended his hand. The gash where Gyaidun had cut the palm still bled freely.

"Gyaidun," said a strong voice, the voice of the singer speaking through Jalan. "Time for you to trust me."

Gyaidun reached out. He grasped Jalan's hand with his own bleeding palm, and their blood mingled anew. Gyaidun gasped, and the gasp turned into a laugh, for he saw whom Jalan had summoned.

Over the wind and crashing waves, through the roar of magic and the crackle of the flames, Amira heard something she had never heard nor hoped to hear: a laugh of pure, utter, unrestrained joy—and it was coming from Gyaidun.

She tossed her hair out of her eyes and looked up from where she'd fallen at the bottom of the stone stairway. The four sorcerers had fanned out in a half-ring at the crown of the hill, and they faced a great wall of fire. But even as Amira watched, the four summoned a great wind off the sea and the flames bent and died.

Amira pushed herself to her feet. Her skin was a mass of bruises, scrapes, and cuts. Her arm still throbbed from where the sorcerer had held her, and she'd twisted both her right knee and ankle in the fall. Agony flared in every injury, but she forced herself up the stairs. The sorcerer had taken her staff and thrown it away, but she knew she dared not take the time to look for it now. She still had a few spells of her own ready. She had to get to Jalan.

Amira passed the body of the fallen sorcerer but did not spare it a glance. The sounds of spells and the incantations of the other sorcerers shook the air above her, and she forced herself to move faster. When her knee gave out on her, she crawled up, tearing her clothes on the rough stone of the stairway.

She crested the hill, pulling herself over the final step and through the rubble of the broken wall, but the sight she saw there stopped her.

Passing the dead tree in a slow, deliberate walk, the four sorcerers advanced upon . . . a god. Amira blinked and shook her head. No, it wasn't a god. It was Jalan, but a power—a *living* power—beyond anything she had ever experienced filled her son, and through him it held back the devil-possessed sorcerers. But she could see that he was at the limit of his powers, and the attacks of the sorcerers were breaking through more and more with each strike.

Kneeling beside Jalan and holding his hand was Gyaidun, but Amira scarcely recognized him. He was still covered in blood, he still bled freely from a dozen scratches and scrapes, and his long hair was still unbound and wild down his back. But in his face and behind his closed eyes was an expression that Amira could only describe as rapture.

Then Gyaidun stood and opened his eyes. They shone like Jalan's, golden and bright. The weariness was gone from him, and he stood with the strength and power of a warrior in his prime. But in Gyaidun, too, Amira saw that the power was not his own, but came from something inside him. Something other.

Recognition struck her. In *Hro'nyewachu* she had seen the last stand of Arantar, watched as these very sorcerers had destroyed his city and murdered him. But there had been that other, that strange power working through Arantar, that being that even the Fist of Winter had been unable to destroy.

Amira recognized that same presence in her son, and standing next to him, shining through Gyaidun, was another.

Combining their strength, Jalan and Gyaidun—or the beings in them—began to beat back the attacks of the sorcerers. Spells of darkness and cold met the power of light and life, and it was the cold darkness that broke and shattered.

A great cry rent the air, and Amira saw the sorcerer who had crouched over Jalan under the Witness Tree, the one who seemed weaker than the others, fall to the ground. The unholy power within him was banished, the black magics that kept his ancient flesh upon his bones shattered, and he was a corpse before he struck the rocks.

The leader of the sorcerers cried out, an incoherent shriek of rage. He loosed a barrage of spells at Jalan, but rather than block them or turn them aside, Jalan leaped into the air. At his summons the wind bore him up and over the sorcerers. He sailed over the boughs of the Witness Tree and came down upon the stone staircase next to the fallen body of Erun.

"NO!" cried the leader.

Jalan knelt beside Erun and took his face in both hands. Erun's body spasmed, strength filling him, and he and Jalan stood together. The body of Gyaidun's son was still emaciated, but the corpse pallor was gone from his skin, and his eyes shone with the same light as Jalan and Gyaidun's.

The three of them—Jalan, Erun, and Gyaidun—closed in on the sorcerers, who stood back to back. Amira scrambled to get out of the way.

"No!" said the leader of the sorcerers. "Mercy! Remember mercy!"

Jalan's smile faded, and an expression of great solemnity filled his face. "Today," he said, "mercy meets justice."

The leader's two remaining fellows forsook him, fleeing in either direction. One leaped over the edge, perhaps hoping to lose himself in the waves below, while the other summoned the winter winds to bear him up. But both ran into a gale summoned by the three beings of light and were flung back. They fell to the ground, writhing and screaming, one of them only an arm's length from where Amira huddled in the rubble. Like the one before them, the power of the devils faltered, their hold on the mortal bodies broken at last.

Before her eyes, Amira saw the body age decades in a few

breaths. The flesh melted away beneath the skin, the eyes shriveled and sank, the remaining locks of hair blew away in the wind, and finally the skin itself peeled away.

The leader stood before them, the tattered remains of his robe fluttering in the wind and sudden silence. He glanced at Gyaidun and Erun, then fixed his gaze on Jalan.

"I will not bow before you, Vyaidelon," he said. "Nor your brothers. I will—"

"Silence!" said a voice. It came from Jalan, but Amira knew it was the being inside him speaking. "Speak no more in this world. Go back to the hell that spawned you."

Jalan, Erun, and Gyaidun raised their hands, and each of them was singing, a melodic chant in words Amira had never heard. The winter winds died, a few last snowflakes fell, and far overhead the gray ceiling of cloud split, and through it shone the noonday sun. A thick beam of light, almost like a great ladder joining earth to sky, fell upon the Isle of Witness, bathing everyone in its pure light.

The leader screamed. Not the cry of a powerful sorcerer or a defeated lord, this was the shriek of a beast in agony. He ran, blinded by his own suffering, but tripped over the rubble that littered the old courtyard around the Witness Tree. He fell only a few paces from Amira. His body twisted and bounced on the rocks like grease dropped on a hot rock. Fists and feet hammered the earth, and with each strike Amira could hear bones snapping.

Vyaidelon—for that's who he truly was now; he only wore Jalan's body—stood over the body and sang. The music was strong, but the melody sounded to Amira more like a dirge or even a sad lullaby than an incantation.

With a final cry that scraped like sharp nails inside her ears, the thing inside the leader lost its grip. The back arched, the body taking in a long breath, then relaxed. There, basking in the light of a sun that was beginning to fade back behind the clouds, Amira caught a fleeting glimpse of the young man he must once have been. A look of peace settled onto his face.

And he died.

CHAPTER THIRTY-TWO

The Endless Wastes

They walked many miles after the great battle of Winterkeep, the Vil Adanrath, the exiles, and the war wizard carrying their dead over the snow-covered steppes. Tired as they were, many of them wounded, the Vil Adanrath would not burn their dead so close to *Iket Sotha*. In killing the Fist of Winter, a great evil had been banished from the world, but many foul things still lurked in the dark places of Winterkeep.

The survivors and their dead gathered in a valley filled with small trees and scraggly bushes. Those not wounded went far and wide, searching for enough wood to burn so many.

Far away as they were, Amira could still smell Yal Tengri on the back of the north wind. The scent filled her with mixed emotions. She had seen so much horror and sadness there on the shore of the Great Ice Sea, but she had also regained her son there—and witnessed what she could only describe as a wonder. A miracle. Whatever beings had worked through Jalan, Gyaidun, and Erun . . . she was glad she had seen them. She didn't understand them, but in her heart she knew they were . . . good. There was no other word for it. In a world filled with so much sadness, so much compromise, corruption, so much light mixing with darkness, she had seen what she could only describe as good incarnate.

Jalan and Erun both slept beside the fire. Watching them, the knowledge she'd gained in *Hro'nyewachu* was confirmed. Anyone could have seen the family resemblance. The same high cheekbones, the slight cant to their eyes—both of them even slept with one arm outside the blanket. Separated by generations they certainly were, Erun only half-human, their relation distant at best, but the blood of Arantar ran strong in both of them.

"Lady," said a voice behind her, and she turned.

Lendri and Gyaidun stood there. Mingan the wolf lingered not far away, and Durja perched on his master's shoulder. Both warriors still bore the wounds of battle—both in the haunted look in their eyes and the many cuts, scrapes, and bruises behind their bandages. Amira had done what she could for them, mixing potions for which she could find ingredients, but she was no cleric, and her knowledge of healing went little beyond dressing battle wounds.

"What is it?" she asked, keeping her voice low so as not to wake Erun and Jalan.

"We must prepare the belkagen," said Lendri. "For the fire. At sunset, the pyres must be lit."

"We?" she asked.

"The duty falls to us."

"But . . . but you're exiles and I'm an outlander. The Vil Adanrath—"

"The belkagen died fighting by *our* side," said Gyaidun. "The duty falls to us."

Amira looked to Lendri. "And your father, he approves of this?"

"It is our way," said Lendri. "The omah nin will not help us, but he will not interfere."

Amira stood. "Show me what to do."

The three of them swaddled the belkagen in the remains of his cloak, wrapped him in one of the spare deerhide blankets, and bound it all with tough leather thongs. When they finished, only the belkagen's head could be seen. Dried blood and dirt still smeared his face and caked his hair. Amira used a little water and the hem of her cloak to clean it off.

Amira looked down on the face and laughed sadly. "A ghost of fire."

"What?" said Gyaidun.

"The first time I saw him," she said, "I was wounded. Half dead, more likely. And delirious. I woke with him bending over me, chanting beside the fire. My first thought was, 'A ghost of fire.' Looking at him now, I see no ghost, no fire."

Both warriors exchanged a look and scowled, probably thinking it some subtlety of Common that they didn't understand.

"Our people believe the body is only a home for our ghost," said Lendri, "and our word for 'ghost' is *uskeche*."

"*Uskeche?*"

"It means fire," said Gyaidun.

Amira looked down at the belkagen's face. There was no fire there. Not anymore. Only a vague remembrance of it, like cold ashes.

"I . . ." said Amira, and found tears welling in her eyes. "I never thought . . . it would be him. Going after my son, chasing his captors, I thought I might die. I half-expected you two to get yourselves killed, but I never thought . . . not him."

They stood in silence over the body a moment before Lendri spoke. "I think he did."

"What?"

"I have thought long about this," said Lendri. "All belkagen are given wisdom in *Hro'nyewachu*. It is said it is the source of much of their power. But Belkagen Kwarun once told me that his blessing was just as much a curse. 'The one burden no warrior should ever bear,' he told me."

"What was it?" asked Amira.

"He never told me, but I think *Hro'nyewachu* showed him his own death. It is the one thing every warrior risks but the one thing he never knows. But I think the belkagen knew."

Gyaidun nodded, his eyes distant and a cold fire burning in them. "Yes," he said. "On Arzhan Island, when he heard Amira's tale . . . she awoke a great fear in him. I think it may have been why he balked at first." His face clouded, his nostrils flaring, and he looked away. "I shamed him. And myself. I . . . should have—"

"No," said Amira. "No, I think you made him proud. He was afraid, yes. Who wouldn't be? But you reminded him of courage and woke it in him. I only knew him a short time, but I think he was proud—*very* proud—of both of you."

The Vil Adanrath built dozens of pyres, arranging them in a wide ring on the hilltop. Finding enough wood for so many had been no easy task, but the survivors had roamed many leagues and brought every scrap they could find. When that was not enough, they dug through the snow, cut the grass beneath, and bundled it into tight sheaves. The heavy snowfall—already melting with the return of autumn weather—made everything damp, but the Vil Adanrath had lived in the Wastes for many generations, and building fires in the snowfields was the least of their skills.

The belkagen's pyre was the tallest of all, a waist-high bed of grass and sticks that stood in the middle of the great ring of dead Vil Adanrath. The belkagen lay upon it, his staff beside him.

The sun touched the rim of the world in the west, and a

great howling filled the air. The surviving Vil Adanrath, elves and wolves, stood just outside the ring of pyres. Each stood over a fallen comrade, brother, sister, or lover. Some few of the older elves stood over the body of one of their adult children. All stood honor's distance away from the *hrayeket,* Lendri and Gyaidun, who stood witness over the belkagen. Amira had chosen to stay with them, as had Jalan and Erun.

"It is time, Lady Amira," said Lendri. "The sun sets, and the song of the people will sing their brothers home."

Amira raised her staff, the gift of *Hro'nyewachu* that the belkagen had named *Karakhnir,* and she spoke the words of power. Fire roared to life beneath the belkagen's body, flames the same color as the sunset consuming the shell of her friend. She forced herself to watch. The old elf's hair, the hoary gray mixed with glistening silver, lit at once, curling and blackening in bright, tiny blue flames that produced a thick, black smoke. The skin tightened, shriveled, and blackened. Amira could hear it sizzling. Bile rose in her throat, but she would not let herself look away. The old elf had risked his life for her and died protecting her son. She would not look away from his death. The flames quickened and soon she could see no more than a dark form amid the flames.

Lendri half-spoke and half-chanted a long string of words in his own tongue. When he was finished, Gyaidun translated for Amira and Jalan.

> *Flames of this world, bear our brother's flame to our ancestors.*
> *Kwarun burned bright. His exile is ended, his rest assured.*

The five of them stood in silence, watching the smoke in flames, then Lendri spoke again. "Lady, someone must take fire to the omah nin, that the other pyres might be lit."

"Me?" said Amira.

"Gyaidun and I, we are *hrayeket.* We cannot."

Amira tore her eyes away from the fire and looked to the omah nin, standing several dozen paces away over the body of his younger brother. Leren stood beside him.

"After all you did," said Amira, "risking your lives. Still he stands behind his *honor*"—she made no attempt to keep the bile from the last word—"rather than beside his firstborn."

"Your ways are not our ways, Lady."

"Indeed," said Amira. "Let the omah nin get his own damned fire."

Lendri scowled. Amira looked to Gyaidun and caught the flicker of a smile before the sternness returned to his face.

"Lady," said Lendri. "That is . . . most discourteous."

"My ways are not his ways."

"Lady—"

"I will take it."

Everyone turned to look at who had spoken. Erun. He still bore the scars of his . . . ordeal. Amira felt stupid calling such torture an "ordeal." Monstrous, she had named it to Gyaidun. Blasphemous. Even those words seemed to fall short. Yet already the young man showed signs of recovery. Whatever being had come to him—no, Amira corrected herself—*through* him, much of that strength remained. Yes, his cheeks were still sunken like a corpse—far beyond the natural thinness he'd inherited from his mother's people—his bones showed under his skin, and much of his color had not yet returned, but there was a light in his eyes. Not burning, precisely. But smoldering. A glow of promise, perhaps, like the bright sky before sunrise. Looking at him now, standing next to his father, Amira thought it would be a wonder indeed to see what would happen when the sun fully rose in him.

Erun stepped forward and pulled one of the larger sheaves out from the bottom of the pyre. Half of it was already well ablaze. He stood, his back straight, and looked to his father. "My grandfather will take fire from me," he said, and Amira heard a deeper meaning in his words.

She watched him walk away, strength and confidence

in his gait, and in that moment an image struck Amira—
Arantar, wise and powerful, walking the steppes. She turned
to Gyaidun and saw a dark look on his face.

"What is it?" she asked.

"What is what?"

"You look as if you just saw your own death."

Gyaidun looked her in the eye. "No. It . . ."

"What?"

He returned his gaze to his son, walking without fear
to the omah nin. "Things happen quicker than I thought
they would."

"Things?"

It hit Amira then that in the past day—the joy at being
reunited with Jalan, the grief at finding the belkagen,
funeral preparations, not to mention being tired beyond
all rational thought—she had forgotten to ask Gyaidun
exactly how he had turned up on the shore of the Great Ice
Sea knowing what had to be done. Standing over the pyre
of her friend, she remembered Gyaidun's argument with
the belkagen, asking why he could not seek *Hro'nyewachu*
if she knew something about Erun.

"You did it, didn't you?" she said.

Even Lendri and Jalan turned to look at Gyaidun. Durja,
resting on Gyaidun's shoulder, squawked as his master
looked down on all of them. His gaze raked over each of them,
his jaw grinding, then he stared into the fire.

"You went to *Hro'nyewachu*," said Amira. "Didn't you?"

Still he said nothing.

"*Rathla?*" said Lendri, awe in his voice. "Is this true?"

Durja squawked again and flapped his wings but did not
leave his master's shoulder.

"I had no choice," said Gyaidun.

"You sought the Mother's Heart and lived?" said Lendri.
"How . . . ?"

"You are not Vil Adanrath," said Amira. "The belkagen
said—"

"I am *athkaraye*," said Gyaidun. "Human, yes, but the
blood of the Vil Adanrath lives in me through Lendri." He

raised his right hand, opened it, and the gash showed plainly across his palm. "And through Hlessa, and through Erun."

"But the belkagen said you couldn't, said you hadn't studied the arcane or the ways of the gods, said—"

"The belkagen was one of the wisest I have ever known," said Gyaidun. "And I sometimes ill-treated him, to my shame. But he did not know everything."

"What do you mean?" said Lendri.

"Hro'nyewachu," said Gyaidun, "she . . . she is a being of . . . need."

"So said the belkagen. Yes."

"A mother's need," said Amira. "That's what he said. What the belkagen told me. 'Hro'nyewachu has a mother's heart.' He said I had a mother's need, and that our hearts would beat the same song."

Gyaidun looked back at his son, who had reached the omah nin and was presenting him with the fire. The Vil Adanrath chieftain stood tall and proud, almost rigid, but he took the fire.

"So how did you survive?" Lendri asked Gyaidun.

"I introduced her to a father's need."

"At the shore," said Amira, "after you came back, you were covered in blood. Much of it your own."

Gyaidun shrugged. His wounds had been tended, but he still bore many new cuts and scrapes. "It was not an easy . . . conversation. I . . ."

"What?"

Gyaidun stared into the fire a long while before answering. "I was blinded by grief, despair, anger. Kehrareth we would say. I . . . I think I went there hoping she would kill me. At least grant me a warrior's death. I went with no sacrifice."

Lendri gasped. Amira remembered what the belkagen had told her—"Hro'nyewachu is . . . akai'ye. There is no good word in your tongue. Ancient. Primal. Tame blood will not sate her. She needs the blood of the wild."

"The blood of the wild," said Amira. "She took your blood instead. As sacrifice."

Gyaidun flinched and looked back to his son, who now stood beside the omah nin, the pyre in front of them burning. "No," said Gyaidun. "Not me."

Amira followed his gaze. Erun stood beside his grandfather. The young man was considerably shorter, and emaciated as he was, still his countenance radiated power. He stood beside the omah nin an equal. What was it Gyaidun had said, what had prompted this entire conversation? "Things happen quicker than I thought they would."

"Erun," said Amira. "She wants Erun. Doesn't she?"

Gyaidun said nothing, but the look on his face was all the answer that she needed.

"I wouldn't worry," said Amira. "I saw Erun on the island. I think he might give even *Hro'nyewachu* pause."

Lendri looked to his *rathla* and said, "What did she say, Brother?"

" 'I will require your blood,' " said Gyaidun. "Her words. I . . . I thought she meant me, and I did not care. But now . . ." He looked back to his son.

The omah nin had lit his pyre, and Erun was carrying the flame to the next one.

"Rathla," said Lendri, "do not dread. I do not think *Hro'nyewachu* would help you find your son only to take him again. 'I will require your blood.' Erun? Perhaps. But consider this. A belkagen—perhaps one of the greatest to have ever served our people—has left the world. His presence will be missed, and *Hro'nyewachu* . . . I do not think she will tolerate such an absence for long. Besides, look at him."

They did. All of them, even Mingan and Durja.

"Who does he remind you of?" said Lendri. "His gait. His confidence. 'My grandfather will take fire from me.' Such boldness."

Arantar, Amira wanted to say. *He reminds me of Arantar.* But she held her tongue.

"You think Erun might be a . . . belkagen?" said Gyaidun.

Lendri considered this a moment, then said, "I think you should heed the lady's advice. Do not fear for Erun."

"Gyaidun?" said Amira.

He looked to her.

"The night you left the encampment, you made it all the way to *Akhrasut Neth,* and from there all the way to here. So far so fast, that's . . . impossible. Even for you."

Gyaidun held up his right fist. A ring of some dark red metal—copper perhaps—was on his little finger. Runes, in the same style as those she'd seen on the belkagen and the omahet, were carved along its surface. "Before I left," he said, "the belkagen gave me this. It performs the same magic that you used on the steppe, able to send me great distances in the blink of an eye."

"Will you keep it?" asked Lendri.

"I have walked all my life," said Gyaidun. "I see no reason to stop now. Still, I might have need of it again."

With the sun gone, all warmth left the air. Cold seemed to radiate from the endless miles of snow, and the northern breeze had the bite of ice. The pyres smoldered, giving off a little heat, but their flames were gone, so that the only light was the thick sliver of moon and the hundreds of stars surrounding it. But with so much snow still on the ground, the land around them reflected the light of moon and stars, so that Amira could see surprisingly well. Still, the Vil Adanrath kept vigil over their dead, and Amira and her companions sat huddled in their cloaks and blankets next to the great pile of ashes.

Durja huddled inside Gyaidun's cloak, and Mingan crouched at Lendri's feet. Erun and Jalan slept in their blankets between the men and Amira. No one had spoken in some time.

"We wait here till morning?" asked Amira.

"Yes," said Lendri. "At sunrise, we help the wind to scatter the ashes. You may sleep if you wish. I will keep the vigil."

"I'm not tired," said Amira, and she was surprised to find it true. After the past several tendays, she ought to have been exhausted, but a growing apprehension filled her and would not let her mind relax.

"So," said Gyaidun. "What now?"

"What?"

"You have your son. What now?"

Amira looked down at Jalan, breathing steadily inside his blankets. "Jalan has been through something that no boy his age should ever have to experience. He's alive, and I have him back. The rest . . ." Her lips curved in a sad smile. "There will be time for the rest later."

Gyaidun said nothing. Listening to the fire smoldering, Amira found the lapse in the conversation unsettling.

"I . . . I owe you both a great debt. Without you and the belkagen—and the Vil Adanrath, I suppose—I never would have been able to get my son back. If there is ever anything—"

"So you're leaving, then?" said Gyaidun, anger in his voice. "That's it?"

"What did you expect?" said Amira. "Jalan deserves a good home, a safe home, a family that cares for him—"

"And he has this in Cormyr?"

Stung, Amira turned her gaze fixed to the snowfield. "What are you asking?"

"Are you—you and Jalan—returning to Cormyr?"

"If we don't, they'll come looking for us. My family might well leave us for dead, but the war wizards . . . they'll come."

"And you will go with them?"

She looked back to him. "I won't fight my own people, Gyaidun."

He returned her gaze, and in the moonlight she could see a small smile crack his stern features. "*You* won't have to, Amira."

He motioned with his head to Lendri and Mingan and patted the long knife in the sheath at his belt.

Amira's eyebrows rose, and she looked at Lendri. The elf said nothing but gave her a feral grin that did nothing to hide the wolf in his nature. Again he looked on her with those predator's eyes, the moon and starlight catching therein and shining out, but for the first time Amira did not feel caught in the wolf gaze. She felt part of the pack.

She took a deep breath and looked back out on the endless miles of rolling steppe, now covered in snow. For the first time since she'd come to this land, she took in its beauty. It was a hard land, Lendri had said, and it bred hard children. But right now Amira was almost awestruck by its splendor.

"I used to hate the Wastes, you know," she said.

Gyaidun chuckled. "I can't imagine why."

A Guide to the Words and Phrases of the Vil Adanrath

akai'ye: "ancient," "primal," or "primeval."

Akhrasut Neth: "the Mother's Bed," a hill sacred to the Vil Adanrath.

alet: a command, meaning "come here."

amrulugek: "council" or "meeting."

aniq: A command, meaning "ready" or "be ready."

athkaraye: "friend of the elves."

belkagen: "good seer," the name given to the holy men of the Vil Adanrath.

besthunit nenle: a proverb, meaning "hurry up slowly;" in other words: be quick, but not so quick that you do it badly.

chu set: "hold calm;" a more general translation would be "control yourself," "be still," or "calm down."

crithta: "sunbeam"

crith kesh het: "sun-shield to me."

dilit: a command, meaning "be quiet."

gaudutu: "burning legs;" the Vil Adanrath name for an extremely venomous centipede common to some parts of the Endless Wastes.

Hinakaweh: A clan of the Vil Adanrath.

hrayek: "cut off," but most often used to mean "exile" or "outcast."

Hro'nyewachu: "Heart of the Piercing," the name of one of the most sacred sites of the Vil Adanrath.

Iket Sotha: "fort of winter," the Vil Adanrath name for Winterkeep.

ikwe: a command, meaning "get back" or "get away."

Inisach tin Nekutha Hro'nyewachwe: "Seeker and survivor of the Heart of the Piercing."

kaharenharik ket: Literally "fires of heaven fall."

kanishta: A type of root, the juices of which help the body and stay warm and provide energy.

Karakhnir: "sharpens the bite."

kaweh rut, kyed: "speak out, now."

kehrareth: "intense grief" or "despair;" "fey."

kweshta: "a special one," but in the sense of one who does not quite fit in, but in a good way; a looser translation might be "dear" or "unique."

na kwast wahir athu kyene wekht unarihe: a proverb, meaning "better a cold truth than a warm lie."

newetik: "without heart"; an insult that means "without honor."

omah: "leader" or "chief."

omah nin: "highest chief."

rathla: "blood-bound," but most often used to mean "blood brothers."

Siksin Neneweth: "Ice Skins," the Vil Adanrath name for the Frost Folk.

sumezh: "stray dog;" it is commonly used as an insult.

te?: "well?" or "huh?"

uskeche: "fire" or "flame," but more commonly used as the Vil Adanrath word for "spirit" or "ghost."

u werekh kye wu: "great winds be born."

uwethla: "skin-bound," the Vil Adanrath name for the holy symbols etched onto the skin of omahet and belkagenet.

vil: wolf.

viliniketu: "wolves of the ice fields." the Vil Adanrath name for winter wolves.

wutheh: a command, meaning "find" or "seek."

Yastehanye: "Honored Exile."

FORGOTTEN REALMS®

PAUL S. KEMP

"I would rank Kemp among WotC's most talented authors, past and present,
such as R. A. Salvatore, Elaine Cunningham, and Troy Denning."
—Fantasy Hotlist

The *New York Times* best-selling author of *Resurrection* and The
Erevis Cale Trilogy plunges ever deeper into the shadows that
surround the FORGOTTEN REALMS world in this
Realms-shaking new trilogy.

THE TWILIGHT WAR

BOOK I
SHADOWBRED
It takes a shade to know a shade, but will take more than a shade to stand against the
Twelve Princes of Shade Enclave. All of the realm of Sembia may not be enough.

BOOK II
SHADOWSTORM
Civil war rends Sembia, and the ancient archwizards of Shade offer to help. But with
friends like these . . .

September 2007

BOOK III
SHADOWREALM
No longer content to stay within the bounds of their magnificent floating city, the
Shadovar promise a new era, and a new empire, for the future of Faerûn.

May 2008

Anthology
REALMS OF WAR
A collection of all new stories by your favorite FORGOTTEN REALMS authors digs
deep into the bloody history of Faerûn.

January 2008

THE KNIGHTS OF MYTH DRANNOR

A brand new trilogy by master storyteller

ED GREENWOOD

Join the creator of the FORGOTTEN REALMS® world as he explores
the early adventures of his original and most celebrated
characters from the moment they earn the name "Swords of
Eveningstar" to the day they prove themselves worthy of it.

BOOK I
SWORDS OF EVENINGSTAR
Florin Falconhand has always dreamed of adventure. When he saves the life of
the king of Cormyr, his dream comes true and he earns an adventuring charter for
himself and his friends. Unfortunately for Florin, he has also earned the enmity of
several nobles and the attention of some of Cormyr's most dangerous denizens.

BOOK II
SWORDS OF DRAGONFIRE
Victory never comes without sacrifice. Florin Falconhand and the Swords of
Eveningstar have lost friends in their adventures, but in true heroic fashion, they
press on. Unfortunately, there are those who would see the Swords of Eveningstar
pay for lives lost and damage wrecked, regardless of where the true blame lies.

August 2007

BOOK III
THE SWORD NEVER SLEEPS
Fame has found the Swords of Eveningstar, but with fame comes danger. Nefarious
forces have dark designs on these adventurers who seem to overturn the most clever
of plots. And if the Swords will not be made into their tools, they will be destroyed.

August 2008

FORGOTTEN REALMS

You cannot escape them, you cannot conquer them,
you can only hope to survive . . .

THE DUNGEONS

DEPTHS OF MADNESS
Erik Scott de Bie

Twilight awakes in the dungeon of a deranged wizard surrounded by strangers as
lost as she is. Twisted magic and deadly traps stand between her and escape, and
threaten to drive Twilight mad—if she lives long enough. . . .

March 2007

THE HOWLING DELVE
Jaleigh Johnson

Meisha returns to find her former master insane, and sealed in his dungeon home
by Shadow Thieves. She must escape, but her survival isn't enough: she must also
rescue the mentor she left behind.

July 2007

STARDEEP
Bruce R. Cordell

The seals that imprison an eldritch wizard within his prison are breaking
down, and the elves scramble to find the reason before the wizard's
nightmarish revolution begins.

November 2007

CRYPT OF THE MOANING DIAMOND
Rosemary Jones

When an avalanche of stone traps siegebreakers undermining the walls of a
captured city, their only hope lies deep within the tunnels. With water rising around
them, and an occupying army waiting above them, will they be able to escape alive?

December 2007

R.A. SALVATORE

The New York Times best-selling author and one of fantasy's most powerful voices.

DRIZZT DO'URDEN

The renegade dark elf who's captured the imagination of a generation.

THE LEGEND OF DRIZZT

Updated editions of the FORGOTTEN REALMS classics finally in their proper chronological order.

BOOK I
HOMELAND
Now available in paperback!

BOOK II
EXILE
Now available in paperback!

BOOK III
SOJOURN
Now available in paperback!

BOOK IV
THE CRYSTAL SHARD
Now available in paperback!

BOOK V
STREAMS OF SILVER
Coming in paperback, May 2007

BOOK VI
THE HALFLING'S GEM
Coming in paperback, August 2007

BOOK VII
THE LEGACY
Coming in paperback, April 2008

BOOK VIII
STARLESS NIGHT
Now available in deluxe
hardcover edition!

BOOK IX
SIEGE OF DARKNESS
Now available in deluxe
hardcover edition!

BOOK X
PASSAGE TO DAWN
Deluxe hardcover, March 2007

BOOK XI
THE SILENT BLADE
Deluxe hardcover, June 2007

BOOK XII
THE SPINE OF THE WORLD
Deluxe hardcover, December 2007

BOOK XIII
SEA OF SWORDS
Deluxe hardcover, March 2008

A world of Adventure awaits

The FORGOTTEN REALMS world is the biggest, most detailed, most vibrant, and most beloved of the DUNGEONS & DRAGONS® campaign settings. Created by best-selling fantasy author Ed Greenwood the FORGOTTEN REALMS setting has grown in almost unimaginable ways since the first line was drawn on the now infamous "Ed's Original Maps."

Still the home of many a group of DUNGEONS & DRAGONS players, the FORGOTTEN REALMS world is brought to life in dozens of novels, including hugely popular best sellers by some of the fantasy genre's most exciting authors. FORGOTTEN REALMS novels are fast, furious, action-packed adventure stories in the grand tradition of sword and sorcery fantasy, but that doesn't mean they're all flash and no substance. There's always something to learn and explore in this richly textured world.

To find out more about the Realms go to www.wizards.com and follow the links from Books to FORGOTTEN REALMS. There you'll find a detailed reader's guide that will tell you where to start if you've never read a FORGOTTEN REALMS novel before, or where to go next if you're a long-time fan!